I0561591

Royal Storm of Atlantis (2nd edition)

The Complete Series

Copyright © 2023 by Sedona Ashe

Gobble Ink, LLC

www.sedonaashe.com

Cover artwork by Fantasia Cover Designs

www.fantasiacoverdesigns.com

Interior formatting by Cauldron Press

www.cauldronpress.ca

A huge thank you to-

Maxine Meyer for Copy Editing.

Imogen Evans for Proofreading & Editing.

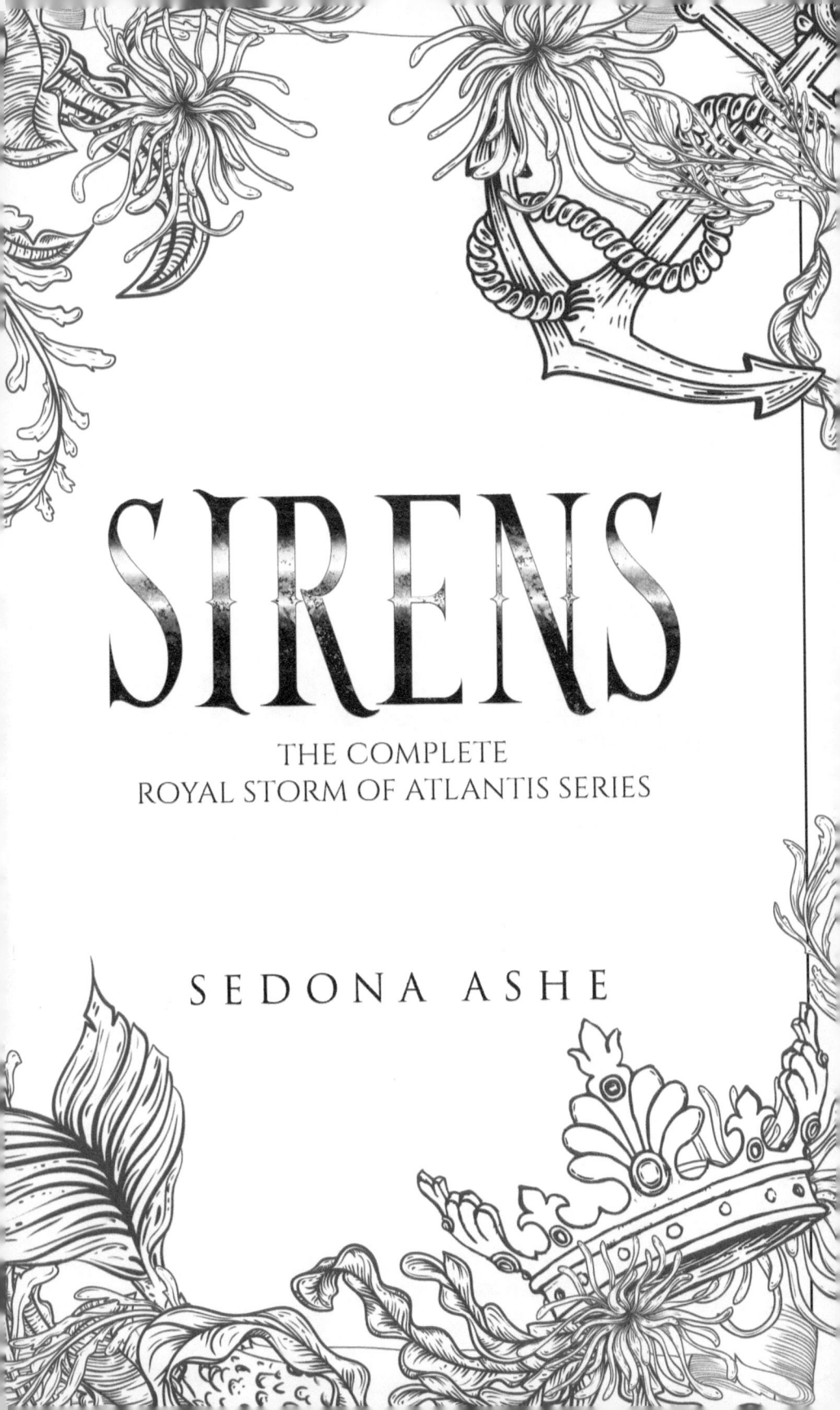

SIRENS

THE COMPLETE
ROYAL STORM OF ATLANTIS SERIES

SEDONA ASHE

CONTENTS

SIREN'S HUNT

SIREN'S THRONE

SIREN'S TRIBUTE

SIREN'S HUNT

ROYAL STORM OF ATLANTIS, BOOK 1

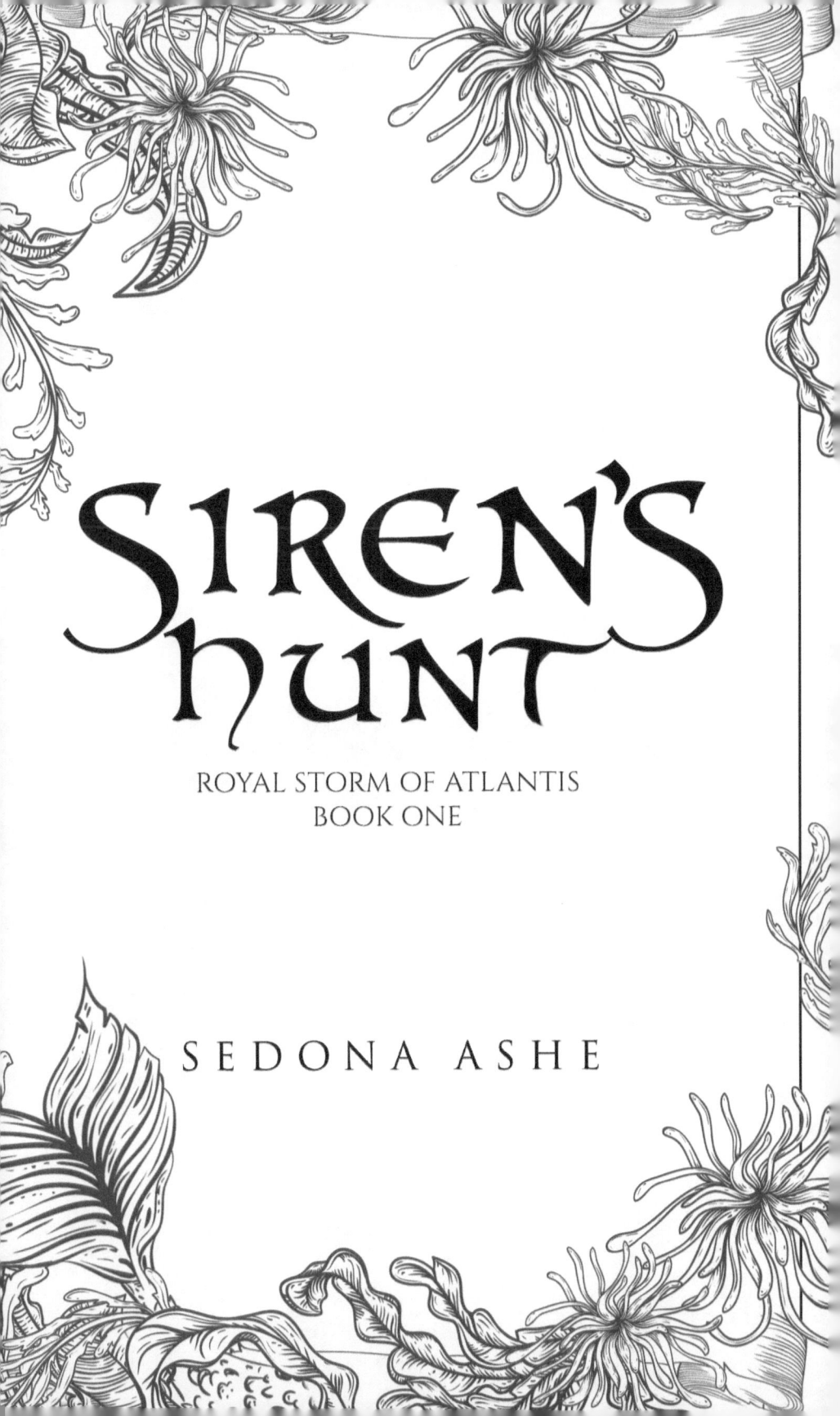

Siren's hunt

ROYAL STORM OF ATLANTIS
BOOK ONE

SEDONA ASHE

CHAPTER ONE

ZOSIME

I circled beneath a small fishing boat that bobbed on the ocean's surface above me. The moon was mostly hidden behind clouds; the lack of light turned the sea obsidian. Light or no light, I could track my prey with ease thanks to my gifts.

I had been drawn here by the *call*. You would think that taking the longest nap in history would have dulled the strength of the pull. No such luck. It was far worse than I remembered. Of course, that had been centuries ago, so my memory might be foggy.

Echoes of deep male laughter vibrated through the water. For several minutes I clung to the underside of the rocking boat. The man's thoughts slammed into me, nearly causing me to lose my tenuous grip on the boat. I shivered—and it had nothing to do with the dark sea around me. The call drummed in my head, growing louder with each minute I waited. I breathed deeply.

My heartbeat slowed to a steady rhythm in my chest. I knew what had to be done, the same thing that I had done hundreds of times before. I gripped the side of the boat and lifted my upper body from the water. Cold saltwater slid down my face and shoulders, seemingly washing away what little was left of my emotions.

It was time.

I used my arms to brace myself on the edge of the boat.

"Good evening."

At the sound of my soft raspy voice, the loud human male startled. His eyes grew wide, and his breathing shallow as he stared at me. He recovered quickly, swallowing a large gulp of his foul-smelling drink before tossing the can into the sea. It bobbed on the surface alongside several others he had discarded. The humans of this time appear to have little respect for the earth.

He stumbled toward me, a smile curling his lips. "What's a little thing like you doing out here? Did your boyfriend toss you out of his boat for misbehaving?"

I forced an answering smile. Only a few steps further and it would be too late for him. "I need help."

"I'm happy to help, little lady. I think there are some ways you can help me, too." He wiggled his eyebrows suggestively, making sure I didn't miss what he was implying.

One more step.

"Mm." I had never lied, so I found it best to speak to my prey as little as possible. He interpreted my hum as encouragement and took that last fateful step. Leaning down, he brought his face near mine. The putrid smell of his hot breath made me want to gag. Are all human males from this era gross? I would have recoiled, but the call drove me into action.

I threw my arms around his neck, locking them in place. Letting myself fall backward, I yanked him with me. Hard. My momentum knocked him off balance. He uttered a shocked scream and toppled into the sea.

The night was filled with his curses and frantic splashing. On land, his size would have given him an advantage against most women, but he was in my territory now. I took no pleasure in hearing his struggles. I was an efficient hunter. Keeping my arms locked around his neck, I spun around until I was behind him. His cries cut off abruptly when my grip tightened.

He struggled helplessly against my hold. I sank below the surface, allowing the murky depths to engulf me. The man had relaxed in my grip, no longer conscious. His pulse grew fainter with each passing second. The pressure that had steadily built inside me since I first heard tonight's call had turned painful. My stomach clenched in agony. A wave of dizziness blurred my vision. I knew from experience that it would get worse the longer I waited.

My teeth lengthened, allowing me to bite deep into the man's neck. The sour taste of his blood filled my mouth, causing me to gag as I swallowed. His heart gave a final stuttering beat. The pressure inside me released with a pop. It was over.

With a thrust of my powerful fluke, I swam deeper, effortlessly dragging the large male with me. A shadow passed near me, announcing the arrival of another predator. The shark turned, sleek grey skin gently bumping into me. I had met the magnificent female when I surfaced near the small fishing town several days before. She was a warrior like me.

Having taken what blood I needed, I released the man to the ocean and her subjects.

Tonight's hunt had been successful.

CHAPTER TWO

STORM

"I don't understand why they pulled us from the field to send us to a fishing town in the middle of who-knows-where just to look at the bloated remains of idiots who likely got drunk while fishing and fell overboard." Kye tossed aside the briefing he had been reading.

I looked up from my own copy and met Kye's irritated green gaze. It was ironic that my name was Storm, yet I was the calm one. Kye didn't hide his emotions, and we were never left in the dark about how he felt at any given moment.

Eason spoke without looking up, "Stop being a baby. They want to get a handle on this situation before the media gets ahold of it. There have been eight bodies found over the past month around Apalachee Bay. A predator is hunting there, either on the land or the sea."

Kye gave a snort of derision. "Did you read some of their theories? They suggested it may be an unknown, or long extinct, species of shark! This whole thing sounds like a low budget horror film."

He wasn't wrong. Some of the wild theories were absolutely laughable. However, the alternative was chilling. If it wasn't a sea creature, then a deranged serial killer was stalking the quiet coastline.

I sighed. "They have also called in a marine biologist to analyze the wounds," I responded. "Hopefully there'll be a simple explanation for these deaths."

Kye sighed and slumped back onto the SUV's soft leather seat. "We were so close, Storm. If they hadn't pulled us, we would have had them."

I may not express my emotions as easily as Kye, but they are still there. Anger and disappointment roiled in my stomach. We had been tracking an illegal drilling operation for three years, only to be moved on to this new case.

Orpati was discovered by scientists while exploring uncharted deep sea rock formations five years ago. They took samples of the glowing rock. The world was mesmerized by the beauty of the turquoise stone. When it was found that Orpati could be used as a safe natural energy source, there was a mad rush to mine it as quickly as possible. It was a modern-day gold rush.

Governments fought over mining rights, and for a time

it seemed that World War III loomed on the horizon. To prevent a devastating war, an agreement was signed that called a temporary halt to all mining of Orpati. This gave the heads of each country, as well as leading scientists, time to create ethical and fair mining practices.

The small amounts of Orpati that had already been mined become the most valuable resource on earth, subsequently driving the prices up beyond belief. Unfortunately, this led to modern day 'pirating.'

Orpati had been scattered around several thousand miles of the Atlantic Ocean. This made it impossible to fully patrol the area, especially in a world where the rich could buy their own underwater vehicles and robots. Which is exactly what happened.

The rich paid those willing to bend the laws to continue to mine. Since there was no way to distinguish legally mined from illegally mined Orpati, it was easy to sell everything the pirates mined.

The damage these men were doing to the ocean was alarming. Tremors on the ocean floor were being picked up at an increased rate, and a small earthquake had been registered a month before. It was possible that it was simply nature doing her thing, but the scientists were concerned that it was directly related to the crazed mining.

Kye, Eason and I had been working to track the largest of the illegal mining operations. This group had not been careful when mining and had caused some serious damage. We suspected that it was going to trace back to several high-ranking officials inside the government, but we had to obtain concrete proof before pursuing them. Our team had received intel that there would be another mining dive that night, and it would have been a huge break in the case. But that wasn't going to happen now, since we had been sent to investigate a string of mysterious deaths in fishing towns that no one had ever heard of.

On the one hand, I understood why we had been sent. We had spent our lives dedicated to various branches of government and law enforcement. Tracking killers had become a specialty of ours, and our ability to find the most slippery of people had become something we were known for.

However, there was something about the ocean that had always called to each of us, and we spent every minute we were not on a case either in the sea, or studying it. We had dived shipwrecks, caves, archeological sites. Other times we had been included on deep sea exploration trips to the ocean floor, or trips to film and study different ocean species. We had studied the mechanics of ocean drilling, as well as the risks, and had used that knowledge to help implement better options.

Our knowledge of the ocean and advanced military training gave us unique qualifications. This led to our team being brought in on strange and difficult marine cases, both above and below water. I was not surprised our expertise was requested for this string of deaths, but another part of me wondered if the sudden change in assignment had something to do with how close we were getting to the miners. Was it possible that our theories were correct, and that someone had tipped off the higher-ups?

The sound of the car door opening broke me from my thoughts. We had arrived and Kye, who hated being confined, had jumped out before the vehicle had even come to a complete stop. Eason shook his head at Kye's antics, but he wasted no time getting out of the vehicle as well. Our team was always more comfortable in open spaces, preferably surrounded by the ocean.

I stretched my aching muscles and glanced around. The smell of saltwater and driftwood filled my lungs. The small town had an aged look, but it had never been a bustling metropolis. This was the type of place you either retired to, or you were born and raised in.

It seemed we were in the town's center. There was a quaint town hall building that had the sturdy elegance of buildings that had stood for a long time. A gas station with a small deli inside was bustling. That must be the local hangout for lunch. Large trees were scattered around the area draped in moss, they reminded me of creatures from a fantasy movie, as if they would begin to move and talk at any moment.

An officer approached us and quickly introduced himself, "I'm glad you guys have arrived," he said, after offering us all a firm handshake. "The fish guy got here a few minutes ago, so we can explain everything at the same time. Follow me."

The officer turned and moved toward the small building marked by the county medical examiner sign. He didn't bother checking to see if we were following. I got the distinct impression he was eager to get us briefed and hand this case off to us. It was always nice when local law enforcement was friendly, but I didn't think he wanted anything to do with whatever was going on.

The interior was cool and dry, a stark contrast to the stifling humidity and heat of the Florida coastline. My nose burned with the overwhelming chemical scent permeating the air. We stepped into a large open room with several gurneys spread around, each containing a victim. Glancing around the room, I was thankful for the chemicals that had taken my sense of smell.

"Dr. Fynn, the other investigators have arrived," the officer said in the direction of a tall man in a lab coat. "If you want to join us in the meeting room, we'll go over the full briefing." The officer barely glanced the doctor's way before moving into the next room.

Kye snickered behind me. I rolled my eyes, already knowing exactly what he was thinking. "Don't say it, Kye."

"But—"

"No." My tone was firm, but Kye didn't care.

"*Fynn*, like *fin*." He had whispered it, but in the bare room the sound carried.

"Yes, Fynn, like a fish's fin," the doctor chimed in. "I am a marine biologist, with a focus on marine mammals. The perfect name for the job, or so I am constantly being told."

The man gave a friendly smile as he strode toward us, not offended in the least by Kye's pun.

"Yes, we are well aware of who you are, Doctor," Kye said. "It's a pleasure to work this case with you."

"Please call me Fynn. If you knew me, you'd know I don't enjoy formality." He laughed and held out his hand.

We shook hands and exchanged names before making our way to the main meeting room where the officer waited with the other county officials. The faces around the room looked exhausted. From my research, outside of natural disasters, the area had not seen this many deaths in a row in its history. These officers were great at their jobs, but this was outside their comfort zone. Who could blame them?

I listened as the officers took turns going over the information they had gathered. My sources had provided all the same details, so I used the time to study the faces around me. If there was a serial killer hunting the area, he or she could very well be in this room.

The cause of death varied among the victims, but it included heart attack, drownings, and apparent shark attacks. They'd all happened within a period of a month, and all the bodies were discovered in the water, nibbled on by various sea inhabitants. In a large city, eight deaths wouldn't have been noticed, but in a community of this size it was alarming.

After the briefing, we followed Dr. Fynn back into the medical examiner's part of the building.

"Now the fun part," Kye groaned. We had all spent

time observing autopsies, but it wasn't something I ever looked forward to.

"I only had a few moments to inspect the wounds before the briefing," Fynn said as he slid on a pair of latex gloves. "The first thing I need to do is compare the bite marks. We need to see if it's one species, and possibly one individual of that species, who is conducting most of the attacks. If an aggressive predator is in the area, maybe it's going after anyone that hits the water."

"Do you have a theory on the different causes of deaths?" Eason asked.

"I think it's possible that a shark attack may have been behind each. The victim could end up in the water, then they see the shark circling and suffer a heart attack from fear. It's also possible that the victims could have drowned during an attack, dying from inhaling water."

"Are you sure it's a shark?" Kye had moved to stand near Fynn and was inspecting a man's leg with a particularly vicious bite. I was surprised the limb was still attached at all.

"Yes, and no," the Doctor replied. "There is definitely a shark involved, but there are a number of other more curious wounds on these bodies. A few of the bites do not match the bite marks of sharks known to inhabit the coastal waters in this area. I'm going to need to take some photos and compare them to other species. Perhaps one has moved into this area."

"What about an alligator?" Kye asked.

Fynn glanced up. "Unlikely, but I guess it's possible."

"Please tell me you don't believe an extinct creature has suddenly emerged like something from a movie." Kye couldn't mask the derision in his tone.

Chuckling, Fynn turned back to the bodies. "I've heard the theories being spread around locally. No, I don't believe that. Although, until we have matched the wounds, nothing is certain. Wouldn't it be amazing to have the chance to study a living member of a long extinct or even completely undiscovered species?"

I had to admit that would be amazing, but we were here to track facts, not conduct a hunt for a cryptid.

It was time to get to work. I turned to the doctor. "Show us how to help."

CHAPTER THREE

ZOSIME

I sped through the ocean, each thrust of my fluke propelling me forward through the murky water. The moon sparkled on the surface like glittering diamonds. It would have been a perfect night to explore the waters I now found myself in, but instead the call had come again. If I wanted peace, I needed to deal with this quickly.

I slowed as the ocean became shallower. Boats of all sizes floated on the surface above me. Debris littered the sand beneath me, with small fish and crustaceans darting among the trash. Carefully, I wove through broken wood crates and submerged netting.

I gagged as I drew in a breath of the filthy water and

wished like crazy that I was back in the clear depths far from shore.

Just get it done, and you can go rest.

I tried to give myself a pep talk, but my anxiety continued to climb. Voices from the humans near the docks began to bombard my mind. I could handle one or two voices, but so many voices at once was unbearable.

When I had awakened, I had found myself being pulled by a current from cool waters to these warmer ones. During that journey, a large metal vessel had floated above me. I was still struggling to comprehend the human speech of this time, but I had understood enough to know that they were soldiers. They thought about missions, leaders, training, and battle. All things that I understood well.

The problem was the number of humans that resided on the vessel. There had to have been more than two hundred men, and I could hear every single thought that went through their minds. To escape the mind-shattering pressure, I descended deeper into the icy abyss beneath me, much further than I had ventured before.

Thankfully, my body had adjusted to the drastic change in temperature. My body still shivered, but I hadn't frozen. Another surprise had come when my body had lit up like a lantern as the sea around me turned midnight blue and then obsidian. My scales had pulsed with a soft phosphorescent green light. I had avoided the depths. Just the thought of that absolute darkness and the odd creatures that dwelled there made my insides churn in fear, and the skin on my arms and neck prickle.

While it wasn't an experience I was eager to repeat in the near future, I couldn't deny the peace that had come over me as the voices had faded and my mind quietened. My vision blurred as white-hot pain sliced through my skull and I slammed hard into a wooden beam supporting a dock. The water vibrated with groans from the old wood and my pain.

Letting out a string of curses in a language I imagined was long dead, I began to move forward again, far more cautiously this time. Several male voices cheered and shouted like they were watching fierce gladiators, while their private thoughts were a drunken jumble. Another male shouted orders at the men working on his boat; they obeyed, but their thoughts were filled with nasty comebacks they weren't brave enough to voice aloud. The pressure in my skull built with each passing moment as thoughts of love, heartbreak, sorrow, joy, hope, and anger overwhelmed me.

Desperation bubbled up inside me. I needed to hurry, answer the call, and get the Tartarus away from the humans and their incessant thinking. The number of changes to my body and the world around me were overwhelming. For the past few weeks I had shoved down my panic. I focused on surviving; emotions would have to wait. Hearing the call had been both relieving and terrifying. It was the one single thing that was familiar to me in this new world, but to answer, I had to venture closer to the humans and away from the relative safety of the ocean.

I was near the source of tonight's call. She sat on the peer, her bare feet swayed, kicking up glittering sprays of saltwater. Her thoughts pushed forward from the rest of the din in my brain. Sadness. Rage. The small female hadn't always been this way; something had changed in her life, and it left her open.

Surfacing slowly, I allowed her to see my face. With some of the others this had shocked them, and they had toppled into the water. This girl was not easily scared.

"Haven't you heard?" she said softly. "There's some freaky fish in the water attacking people. The people on the news are telling everyone to stay away from the ocean." She studied the scales on my face, her eyes showing only curiosity.

"Why then do you have your feet in the sea?" My voice was throaty. A lack of speaking and the constant salt of the sea had taken a toll on my vocal cords.

I watched as she threw back her head and laughed, the sound melodious as it filled the humid air around us.

"Maybe I want to meet this predator." Her gaze was steady as it met my eyes. She brought a small metal container to her curled lips and took a long sip.

I sniffed, prepared to feel the burn of the foul-smelling beverage. To my surprise, it didn't come. Squinting at the scribbles on the container I tried to decipher the language. Thanks to my unique heritage and the gifts that came with it, and the thoughts of the humans that forced themselves into my mind, I was catching up quickly with the modern world and the language spoken in this area. I recognized the individual letters on the can but couldn't yet read them as words.

"It's called soda." She answered my unspoken question. "Here, try one. It's a sugar drink with caffeine."

I caught the can she tossed to me, some of the bubbly liquid sloshing out. My head pounded mercilessly from the call, but my curiosity got the best me. Lifting the can, I took a careful sniff before cautiously taking a sip. It was unlike anything I had tasted before. The sweet beverage tickled my tongue and throat as I swallowed.

"Pretty good, right? I'm Yashy, by the way."

"Yes. Strange, but not unpleasant. I'm Zosime."

"So, you're the one killing off the people around the bay?"

Her tone was indifferent, as if she didn't really care about the answer. How was I supposed to respond? I had never told a lie; I would not start with this female. I simply nodded, sipping more of the syrupy drink.

"Huh. Why? Just for fun? Or is there a deeper reason?" She leaned toward me. I wished she would lean away; the call drummed louder with each passing moment.

"I swore an oath to answer the call," I replied firmly. "It pulls me where I am needed, to where the Lure has taken hold and eroded. Please, you could turn back."

Even as I spoke the last words, I knew it was too late.

Her thoughts of knives, pain, and revenge ran in circles in my mind. She had been hurt beyond what a human should ever have to bear. The Lure had eroded away every bit of human decency from the men who had tormented her and left her broken. In turn, she had allowed the Lure to seep into her soul and numb her pain. She had served up her revenge with an ice-cold heartlessness that was both terrifying and inspiring.

"I can't though," Yashy replied. "I made my decision knowing what that meant for me. Those men paid, and they will never touch another human again. The desire for bloodlust hasn't died along with them though, but I don't want to hurt someone. I've gone past the point of return, but I don't regret my decision for a single second."

Her words held a touch of sadness, but her lips and eyes twinkled at her remembered revenge.

"Alright, so what's next?" she said with a sigh, turning to face me. "Do you morph into something terrifying? Do I jump in the water? Do you sing? Ugh, please don't tell me you sing country music." She yanked free the two bloody knives she had stabbed into the wooden dock and tossed them into the ocean.

I had never taken a willing victim, not in all my time on earth, and my hesitation must have been written on my face.

"Zosime, you know your job, and I know that I cannot fight the evil inside of me forever." Yashy looked at me with pleading eyes. "Please, I'm tired."

"I will make it quick. If I knew of a cure—"

"We both know this isn't your everyday kind of bad vibe. I'm sure you know more about it than me, but I can feel it consuming me like a plague. This is a curse, and it isn't human."

She had no idea how correct she was. It wasn't human, it was created with the magik of an Ancient. I thought of how many from the human population were now contaminated, and it distressed me. Was I the only one left of the Promised? Had anyone been working on a cure to combat the Lure?

I was yanked from the thoughts as Yashy plunged into the water next to me. I caught her arm and held her head above water.

"Let's go for a swim, mermaid!" She continued to laugh as my fangs descended. We slowly sank beneath the sea, the cool water a contrast to the fiery rage that burned inside me.

In another life, I'd have liked having this tiny warrior female as my friend. Yet one more thing this cruel world had stolen from me.

Also, what is a mermaid?

CHAPTER FOUR

STORM

I slid my sunglasses on as we stood around the body of the latest victim. The morning light was painfully bright as the sun rose and glinted across the water. An early morning jogger had found the body of the young female.

"It just doesn't make sense." Fynn kneeled in the sand beside the body. "I spent most of the night studying the different wounds on each body. This female only has one wound, the single bite to her neck. There are no other obvious signs of trauma to the body."

"Does the bite match any of the bites on the other victims?" Eason stepped forward, looking over Fynn's shoulder.

"Yes," Fynn replied. "But it's the one bite that doesn't

match any known species, which means we still don't know who, or what, killed them." Fynn rocked back on his heels, a frown on his face.

"I wonder what made this kill different," Eason mused. "The others were found in the water and had been nibbled on by local sea life. She is the first to be found dry on the shore. If it weren't for the obvious bite mark, I wouldn't have guessed she was linked to the other victims." Eason leaned in for a closer look at that telltale bite, before turning to Kye. "Have we gotten the full backgrounds on each victim?"

"They sent them to us last night, but the files were bare," Kye replied. "It seems the locals were hesitant to include the full details for each person. I'm guessing there are some small-town politics at play. I put in a call to my guy back at the base, and he'll be sending backgrounds within the next few hours. By the time he finishes, we'll know if they so much as jaywalked."

I nodded at Kye, appreciating the fact he had already taken care of this. My team worked smoothly and efficiently; everyone pulled their weight.

"What can you tell us about the bite, Fynn?" I asked the doctor.

He walked toward me, slipping on his own pair of sunglasses. "The more I study it, the more confused I become. Without doubt, it's the bite of a predator. It's strange, closer to a human's bite mark than the mark of any marine species I've studied. Both the canine teeth and the lateral incisors are longer than the other teeth. It also appears that there's a smaller row of teeth behind the larger teeth."

"Are you sure it isn't a shark? They have multiple rows of teeth." Kye asked the obvious.

"I can't be positive until I am able to exam the predator myself, but the second row is different than the known shark species. Perhaps it's a deformed shark, but that wouldn't explain the clean bite this victim has on her neck. There would be torn flesh, but this is a clean impression. Hopefully the medical examiner can figure out the cause of death."

My gaze was drawn to the expansive ocean. Waves lapped at the shore, scattering seaweed and shells along the beach.

Suddenly, I was overcome by a strange and powerful urge.

Closer.

The need to move toward the ocean was sudden and demanding. I always felt the call of the ocean when I was near it. I longed to slip on my fins and find peace under the surface. But this was a pull so strong that I moved automatically toward the water. My feet stumbled as I was pulled between the urge to obey and the desire to fight the irrational demand. I was working, this was not the time to enjoy a quick dip.

Eason's hand clamped down on my shoulder. "Are you okay, man?"

I staggered to a halt. "Uh, yeah. I'm fine. It's probably just jetlag."

He looked at me with a serious expression. "You feel the urge to swim too, don't you?" His voice was barely above a whisper.

"Yes," I said, frozen in place. "It's so strong that I am afraid to move at all." I couldn't hide the tension in my voice. This wasn't normal.

A splashing sound to my left startled me from the trance and I snapped my head in the direction of the noise. Kye must have felt it too because he now stood knee deep in the foamy sea. Eason and I covered the ground between us in a few short strides, stopping just shy of soaking our shoes.

"Kye! Kye!" we called.

His eyes were full of longing when he turned his head toward us. "I thought I saw something, or someone, in the water. Maybe it was just sea grass."

I shook my head in disbelief. What was going on? I couldn't fight the feeling that we had been watched from the moment we stepped onto the beach, but I didn't want to worry the guys by mentioning my own paranoia, so I remained silent.

"Is everything okay over here?" An officer walked toward us, eyeing Kye like he was an idiot.

"It's fine, officer," I said. "Our colleague thought he saw something and wanted to make sure it wasn't a piece of evidence." I turned to Kye in the water, then to Eason. "Let's head back."

As we walked back, we saw that the body was being loaded into the back of the coroner's van. Fynn joined us as we headed toward our rented SUV. It was odd that we had known him for less than twenty-four hours, yet somehow, he seemed to fit into our team like a missing puzzle piece. We had worked with men and women around the world for many years. Their backgrounds had ranged from academia to law enforcement, military to the tough-as-nails working class, and we had managed to do our jobs and work well with them all. But they were outsiders, never part of our team. Until we arrived here and met Fynn.

This case got weirder with every passing hour. The hair on my neck rose and I could feel eyes on me even as I opened my car door, but not from the bystanders outside the tape. No, I was being watched from the ocean.

The sooner we wrapped this up, the better.

"DO YOU THINK WE'LL ACTUALLY CATCH THE CREATURE in action?" Kye tossed me a water bottle as he spoke.

"I don't know, but I can't sit idle in the hotel room waiting for another body to show up."

Fynn and Eason leaned against the railed sides of the small boat. We had moved a little way from shore, hoping we might be able to hear any screams in our vicinity. It was a long shot, but we didn't have a lot of options at that moment.

Fynn's phone vibrated, and he checked the notification. "It looks like we got some preliminary reports back on the latest victim. The body showed signs of long-term trauma, but the wounds were old or nearly healed." He paused and seemed to zoom in on something on his screen. "Huh. That's odd. There are traces of a toxin in her bloodstream."

"What type of toxin?" Eason asked. "She ingested something?" He leaned toward Fynn's phone. He had spent years studying toxins and had a bit of an obsession with them. To my surprise, Fynn angled his phone toward Eason, allowing him to read the report at the same time.

"It's a neurotoxin called tetrodotoxin, or TTX," Fynn explained. "The blue-ringed octopus is the only thing with a comparable bite, but the marks don't match. This venom is no joke—it's one of the deadliest venoms found in the ocean. If bitten, death would be quick. A victim wouldn't even realize they needed medical help until it was too late. Not that medical help would save them anyway." He sounded more fascinated than horrified.

"Did they find traces of the toxins in any of the other victims?" Kye asked the question before I could voice it.

"That's the odd thing, it's only in the latest victim," Fynn replied. "If it weren't for the distinct and unique bite imprint, I wouldn't have believed this victim was killed by the same predator."

Eason leaned back against the rail, crossing his arms and wrinkling his brow. "It almost seems like this girl was killed with mercy. Which is impossible since this is an animal, right?"

"Right..." Fynn elongated the word, his voice trailing off. He pinched his brow and sighed.

"Any idea what we're looking for?" I asked, but I didn't expect an answer.

Kye's laughter broke the quiet of the night. "A mermaid! Not the cute cartoon type of mermaids, but the type that lure sailors to their death."

Eason smacked Kye on the back of his head, cutting Kye's laughter off abruptly.

"Ow, man. What was that for?"

"I was trying to knock some sense into you, fool."

A chill slammed into the boat, and the hair on my neck rose. The night had been hot and humid, without so much as a breeze. I looked to the other guys, but they looked just as confused. Eason and Kye had dropped their easy-going banter and had taken up defensive stances.

I waited for another gust, but it never came. Around us, the night was calm. Unnaturally calm. The water's surface was still, a perfect glass mirror. Not a single wave broke the illusion.

"There's something fishy going on," Kye whispered.

Fynn and I groaned in amused exasperation. Eason

gave Kye a playful shove. Unfortunately, it was a bit harder than he had intended. Kye stumbled, losing his footing. Eason grabbed for Kye's shirt but missed, clutching at thin air instead. Kye tumbled off the back of the boat, his head made a sickening crack against the small platform at the boat's stern. He hit the water with a crash and sunk below the surface.

Another splash sounded from nearby. My stomach dropped like lead. Whatever made that splash was much larger than a normal fish.

A predator was in the water.

CHAPTER FIVE

ZOSIME

T he four men in the fishing vessel talked and joked, the music of their laughter reaching me even beneath the surface of the water. I had been drawn here, but it had nothing to do with the call.

That morning I had hidden in the reeds, watching to ensure the female had been found. She was brave and deserved to be treated with respect. Emotion stirred in my chest when I thought of her. Even before the battle that sent Atlantis into the sea and me into suspended animation, my emotions were dulled.

I had sworn to fight the Lure that was spreading across earth. To do my job properly, I couldn't be distracted by emotions. The call led me to my targets, to those with souls already damaged by the Lure. Some were evil and had done despicable things, making it easy to complete my mission. Others were like the female, Yashy—good humans that the Lure preyed on. The mission had to be completed regardless. There was no coming back from the Lure, but emotions made it harder to kill those whose souls weren't completely eroded away.

The Ancients took pity on the Promised, and buried our emotions, giving us the ability to destroy the Lure without hesitation. Once the Lure was defeated, we were to have our full emotions restored. It clearly wasn't defeated, so why were my emotions trying to surface?

The female had been found quickly that morning. I was forced to remain still in the water to avoid detection. They wouldn't have been able to catch me in the water, but a hunt would have started. I wasn't ready for that, not yet. As more officers and bystanders arrived on the beach, my head pounded with the chaotic thoughts.

Just when I thought my skull might crack from the pressure, a man had walked on the beach. He wasn't as tall as the Atlantean guards, but he carried himself in a way that made him seem taller than the rest of the men on the shore. Unlike the other men, his hair brushed against his shoulders. It was the pale color of the sand, a contrast to his tanned skin. This man spent long hours outside, not hidden away from the sun.

The closer he came to the water's edge, the more the pressure in my mind eased. I was still in pain, but the sharp edge had softened. The man moved around the body, paying special attention to my bite mark on her neck. I wondered what he had thought about it. Would he recognize the bite? Were there others out there like me?

The arrival of three more men caused a shift among everyone on the beach. Their presence commanded attention without them speaking a word. These men could have stood proudly among the Atlantean warriors. People avoided eye contact, and unconsciously moved out of their way. Everyone reacted, except for the man studying the bite mark. His body remained relaxed, even when the others moved close enough to peer over his shoulder.

The pain in my mind eased a little more. The voices were still there, but quieter. My heart did a strange flutter in my chest, and I had to search my memory to recall the sensation. I had felt this once before, before I became a Promised and swore my life to destroying the Lure. Centuries had passed, but I would never forget him or that single day we had spent in a haze of passion. Now these four men had my heart stirring and my body desiring things that made my cheeks flush.

I remained motionless, but somehow the men sensed my presence. The man with the easy smile and eyes the same color as sea grass had strode into the water in a trance. His eyes were searching, although he had no idea what he was looking for. I knew humans were drawn to me, but only after seeing me. This new form gave me an allure I had yet to figure out. Why were these men feeling it without even seeing me?

A sense of longing washed through me, stealing my breath and forcing salty tears from my eyes. I couldn't stay here any longer. I carefully sank to the shallow seabed, hoping that would cover my retreat. It took several long minutes to ease myself into deeper water since I didn't want to risk an accidental splash of my large fluke.

I spent the remaining hours of daylight resting in a small sea cave I had found. There wasn't a lot of room to move around, but I like the security it provided me. I preferred sunlight (the Atlanteans were a people who thrived in the sun) but it also increased the risk that I would be spotted.

There was only so long I could remain hidden. I had work to do and an oath to keep. At some point, I needed to make contact with the humans of this time and figure out what had happened during the years I was asleep. The problem was figuring out who to approach. I didn't relish the idea of becoming someone's dinner, trophy, or pet, and I wasn't sure how the humans would react to me. The female had been kind, but the others had been cruel, and their thoughts corrupt. I had yet to speak with a human that the Lure hadn't touched. Maybe I needed to approach the men from the beach. Perhaps that was the reason for my pull toward them.

That is how I ended up watching their boat from a small rock outcropping. I was hidden, but able to observe them. Their thoughts pushed at my mind, and instead of trying to stifle them, I opened my mind, allowing their voices to fill my mind. I needed to know more about these men. The Lure hadn't touched them, but that didn't mean they were good. There was evil in the world that had nothing to do with the magik of the Lure. It was possible to be one without the other.

The men's laughter echoed across the water, sending warm tingles through my body. The largest of the men, I heard them call him Eason, reached out a hand with impressive speed and slapped the emerald-eyed man who was called Kye. Unexpected anger surged through me with a force so strong it forced a startled exhalation from me. What was even more shocking was my breath transforming into a gust of wind that rushed across the water and slammed into the small vessel. I clung to the rock, limp and confused.

The men had just been joking. They were like brothers, relaxed and comfortable with one another. Their playful exchange shouldn't have caused me to feel anger; I wasn't supposed to be able to feel any emotions that strong.

I didn't like to see anyone touch what was mine.

The realization made even less sense. Yes, I was curious about them, that's why I was stalking them. But they weren't mine, they were strangers. My mother had told me stories of instant bonding, but it was a myth, not something I had ever seen happen among my people. I couldn't be feeling a bond with strangers, could I? They were humans, and I was… I didn't even know what I was.

My body had continued to adapt and change since my wake-up call. Tonight, I had manipulated the air around me. What if I did it again and hurt an innocent? Or gave away my location? Atlanteans possessed gifts, but nothing that would explain the continued changes I was experiencing.

I focused back on the men. Their expressions were serious, and their thoughts told me they worried for the safety of the humans. It seemed they didn't know what had caused the deaths, but they were determined to figure it out. They had been sent here specifically to hunt down the killer, whether it was a human or an animal. The fact that I was neither might have been funny if I hadn't been just as clueless as to what I'd become.

"There's something fishy going on," the man named Kye had whispered.

I had laughed before quickly clamping a hand over my mouth. I hadn't laughed since I awoke, and even in my previous life I remembered laughing only on rare occasions. I didn't get time to dwell on this latest development. A crack, followed by a heavy splash, yanked my focus to the disturbed water at the back of the boat. Ducking my head beneath the water I searched for the human, expecting to see him kicking back to the surface with a smile on his face.

Instead, I saw Kye's limp body sinking like stone toward the seabed, twenty feet below the vessel. The coppery taste of his blood sent my body and mind into a tailspin. Sharks weren't the only creature of the deep who could taste blood in the water. I wanted to save him from drowning, but I also wanted to sink my fangs into his neck and taste him. My new nature required blood to survive, but I hadn't craved blood in the way that I wanted Kye's.

All thoughts of staying hidden fled from my mind. I wanted him safe, and I wanted to taste him. I shot like a torpedo through the water, not bothering to hide the sounds of my fluke as I used it to propel myself faster than I had ever moved before.

Mine. Mine. Mine.

Sand and silt puffed around him like a cloud when he landed with a soft thump on the seafloor. He remained motionless, a thin line of crimson blood drifting up from his head. His team shouted out orders, I could hear them scrambling for the back of the boat. They were going to jump in as well.

I had nearly reached him when a silver glimmer caught my attention. The panic inside me tripled and I forgot to breathe. I wasn't the only predator in these waters tonight, and the large female shark that I had grown fond of had smelled the blood as well. She must have been nearby to have arrived this fast.

I was faster than her, but I wasn't sure if I could outrun her while carrying a body. The beautiful female didn't deserve to be attacked for simply existing in her own habitat and eating what was available in the ocean. I wasn't sure I could take her down without a weapon, even if I had been willing to.

If the men jumped in, she was going to have more than one target and I couldn't keep them all safe. I could try to toss him up on the boat and then get out of there. That was the best choice, the logical choice. But I couldn't do it. He was mine and he was hurt. I needed to be with him, and I didn't think they would trust me. With the way my gums ached, I wasn't sure I trusted me completely either.

I wrapped my arms around Kye's lifeless body and thrust my fluke hard to send us hurtling toward the surface. Our heads broke the water, and I rushed to expel the water from my lungs. I could breathe above or below the water, but I couldn't communicate with humans with water-logged lungs. Despite this, I still struggled to speak.

"His...his heart beats. I will not harm him. There is a large shark heading for the boat. Do not enter the water tonight."

I didn't give them time to react. Leaving them frozen in stunned disbelief, I sank beneath the waves again. I had to get Kye out of the water so I could get him breathing. I knew just the place, but first I had to outrun a hungry shark who had just realized that I had stolen her meal.

I swam like my life depended on it, and maybe it did. My heart told me that I might not make it if the stranger in my arms died. My teeth had lengthened and need began to pound out a beat that matched the frantic pounding of my heart. He was being hunted by two predators tonight. I might not be able to save him from both.

I pulled his body tighter against mine, trying to reduce the drag as much as possible. My powerful fluke displaced enormous amounts of water, surging me forward. My body undulated, but my companion's limp body made my movements jerky. Glancing over my shoulder, I saw that the sleek queen of the bay had turned from the boat and was streaking toward me. Her entire body was built for speed and efficiency in the water, so it wasn't a surprise that she was closing the gap between us horrifyingly fast.

Gritting my teeth, I dug deep inside me, and something shifted in my chest. Water curled and spun around us, and my burning muscles moved through the water without any strain. We were being sucked along a current. A current that just so happened to be taking me exactly where I wanted. I would have been more concerned over the fact that I now had the ability to manipulate water, but in that moment all I felt was relief.

I bolted into the stone opening next to my cave. My scales shimmered, bathing the dark tunnel in eerie green light. The sharp cave walls angled upwards, and I followed the curve without slowing. We shot up out of the water, slamming hard into damp earth and cool stone. I had moved fast, but Kye had still been underwater for ninety seconds. Wasting no time, I rolled him over and began working to clear water from his lungs.

Water bubbled from his mouth, but he didn't take in a

breath. I slammed my fists against his chest and snarled in frustration. Leaning down, I pressed my warm lips against his pale ones. The coolness of his open mouth was a stark contrast to the burning heat of my own. We were both motionless; the moment frozen in time.

A soft gurgle came from his throat, and I jerked back. Nothing happened. Kye remained still. I wanted to see his playful smile and bright green eyes. I reached out and brushed a finger along his stubbled jawline. Water trickled from the corner of his mouth, but instead of submitting to gravity and slipping to the ground, it moved toward my finger that rested against his jaw.

In disbelief, I slid my finger up his cheek. The water trailed after my finger like an obedient pup. Lifting my finger away, I held it several inches above his face. Water followed my finger like a snake responding to a charmer. I dropped my hand, absolutely dumbfounded. The thin stream of water fell to the ground.

Clarity smacked me in the face. Moving forward, I pressed my hands against his chest where I guessed his lungs would be. Focusing hard, I thought about what I wanted the water to do and crossed my fins that it would work.

I moved my hands up, trying not to be distracted by the incredible feel of the hard muscular planes of his chest. My body flushed with desire, missing the note that this was not the time.

My hands slid along the column of his neck and along

his jawline to his mouth. Water gurgled and bubbled out of his mouth again. Keeping my hands steady, I lifted them away from his mouth and toward me. The water began to rush from his lungs, following my motions. It splashed against me, soaking the ground around me.

Kye choked, automatically rolling to his side. Powerful coughs wracked his body as he worked to clear the remaining water from his lungs. I scooted toward him, patting his back and supporting him as he propped himself up. It took several minutes before his breathing grew less raged and more natural.

He lifted his shirt hem, rubbing at his face. The damp material did nothing to dry his face, and when I caught a peek of his abs, the shirt wasn't the only thing that was wet. I wanted to smack myself. Sure, it had been centuries—fine, millennia—since I had felt my body intertwined with a man. But that was no reason to be this easily aroused.

I bit my lip and tasted blood. The sharp tips of my fangs were still strange to me, and I forgot about them far too often. In this moment I was struggling to hang onto the human traits I had learned. It was futile attempt because I wasn't fully human. I was beginning to question if I was human at all.

With a pained groan, Kye turned toward me. He took in my appearance for the first time. His eyes grew round, and his pupils dilated until the green of his irises disappeared. Chaotic thoughts tumbled through his mind while he tried to make sense of his current situation—and me. I waited, not wanting to admit how much I dreaded hearing his reaction out loud. But nothing on this earth could have prepared me for his reaction.

The tension in his face eased, and his heart slowed from erratic to only slightly faster than normal. He lifted his arm and rubbed the back of his neck in an adorable, but practiced, gesture that was designed to show off his toned abs. His biceps flexed as he moved, affecting me more than it should. I was a warrior that had trained among gladiators without my body reacting. Yet this human man with the kind smile, boyish charm, and gentle thoughts, was stirring the desire to hunt inside me. The desire to hunt and devour him. My mouth watered.

Through the eyes of a predator, I watched him catch his lower lip between his teeth for moment, biting gently before letting go. I stopped breathing, unable to look away. His chest rumbled as he spoke, his voice a deeper pitch than I had heard him use before. Was the human male attempting to lure me with his voice, just as I had done with several of my recent victims?

"Hey baby, are you a mermaid or am I the one who made you all wet?"

CHAPTER SIX

KYE

How hard had I hit my head? I remembered making a joke about mermaids, Eason giving me a playful shove, and then whacking my head as I tumbled off the boat. But I don't remember going into the water. Although, from the water I had coughed up and my soaked clothing, it was obvious that I had not only fallen into the water, but I had nearly died.

Where were the guys? Shouldn't they be here trying to save me? I turned to look for them, and locked eyes with a— mermaid? I was dreaming. Maybe I was still unconscious. That explained the strange cavern and my missing friends. The last thing I had said before losing my footing was a joke about mermaids, and my mind had conjured one.

Long dark hair fell down her back, hiding much of her face and body. Glowing eyes watched me from behind the curtain of hair. When I say glowing, I mean they literally glowed. The effect reminded me of the golden light reflecting in a cat's eyes in the dark, except her eyes glinted turquoise, the color of Caribbean waters.

I followed the damp strands of her hair down her body. Her skin was pale, shimmering scales, the same color as her eyes, and they pulsed in a faint rhythm. It took me a minute to realize why the sight was familiar, why I was convinced that I had seen a similar light show. Then I remembered my work with a research team at a large aquarium. I had spent a summer studying bioluminescence in jellyfish. Their mesmerizing display had caused the entire team to lose track of time on more than one occasion. This affect, now on the mermaid, only added to her allure.

My eyes drifted lower and came to a halt. Books and movies normally portrayed mermaids as having either shells or seaweed styled into a bra, or being completely topless. Turns out they all had it wrong. The reality was more like the armor given to females in video games. You know, the kind that appeared more sexy than practical. A thick piece of 'armor' covered her breastplate and sternum. Smaller individual pieces protected her ribs and connected to the sternum, creating an elegant draping design.

The armor was black and red, but I couldn't figure out what it was made from. I would have guessed leather, but that wouldn't be a logical choice for a sea dweller. I wanted to reach out and explore her body with my hands, not just my eyes. If I was being honest with myself, I didn't just want to explore her body for science. No, I was being drawn to her, ignoring the pull was becoming increasingly difficult with each passing second. It was as impossible as resisting gravity.

Water droplets slid down her body, and my eyes trailed after them. Trepidation and excitement warred inside me. It wasn't every day, or every dream, that you got the chance to study a mermaid. Her skin shifted colors when it came to her hips, the transition from her pale skin to the charcoal of her tail was smooth and gradual. She hadn't just slipped into a tail from the internet to indulge in her own fantasy. No, she was the real deal. The fluke was submerged in the water at the center of the cave, so admiring it would have to wait.

Our eyes locked, and I sucked in a breath as I watched her pupils shift back and forth between rounded and slitted. She wasn't like the mermaids of my daydreams. She was more than I could imagine. Emotion surged inside me, things I thought you could only feel for someone you had known for years. How could you feel so strongly for someone you just met? If I'd had a ring, I would have proposed on the spot. I wasn't going to waste this opportunity, even if it was just a figment of my imagination.

I opened my mouth and the voice that came out was one I didn't recognize. She was affecting every part of me.

"Hey baby, are you a mermaid, or am I the one who made you all wet?"

I wanted to jump back on the boat so I could knock myself out again. Sure, I may be obsessed with cheesy pickup lines, but that one had come out of nowhere. Where had I even heard it?

I watched her reaction and prayed she couldn't speak English. Her aquamarine eyes shimmered with intelligence, and her head tilted as she worked to decipher something. Scales began to flicker, colors flashing like lightning while traveling along her body in a brilliant display. Intuitively, I recognized it as a visual display of her emotions, but couldn't figure out if it was fear, anger, curiosity, or something else.

"You desire me?" The words were spoken in the low sultry tone of a 1950's female blues singer. Her voice hit me like a bolt of electricity, surging through my body and leaving a burning path of desire in its wake.

I huffed out a laugh. "Sweetheart, you have no idea. Yes. Yes, I want you so much it hurts, and that isn't just a figure of speech."

Again, her head tilted as she thought over my words. She worried her bottom lip between her teeth—fangs.

She has fangs.

This wasn't a mermaid, this was a Siren. And if the legends were anything to go by, I was sharing a tiny cavern with the most devious and accomplished predator of the sea. If she decided to attack me, my larger size wasn't going to be enough to save me.

She started to move forward but stopped and glanced down at her tail. I wondered if her hesitation was due to the weight of her tail and fluke. Once that was pulled from the water, the weight would likely be significant. It would slow her down giving me a bit more of a fighting chance should she decide to attack. On the flip side, it would make her more vulnerable, and I doubted that was something she would be okay with.

I hated to think of her feeling uncomfortable, even if I knew she had no reason to fear me. Moving slowly, I scooted toward her. Glinting eyes lifted at my movement, and a predator stared back at me. My heart tripped over its own beat for a split second, but then I remembered this was a dream and you couldn't really die in a dream. At least, I hoped you couldn't.

Inch by excruciatingly slow inch I edged toward her. I stopped when my leg brushed against her thigh. I wondered about the skeletal structure of a mermaid. Did she have two thigh bones? Silencing my inner scientist yet again, I reached out, brushing her check with my knuckles. I couldn't hide the small tremor in my hand as it shook in much the same way it would if I were petting a wild tiger.

She stiffened but remained still. I didn't get bit, so I took that as a good sign. Cupping her face in my palm, I stroked her cheek with my thumb, enjoying the contrast of her slick scales against my roughened skin. Some of the tension left her body and she relaxed into my touch.

"May I kiss you?" I wish I could say my voice came out sexy and confident, but the truth was that the words were little more than a whisper.

Glowing eyes watched me steadily. Her pupils had stopped shifting shapes and now remained slitted like the eyes of a cat. It should have freaked me out more. Maybe I just had a previously unknown kink for the dangerous because something about the unnatural beauty of her predatory features had my body burning with a need like nothing I had experienced before. I wanted her, even if having her was the last thing I would ever do.

"Yes."

My heart soared at that single word. Leaning in, I pressed my lips to the curve of her jawline. Wanting to savor every second of this incredible illusion, I kissed my way to the corner of her mouth, my pace unhurried. Her breathing hitched and she shivered. I smiled, knowing that she was experiencing the same crazy desire that was currently threatening to burn my insides to ash.

I caught her bottom lip between my own, sucking gently. The salty taste of her skin was a reminder that this wasn't your typical kiss. Another taste met my tongue, one that I couldn't place. It was sweet like nectar or honey. My body trembled with desire. I should have been embarrassed to be so affected by simply kissing her, but I didn't care about anything but making her my own at that moment.

Her lips began to move with mine, and our kiss took a turn from sweet to steamy. A soft little hum escaped her mouth, the sound vibrating through me. Dizziness washed over me. The sensation was that of holding your breath for too long, then releasing it and desperately gulping in lungfuls of air. Except in this case, it was her that had me gasping in need. If things stopped at that point, I'm sure I would have passed out.

I needed more. Sliding my hand into her hair, I pulled her lips more firmly against my own. Her hands trailed up my water-soaked shirt. It clung to my skin, and she traced along the lines of my chest through the fabric.

When she sighed out another hum, blood rushed to my groin with a suddenness that caused me to jerk. The movement caught us both off-guard and she nicked my lip with her fang. We both froze. The faint acidic taste of blood was in my mouth, which meant she likely tasted it too. Would she turn full predator now and eat me? Somehow, instead of the thought dousing my desire like cold water, it turned me on even more. Sweat trickled down my forehead and spine, not from fear, but from desire.

"I am sorry. This is not normal for me. I cannot resist any longer." Her soft textured voice trembled.

If she was going to go all predator, I was more than happy to go out this way. Just so long as I got to have her as my last meal.

"Whatever you need, babe. I'm yours." I wasn't the type to make promises and declarations of love during sex, but in that moment, I knew without a doubt that she would have my heart until the day it stopped beating. Whether that was five minutes from now, when she ripped it out and ate it, until I died as an old man, or until I woke up from this way-too-real dream.

She wasted no time, lunging forward, her arms wrapping around my neck. Yanking hard and popping her fin to push herself off the ground a few inches, she twisted me around. I landed with a soft thud on the ground, surprised to find she had moved her hand to the back of my head to ensure it didn't bang against the stone floor of the tiny cavern. A thoughtful gesture that made me think that she might not be planning to eat me. Why would she care if her dinner was braindead?

Her hips and fin settled between my legs, and her hands slid under my shirt. The skin-to-skin contact sent another wave of dizziness through me. How hard had I hit my head? She shimmied, attempting to pull herself up my body. Grabbing her waist, I hauled her up my body until our faces met. The delicious friction of her wiggling body against my erection was a special kind of torture.

She kissed my lips again and then pulled away before I could deepen the kiss. Sucking and licking, she nuzzled her way down my neck. My heavy-lidded eyes jerked open wide when a sting of pain shot through my neck. She had bitten me, and her teeth were still embedded in my skin. As quickly as the pain had come, it disappeared. Instead, lust slammed into me like a tsunami.

This wasn't your typical lust-filled haze. No, this was the type of lust that made you feel like ripping your clothes off and going at it like an animal. Pure, unadulterated, raw need. Imagine being bitten by a venomous animal and feeling the venom move through your body, affecting nerves and muscles, and burning you up on the inside? The only thing that can save you is antivenom, otherwise you'll die. In my case, lust was burning through my body, and I was confident I wouldn't survive if I didn't get to sink inside her and feel her body wrapped around mine.

My mouth was dry, my heartbeat erratic, and my breathing shallow. My erection jerked against the constraints of my pants. Her soft sucking sound just below my ear hit caused my stomach to flip as though we had just gone into zero gravity.

"Please. I need you." If the guys ever found out that I had begged her, I would be ribbed for the rest of my life. I didn't care. But nothing mattered in that moment except her. The only problem was that I wasn't sure how exactly a mermaid, or whatever this sexy little thing was, mated.

She released her hold on my neck, licking at the wounds like a cat. She rolled to the side and out from between my legs. I ached at the loss of contact.

"Remove your clothing." Her eyes were hooded as she watched me. The white of her fangs glinted as she licked her lips.

My hands shook as I moved to do as she asked. I felt weak and feverish. How could my need for her be making me physically ill? It took some work to remove my soaked shoes and jeans, the material clinging to my body. I didn't wear anything under my jeans, so after removing them and my shirt, I was bare in front of her. My pulsing erection made the extent of my desire fully known.

She moved back toward me, shimmying her way between my legs again with a little help from me. I sighed in relief as soon as our skin touched again. My shaking eased as I wrapped my arms around her body.

"Come into the water with me, Kye." She hummed the words against my lips.

I should have questioned how she knew my name. Red flags should have waved like crazy at the idea of getting into the water with a fanged Siren who had already proved she liked human sushi. I was having a hard time keeping it straight in my mind that this was a dream. It felt far too real. In the end, it didn't really matter whether it was real life or a dream; I would follow her into the water without question.

The end of her tail and her fluke was still hidden in the small hole in the cave's center. I assumed that was the water she wanted me to enter. Refusing to release my hold on her, I half-scooted half-shuffled my way to the edge of the hole. My legs were submerged up to my knees, and her body dangled from my arms.

"You have to release me, handsome."

Reluctantly, I loosened my grip and let her slide down my body and into the pool. She stopped herself right at my hips and nuzzled my thigh. Her head moved nearer to my aching member. If she touched it, I was going to explode.

She licked up my shaft, and my vision shifted as blackness threatened to swallow me. This was not the time to pass out or wake up. Her teeth sank gently into my most prized body part, and again that all-consuming lust tore through my body, ripping away at my humanity. My erection grew hotter, my blood turned to lava by her bite. I had to be dreaming because my erection swelled and ached as it stretched. Nothing crazy dramatic, it was more like I had never been fully erect in the past, and additional blood now pumped into it making my muscles swell and pushing me to a fuller erection.

Licking the tiny prick marks, she slipped into the water. I wasted no time in joining her. The cool water was a welcome relief to my feverish body and aching muscles. The moment I was in the water, she pressed her body against the length of mine.

"Stop trying to swim. Just hold me close." Her words felt like a caress, and my body obeyed her instantly. It was no wonder there were countless stories about Sirens luring men to their death.

With the added length of her tail, she was much longer than me. As I held her against me and stopped treading water, my body floated with perfect buoyancy. Her beautiful face held no signs of strain, and I was reminded again that I was in her territory now. We swayed as her tail undulated in lazy motions, keeping our heads above water. Each time her tail moved, it would rock against my erection, continuing to build my need past the point I thought possible.

I felt her shudder against my chest, and I wondered if the friction was as innocent as it seemed, or if it was affecting her just as much.

"What's your name, beautiful?" I was about to make love to the girl of my dreams, literally. It wasn't just my body that was being affected by her, my heart was too. I wanted her more than anything I had ever wanted before, and I wanted to have her for the rest of my life. This was more than lust—I wanted to know the name of the woman I would give up my entire world for.

She paused from licking and nipping my chest. "Zosime."

She pronounced Zo, like Joe. Her name sounded like 'zo-see-mae.'

"Zosi. I like it." Smiling, I nipped at her earlobe.

"Zosi?"

"Yes, like Josie. A girl's nickname."

She stiffened and then stunned me with a growl. It was a sound I had never heard before. It was a cross between a wolf's growl, a jaguar's hiss, and a creepy alien sound from a horror movie. She pushed away from me.

"This Josie, she is bonded to you?"

Was I imagining it, or had her fangs grown longer? That wasn't possible. I think. We bobbed, water washing over my head. She was twitching her tail like an irritated cat. I wanted to laugh at the absurdity, but I was currently in the water, butt naked, and at the mercy of an angry fanged mermaid.

"No! Josie is a common female name. One of my commanders had a wife with that name."

She continued to glare at me through slitted eyes, not bothering to hide her fangs. Water washed over my head, forcing me to begin treading water. The water stirred violently, her tail stirring it up.

"What...what does 'bonded' mean?" I asked between spitting out mouthfuls of saltwater.

The tightness around her eyes eased slightly, and although her tail continued to churn the water around us, the movements were less erratic.

"Among my kind, bonded is a covenant between two people to become mates for life."

"Oh! Like marriage!"

She tilted her head, considering my words. As stupid as it sounds, I could have sworn she was downloading information or talking to someone telepathically.

"Yes. That word is the closest in meaning to my people's word for bonding."

"Then no. I am not bonded, and I have never been bonded." I huffed a laugh. "I haven't ever wanted to be bonded. Not until tonight. Until you." I couldn't believe the words tumbling out of my mouth, perhaps it was because this was just a dream. But that didn't change the fact that every single word was true. I would bond to her that very night if given the chance. I imagined someone officiating a ceremony from the side of the cave to marry a naked man and a mermaid, and chuckled.

Zosi floated back up against me. I wrapped my arms around her and relaxed as she took over swimming for both of us.

"You would bond with me tonight?" Her sultry voice sent goosebumps across my skin.

"Without question. I'd love nothing more than to bond with you tonight."

"Okay." She smiled and moved up to capture my lips. This taste of honey and salt danced across my tongue, and just as before, my body instantly flared to life. The effects from our previous make-out session hadn't worn off, and I had been growing more tired with each minute that passed. When she had pulled away, the symptoms became worse. I could think of nothing but sinking inside her and claiming her as mine.

Now.

CHAPTER SEVEN

ZOSIME

The things this man was doing to my body shouldn't be possible. My emotions were bound by the Ancients, and only they were able to undo it. Yet the stone encasing my heart had begun to fracture just being near these men. With Kye's hands and lips on my body, the walls had started to crumble, and pieces of my emotions slipped through unchecked.

It was utter chaos inside me. Atlantean, warrior and Siren all struggled against each other. Each nature trying to push forward and gain control. I fought against my inner turmoil, determined to have this time with Kye. I wasn't sure how long my control would last, so I needed to make every moment count.

My immense relief at knowing he was not bonded surprised me, but the bigger shock came when he said that if it were possible, he would bond with me that night. His thoughts were jumbled, so I couldn't understand every sentence, but those words were crystal clear, and he meant them. The turmoil inside me stilled instantly, the abrupt silence deafening.

That's when it happened. The three sides of me decided in that moment to become one. I had been able to use one or two aspects of my nature at the same time, but never all three. We weren't prepared, but that made no difference. The Atlantean had found her forever love, the Siren had found her delicious mate, and the warrior had found her perfect partner. The fractured parts of me were in agreement for this small window of time.

I wrapped my arms around his neck, pressing our bodies together. Water twirled around us in a sensual dance and our mouths joined in the motion of the dance. Kye grew impossibly harder, and his kisses turned from gentle to hungry. I had a sneaking suspicion of why that might be, but I would have to explore that line of thought later.

Kye's manhood pressed against the apex of my thighs. Yes, my sex was in approximately the same area as it would be on a woman with legs. My skin tingled and burned, and I couldn't wait any longer to feel his touch inside me. I slid my hand down until I touched the most sensitive scales. While all my scales were just as sensitive as my skin, the scales in this area were extraordinarily so. Using two fingers, I pushed aside the scales on either side of my most private spot. The tiny, scaled lips blended seamlessly with the rest of my scales, hiding my sex completely.

My finger slipped inside the heated channel, ensuring I was well lubricated. I needn't have worried. Moving my other hand away from his neck, I maneuvered it between us until I could wrap my fingers around his thick erection. Kye gave an involuntary jerk and groaned into my mouth.

His unexpected lurch caused me to again nick his lip. The delicious spicy taste of his blood exploded in my mouth. Nothing had tasted this amazing since I had awakened. I was forced to drink blood to survive. The taste didn't repulse me, but it was more about survival than savoring a meal. It had been a challenge to pull back the first time I tasted Kye's blood. I needed him. His body, his blood, and his love.

Kye's hips jerked, his heavy erection moving in my hand as he sought relief. No more waiting, we had a lifetime to explore each other's bodies. Moving away from his mouth, I sank my fangs into his neck. At the same moment I lined him up with my slit and with a flick of my fluke, I sheathed him inside me in one hard thrust. Our bodies slammed against each other; his hot member buried as far as it could go.

My eyes rolled back in my head and for a moment I thought I might pass out. There was a sharp pain as he stretched me past the point that was comfortable. I hadn't given myself time to adjust to his size slowly in my eagerness to have him in me. To my surprise, the edge of pain aroused me even more and I teetered on the edge of my release.

Kye must have experienced similar sensations. When his pulsing erection had been shoved inside me, slamming against my walls, he had growled through clenched teeth. He grasped me tightly against him, his chest shuddering with each breath he sucked into his lungs.

"Don't move. If you move, I will lose it. Give me a minute, please." His teeth were still clenched. "You are so tight, Zosi. So tight."

His voice sounded pained, and I worried I had hurt him. I released his neck to say, "Are you injured?"

"No, nothing like that. I've never felt anything this good."

I said nothing, instead sinking my teeth back into his neck, unable to resist the aromatic scent of his blood that made my mouth water. I felt his body pulse inside me in response to the bite.

Gradually his grip eased, and I took that as my cue that he had regained control. I began to undulate my tail in the water, my pace unhurried. The motion moved him in and out of me. The feeling of him rubbing along my walls had me growling against his skin. I tried to go slow, but the Siren could wait no longer. The water around us had continued to swirl, but now it sloshed and splashed as my pace grew faster. The rocking undulation of my fin had Kye's member thrusting in and out of me. Each time he sheathed himself, our groins banged together.

Kye never tried to take over, instead he gripped my hips and allowed my tail to rush us toward our release. His fingers dug into my hips as I moved us faster and faster. Our breathing was little more than small panting gasps. Kye kept his head tilted to the side so I could continue to drink from him.

Stars glittered in my vision, and my stomach clenched. With two more hard slips of my fluke, the coil inside me sprung free and my orgasm crashed over me. My body shook as wave after wave of pleasure rocked through me. Kye shouted my name, his body stiffening as he followed me over the precipice. I could feel his erection pulse as the evidence of release filled me. The feeling of his body jerking inside my tight walls sent another orgasm shuddering through me. I screamed his name in surprise and dug my nails into his skin as I clung to him.

Mine.

He was mine. Forever and always.

I pressed my hand against his heart and my mouth to the spot where I had bitten him. For a moment I stayed still, savoring this moment as we became one. I was no longer alone in the world. I still had so much to figure out, but I would not face it alone. Pulling away, I watched the magik swirl along his skin. It should have been the gold of the Atlanteans, but instead it was the color of my glowing scales. The magik etched a shimmering tattoo from the skin above his heart, up to his shoulder, and finally connecting with the imprint of my teeth. The bite mark was incorporated into the intricate design, not hidden, but a part of the tattoo.

"Αν έπρεπε να ζήσω τη ζωή μου ξανά, θα σε έβρισκα νωρίτερα."

I met Kye's startled gaze. "I understood you," he whispered. "You said, 'If I were to live my life again, I'd find you sooner.' How am I able to understand you?"

"Because we are one. You are mine, and I am yours."

I kissed the full lips of my handsome mate, ready to find more ways to enjoy each other's bodies. I felt the answering stir of his body still inside me. This was going to be a deliciously long night.

Suddenly, the sound of shouting ricocheted around the cave. There were no entrances to the little cave, the only way to get it was to go through the underwater tunnel. The chamber was about sixteen by twelve feet. It was dry, although water sloshed onto the dark rough stones around the mouth of the tunnel. The ceiling was almost solid rock, patches of velvet black sky and stars could be seen through small holes, and it also allowed us to hear some of the sounds from the outside world.

I stilled against the hard muscled planes of Kye's body and

my instincts kicked into overdrive. Emotions were trying to break through the magik barriers that held them back. I had just bonded with my mate, and that left me feeling raw. Atlanteans disappeared from society for several months after bonding. This allowed them to focus on the needs and desires of their claimed mate. It also gave both partners time to adjust to the physical and mental changes that came from an Atlantean bonding. I hadn't had time to explain things to Kye, things that ideally, he should have been told before I sealed our bond.

What I was having more trouble controlling was the feral nature of the Siren. I had grown up as an Atlantean, but I had barely begun to understand the changes that had happened to my body as the ocean swallowed Atlantis. The changes to my body were obvious, but the mental differences and instincts were unfamiliar and less predictable. The second row of teeth dropped down behind the first. My mouth tingled and I tasted the sweet taste of toxin. That had been a shock, one more ability that had manifested when the need arose.

Voices grew louder, carrying across the water. They wanted my mate. He was going to be taken from me. I couldn't go with him unless I wanted to risk being captured. For a moment I thought about dragging them all beneath the waves, then they wouldn't be able to take Kye from me. But recognizing the voices as belonging to his friends on the boat, Storm, Eason, and Fynn, I knew it would be impossible to harm them. They were mine too, although I didn't know how Kye would take that. We had much to discuss and learn about each other.

Atlantis had very open ideas regarding love, and relationships of all types were common. It was not uncommon for there to be several people in one relationship. From the thoughts I had picked up from the humans of this time, multiple partners in a single relationship was less accepted and often considered strange. I would honor his wishes, but I hoped that Kye would consider the ways of my kind.

"Zosi, my love," Kye whispered gently. "My friends are worried, I need to go to them. I don't want to this dream to end, but this may be my call to wake up." He pulled himself from my slick folds. Our bodies were still aroused, and the friction sent a shudder through both of us.

What did he want to wake up from? He wasn't asleep. I focused and his thoughts swirled in my mind. There were memories that seemed to come from a dream—mating with a mermaid, our bodies moving together like an erotic dream, moments when he thought of waking. It was confusing, and the thoughts blended into each other.

"You are not asleep. Stay with me." I could barely hear my own words.

"Oh, how I wish I could, my love. I know a day will never pass without me thinking of this perfect dream, and my incredible dream girl." His lips pressed against my hair, and he inhaled in my scent. He was trying to commit everything about me to memory.

My eyes burned, but I did not cry. I had never heard of

anyone leaving their mate the day they had consummated the bond. These hours were important, but I would not force Kye to remain with me. I would take him to the others; I would do anything for him. He carried a piece of my soul now.

"I will take you," I said. "Even with equipment, a human would struggle to navigate this tunnel. You must breathe slowly and lower your heart rate. When you need air, expel your air fully and seal your lips against mine."

Curiosity stirred in Kye's eyes when he looked back at me. "Don't you need that air? I don't want you to pass out!"

Laughter tried to bubble up inside me, but the barriers continued to force it back. I was surprised to find that I wanted to remember what it felt like to laugh. "I breathe beneath the water. Now, get dressed. if you are truly leaving, we need to go soon."

Kye struggled into his clothes, snagging them. Once he was ready, he turned to look at me.

"Focus your breathing," I told him as I moved toward him.

Nodding his head, he closed his eyes and focused on his breathing. I did the same. I had not told him the challenge this would pose for me. I needed to allow one lung to fill with water, while letting the other remain full of air. If I were human, that level of control wouldn't be possible. However, just because I could do it, didn't mean it was easy. I had practiced this only a few times and each time it was painful, not unlike drowning. But Kye didn't need to know that this was the only way to get him safely from the cave without alerting outsiders to my hidden home.

Propelling myself higher in the water, I captured Kye's lips in my own. I poured what emotions I was capable of into those precious seconds.

"Breath deep." I watched him pack air into his lungs. With a small dip of his chin, he signaled that he was ready.

"Θα σε αγαπάω για πάντα."

His eyes widened but I didn't give him time to respond before dragging him into the obsidian waters of the tunnel. I had traveled this route many times before, and I avoided the jagged rocks that jutted from the walls with ease. My scales pulsed their blue-green light, casting a soft glow around us. The tunnel went deep into the earth before taking a sharp curve up and opening into waters near mouth of the bay. The boat was not far from my cave if you had the wings of a bird, but the maze beneath the ocean took longer to navigate.

We were nearing the steep bend when Kye released a curtain of bubbles and pressed his lip against mine. For a moment, I wanted to pause and savor his lips, but I did not have enough air in my lung for long delays. I opened my mouth against his, my muscles constricting painfully as I sealed the water-filled lung and opened the pipe to my air-filled lung. He drew in what he needed, and then pulled away. His lips lingered against mine for mere second. I reversed the process in my chest, gritting my teeth against the discomfort.

Our surroundings were little more than a blur as my powerful fluke propelled us forward. We streaked into the ocean, and I turned and headed straight for the vessel. The shouts of the men could be heard even beneath the waves. Large spotlights shined on the water; they were using everything they could to locate Kye. I slowed to dodge the blinding lights. Kye's lips pressed against my lips once more, and again I gave him air. This time, I allowed both lungs to fill with water. That first long breath of cool saltwater eased the burn in my chest. I took several breaths in a row, moving faster now that I was no longer functioning on a single lung.

Kye's arms tightened painfully around my waist when I swam deeper. I would not risk being seen. Once we were directly beneath the boat, I began our ascent to the surface. The outline of the back of the boat came into view. When we were six feet from the surface, I halted our forward motion. Kye's questioning look made it clear that he expected me to surface alongside him.

Shaking my head, I wiggled free of his snug embrace. He had already begun to float toward the surface, and I used my newly discovered water abilities to move him the last few feet to the surface. He struggled to reach for me, but I turned and sank into the depths. I lurked beneath the boat until I saw his legs disappear as his friends pulled him from the dark sea. Once he was safe, I made my escape.

I headed straight for the ocean. The shallow water surrounding the bay wasn't going to be safe with the humans looking for me. I needed to hide from them, but I also wanted to escape my hurt. For a beautiful moment, I had thought I wouldn't have to be alone anymore.

Swimming into the black depths of the sea, I realized I had never felt so alone in my entire existence.

CHAPTER EIGHT

KYE

I broke the surface and gasped in the salty warm air. I had fully expected to wake up from unconsciousness when I surfaced. Instead, Eason and Storm shouted exclamations and hauled me from the water. Fynn stepped forward, a thick towel held out toward me. I thanked him and grabbed the towel. I wiped at the salt water that was burning my nose.

"Where have you been? How did you escape?" Fynn spoke first.

"Escape? From what?" I replied.

"The mermaid that surfaced with you in her arms," Fynn almost shouted back. "She told us you were alive, and that she wouldn't hurt you. Then she warned us not to get in the water because a shark was nearby. It's highly likely that *she* is the one responsible for the climbing body count. We worried you were her next victim." His words came out like a torrent, his fear and anxiety apparent.

"She wouldn't do that!" I said it with confidence, but the reality was I had no way of knowing if it was true or not. After we made love, something inside me shifted and I had thought I could feel her. I couldn't clearly read her thoughts, but there was a ghostly impression of them. It had been just another intriguing twist of the illusion.

"Did she tell you that?" Eason's snort of derision had me snapping my head up to lock eyes with him.

"No, we didn't talk about it. She was—" How was I supposed to describe her?

"Kye, I am sure any of us would fall in love with a mermaid that rescued us, but remember that she is a predator," Storm said. "From the little I saw, she is literally built to kill. We were helpless to stop her tonight and that was terrifying." Storm's tone wasn't condescending, and I knew where he was coming from. They were all wrong, though.

"It's a dream. I'll wake up any minute." I closed my eyes tightly, praying that I would wake up and none of this would be real. The most incredible dream of my life was fast becoming a nightmare. Just the thought that this might not be a dream had bile rising up my throat. I was the one who asked to cut our time together short, and I had let her swim away. Her last words to me had been in Greek, but my mind had understood her meaning, even though I knew nothing about the language.

I will love you forever.

Those were the last words she said to me. I hadn't even had a chance to respond before she pulled us underwater. If this was all real, then I had let the love of my life slip through my hands like water and she didn't even know that I loved her too.

Groaning, I dropped onto the deck with a thud and pressed my face into the damp towel. Storm eased down on one side of me, and Fynn settled on the other side.

"What's going on, little brother?" Storm wasn't my brother, none of us were related by blood, but that didn't change the depth of our relationship.

Heaving a sigh, I recounted the entire saga. I did, however, skim over the details of our lovemaking. "How can I be sure I'm not still asleep?" I moaned in frustration.

Suddenly, a fist connected with my stomach, hard enough to knock the wind from me, but not hard enough to truly hurt me. "What the heck, Eason?"

"I was just proving you were awake." His casual shrug was irritating.

"You couldn't just pinch me like a normal person?" I growled.

"That's for wimps."

I wanted to wipe the smug smirk off his face, but I was exhausted and heartsick. I wanted to sleep for the next week straight, but I also wanted to jump in the ocean and find Zosi.

Fynn spoke, his voice coming from far away. "He's going into shock. Our questions will have to wait until he has been rested and checked for injuries." His hands moved along my skin feeling for my pulse and temperature. My eyelids turned to lead, drooping with the weight. Unable to bear the heartache of losing her, I let unconsciousness steal me away.

CHAPTER NINE

FYNN

Kye's body went slack, and he slumped against me. "Guys, we really need to get him back to shore and to a hospital," I said.

"No hospitals, not yet anyway," Storm replied firmly. "We can't explain what happened, which means they won't be able to help him. If she bit him and released venom, the hospitals won't have an anti-venom for that, since Sirens aren't real. We'll get him back to our room and you can examine him there. If you believe there are internal injuries, we will take him for X-rays at the medical examiner's office. If those show internal injuries that require surgery or medical supplies outside of what we can obtain, *then* we will make the trip to the hospital."

Storm's tone made it clear this wasn't up for debate. I understood his decision, but I didn't have to like it. Growing up, books were my friends and they had opened doors to things I had found fascinating. As an adult, I was still a loner, never fitting in with those around me. Even when undertaking my research work, I preferred my home office or visiting the lab after hours to work. I filled the long hours alone by studying, and I had earned degrees in several fields. One of those was a PhD, although I had never practiced as a doctor after finishing my residency. I would have preferred a doctor check him over at a hospital immediately. If there was a problem, the delay could cost Kye his life.

Eason turned the boat back toward the shore, careful to stay just inside the posted speed limits. Storm pulled Kye against him to keep Kye's limp frame from banging against the boat. There was nothing romantic between these three men. Their shared bond was that of brothers, not by blood, but by choice. They were family, and I longed to have that for myself.

In under thirty minutes we were settling Kye on his bed. Eason and Storm stepped to the side, close enough to observe, but far enough to give me space to move around him without feeling cramped.

I started with his head, wanting to check the spot that had impacted with the boat. "That's weird, there should be a lump and a cut here. We know he was knocked unconscious and there was blood on the boat and in the water, but there are no signs of an injury. That isn't possible." I checked again, and then stepped aside as Storm looked for the point of impact as well. There wasn't so much as a lump or papercut to mark the spot. He stepped back, shaking his head in confusion.

"Let's remove his shirt." With a few grunts as we lifted and maneuvered his dead weight, we managed to get it off. As his shoulder came into view, I gasped.

"Has he always had this tattoo?"

"What tattoo? He doesn't have..." Eason's words trailed off as he stared at the markings that traveled down Kye's neck to his shoulder and then lower toward his heart. The design was elegant, reminding me of the swirling sea. The lines were glowing, aquamarine light ebbing and flowing throughout the tattoo. Letters of an alphabet I didn't recognize spelled something about his heart. This type of art piece would have taken days to complete, but somehow it had been done in two or three hours. One more impossibility to add to our growing list.

"What's that on his neck?" Storm pointed to a spot where the design created a beautiful circular seal, the type often used by royalty. In the middle of the circle there were additional words in that unfamiliar script, and a—"Bite mark. He's been bitten!"

Utter panic ensued.

I scrambled to check his vitals for the umpteenth time. Eason grabbed his keys and started putting his shoes on the wrong feet. Storm grabbed his phone and made the motions to call someone but couldn't decide who. I'm not sure what would have happened if Kye hadn't decided to wake up in the middle of our chaos.

"Ugh. Guys? What is going on?" He rubbed at his temple and tried to sit up. His body trembled with the effort. With a groan he collapsed back on the bed.

"We will get you to the hospital. Just hang in there, Kye!" Storm couldn't hide the fear in his voice.

"I'm tired, not dying. Chill." Kye huffed a breathless laugh that helped to reassure all of us that he wasn't truly dying.

"Kye, do you remember being bitten? How long ago did it happen?" I peered into his eyes checking for discoloration.

To my shock, he blushed. "Fynn, I like you a lot, but back up a bit." He was trying to distract me.

"So, you do remember being bitten," I said. "Why did she bite you? Have there been any side effects or symptoms?"

Kye turned a deeper shade of crimson. Roars of laughter startled me, and I jumped. Eason and Storm collapsed into chairs and laughed until tears streamed down their faces. "What's so funny? Kye's life may still be in danger!"

The men tried to speak, but between their gasps for air and raucous laughter, I couldn't make sense of it.

"She bit me while we were being intimate," Kye said with a sigh. "Those jerks figured it out. I'm not going to die from it. It did have, um, side effects, but she fixed that." He wouldn't even look at me as he spoke, and his skin remained red.

"Side effects like what? I need specifics to figure out what we are dealing with." I grabbed my pen and paper, preparing to make notes that we could use later if needed.

Kye's eyes finally met mine and he looked horrified. "You're going to write it down?" His voice cracked in panic.

I looked in confusion at Eason and Storm, but they had been set off into another round of laughter. I wasn't sure how we were supposed to get to the bottom of this if everyone kept acting like children. Clicking my pen over and over, a habit I had developed as a kid, I waited for everyone to calm down. It took about ten minutes for the guys to get ahold of themselves, wipe their eyes, and stop chuckling.

"Fynn, you really need to relax a bit," Storm said with a grin. "I always thought Eason was uptight, but you have him beat." Storm's smile made it clear this was playful banter; he was not belittling me.

"You aren't the first to say that." I sighed. These guys were the first men I had ever felt like I belonged with. It made zero sense considering how long we had known each other. My heart said they were my tribe, even as my mind said that was sentimental and ridiculous.

Eason walked over and slapped me on the back. "Give us time, we'll make you unwind." He turned toward Kye. "Alright kid, you left out a lot of details on the boat when you described your encounter with the mermaid. I don't care if it's embarrassing. It's time to tell us everything."

Kye's shoulder sagged. Taking a deep breath, he began to tell the story again, except this time when he got to the part about their intimacy, he retold it in great detail. I forgot to write; my pen frozen on the paper as he described the encounter. Never in my life had I heard anything this erotic. A hard bulge formed in my pants, and I moved my notebook to cover it, embarrassed that the guys might have noticed it.

When Kye finished speaking, he adjusted his pants and cleared his throat a few times. Eason threw a bottle of water at him but didn't bother to get up. I hid my smile; it turns out I wasn't the only one affected by the tale.

Storm spoke up, his voice low and rough, "It sounds like she managed to counteract her venom. It's good to know that there's a cure, or an antivenom. Maybe it's her saliva? Perhaps she's the cure for her venom."

I choked on my own laughter. Now it was their turn to watch me with irritated gazes as I howled. With herculean effort I managed to speak, "Oh yes, she is definitely the cure!" It took several more minutes for me to pull myself together.

"Care to elaborate, Doctor?" Eason raised his brow, impatience showing in his squinted eyes.

"Yes, yes," I said, collecting myself. "Okay, it sounds like she can control her venom. Based on Kye's symptoms, her venom acted as an aphrodisiac. Maybe a smaller dose has these effects, while a larger dose is lethal. I would need to study that more to be sure. However, what we do know is that it worked as a sexual stimulant in Kye. He was experiencing health issues, until they completed copulation—"

"Did he just say 'copulation?'" Kye's eyes were wide, and his mouth hung open in horror.

"Do you prefer coitus?" I queried.

Eason snorted.

"Coupling? Intercourse? Fornicati—"

Storm broke in. "Sex. You are saying that she injected him with a stimulant to ensure he would perform. What would be the point? Maybe she needed a male to procreate?"

Kye looked faint, his skin turning a sickly green shade.

Eason's eyes glinted in humor. "Did you hear that, Kye? She basically gave you the mermaid's version of a little blue pill."

"It wasn't like that!" Kye cried. "I was already aroused before she bit me, and I came onto her first. We both wanted it and consented to it verbally." He paused and rubbed his eyes.

"Fynn may be right about its affects, though," he confessed. "It didn't force me to be aroused, but it definitely enhanced our lovemaking."

"It would be very interesting to study the effects in person," I added.

All three guys guffawed. My cheeks grew warm from embarrassment.

"Purely for science! I didn't mean it like that!"

They snickered and elbowed each other like they were thirteen years old instead of in their twenties and early thirties.

"Fine, it sounded weird," I conceded. "From what Kye said, the flu-like symptoms of the toxin eased, but didn't cease completely. That might be why he's still shaky." I sighed and turned to Kye. "I wish we had a sample to study. We still don't know why your injuries healed, or how she gave you an intricate tattoo in minutes. If I weren't looking at the evidence, I wouldn't believe it. I wish we could read that language. Maybe I could send some photos to my friends and see if they recognize the script."

"I want to see it, is there a mirror?" Kye glanced around the room. Flicking the blanket off his body he prepared to stand.

"Stay in bed!" I barked. Moving toward him, I pulled out my cell phone and snapped a photo. I handed him the phone, watching his face as he zoomed in on the script. He unconsciously moved his mouth as he studied the photograph. Color drained from his face and the phone trembled in his hand.

"What is it? Why do you look like someone died?" Storm asked what we were all wondering.

Kye moved his hand up and rubbed the tattoo. When he finally met our eyes, I saw the tears in his own. "We bonded, and I left her."

"Bonded? What does that mean?"

My stomach dropped. Eason may not understand, but I believed I knew what Kye was saying. "Are you sure?" I asked him.

"Yes." His voice was barely a whisper. "I can't read the words, but somehow I know what they symbolize. She asked, and I agreed. I believed it was a dream. The thing is, even if I had known it was real, I still would have said yes. I can't explain it because it doesn't make sense. But I knew she was mine and I was hers. Nothing else mattered."

"Is someone going to explain what on earth he's talking about?" Eason asked.

I turned to face Eason.

"I'm guessing there's a lot more at play here judging by her effect on him and the magical tattoos," I said. "But the short answer is, he got married tonight, got his rocks off, and then ditched his new bride."

CHAPTER TEN

ZOSIME

I spent six days hidden in the depths. The obsidian darkness that had once bothered me, now enveloped me in a way that made me feel secure. I lay curled on the sandy bed of the ocean floor. My scales remained dark, not bothering to light the world around me, a world I didn't care to see.

Even when I had held my emotions centuries ago, I would never have been this devastated. I was chosen to be one of the Promised because of my warrior heart. Being soft was nothing to be ashamed of, but it wasn't me. I was the one who helped to protect the tenderhearted. Now I hid in the darkness, nursing a broken heart. Idly, I wondered how

I would have survived this devastation if my emotions weren't still being partially blocked.

It seemed impossible that a stranger could affect me so much. It had to be the instant bonding. Hot salty tears mixed with the cool saltwater around me. I had no one to ask about the bonding legends, and I doubted any scrolls from Atlantis had survived in the collapse. Maybe it was time for me to return to the waters of my childhood and search for any ruins of my home and her people.

Rough skin slid against my own, startling me out of my own little 'pity party.' That was a term I heard in the mind of the female but didn't understand until Kye had climbed onto that boat and left me behind. Rousing myself, I thought of my shimmering scales and slowly they flickered to life. A wave of dizziness washed over me the moment I pushed myself into a sitting position. It wasn't until that moment that I realized how weak I felt. I had gone too long without eating.

Dim green light lit the waters a few feet around me. It was just enough to see the massive grey and white body not four feet from my face. I flattened myself into the sand and silt, gritting my teeth as her rough skin rubbed against the length of my body. It was the same impressive shark that had been lurking around me since I swam into these waters.

I watched as she turned and moved toward me again. The sheer size and girth of her body made her turns a bit slower. This time as she neared me, I pushed at her head, using the force to propel me backwards and away from her.

"Why won't you leave me alone!"

There wasn't an answer, not that I expected one. This female had found me in the depths and shoved at me until I would get up and begin swimming. I would find another spot, only to have her find me the next day and repeat her annoying ritual. It reminded me of the Atlanteans who had tamed wild dogs and kept them inside their homes. The dogs would beg for food, to be petted, and to play outdoors. They were as demanding as children! Secretly, I had always wished for a hound as well, but my life had been dedicated to serving Atlantis and that wouldn't have been fair to an animal.

Now I found myself being followed around by an eighteen-foot shark who acted like one of the small hounds from my memories. Just like everything else in my life, it was disconcerting and made no sense. She glided past me again, much slower this time. I ran my hands down her smokey-colored sides and pearl-colored stomach. Satisfied that I was awake, she moved away, disappearing into the gloom around me. With a sigh, I started my own journey toward land. If I didn't want to die, I needed to find food. It was time I headed back to my homeland, and swimming the length of an entire ocean would require strength.

I HAD MADE IT ONLY A COUPLE OF MILES BEFORE THE call began. The Lure was nearby, and I was needed. The good news was that a meal had just presented itself, the bad news was that I was weakened, and this would be a harder kill if the human was fit and healthy.

I tried to pick up my pace, but my movements remained sluggish. I had snacked on a few fish, which provided small amounts of nutrients, but my new form also required blood in larger amounts than was provided by the tiny fish. What I had taken from Kye should have lasted for several more days. My guess was the binding magik had depleted my body, and since I hadn't taken blood after leaving him, I was suffering from starvation.

Humans could go much longer without food, especially if they had access to fresh water. I was learning about this new body through trial and error, and I had noticed that the cooler water used my energy reserves faster than warm water. This meant that as long as I stayed in the warm waters, I could go longer between blood feedings. Small fish that I caught could give me a tiny boost to last an extra day or two. Between my exhaustion after the binding, the amount of time since I drank from anyone, and the cooler temperatures of the deeps where I had been resting, this was the worst shape I had been in since waking.

There was also a strange throbbing in my chest I hadn't felt before. I guessed it had something to do with Kye, but I didn't know if it was the pain of him leaving me, or if being separated from one's mate was the cause. Anything was possible when Ancient magik was involved. The theory would be tested when I began my journey across the sea and the distance between us grew larger.

The ocean around me turned from pitch black to midnight blue, then to a soft blue as the light penetrated the shallow water. I enjoyed the feel of the silky warm waters caressing my body, but I also felt exposed. The tropical waters in the gulf were clear in most areas, so someone standing on a boat and looking down would be able to see me, or at least see my dark outline. The sooner I answered the call and headed back into the depths, the better.

The vibrations of the boat's idling motor reached me first, with the man's thoughts blasting into my mind moments later. He was thinking of the things he had done to a young waitress the night before, things that made acidic bile make its way up my throat. She wasn't the first he had brutalized, nor did he plan for her to be the last.

My skin crawled and to my astonishment, liquid anger burned through me. I answered the call, but I did not get emotional over it. Disgusted, yes. But anger was one of the emotions that had been buried. It was a messy emotion that simply got in the way of our job, just like pity, sadness, and guilt. This was not good.

I moved faster toward the boat, my fury lending me a

small burst of energy that I would pay for later. Both sets of fangs dropped into place and I could taste the toxin in my mouth. I wished I had better control over the venom, I didn't want this man to die quickly, I wanted him to suffer. See? This is exactly why anger is an issue when you're a warrior. He needed to die, it shouldn't matter to me if his death was fast or slow, only that it was efficient.

His slimy thoughts in my mind stoked my anger into a volcanic rage. I wanted him to suffer like he had forced his victims to suffer. Some of the women had been left alive to relive their trauma over and over in their minds while they tried to rebuild their lives. Others had been killed and their bodies were scattered around the island in shallow graves. Nausea churned in my stomach. I would have to speak to someone on land before I left this place. Those girls deserved to be found, and their families deserved to bury their loved ones. Pushing those worries aside, I focused back on the boat I was circling.

Annoyance. The emotion echoed in my mind, yanking it back from the dark feral place it had been heading. It was a strange feeling to feel an emotion so strongly, but know it wasn't yours. It wasn't coming from the filth above me either; I sensed his emotions, but I didn't feel them, nor did I feel anyone else's emotions. I was far too exhausted to deal with this. Moving closer, I suctioned my palms against the side of the boat, edging myself nearer to my victim.

Worry. Again, an emotion that didn't belong to me washed through my mind, and made my heart skip a beat. I grit my teeth, irritated. I was hunting and struggling to maintain control of my own unruly emotions; this wasn't the time or place to deal with someone else's feelings. The man above me was carefree, not a worry in his mind. He had taken what he wanted and had gotten away with it. I ground my jaw so tightly that my fangs pierced my lip in several places.

Focus. Let the call wash away everything but the mission.

It didn't work. I was hungry and angry. What did the female with the knives call this? Oh yes, she called it being *hangry*. A fitting name for this state of being. Reaching out, I yanked hard on the man's fishing line. He let loose with a string of curses and his feet stumbled on the deck. The boat tilted slightly as he leaned over the edge to peer into the water, no doubt trying to see what he had caught on his line.

I was tired and knew I couldn't waste this opportunity. Using everything in me, I propelled myself up and onto his body. Sinking my hands into his shirt, I pulled him from the safety of his small fishing vessel and into the waters with me. The predator in me uncoiled, pleased with her catch. We sank beneath the surface. His struggles made little difference to me; in the water, I was stronger than he could imagine. I was not one of the helpless young women he enjoyed preying on. The hunter was now the hunted.

Shock. I gasped as the new emotion battered my mind. My heart began to race, experiencing another emotion that didn't belong to me. I struggled to focus on the task at hand, but the damage had already been done. Sharp pain sliced between my ribs. Glancing down, I stared at the small knife that the man had embedded in the softer skin of my side. He shoved at my body, a nasty smirk on his lips.

I flashed my fangs at him in a feral smile. The pain had startled me and that had been enough for me to lose control over the turmoil inside me. The Siren had come out to play. His skin paled to a deathly shade as he took in my fangs and slitted eyes. He was looking death in the face, and he knew it.

Moving forward, my fangs sank savagely into the vein on his neck. The blood tasted like water from a wishing well filled with old coins. Basically, it tasted nasty. This had never truly bothered me until I had drunk from Kye. I drank to survive; it didn't matter if I enjoyed it or not. Now I knew that it could be pleasurable and taste better than any food I had ever enjoyed in my life. That knowledge made it much more difficult to choke down the foul taste of this man's blood.

My claws extended and sank into his shoulders; he would not escape my grip. I was careful to not inject him with venom. The Siren wanted him to suffer, and I couldn't stop her. His blood mixed with my own which poured from my side, and it excited the feral part of me even more. Ripping my fangs from his skin, I released my hold on his neck, turning his neck to bury my fangs deeper on the other side.

Fear. The emotion did not concern me, it was not my own. I felt only the thrill of the hunt.

Panic. Once more, I shoved at the emotion, wanting to enjoy my prey's futile struggles.

Sadness. I froze. There was something familiar...

It hit me with the force of a tsunami. Kye. The emotions belonged to him, and I was feeling them because he was my soulmate. He had to be near for me to be sensing his emotions. I hadn't been able to feel them when I was in the depths. Something was very wrong. He needed me.

I grappled to control the Siren who wasn't finished playing with her meal. She had been careful not to take too much blood right away, not wanting to let him slip immediately into unconsciousness. Unfortunately, that was biting us in the dorsal fin now. I needed to get to Kye, and deal with whatever had put him in danger. He left me, but he was still my mate, and I would always honor our bond.

I sank my fangs into the man one last time and delivered a dose of venom that would have paralyzed a whale. My unique toxin worked fast, and his limbs immediately seized. His face contorted in horrific pain, the toxin freezing the expression on his face like a tribal mask. I released my hold, and he sank toward the ocean floor several feet below. He could see his boat but wouldn't be able to reach it. The Siren despised knowing that he would die in less than a minute, escaping the punishment she had planned for him, but I resisted the urge to go back for more. Twisting around,

I shot through the water, following Kye's emotions like a shark seeking blood.

My warrior's mind blocked out the pain in my side and allowed me to focus on what had to be done.

My Atlantean heart pushed me forward, well past my limits, prepared to give everything to save my soulmate.

My Siren's body shifted and changed, eager to destroy anything that dared to threaten what belonged to me.

I'm coming, Kye.

And I was bringing death with me.

CHAPTER ELEVEN

EASON

W e had headed out this morning, exactly as we had every other morning the past week. There hadn't been any deaths since the night the mermaid brought Kye back to our boat. We had been sent here to determine and then resolve any threats in this area. Now we knew what, or rather who, had caused the death. But she was nowhere to be seen.

However, thanks to extensive research and calls to Kye's computer genius friends, we had a pretty good idea of the 'why' behind her kills. The sleepy little towns scattered around the bay had a habit 'forgetting' to record certain crimes that were perpetrated by individuals belonging to their oldest families. Those roots ran deep, and some of the officers were turning a blind eye to their crimes out of misplaced loyalty. They took the stance that what happened in a citizen's home wasn't any of their business, unless the wife came to them to file a report, or the hospital called them with a victim.

There were many wonderful hardworking people in these quaint towns, but some of the guys had started to rub off on each other. The bar fights were loud, and when they were kicked out to 'sober up,' most went home to vent their frustrations on those they swore to love. The men quickly realized that if they kept their women and kids quiet, they wouldn't face any real trouble from the law.

I had wanted to break every piece of furniture in our room when the information had started trickling in. Kye had printed out files for each of the men that his contact sent information on. When the contact had realized the depth of the cover-ups in the area, he had expanded his digging, no longer focusing only on our victims. Reading through file after file, I had wanted to go pay a visit to each of the men and ensure they never lifted another drunk fist to their family members. Yet file after file, I was shocked to find that the mermaid had beat me to it.

By the time we finished sorting the files, we had discovered that some of the men were missing, some were laying on cold steel tables in the morgue, and only three remained alive. She was a highly efficient assassin, and I admired her for it. In a few weeks' time, she had nearly wiped out a hotbed of cruelty, and changed the lives of two dozen women and children.

The single female victim had been more of a mystery, and it took an entire team of computer guys, as well as us doing our own investigations, to figure out what her backstory was. She had been kidnapped, and reading about the things she had endured made me burn in rage. I wanted to slaughter her tormentors, but somehow, she had managed to do it herself. She had gone in, armed with knives, and had exacted her revenge.

What disgusted me most was how the cover up had twisted the story. If she had been taken into custody, she would have faced charges and would have been incarcerated the rest of her life. She had just gotten her freedom and would have been sentenced to live in a cage again. What kind of justice was that? Instead, she had been given a merciful death, and from Fynn's examination, it appeared that she went willingly. I didn't like it, but I could see a weird logic to it.

We suspected that someone high up in law enforcement was behind much of the corruption, but we hadn't been able to figure out who...yet. It was only a matter of time. Finding people was our specialty, and we never missed a target.

Which was probably why we found ourselves in the middle of an absolute crap-storm. First, our air tanks had malfunctioned, leaving us without air shortly after we had started our dive. Thankfully we weren't down too deep, and after years spent in the water gaining longer breath holds, we were able to ascend without risking serious injury. But things only got worse from there.

Storm grabbed the ladder preparing to climb back onto the boat. The moment he put his weight on the bottom rung, the engine exploded. It was a small explosion, designed to cause maximum damage while not being large enough to draw the attention of other boats that could come to our aid.

Kye, Fynn and I were hit by small pieces of debris that sliced through our suits. Storm had taken the brunt of the explosion and was hurled back into the sea. While I had only minor cuts, he had several pieces of fiberglass embedded in his skin. His body hit the water like a limp ragdoll. Kye scrambled to him, keeping his head above water, while Fynn assessed his injuries and tried to staunch the blood flow.

I was the rock in our friendship, the tough guy that feared nothing. But in that moment, my heart seized. We had all suffered wounds to various degrees, and now our blood was turning the water around us red. It was astounding how even a small amount of blood could tint the water such a brilliant shade. If we could see it, any sharks within a quarter mile radius would be able to smell it.

The boat listed to the right, taking on water fast; it would be underwater within minutes. We had no weapons, and no way to get ourselves out of the water. I moved toward the boat, careful to not get trapped in the suction from its sinking. If I could find our duffel, I could use the satellite phone to call for help. I was five feet from the boat when I came across the shredded material of the bag. It had been destroyed, along with everything that had been inside it.

We were miles from shore, a distance we could have easily swam had we been uninjured. I searched the horizon but not a single ship was in sight. Considering the string of deaths recently and law enforcement's warnings to avoid the waters, it wasn't a surprise. Our team had been in tight situations before, but I wasn't sure how we would get out of this.

A brown dorsal fin sliced through the water ten feet from us, quickly followed by a second fin, and then a third. What little bit of hope I was clinging to immediately vanished. These were bull sharks, one of the most dangerous shark species on earth. I didn't fault them for their instincts. We were in their home, and we were injured. They were simply doing what they had been designed to do, and we were ringing the shark equivalent of a dinner bell with our blood. I would still prefer not to be eaten, but I just didn't see a way to avoid it.

Then, a fourth fin broke the surface, joining the others as they circled the debris from the boat that surrounded us. One fin broke away from the others and headed straight at us. The frenzy was about to start. I pushed in front of my brothers.

My role in our group had always been that of protector,

even when they didn't know they needed one. I was quiet, preferring to listen than to speak. That had earned me many labels from those outside our team. Cold, cruel, arrogant, egotistical, slow—I had heard them all. I didn't care what strangers thought of me, only that I did my job and did it well. This would be the last time I fought by my brothers' sides, and I would go out doing what made me the happiest. Protecting my family.

The shark turned at the last second, its torpedo-shaped body slamming into me. A second shark moved in, and I barely managed to shove into its way, forcing it to turn. The first shark had circled back around and was moving in fast. The remaining two sharks had disappeared completely, likely circling beneath us. I felt sick knowing there was no way we could prepare for their attacks. At any moment, one of us could be yanked beneath the waves.

Both sharks were closing in on us, one veering toward Fynn who was frantically applying pressure to a wound on Storm's neck, and the second shark moved toward Kye who was keeping Storm's head above water. Panic made my limbs numb. I couldn't stop both sharks by myself.

But it turned out we weren't alone.

If I hadn't seen it with my own eyes, I never would have believed it. To be honest, I wasn't sure it had really happened.

The sharks were only seconds away from attacking when water exploded into the air in front of us and rained down on our stunned faces. A great white surged up out of the ocean like something off a television drama documentary. The beast had to be nearing twenty feet long, by far the largest living shark I had encountered in the ocean.

I believe I would've had a heart attack on the spot had it not been for the shock of seeing what, or rather who, was clinging to the dorsal fin of the great white. The elusive mermaid was pressed against the shark's side, gripping the dorsal in one hand and a knife in the other. Confidence radiated from her as she held onto one of the world's most terrifying predators as if it were her trusty steed and she was riding it into battle. Dark hair fanned around her face and her glowing eyes quickly assessed our dire situation. She was a breathtakingly stunning warrior. Fury spread across her face, and I wondered who I should fear more—the shark, or this lethal goddess.

I didn't have to wait long to figure it out. She flung herself off the great white, twisting gracefully in the air and slamming into the shark headed for Kye. Burying the knife into the shark, she clung to it as it began to thrash. White fangs flashed and sank into the base of the bull shark's dorsal fin. At the same time, the great white crashed back into the water, her mouth open and snagging the bull shark heading toward Fynn, dragging the much smaller shark beneath the waves.

Looking back at the guys, I saw they weren't even breathing as they watched the scene unfold with wide unblinking eyes. A battle cry rang out, raising every hair on my body. This was a war cry you read about in books on ancient civilizations, not the type of battle cry that's portrayed on modern television. It didn't matter how eloquent the author was in their description, or how talented the actor, it would never compare to hearing a long dead call to arms with your own ears. I'll never forget that eerie sound. It was a sound that made you want to run for your life, while also making you want to pick up a sword and follow her into battle.

Releasing the first shark, the mermaid disappeared in the churning water. The third shark had decided to join the frenzy and sliced through the water directly toward us. He didn't even manage to get within ten feet of us. The beautiful warrior surged up out of the water, impacting against its muscled body with a slap that left my ears ringing. The knife was nowhere to be seen, but it turned out she didn't need it. Her nails were pointed claws and she sank them into the shark, anchoring herself to him. The claws should have been grotesque, but instead the long-tapered nails on her elegant hands added to her otherworldly beauty. Faint lace-like webbing appeared between her spread fingers, something I had noticed the night she had saved, kidnapped, married, and finally returned Kye.

The shark veered sharply away from us, lurching from side-to-side in an attempt to throw the mermaid off. She clung to him like a world champion bull rider, or in this case, a bull shark rider. Even in my panic, I found myself wanting to laugh at my stupid joke, but I had forgotten how to breathe the moment she had burst out of the water.

This time when she sank her fangs into the shark's dorsal fin, he jerked hard, and his fin slammed into her face with a sickening crack. She crumpled from his back and disappeared. The shark swam a few more feet before the effects of her venom set in and with a few halting movements, he too sank beneath the choppy surface of the water.

The abrupt silence that followed was unnerving. Were all the sharks gone? Or was the great white going to pop back up like a scene from *Jaws*? Was the mermaid still alive? My mind said I should be worried. We were still in the water with her, and she had proven herself to be lethal. Instead, my stone heart cracked with worry for her. I could continue trying to deny it, but I had known she was mine the instant her face popped up holding Kye's limp body. There was nothing I wouldn't have given to have swapped places with him that night.

Suddenly, her head surfaced in front of me. I stared into her eyes, studying the slitted pupils lost in the aquamarine depths. She studied me in return, her expression a curious mix of defiance and vulnerability. I opened my mouth to speak, but before I had the chance she screamed in pain and was yanked below the surface. I yelled and tried to grab her, but it was too late.

"Zosime!" Kye cried in anguish.

Another wall of water exploded to our right. The monster shark broke the surface, the final bull shark crushed in her jaws. My stomach dropped and Kye roared behind me. The dying bull shark still held the mermaid's tail clamped in its jaws. Blood poured from her tail, but that didn't stop her. She fought like a wild cat, striking out at the bull shark. I watched in amazement as she pressed her fingers into her mouth, and then sank her claws into the thick skin of the shark. The trio sank under the foamy water. My heartbeat pounded in my ears. I knew we should start swimming toward the shore. Storm needed a hospital, but I couldn't leave her.

Tears of relief burned in my eyes when I saw the mermaid's head surface. She had survived, but she was struggling. I swam toward her and pulled her against my chest. Exhaustion was etched on her face, but the feisty little vixen tried to wiggle free.

"Stop wiggling," I said. "You're injured and fighting me is only going to make it worse."

"I do not need your assistance." The words were hissed, but her tone lacked any fire.

"Woman, listen to me! Not only did you save our useless hides, but you did it like a freaking rockstar! Human girls daydream of a prince on a white horse coming to their rescue, a fairytale I had always believed to be ridiculous. But that changed when I watched you burst out of the sea. A warrior princess riding a great white shark to our rescue."

Her eyes narrowed in suspicion when I said the word *princess*, but she stopped resisting my hold.

"I hope Kye isn't a jealous man, because I just fell head-over-heels in love with you, soldier."

CHAPTER TWELVE

ZOSIME

T he giant man declared his love for me, then shushed me. He pinned me against his chest, careful not to hurt me, while also not giving me enough room to wiggle free. I wanted to be angry with him, but the truth was that I didn't know if I could make it on my own in my current condition.

The knife wound in my side had widened during the shark frenzy, and lacerations covered my body. The worst was the damage to my ankles and fluke. Skin hung from my tail, and I thought I saw the flash of white bone. Blood was leaking into the water at a rate that didn't bode well for my long-term survival.

I was in a bad position. If I were able to drink my fill of

blood, my body would stitch itself back together. I shuddered, remembering the incident with boat blades that happened shortly after I had awakened. If I had healed from those injuries, then I could heal from these. The main issue was my inability to hunt due to being unable to swim, and I couldn't heal until I got blood. Groaning, I dropped my head onto Eason's chest.

"I know it hurts. Is there anything I can do to help you?" he asked gently.

"Not unless you are willing to let me sink my fangs into you and drink my fill. Also, if I drink from you, it's likely my venom will have...uncomfortable side-effects for you."

His heart stuttered. If he feared me, why would he be working so hard to keep me alive? I wished I could hear his thoughts, but my mind was silent. My body must be in worst shape than I thought for my abilities to be so weak.

"What type of effects?" His husky voice sent another shudder through me. The longer I was around these men, the stronger the pull toward them became.

"It will intensify your sexual desires," I muttered. "I will likely be lost to the Siren's nature and unable to resist my own desires."

"You desire me?" He sounded hopeful.

"Of course. You are meant to be mine, and I am meant to be claimed by you." I wanted to close my mouth and stop myself from rambling, but exhaustion had loosened my tongue. "I don't know how Kye would feel about it, and I do not want to hurt him. I understand he changed his mind, and I will honor his decision. Among my people, the bond is not something we are able to dishonor, so I cannot take another mate without his agreement."

"But if he agreed, you would want to complete the binding with me?"

"Yes, without question. I would do it, even knowing you might leave me behind." My eyes were growing heavier with each passing second.

"What will my blood do for you?" I heard Eason whisper.

"It is my best chance at survival. I cannot heal without blood. Even if I drink from you, it may not be enough. I'm not a medical doctor, but I think I am bleeding internally."

"What if you drank from Kye and me? Would that be enough for you to heal?" Worry strained his voice.

"Yes. I would be able to heal Storm's injuries as well. I can smell his blood. Too much blood." I wished he would stop talking; I was tired and wanted to sleep.

"We thought you might be able to heal him. Kye's head injury was healed when you brought him back to the boat. You really could heal Storm? Are you sure?"

"Yes."

Numbness wrapped me in its embrace, freeing me from the excruciating pain that clawed at my sanity. My heart stumbled, no longer a steady rhythm, but all I felt was relief. I could sleep now.

WARM LIQUID SPICE COATED MY THROAT, REMINDING me of the chai tea I had tasted while traveling thousands of years ago. I sloshed the liquid around my mouth, wanting to savor it. The scent of saltwater, sweat, aromatic spices, and manly musk threatened to overwhelm my senses. Sunshine warmed my aching body, making me want to arch my back in a deep feline stretch. Cool water lapped at my waist, occasionally splashing over my shoulders. I doubted anything could have made the moment more perfect.

Then, a husky male growl vibrated through my body. Coming out of my drunken daze, I snapped open my eyes. The world around me was unfocused and I struggled to clear my vision. I retracted my fangs and tilted myself back in the arms of the man holding me. Eason's lust-filled amber eyes bore into mine. I gasped in a shocked breath, as pieces started to click into place.

I had passed out, and Eason had found a way to get me to swallow enough blood to begin the healing process in my body. At some point, my body, or more likely the Siren, had taken over and decided to take what we wanted...and that was Eason. I felt the hard length of him press against my stomach, leaving no doubt in my mind that he wanted me too.

My voice croaked as I tried to recall how to use my vocal cords.

"Did I hurt you?" I didn't even recognize my voice. Since waking, my voice was lower and huskier than it had been before the battle. This low-pitched voice was pure silky seduction. I hadn't sung the words, but they carried a lilt that suggested naughty things that made me blush. I had coped each time my body changed and adapted, but I wasn't sure I could handle having a voice that made me blush every time I spoke.

Eason moaned, and I felt his body press harder against mine. To my utter surprise, another body pressed against my back, trapping me between two people. The moment his skin touched mine, I knew it was my Kye. He trailed kissed down my spine, while his hands gripped my hips and held me in place against his rock-hard manhood. My voice might have made me blush in embarrassment, but it appeared to have a much larger impact on these men.

Eason and Kye continued to kiss and lick at my skin, neither man seeming inclined to answer me. I would not allow things to go any further until my questions were answered.

"I need to know if I have injured anyone," I said. My skin flushed at the sound of my voice and their hard muscled bodies trembled against mine.

"You haven't hurt anyone. Eason was bitten, but he wanted that." Kye sounded as if he were speaking through a throat filled with gravel. Parts of me grew wet, and it had nothing to do with the water surrounding us.

"Kye, I need to know you are okay with this," I continued. "I can stop now but if I take more of his blood to heal myself, I will end up claiming him. It cannot be undone. Being bonded to multiple mates was common among my people, but I do not believe it is the same with the humans of today." As I spoke, my body quivered in need. I needed blood to heal, but I needed so much more.

"Yes, Zosi," Kye said with a smile. "Eason and I spoke, we're in complete agreement. If you want us, then we are yours."

I had so many things I wanted to ask them, but I had held back the Siren as long as possible. I needed to hear one more thing though.

"Eason, do you truly want to be claimed by me?" If I thought my voice was seductive before, this time it was full of sin. It had escalated from hinting at things to come, to making you believe you were in the middle of passionate sex from your wildest dreams.

"Yes, mi amor," Eason whispered. "I felt the pull to you that day on the beach. When you surfaced with Kye in your arms, I wanted you. I'm ashamed to admit I was jealous when he returned bearing your mark. I am yours. Please."

The words were strangled but spoken with conviction. His voice had cracked with the last word, a desperate plea. His need, and likely my venom, ran wild through his veins.

Mine.

So, I sank my fangs back into his neck. My own need was a living thing inside me that was trying to claw its way out. The taste of my venom mixing with the exotic spice of his blood was too much. My skin felt too tight, and my blood too hot. Sweated coated every inch of me that bobbed above the water's surface. Every few minutes, pain from my wounds would surge through my body like a lightning bolt streaking across an angry night sky. Instead of dousing my lust, the pain, in some twisted way, added to my pleasure.

In my feverish haze, I must have injected Eason with more of my toxin than I intended to, or perhaps my Siren nature did it purposely. It wouldn't surprise me in the least. With some of my emotions beginning to break through, I was beginning to believe she hid a wicked side. Each time I sucked in a mouthful of his rich blood, Eason's hips bucked against me. His hand tangled in my hair, cradling my head in the crook of his neck, and tempting me to drain him of every last drop.

I couldn't unlatch myself from his neck, my need for nourishment too demanding. Other parts of my body clenched in a different kind of need, one that grew more frenzied as the two men continued to arch and grind against me. Their erections burned against my skin even beneath the cool waters. Eason's fingers dug harder into my hips, his breathing becoming labored as he moaned and jerked against me. The dose of venom he had received was pushing him to mate with me and seek his release. I moaned into his skin; the overwhelming sensations were almost more than I could bear. I felt the Siren's satisfaction with her work; she was enjoying his growing roughness, she wanted him to lose control.

Hands stroked along my skin, moving lower until fingers teased across the scales that hid my secret place. I arched and whimpered. Eason responded to the sound by slamming me impossibly tight against him.

"Chill, man. I'm trying to help you both." Kye's voice was harsh, but it wasn't from anger.

Eason growled. The absurdity of a human male growling should have been humorous, but my body responded to it by sending another wave of slick to my core.

"Eason!" Kye snapped. "My hand's trapped between your bodies. I don't want to be anywhere near your junk, so ease up so I can help, or at least give me enough room to pull my hand free." Kye's voice was sharp, the command permeating through Eason's lust.

Eason not only eased back, but he angled to the side, giving Kye more room to work without accidentally touching Eason's 'junk.' What a strange human word. Kye wasted no time and without hesitation, his fingers zeroed in on my most sensitive scales as if flashing lights were showing him their location.

The first soft brush had my body lurching forward, although with Kye pinning my back against his chest, I didn't move much.

"Be still, mermaid."

My body obeyed his command, relaxing back against

him. It was then that I noticed something that had escaped my attention. Both men were nude. They had been smart enough to realize how quickly things would accelerate once I was given a taste of blood.

It took Kye several tries to find the hidden slit; I could have helped him but the heavy petting was far too pleasurable. With a jolt, his finger buried itself inside me. My walls quivered as his finger stroked and explored. He brushed over the tiny pearls that formed a row on the bottom wall of my slick tunnel. They weren't true pearls, but I didn't know what else to call them. My previous body hadn't possessed these sensitive spots. His finger circled them, and then flicked down the delicate strand several times in a row. My pleasure built with a speed that made me light-headed.

"Do these give you pleasure—"

Kye's words were cut off as I retracted my fangs from Eason's skin and screamed my release. The sun was low in the sky, and the briny air around us had grown cool.

"I guess that answered my question." I felt his satisfaction leak through the bond.

Ignoring him, I reached down and captured Eason's erection in my hand. I enjoyed the heavy weight of it as I worked the rigid length in my hand.

"Babe, Eason isn't feeling so well. You whammied him with a massive dose of your kinky cocktail." Kye snickered for a moment at some joke I didn't understand before continuing. "I continued feeling worse until we both orgasmed, and you claimed me. I wish this could be longer for you, but our current situation is a bit dire."

Guilt washed over me. He was right. Eason's breathing was shallow, and his heartbeat was too fast. The skin that normally reminded me of the golden sands of my homeland had turned grey. Would my venom kill him? I didn't know. Tartarus! I was still figuring out how it worked and trying to control the fickle toxin.

It was now or never. Bracing one hand on Eason's shoulder, I steadied myself so I could guide his length inside me with the other hand. His erection jerked in my hand like a living thing, making the task far more challenging than it should have been. I finally slid the first two inches inside me, gasping and sinking my nails into his shoulder. He was too far gone with the venom in his blood, and with a single hard thrust he sheathed himself inside me completely. I ground my teeth together. Ecstasy and pain blended together until I couldn't tell where one ended and the other began.

Eason's body shivered against my own, his strong arms trembled where they wrapped around me. His skin was clammy, the toxin and blood loss taking a toll on him. The good news is that I am able to control my buoyancy, as long as I'm conscious. He wouldn't sink while holding onto me. The bad news was that my fin wasn't healed enough for me to move it. I had been careful to keep it still since awakening to speed the healing process. What a pair we made—both eager to bond, yet one of us sick and the other injured.

I shouldn't have worried, though. Kye had also realized our problem. His hands shifted to my hips, and with steady movements he began to pull my hips away from Eason. Just before Eason's shaft would have sprung free, Kye pushed me forward. It should have been strange and off-putting. Instead, it stole the breath from my lungs. I was bonding with my second soulmate, and my first was helping me with a tenderness that brought tears to my eyes. I hated the circumstances that forced this situation, but deep in my heart this moment would be one that I treasured forever. The warrior who hid her loneliness behind a shield was now hidden between two men who loved her.

He began to move my hips faster, my desire galloping through me like a herd of mustangs. My heartbeat pounded in my ears, drowning the sounds of the world around me. I climaxed, stars bursting in my vision in a sparkling shower. I buried my fangs into the shoulder of the man who roared and pulsed inside me as he found his own release. I repeated the Greek words I loved so much and watched as the aquamarine light etched my mark on his chest and shoulder, a visual sign of my claim.

We heaved against each other for a minute. Relief flooded me as his heartbeat slowed and color returned to his skin. He would be okay.

"I am sorry, Zosime," Kye said gently. "Storm is worse and there isn't a boat in sight. We are capable of swimming the miles back to shore, and pulling you and Storm with us, but we won't make it in time. You are his only hope."

He pulled me away from Eason, spinning me in the water until I pressed against him. Angling his neck, he pleaded with me, "Drink, baby. Take it all if you need to. Heal yourself and heal my brother. Please."

Unshed tears shone in his eyes, and I felt an answering tear well up in mine. I wrapped my arms around him, embracing this man with a heart too big for his chest. With gentleness, I kissed his neck and then pressed my fangs into his artery. He twitched but didn't jerk away. One of his hands moved to rub soothing circles on my back. He was trying to comfort a monster of the deep, even as her toxin pumped into his veins.

I knew in the end the toxin would amplify his pleasure, but that didn't negate the reality that combined with the blood loss; it would make him feel ill and weaken him. Tears of shame leaked from my eyes and fell onto his neck. I had to figure out how to control this curse before they grew tired of the side effects of loving me. I also needed to get a grip on my emotions before they distracted me and cost someone their life.

CHAPTER THIRTEEN

KYE

I felt her tears falling on my neck and my guilt made me sick. She must feel like we were using her, yet she was allowing it. In exchange for our blood to heal herself, we were asking that she heal us as well. Her heart had stopped beating earlier and my tattoo had burned like a fiery brand. She had died, and here we were using both her body and her abilities.

Eason had sliced open his arm, prying her mouth open until he was able to let the blood pour into her mouth. She hadn't swallowed and it began to flow from the side of her mouth and into the ocean. I had massaged her throat, working the blood down into her stomach and praying it wouldn't get into her lungs since I wasn't sure if that would drown her or not. Her heart fluttered one, two, three times before beginning to beat. Her pulse so faint it was hard to find.

Once she was swallowing on her own, we had shifted her up against Eason's chest, her head lolling against his collarbone. With a piece of floating debris, I nicked his neck and angled her mouth over the spot. We held our breaths, waiting to see if her instincts would kick in. I barely kept from whooping in relief when she began to suck, and then sank her fangs into his skin.

I moved quickly to help him out of his tattered wetsuit before removing mine as well. If she woke as a predator, we were willing to accept whatever she demanded. If she managed to regain control, we hoped to plead our case for her to save Storm. We didn't want anything in the way.

Storm had regained consciousness while we had been working with Zosime, staying conscious just long enough for us to ask if he would be willing to bond with her if it became necessary for his survival. He admitted that he was pulled toward her, but he begged us to wait if possible.

Storm was a man that walked into a room with a confidence that made lesser men cower, but he was also a hopeless romantic. He wanted to plan a romantic evening for their bonding, a special night to show her his love first. Unfortunately, that wasn't going to happen. He either bonded with her now, or not at all.

"Eason, you need to rest," I said to my brother. "The effects will take a while to wear off, but from my experience, sleep will speed the process up. We are going to have a long swim ahead of us once Storm's injuries are healed, and we may need to drag him with us until the toxin leaves his system."

Eason nodded, still dazed. He managed to slip back into his wetsuit, and then floated on the surface of the water on his back. His eyes closed almost immediately.

I could feel my blood beginning to heat, Zosi's sweet toxin exciting my every nerve ending. Blinking my eyes to clear my blurred vision, I locked gazes with Fynn.

"How is he?" I asked.

"His heart rate is steady, but it is continuing to slow," he whispered. "Blood is no longer pumping into the sea, but I'm worried that is because he has lost too much blood." He didn't bother to hide his fear. Storm wasn't going to make it.

"Drink, Zosi, drink." My voice cracked. I didn't care if she heard me beg. All five of us had to survive this. I couldn't handle losing another family. My parents, my twin, and my baby sister. I hadn't been able to save them, and I had lived with the guilt of being the only one to survive. Eason and Storm had pulled me from that dark place and had given me a family to anchor myself to. That family now included Zosi and Fynn.

"Zosime, I want you to know I didn't mean to leave you that night," I said to the beautiful mermaid. "You were so perfect, and our time together was mind-blowing, far exceeding anything I thought was humanly possible. I thought I was unconscious from the blow to my head, and that it was all an illusion my battered brain had conjured. When the guys called, I thought that was my brain telling me the dream was over and it was time to wake up, whether I wanted to or not." I took a breath, fighting to concentrate through the effects of the venom.

"When I realized it wasn't a dream, that it was all real and that I had left you behind like a cold-hearted jerk, I ran into the ocean," I continued. "The guys had to wrestle me back onto land, and I finally caved when they promised we would search for you. That's what we were doing today, looking for you. Just like I have every day since the night I left you crying in the ocean."

Her hot tears fell faster on my neck, a soft sob was muffled against my neck.

"Please, don't stop drinking," I pleaded. "Storm needs you. I need you."

Her grip around my neck tightened, and she pressed her body against the length of me. She couldn't speak around her fangs in my neck, so it seemed she was trying to show her feelings the only way she could.

"I want to make love to you, okay?" I asked gently.

She nodded against my neck, continuing to suck.

"One day we will do this slow. I will take my time kissing every inch of you. I cannot wait for that day." She only hummed in response. I felt her gag against my neck, but she doggedly began swallowing again. She was full, but she was making sure she was prepared to heal Storm.

I lined her hips up with my groin, using a finger to

locate those hard-to-find scales. Finding her entrance, I slid a finger inside, wanting to ensure she was ready for me. This had to be hard and fast. I couldn't risk the venom weakening me too much, since I would likely be hauling either her or Storm back to the beach when this was over.

With my other hand I lined myself up with her hot slit and pushed myself inside. I couldn't stop the groan that escaped at feeling her around me. As soon as I was buried to the hilt, I slid out and thrust in again. The venom in my system threatened to steal all my thoughts except the need to find release, by whatever means necessary. I fought it, not wanting to lose myself and injure her more.

I was relieved to hear her soft moans of pleasure against my neck. The sounds urged me on, each stroke faster and harder until water splashed into the air each time I rammed into her.

Mine.

She was mine.

Her fangs disappeared from my neck and her back arched. She cried out my name as pleasure washed through her. I tilted her pelvis up a bit and thrust into her one final time. The new angle allowed me to hit her sensitive string of pearls with the head of my erection. Her scales exploded into light, and she screamed my name as we found our release together. Blue-green light pulsed in time with her shudders, allowing me to not only feel the after-effects of her orgasm, but also to see it. She was perfect.

"I love you, Zosime. From now until forever."

She opened her mouth, but no words came out. Her luminous eyes stared up at me. Her lips did not move, but I heard her clearly.

"And I love you, my Kye."

She was telepathic. I starred at her in wonder. Would I ever know all the secrets inside my mysterious little soul-mate? I hated that out entire encounter had taken less than two minutes, but I had a lifetime to make it up to her.

"Kye, I need you to take me to Storm. Hurry."

No sooner had her words registered in my mind, than I heard Fynn scream my name.

"Kye! His heart stopped!"

CHAPTER FOURTEEN

FYNN

A tornado created by my swirling emotions shredded my insides and tore at my heart. I had watched as Eason and Kye fed her their blood. When the venom sent their sex drive into overtime, I had looked away. While I might not have seen the act of them bonding, I had heard everything. Her whimpers and moans of pleasure, the sloshing water that made it clear what was happening beneath the surface, and finally, her screams.

To my shame, I did sneak quick glimpses. Once, when Kye was helping the weak, battered pair claim each other, and again when Kye brought her to another orgasm. She glowed the color of the sea, her eyes bright, and her face radiant as she screamed Kye's name. His roar of pleasure mixed with hers, and ugly jealousy shot through me. I was happy for them, but I was also heartbroken.

I had never felt as happy as I had those past few days. The guys had welcomed me into their group as one of their own. There was no awkwardness. It was just assumed that whatever decision was made, I was part of it. If they wanted to investigate, it was assumed that I was going with them.

They had even been surprised by my absence when I left to pick up some of my personal stuff from my hotel. We hadn't been staying at the same one, and I had been gone less than an hour before Kye called to ask where I was. He said I should have told him, and he would have ridden with me to keep me company.

They weren't investigating me or stalking me. They were treating me exactly like they treated each other, like brothers.

What I hadn't expected was that I would feel so drawn to the mermaid that we spent days trying to track. I thought my obsessive interest was because of my curiosity as a scientist. But when she had fought the sharks, and then died in Eason's arms, I knew I had been so wrong.

I wanted her love—and I wanted her to mark me.

I tried to convince myself it was simply my brain wanting to study the effects. But just the thought of a scientist studying her or putting her in a display tank in the name of science sent white hot rage coursing through me. I didn't want her anywhere near land, it was better if she stayed as far away from those prying eyes as possible. My identity as a scientist began to crumble at the realization that science was no longer the most important thing on this planet to me.

Then the men created a plan to save Storm. As long as the beautiful mermaid agreed with the plan, it was the best option we had. I understood the logic. But as I tried to ignore the sounds around me, loneliness weighed me down as surely as if I had swallowed lead. I didn't know where I would stand with the men once they had each bonded with Zosime. There was no way my heart would be able to handle working alongside them, knowing Zosime could never be mine.

I had gone from a world-renowned marine biologist and doctor, to feeling like an imposter. If possible, I would hide Zosime from the world forever. Could any self-respecting scientist hold his head up after knowing he purposely hid one of the most important marine discovers to ever be made?

I would help them get to shore, and make sure that both Storm and Zosime were recovering. Then I would destroy all evidence pointing toward the mermaid, and release a statement saying we had found a shark with a deformed jaw. The crooked cops wanted this to disappear, so they wouldn't question me. Storm would take them all down once he recovered and finished the investigation he had started secretly.

Then I would allow myself to disappear. I would travel to my favorite place on earth, hidden from the rest of the world, and do... Well, I didn't know what I would do. But at least I had a plan.

Storm's heart tripped beneath my fingers, and then it stopped. I screamed for Kye and Zosime. I knew his outside injuries were bad, but for him to have passed this quickly, there must be significant internal damage too. I wanted to believe he could be saved, but logic screamed that it was too late.

Kye swam to my side, Zosime clinging to him. Fatigue showed on Kye's face, but he seemed to have handled the toxin better than his first time, and far better than Eason. For a moment, my curiosity flickered. Had Kye received a lesser dose because she had bitten Eason first? Or was it possible that with each exposure, the effects would lessen? I shoved the errant thoughts into the dark recesses of my mind, reminding myself that I was finished with this life.

Kye tucked Zosime against Storm's side. I'd kept his head above water, but quickly released my hold once she was against him. I had watched her with Eason and knew as long as she was with him, Storm would stay above water.

We both watched in surprise as she wrapped one arm around his neck and tucked the other beneath his arm. Water sloshed around them, and then stilled. Storm's body tilted back, his legs floating to the surface. Zosime had curled her tail around his legs, careful to not injure him further. Storm now floated on top of the water, the mermaid's body acting as a giant foam pool noodle for him. If she could stay in that position, it would make getting them back to shore far easier. But first, she would have to be able to save him.

I am not sure what I expected. Maybe I thought healing magic would shoot from her palm, or she would bite him and kick-start his body with her toxin. What I hadn't expected was for her to rip open her wrist and press it to his pale lips. That done, she sighed and sagged against him.

For several minutes, nothing happened; she seemed to fall asleep, and a tiny trail of blood trickled from the side of his mouth. Then his lips pressed to her wrist, the movement so subtle that I thought I had imagined it. His Adam's apple bobbed with each swallow. I jumped in surprise when his hand flew to her wrist, pinning it in place. The movement had been inhumanly fast.

A growl rumbled in his chest, and I could have sworn I saw a flash of teeth as he gulped at her wrist with a hunger that worried me. Would he be able to stop before he hurt her? Surely, she would stop him before that happened, right?

Anxiety and fear churned in my stomach. She wouldn't stop him. If she had been worried about her safety, she wouldn't have leaped into the middle of a feeding frenzy to save us. Between our knowledge and survival skills, we should have at least managed to put up a bit of a fight. Instead, we had been caught so off guard, we had needed to be saved by a mermaid. A terrifying, deadly, ruler-of-the-sea type of mermaid, but a mermaid, nonetheless.

A mermaid that I longed to hold and protect from the world.

I began taking inventory of their wounds. The open wounds scattered down Storm's body had sealed themselves closed. His lips and skin grew flush, the sickly grey fading with each long pull from her wrist.

Turning my focus to Zosime, I studied her face. She was pale, but most of the cuts on her neck and face were pale pink lines. I continued my inspection, moving down her body. A jagged slash ran between her ribs, the angry puckered skin was still trying to heal. My heart slammed into my ribcage. If that was a knife, it was likely she had life-threatening organ damage. She had proved she had the ability to heal, but could she heal herself fast enough to survive internal trauma?

My eyes darted across her body. Other than pale pink lines indicating healing flesh wounds, it seemed her body had escaped injury. I began my visual inspection of her tail. We had known it was bad, but since the attack it had remained below the water. When my eyes took in the damage, I turned and emptied what little bit remained in my stomach.

It wasn't the sight that made me ill, it was the thought of the excruciating pain she had to be experiencing. The shark had nearly detached her fluke from her tail. Rows of serrated teeth had sawed into her skin and muscle, shredding it with ease and exposing bone.

I struggled to understand what I was seeing. She said if

she drank blood, then she could heal herself and Storm. The blood Eason had dripped into her mouth had restarted her heart, just as the blood she spilled into Storm's mouth restarted his. His wounds had healed quickly.

Looking toward Eason and Kye, I searched every inch of visible skin, but they were flawless. In fact, a rather distinct scar that had been on Eason's temple was gone. She didn't just heal their new wounds; she healed all signs of damage.

I was getting frustrated. Inspecting her tail, I noticed it wasn't bleeding. You could bleed to death from wounds half this serious. Looking at her beautiful pale face, it hit me like a sledgehammer. She had healed herself just enough to survive and then stopped. She had drunk as much as she dared to take, not for herself, but to use on each man.

Swimming closer, I reached out to check her pulse, but yanked my hand back when Storm's eyes flashed open. Glowing eyes locked onto me, and they didn't belong to the mermaid. I held my hands up, trying to show him I meant no harm. He snarled in response. The tables had turned, and it wasn't the mermaid who was the feral one now.

"Guys?" I called out to the others. "We have a situation. I need you guys to swim toward me. Move very slow—do *not* touch Zosime or Storm." As I spoke, I never broke eye contact with Storm.

He shifted his body, no longer using Zosime as a float. Storm's upper body remained out of the water, with Zosime's chest held against him. I couldn't see her tail and worried if he was jostling it beneath the water.

"Storm, listen to me."

The narrowing of his eyes was the only response I received.

"Zosime is hurt, she isn't healing properly. We need to get her to safety and let her rest so she can heal."

He made no move to release her.

"Storm would never hurt her, and we gave her blood to heal them both." Kye tried to reassure me.

"Well, apparently you three had more severe injuries than we thought, because she used very little to heal herself. I am stunned she's even conscious; her body should be going into shock. The shark nearly ripped her fluke off."

Kye moved immediately toward her, only to be stopped short when Storm's glowing eyes locked on him.

"Mine." The single word was more of a growl than an actual word, but his meaning was crystal clear.

"Yes, she is yours," I said firmly. "She is willing to die for you, now is not the time to claim her." I hoped my words were sinking in.

"Why is he acting like this?" Eason asked. "I know we get a little crazy when she bites us, but this is insane! She didn't even bite him." Eason sounded exhausted. His injuries were healed, but his body was still dealing with the blood loss and the toxin.

"It's my blood."

At the sound of Zosime's voice, four sets of eyes snapped to her face.

"Are you okay, Zosi?" Kye was the first to speak.

"Don't worry, it will be okay," she said gently. "I wasn't thinking clearly. I've known my blood could boost healing, but I didn't stop to think about how I had ingested my own toxin while drinking from you two. When I gave Storm my blood, he got the boost from my blood, as well as the toxin that I had ingested. He's acting like my Siren, the combination must be potent."

"Your Siren?" I asked.

"What you call a mermaid," she replied. "Although mermaids seem to be gentle and happy from what I have gathered. I don't think that fits me at all."

"We can discuss all this later. Zosi, what do we do now?" Kye asked. He looked ready to pounce on Storm, but with the latter juiced up on Siren's blood, I doubted that would end well for Kye.

"Let me talk to him."

Sliding her arms around his neck, she rested her head on his shoulder. They looked like a normal couple sharing a sweet embrace. When she spoke again, her voice was pure velvet, each word brushing against our skin.

"Storm, listen to my voice," she said. "Focus on it and ignore the whispers from my blood. This isn't you. Come back to me. I want to be us to be bonded, but I want you to remember it and not have regrets. It is your choice; I will be proud to have you as my mate regardless of how you choose for that to happen."

Her breathing was rough when she finished speaking. The scientist in me was curious if speaking in the voice of her 'Siren' required energy. The man in me worried that she was taking a turn for the worse.

Storm held her against him, not a single muscle twitching. His breathing leveled out, and the color of his eyes flickered several times between the glowing green and his natural grey. We watched warily as his muscles relaxed one by one, and his hold on Zosime changed from crushing to tender. I exhaled in relief; he was back and no longer a risk to our girl. I mean, their girl.

"I believe I have a lot to apologize for later, to all of you," Storm said. He nodded in our direction, but his focus remained on Zosi.

"Zosime, if you feed from me, would you be able to heal yourself?" I asked. I was the only one that could spare some blood.

A sad smile passed across her face. "It will take several hours, possibly even a day to finish healing myself. Your blood would provide much needed help, but it will not heal me instantly. There is no reason for you to be weakened like the rest of us. It is best we all get to safety first, then you can decide if you are willing to feed me or not."

The thought of her pain was making me physically ill, but I did understand her logic.

"Darling," Storm began, "I need you to move onto my back so we can swim to shore." Storm tried to shift her around to his back.

I knew these men had been trained to swim with large

amounts of weight on their backs. Zosime's body was long with the added length from her tail, but she was lean.

"I can make my own way back," Zosime said firmly.

"Absolutely not, you will keep that fin still." Kye's tone was firm.

"I wasn't going to swim back. Sheba has been waiting."

"Who is Sh—"

Eason broke off mid-sentence when the massive fin sliced through the water between us.

CHAPTER FIFTEEN

FYNN

"Please tell me you didn't adopt a great white and name it Sheba." Eason's tone was equal parts horror and awe, the same thing we were all feeling at that moment.

Zosime tilted her head to the side, considering his words. "No, you cannot adopt a shark." Her voice was condescending, as if we were the crazy ones here.

"This from the fish girl who rode the twenty-foot-long behemoth like a knight into battle," Kye retorted. "Great whites terrify nearly all of earth's current population, yet you made one a pet and named it Sheba." Kye rolled his eyes, not angry, just bemused.

Her pale cheeks flushed, and she snorted. "She is *not*

a pet; she is like me. A warrior who has seen battle and survived to fight again, a lethal predator designed to kill, a keeper of the balance, and protector of her territory. I came into her waters, and we grew to respect one another. I do not understand it myself, but we have become connected. She is near because she senses I am vulnerable, just as I would go to her aid if she required my assistance."

Eason pinched the bridge of his nose, trying to stave off the headache of her logic. "Zosi, you do understand how insane that sounds?" he asked. "Maybe she's nearby because you are vulnerable, and she's hungry. Please tell me that this isn't shark that chased you and Kye when he hit his head?"

Zosi narrowed her eyes but stayed quiet.

"It is the same shark," Eason said, answering his question himself. "Is this also the same shark that has been chomping on your victims?"

This elicited a response from her. She gasped, her eyes widening. "You knew?"

"We aren't idiots, Zosi. I also think we know why, but that talk will wait until later. How can you be so confident that this shark will take you to shore?"

Her chin lifted in defiance. "We have come to an understanding. I would not have made it to you in time yesterday if not for her assistance, I was not at my full strength. Without her help in the frenzy, we would all be dead. She has stayed in the waters near us since the attack, keeping away other predators who have been attracted by our blood."

I had dedicated my life to studying the sea and her inhabitants. It wasn't just a career; it was my passion. The behavior Zosi was describing was thrilling. There were cases of sharks recognizing divers that they form a strange type of bond with, that even seemed to enjoy being 'petted.' I had also reviewed hundreds of cases where a shark had every reason and opportunity to attack the humans in the water with them, but they showed patience.

It was amazing that a species portrayed as the bloodthirsty villain of the ocean could also show such restraint in not attacking the idiot tourists who harass and ride them, all for a photo to show their friends. I wasn't particularly fond of humanity and doubted I would have such restraint if I had been in the sharks' position. Movies and books had given sharks a bad reputation and stoked an irrational level of fear in the minds of most humans. It was important to be cautious, aware, and respectful of these powerful predators, but we didn't have to fear them.

We needed to find a balance when it came to these magnificent beasts. They weren't dolphins, and they shouldn't be expected to act like one. As humans, we have rather limited abilities in the water, putting us at a distinct disadvantage when it comes to shark encounters. But humans aren't exclusively on the sharks' menu. They aren't actively hunting humans, nor are they just waiting for us to dip a toe in the water so they can attack. Considering the tens of millions of sharks that humans slaughter each year, along with the fact that the creatures are found in all of the world's oceans, there are very few attacks on humans. There are more than three hundred shark species, but only about a dozen species are involved in those attacks.

Sharks are curious by nature and certain things make them want to investigate further. The disturbance in the water from our boat fiasco, our panicked splashing, and the blood from our injuries had ticked nearly every box. Unfortunately for us, bull sharks were one of the more dangerous species.

If Zosi truly had formed a bond with this great white, the potential for what could be learned about these enigmatic rulers of the deep made me nearly faint from excitement. Knowledge is power, and with that type of inside knowledge, we might be able to find ways to keep humans and sharks safer from each other.

"Zosi, are you sure she will take you to the shore?" I asked. "It would be dangerous for you if she took you out deeper and you became stranded."

"She cannot take me all the way to the shore," Zosi replied. "In shallow waters, her size makes it difficult for her to remain unseen. I will not risk the humans seeing her and deciding to hunt her."

"You can't be alone in the water! It will take us a while to reach shore. If a fisherman saw you—" I shuddered, unable to finish the sentence.

"I can have her leave me at the buoy, I can wait for you

there. If a boat comes near me, I will sink to the ocean floor and wait for your arrival."

"I don't like it," Kye interjected. "You can't swim, you shouldn't be alone." He had voiced what we were all thinking.

"Do not forget what I am." Zosi's pupils flashed to slits and her fangs lengthened. Her features shifted from injured prey to stone cold predator.

The fine hairs on my body stood on end and my heart beat faster; the automatic human response to knowing you're in danger. She eyed each of us in turn, wanting to make sure we saw this side of her. It was a reminder that while we wanted to coddle and protect her, she wasn't human. She possessed intelligence, venom, a Siren's voice, and skills as a fighter. And those were only the things we knew about. Who knew what other secrets she possessed? The delicate mermaid we had all been fussing over posed a greater threat to life and limb than anything else currently swimming in the sea.

Her facial features shifted back to normal. The change was so swift that if I had blinked, I would have missed it. I also caught the wince of pain that flashed across her face. My heart ached. I didn't care if she accidentally ate me in my sleep one night, it was a risk I was willing to take. I loved her.

"Zosi, thank you for the reminder, but it wasn't needed," I said gently. "You are the baddest monster in the ocean, but you are ours to worry over." Her eyes were soft when she looked at me, and I realized too late what I had said. *Ours.* I didn't dare look at the guys.

"There is another option," Zosi said to us. "One of you will go with me."

"With Sheba?" Kye's voice squeaked.

I knew which one of us wasn't going back with her. I couldn't help the snicker that escaped. Kye shot me an annoyed look that only made me laugh harder.

"She is impatient. Do I go alone?" Zosi pressed.

"Fynn should go," Eason said. "My large size might annoy the shark, I mean, Sheba. Kye is the strongest swimmer in our group. Storm is still on a weird mermaid blood high. He will probably pay for it later, but right now it's an advantage. Fynn's the only one of us that grinned when you spoke about Sheba. He will be most comfortable with the experience." Eason turned to me and the guys and added, "Fynn can start treating Zosime's wounds once they are safe, and he's the only one left of our group that can feed her." His logic was sound, and no one argued.

"It is decided?" Zosi's tone was impatient. From exhaustion, not anger, if her drooping eyelids and limp body were anything to go on.

"You understand what might happen if you feed her, right?" Kye asked me. "You need to be sure." His tone was soft, not a hint of jealousy.

"Yes." My mouth turned as dry as the Sahara Desert as I spoke the one word I could manage.

Zosime's eyes met mine over the back of the large shark that surfaced between us, and she smiled.

"Come, my love."

I didn't need to be asked twice. Storm held her waist and moved her against Sheba's side. To my surprise, she didn't grab the shark's dorsal or pectoral fin. She pressed her palms against the shark and flatted her body along the length of the thick bodied great white. Her hands must have the ability to suction. I would give anything to explore her body.

"She looks like a remora attached to the shark like that!" Kye's laughter was contagious. He wasn't wrong, she was doing a dang good impression of a suckerfish.

"Come on, fish boy. Let's see you pull that off!" Kye said, slapping me playfully on the back.

I gave Kye the stink eye. I had to hold Sheba's pectoral fin since I lacked Zosi's unique adaptations.

"Flatten yourself against her body," Zosi instructed. "You are not hurting her, but your clumsy body will create drag when she moves. She does not need your help to swim. Stay tight against her. She will surface every two minutes for you to breathe. Do not waste time, take a breath quickly."

I didn't get a chance to respond. With a hard thrust of her tail, we were underwater.

I laid Zosime on a small cot in the medical wing of the local marine conservation center. My arms shook from fatigue. After Sheba brought us as close to the shore as Zosime allowed, I had swum to shore, bringing Zosi with me. I was a strong swimmer and enjoyed working out, but my body was strained. The events of the day, combined with dehydration and hunger, were getting to me.

I had hidden Zosi in a tiny, abandoned boat. Splashing onto shore, I rushed into the small dock office. When things started to not add up, I had asked a trusted friend to bring his boat and discretely hang out offshore. I called him and asked him to go pick up the guys, hoping that my vague directions were enough for him to find them.

I then called in a favor at the marine conservation center. They were happy to lend me their lab and medical supplies for my 'research.' In exchange, I would have to give a lecture at a charity dinner the following year.

With that done, I jogged to the hotel where my car was parked. Reaching under the fender, I located the tiny magnetic box where I kept a spare key. I tended to forget things when I was engrossed in research, and having extra keys became a necessity. It had been a challenge to get Zosi loaded into the car. She had to be in extreme pain in the small confines of the interior, but she never said a word.

Now that it was time to begin tending to her wounds, I was frozen; with fear that I wouldn't be able to figure out her unique medical needs, worry that I would hurt her further, and disgust at the part of me that was excited at the opportunity to examine her unique physiology.

"I don't mind." A smile played around her lips.

It was the first time she had spoken since we left the others, and I was confused by the randomness.

"What don't you mind?" I asked.

"That you want to inspect me like one of your specimens." She gave a small chuckle and then winced.

"You can read my thoughts? Can you read everyone's thoughts?"

"I do not read thoughts," she replied. "I *hear* thoughts. Yes, I can hear everyone's thoughts, although some people are easier to hear and understand."

That might explain the mystery of how she picked her victims, I thought. *If she heard their thoughts, she would know what sick things they had been up to.* But we had time to discuss things later.

I moved to her tail first, it was the worst of her external injuries. The skin and most of the muscles were still ripped open. The tissue around her bones had woven itself back together so that the bones were no longer visible.

"If I stitch this back together, it may heal faster," I said gently.

"Do it," she replied.

I gathered the supplies I needed, thankful the small

center was well stocked. Pushing a small stool to the foot of the cot, I got to work. She twitched when I injected the local anesthetic. I didn't want to risk putting her to sleep or giving her a large dose of painkillers while she was so weak. She was tough, but her breathing had grown ragged and her pulse faint. Once she drank blood, I would give her enough to let her slip into a painless sleep so she could heal.

After an hour of tedious work, I pushed away from the cot and stretched my aching back. Her eyes tracked my movements, but her body remained motionless.

"You did well, princess."

They only response I got was her eyes becoming slits. It was going to take me a while to understand her behavior. I was looking forward to it.

Then I moved to her head, slipping my hands into her hair. Careful to not hurt her, I massaged her scalp searching for bumps or swelling. I didn't find anything other than dried bits of what appeared to be shark skin.

My hand brushed across the scales on her face. She studied my face while I studied hers. I leaned down and inspected them closer. The scales lay tight against her skin, similar to fish scales. Her scales were much thicker though; they must provide protection against some injuries, just not a full-blown shark attack. Soft light began to emanate from the edges of each individual scale. Did she control the glow, or were they a natural response?

"Both," she said. "Our eyes blink without our conscious thought, but we can also choose to blink or not blink."

She was listening to my thoughts again. It should have felt invasive, but instead it felt intimate. Moving down, I teased the skin of her neck and shoulders, trying to find any shifting bones or swelling. My relief was growing. She would be okay.

My hands froze and a flush went up my neck. I was struggling to keep my examination impersonal, and I was quickly losing the battle. Taking her arm in my hand, I decided to check it for injuries instead of continuing down her torso. Sliding my hand down her lightly muscled arm, my stomach lurched as the bone in her forearm shifted under slight pressure from my fingers.

"Why didn't you tell us your arm was broken?" I asked.

"It served no purpose. Our situation would not have improved had you known, and the knowledge likely would have caused additional stress to the four of you."

As a scientist, I loved and understood her logic. However, as a man who loved her, I was horrified.

"Did you conceal other injuries?" I demanded, trying not to sound too forceful.

Her silence was answer enough. Anger began to simmer inside me. It was irrational, and I knew it, but I couldn't help it. I hated knowing she was in pain, and I hated that she felt the need to protect us.

My eyes burned and I blinked hard, working to focus back on the exam. I held her slender hand between my own. A flexible piece of webbing draped between each pale finger. The webbing was translucent but had a delicate green lace design etched into it. It was beautiful and functional.

"It is new," she explained. "My body continues to adapt."

"You haven't always been a Siren? And this form can change your features?" I was a man of science and facts, and she was throwing it all out the window.

She didn't answer right away. I braced her arm to keep it from shifting as it finished healing. After finished with her arms, I began to examine her torso and rib cage. The exam went smoothly until my fingers found the jagged wound between her ribs. Again, I wondered if it was a knife, and if there was internal damage.

"It was a knife. There was internal damage, but I stopped the bleeding." Her tone was so matter-of-fact.

"What organs were injured?" I asked the question but wasn't sure I wanted the answer.

She shrugged. "My lung and liver were perforated."

I gathered her into my arms, holding her against me, careful to not jostle her fluke. Her hand patted me awkwardly; trying to comfort people wasn't something she did often. She was a lethal predator, designed to kill with cold efficiency, yet she was trying to ease my devastation over how close we had come to losing her, and the pain she endured coming to our aid.

"Who stabbed you, Zosi?"

"A fisherman. I had him beneath the water. Kye's emotions distracted me, and the man stabbed me."

My mouth dropped open. I didn't even know where to begin. I had seen her soft side, and I had tried to push the memory of the victims I had examined to the dark recesses of my mind. Her victims. If I asked her why he was in the ocean, would she tell me the truth? Did I want to hear her say what I already knew in my heart?

"I do not lie," she said. "I was killing him when I became distracted. The stabbing was a futile effort on his part to escape me. He did not escape. I know my purpose, and I will do what I must to fulfill it. Will you be able to accept me for what I am?"

I couldn't even begin to decide how to respond to this. Could I? If her existence was found out, would I be willing to go on the run with her? It would mean throwing away the career I had worked so hard for.

Tilting her chin back, I leaned down and kissed her closed lips.

Yes.

CHAPTER SIXTEEN

ZOSIME

"Y*es.*"

His answer resounded in my mind. It was filled with confidence and absolute certainty. He was mine. I moved to return his kiss, but he pulled away.

"You have no idea how much I want to experience your bite," he said, "but I want to make love to you the first time without the venom in my system. You need blood, and I think I have figured out a solution."

He moved to the cabinet, grabbing several items before returning to sit on the edge of the cot.

"My blood will flow through this tube," he explained, holding up a long, thin tube, "and you can drink me like juice pack."

I didn't know what a 'juice pack' was. The only human beverage I would like to drink was bubbly soda. But my mouth watered when a drop of blood appeared on his skin next to the needle. He had inserted the needle directly into his vein, I would have to be careful to not take too much. It was easier to monitor how much I had taken when my fangs were embedded in a pulsing vein.

He placed the tip of the tube between my dry lips. "Bite down gently, love. You don't want it to slip free."

I bit down on the tube, scrunching my nose at the odd taste of it. My gums ached with the desire to sink into his neck, but I fought off the urge. This seemed important to my mate. He secured the needle with tape, did something to the tube, and blood speed through the clear tube.

When the warm crimson liquid poured into my mouth, I moaned in pleasure. My eyes closed of their own accord, wanting to savor the taste of his blood. It tasted like the sweet spice of cinnamon, a treat I had tasted when traveling with my battalion long ago. The Siren was just below my skin, eager to pounce on Fynn the moment my control slipped.

Hot lips pressed against my stomach and my back arched in response.

"Be still, Zosime. You need to heal. Let me explore your beautiful body while you drink what you need."

There was something seductive about hearing him speak directly to me in my mind. I had considered hearing the deluge of voices in my mind as a curse, but I might have to change my opinion.

Fynn trailed tender kisses up my stomach. My breath caught when he kissed between my breasts. His hand teased up my uninjured side, and I squirmed into his touch.

"Behave, or I will stop until you have healed."

I stilled, not wanting him to stop. My stomach clenched in desire at his command. Fynn had seemed like a gentle, shy man. This confident, self-assured man was an exciting surprise.

His hand teased along my torso again, this time brushing against my breast. I moaned around the tube in my mouth. Hot lips joined his talented fingers, tracing the lines of my scaled breastplate. I focused on staying relaxed, a hard task since I wanted to jump up and sink my fangs into him.

Agile fingers made their way to my tail, paying attention to each scale. I wanted to beg him to move lower and couldn't seem to stop my hips from shifting a fraction toward his fingers.

Immediately, his hand stopped. I growled in frustration.

"You may rule the sea, but when we are intimate on land, I am the boss. Do you understand, princess?"

My body became impossibly wet. Something must have happened to me while I was suspended in time. I had never allowed a man to command me. This man gives an order, and my body becomes even more aroused. I wanted to obey him. The Siren wanted to disobey him to see if he would punish us. There was something wrong with this body. Lost in my thoughts, I forgot to answer him.

"I asked you a question, Zosime. I expect an answer."

"Yes."

His eyes widened in shock at my voice in his mind. It seemed the Siren was very intrigued by his new game and wanted to play. I had never been able to speak in a human mind until I spoke in Kye's, and I assumed that was because we had bonded. This Siren body continued to change the rules.

"Good girl."

I meant to curl my lips in derision at the ridiculous praise, instead my core throbbed. The Atlantean Queen had appointed me the commander of her entire army, and now my traitorous body was eager to obey Fynn's orders. Oh! How the mighty had fallen.

I was relieved when he began his exploration again. My body screamed for him to hurry, but I remained quiet. His body slid along the length of mine, setting every nerve ending on fire. I almost cried out when he bumped against my hidden channel.

"Kye told us about your scales, and how they hide your sex. I am going to enjoying finding it for myself."

Kill me now. My body was going to burn from the inside out. Fynn inspected each scale like the scientist he was, and then he licked and kissed it before moving to the next. My body had been stirred into a frenzy worse than any shark frenzy I had witnessed in the ocean.

"Fynn. Stop your blood flow, you have given me enough."

For a moment I thought he might scold me, but instead he paused and removed the tube from my mouth and the needle from his arm. He bandaged his arm and then looked into my eyes. His were filled with a wild hunger that I recognized.

"No biting."

I nodded.

He resumed his mission of kissing every scale on my tail. My entire body was shaking by the time his tongue licked along the edges of the most tender scales.

"Fynn!" I cried out his name.

His soft chuckle blew warm air against my sex, nearly causing me to climax.

"It seems I have found the hidden treasure."

Talented fingers rubbed and teased, working to figure out the secrets of my body. I didn't have to wait long. His strong finger slipped inside me, alternating between stroking and probing my slick walls.

"I want to taste to you so much it hurts, but we don't fully understand your toxin. Next time I am going to devour you until you scream my name."

"Please." I couldn't take anymore.

"Please, what? Tell me what you want, princess."

"Claim me, make me yours."

I heard rustling and then the sound of his pants hitting the floor. He had slid on a pair of borrowed pants after we arrived at this building. He called them scrubs. A strange name for an article of clothing that made him look edible. He hadn't bothered with a shirt, and with the pants hanging loose around his hips, I had been given an amazing view of his body. The outline of his manhood had been clearly visible as he moved around the room.

The shy scholar had transformed into a man that the artists of my homeland would have begged to sculpt. My gums throbbed with the need to mark him as mine. His hand wrapped around his erection. I watched transfixed as he slid his hand along his length. He was tempting a predator, and it was taking every ounce of my willpower to maintain control.

After his show of dominance, I was surprised when he gently moved me to the side of the small cot and eased down beside me.

"I love you, Zosime." He spoke the words out loud.

"You have my heart, now claim the rest of me, Fynn," I whispered back.

He needed no further encouragement. I felt his erection press against my scales, seeking entrance. His fingers found my entrance. I gasped as I felt the head of his erection slide inside me. Inch by slow inch, he moved deeper. When I felt our bodies press against each other, I moaned in satisfaction.

"Full. So full."

"Princess." He groaned into my hair.

With the same slow tenderness, he slid in and out. His

rhythm was smooth and unhurried, as if we had all the time in the world. Part of me, the Siren, wanted to ride him like my I rode my favorite mount into battle thousands of years ago. The other part of me was basking in the love Fynn was showing me.

I knew from his thoughts that he had experienced sadness in his past and had learned to wall himself off from others to protect himself. He was giving me every part of himself and trusting that I would not rip his heart in two. We were both broken souls, but together we had a chance to be whole again.

I forced myself to relax and enjoy this time instead of turning it into crazy frantic sex. We could do that when I healed. Resting my head on his chest, I listened to the steady sound of his heartbeat.

Our breathing grew ragged, and while his pace remained unhurried, he began to thrust in a little harder. His hand on my hip kept me steady, ever mindful of my injuries. I felt the pleasure building inside me. We were both nearing our release, but still he refused to move faster. I thought I would die from the overwhelming urgency of my need, but when I toppled off the precipice into pleasure so incredible, I forgot how to breathe. Wave after wave of pleasure rocked my body, the torturously slow build up created an orgasm that I thought would go on forever. I clawed at his chest, drowning in sensation, and struggling to take a breath.

"Bite me, princess. Now."

His voice was strangled, my body had clamped around him and he was fighting to stave off his own release. I didn't need to be asked twice. I sank my fangs deep, my out-of-control hormones pumping my toxin into him. The Siren smirked. She had enjoyed his dominance, and now she was enjoying having the upper hand.

"Fynn! I'm sorry!" I didn't need to tell him why I was sorry. It was written in the strain on his face.

"Oh. This is— I can't—"

The man couldn't finish a sentence. She had broken him and felt no remorse about it. And then I felt it and knew why she was pleased with herself. When I bit Kye's manhood, the toxin going directly to the area had sent it into overdrive, muscles straining and blood pumping. She had just pumped enough toxin into Fynn to affect his erection as well.

My slick walls suddenly felt tight, too tight. His hard member swelled as his body continued to pump blood into it. My eyes burned; if this didn't stop soon, I was going to be ripped in two.

"I'm sorry, I can't control it. Breathe, baby."

Of course he couldn't control it, no more than I could control how much venom was injected into him.

"It is not your fault, Fynn. Please, don't move. I need time to adjust."

I doubted I would ever adjust to this. The men may find us dead tomorrow, still stuck together.

Several minutes passed with neither of us moving so

much as a muscle. Fynn's erection seemed to have swelled as much as the venom and his body could force it to. I could feel him pulsing inside me as my channel squeezed him.

My body slowly relaxed, adjusting to his size. The pain gradually eased and with it came small ripples of pleasure. Cautiously, I moved my hips a fraction, startling myself when a moan of pure bliss bubbled out of my chest.

"If you make a sound like that again, I will come on the spot."

Ignoring him, I shifted again. This time the pleasure caused me to bite my lip hard enough that I tasted blood.

"My turn, princess."

By the time he fully unsheathed himself, we were both panting hard. He hesitated for a moment, searching my face for permission.

"Claim me." My voice had shifted to that of my Siren. He didn't have a chance.

With one hard thrust, he rammed himself deep inside me. Our cries of pleasure echoed in the stark room. I could feel every pulse of his release, my body shuddering around him with my own climax.

I repeated my chant, bonding with Fynn. His skin glowed and swirled, inking my mark like a brand on his skin.

When the aftershocks finally ceased, we lay panting, our skin covered in a sheen of sweat. He was still inside me, both of us too exhausted to move.

"I should get up and check your wounds," Fynn said. He made a move to rise.

"Or you could hold me while we both get some rest. I've never spent a night being held by a man." I cuddled into his chest and wrapped my arm around him to hold him close.

"I'm not just a man, I'm your soulmate." His body relaxed, and his arm slid around my waist and pulling me closer.

"That makes this even better."

CHAPTER SEVENTEEN

ZOSIME

Things moved fast the following morning. It was a relief to discover that Fynn and I were no longer stuck together. Fynn checked my injuries and was stunned to find they had healed so quickly. Little did he know this was the slowest I had healed since awakening. I couldn't be too critical of my body though; it had been given a challenging task.

I had already been weakened from not drinking, I then used additional energy I didn't have to answer the call. If I had been human, the knife would have been fatal. I had stopped the bleeding as best I could, but healing wouldn't happen until I could feed myself. Battling a group of sharks was the last thing I should have done, but only death could have prevented me from fighting for my men. Incidentally, death almost did take me out.

The frenzy reopened the injuries from the knife, and I began to bleed out internally. That was right about the time the last shark attempted to rip my tail in half. I had told Fynn the truth about my injuries, but I had not told him how extensive they were.

I also did not tell the men how bad Storm had been wounded. Debris had embedded in him like shrapnel, slicing vital organs. His bowel had been sliced through, his spine injured, he had massive internal bleeding, and a small piece of metal had slowly sawed away at his aorta with each breath he took. It was a surprise that he had stayed alive for as long as he did after the explosion.

I could have healed myself in an hour or two, with only Eason's blood. But I needed all the blood they could spare to heal Storm's human body. He had come back to us, but he almost drained my body of blood in the process. Once Fynn gave me blood, I was able to start the healing process on my body again.

After reassuring himself I wasn't in pain, Fynn had gathered me into his arms and carried me to a small steel tub. It was a tight fit, not at all like the elegant bathing pools of Atlantis. He turned several knobs until warm water sprayed over me.

Kye, Eason and Storm strode into the room and froze. Kye burst into laughter, doubling over to brace himself on his knees. Storm began to chuckle as well, and even the stoic Eason tried to hide a smile. I didn't see what was so amusing.

He finally got his laughter under control long enough speak, "You are bathing her in the sink where the lab cleans their dead specimens?" Eason spluttered. "Talk about romance being dead in the world nowadays."

I was indignant. "Is he speaking the truth?" I said to Fynn. "You are bathing the leader of the entire Atlantean military force in a tub for cleaning dead fish?" No wonder the cold tub had a strange odor.

Silence fell on the room. I glanced at the men, but they were frozen in place. My mind flashed back to the final attack on Atlantis; the strange frozen moments in time. The sudden silence after the loud shouts of battle and then the terrified wails as the sea swallowed an entire civilization. I jerked my mind back to my current reality and was relieved to realize they were still breathing and blinking rapidly. They had frozen in shock, not from a trick of magik.

"When you say Atlantean—" Storm started.

"Do you mean Atlantis?" Fynn finished.

How could these men be so highly educated on a vast number of topics, yet not know basic history?

"Yes, of course." I tilted my hand to allow the clean water to rush through it.

"Soldier, are you from Atlantis?" Eason asked. I continued washing my hair as I eyed him and the other men.

"Why are you all acting so strange?" I asked.

Their hearts had begun to race, and I was growing uncomfortable. Eason moved to the tub and lifted me up into his arms, not caring that my body soaked his dry clothing. He found a seat and sat with me on his lap.

"I think we need to tell you about the legends of Atlantis," he said gently.

And he did. He told me how my home was a bedtime story told to children, and a tale that had many pirates searching for our treasures. It had become a legend that morphed and changed—some claimed we were human, other claimed we were mermaids. Our true history had been wiped from the minds of men and from their historical records. The brave heroes, the wise rulers, the brilliant scientists, the talented artists... All had been forgotten.

We didn't exist.

I didn't exist.

Tears blurred my vision and the sound of blood rushed in my ears. I had awakened in a strange body and in a world far different from the one I remembered. It had been hard to accept that my people were gone, but I had found solace in the belief that my people would be honored in history for the sacrifices we had made.

Humans would have been destroyed had we not stepped up to protect them and fight back against the Lure. Rage burned in my chest. We had given up everything in an effort to protect the humans, and the humans had repaid us by turning my people into a silly myth.

"Soldier, listen to me!" I snapped my head up at Eason's

sharp tone. "You *do* matter. It is unfair what has been done to your people. We will listen to you recount the history of Atlantis. Heck, I bet you'll get sick of all our questions!" He gave me a winning smile. "This is incredible. We will help to honor those you loved and admired. It will not right the wrongs done, but it is a start."

I threw my arms around his neck. My emotions were continuing to chip away at the cage locking them in, and I was already struggling with the ups and downs.

"I need to go home," I mumbled. "Atlantis is there. It has to be." His shirt muffled my words.

"You think you can find Atlantis?" Storm asked, his tone incredulous.

"I know I can. If I get near enough, it will call to me."

I jerked, startled by a loud thump. Peering around Eason, I saw Fynn passed out on the cool tile floor.

"What happened to him? Is he okay?" I gasped.

Kye laughed, moving to help Storm check on my unconscious mate. "He'll be fine," he reassured me. "Every marine biologist and marine archaeologist on earth is in love with the legends of Atlantis. You just told the biggest nerd of them all that Atlantis is real. He was already struggling to keep his excitement under control over you being a mermaid, this just pushed him over the edge."

They moved Fynn to the tiny cot, and then turned back to me. Kye plucked me out of Eason's lap and twirled me around.

"Zosi, we will follow you wherever you go," he said. "Whether it is a modern city, or a city of legend."

I couldn't help but smile. These men had brought such love and light into my life. Kye took a seat and settled me on his lap. Storm held out a small brush. I reached for it, but Kye snatched it and began brushing my damp tangled locks.

"After we made it to shore last night, we all went straight to bed," he began. "This morning we woke to a message from our commander. He wants us to go in person to brief him on what's been going on and to look at some data he has collected regarding our previous mission. I tried to get out of it, but the officials here have ruled the recent deaths as accidents and shark attacks. They are trying to get us out of here, to stop us from investigating them.

"We are in a bad position. If we disagree with their findings, we will be asked to show proof. Obviously, we aren't going to show them proof that you exist. It is best for your safety if we just go along with their reports. However, if we agree with their medical examiner's reports, we are going to be removed from this case and shipped off to our next mission. Whoever has been orchestrating things behind the scenes around here will get away with it."

The cot creaked as Fynn sat up. He rubbed at the back of his head and winced. Kye snickered.

"You guys go ahead and report back to your boss," Fynn mumbled slowly. "I have private use of this part of the facility for the weekend and will use the time to arrange for some things that will help us to assist Zosime in her search."

His logical brain had kicked back in, ready to efficiently do whatever needed to be done.

"How did you arrange the private use of this facility?" Storm asked. "This may not be the most populated coastal city, but this center is well known for their snotty treatment of those outside of their little clique. I had a very hard time getting copies of some of their research a few years back, even though it had been funded by my boss and he was the one requesting the documents." Storm's eyes were narrowed on Fynn.

Fynn just waved his hand casually in the air and replied, "I'm giving a talk at their private charity event next year."

Eason's laughter was so loud that I squeaked in surprise and clung to Kye. "They suckered you!" he said. "I bet they're bragging to the entire marine biology and conservation community."

I looked questioningly at Fynn, but he only shrugged. Eason got himself under control enough to answer my unspoken question.

"Fynn is a renowned leader in marine biology," he said. "His lab is cutting edge, and their research provides massive breakthroughs in the field. If a new technique is announced that will reduce pollutants in the ocean, it's Fynn's lab that created it. If a new species is discovered, or new research is released about an existing marine species, ninety-five percent of the time it comes from Fynn's lab.

"What makes this so ridiculously hilarious, is how they

managed to rope the most elusive man on earth into a private lecture. Fynn has given exactly three lectures in the last decade. People pay absurd amounts of money for those highly sought-after seats. I know, I could have bought a sports car for what I had to pay. Your newly claimed mate is the darling of his field. They should have allowed him use of this facility out of courtesy for all he gives to conservation, instead they extorted him. And he is so besotted with you that he agreed without question to their demands, even knowing the stress it will put him under. You caught him hook, line and sinker. It turns out our little fish is quite the talented fisherman."

My mouth hung open. I was not surprised to discover exactly how talented my scholar mate was, I already knew that. However, finding out that the shy humble man was a man of fame in his world was a shock. None of his thoughts had even hinted that he was more than a private man that thrived in research.

"Look!" Kye cried. "She just realized she married a rich man. Wait until she finds out the rest!" He cackled in glee.

I bit the inside of my cheek. Laughter welled up inside me and tried to break free, the feeling was still foreign and strange. I wondered how Kye would react when he knew the secrets of Atlantis.

"Now's not the time, Kye," Storm interjected. "We have a lifetime to discuss the details of our lives. Let's focus on creating a plan to keep her safe and help her find her home."

"Storm's right. The sooner we report to command, the sooner we can return," Eason said. He was back to his serious self, his face an emotionless mask. Then he winked at me.

Butterfly wings tickled my stomach at his gesture and my heart skipped a beat. I found myself wanting to roll my eyes. These men were making me soft, something I couldn't afford to be. Not yet.

"We are going to request a leave of absence," Storm said, turning to Kye and Eason. "If they deny it, we will hand in our resignations. We like to serve, but not at the expense of Zosi's safety. She is our priority until we get things figured out. The helicopter to fly us out will arrive within the hour. Fynn can padlock the doors to this facility, while he goes and arranges what he thinks we will need. That will keep any nosy staff from wandering in here." Storm turned to Fynn and added, "Fynn, you can contact me on my private cell if you need to use any of my resources for the arrangements. I want all our communications to be on untraceable lines only. Kye will give you a new cell before we leave."

Fynn nodded and Storm continued, "Zosi, I know you aren't going to like this,"—he turned to face me, his expression solemn—"but we need you to stay in here until we return. We hope that we can make it back tonight, but it may be morning before we return. It is too risky for Fynn to try sneak you out in broad daylight by himself. I am also selfish, but I don't want you to be separated from all of us at once. I know you can sense us in the water, but we are still new to this, and I want to be able to communicate with you while we prepare for this expedition."

I hated the thought of being forced to stay on land. I had a secret hope that one day I would walk on land again, but this body was made for the sea. While on land, I was more vulnerable, a feeling I didn't enjoy. Storm's logic made sense, so I would not argue with his plan. They were sacrificing much for me; I could spend a few hours hiding in this room to please them.

"Zosi, how long can you stay on land?" Fynn asked. "Will you be uncomfortable?" His worried eyes bore into me.

"To be truthful, I don't know," I replied. "This is the longest I have been out of the water since awakening. I am thirsty, and my skin itches a little, but I am not in pain. It will be fine. Let us get started on this plan."

"Do you have things you need to collect before we leave the area, soldier?" Eason's question caught me off guard.

"No."

"Are you sure?" Kye pressed. "We don't mind getting them before we sail out." He was being so sweet.

"I have nothing," I said and their collective sadness was so powerful that it slammed into me like a physical blow. "As long as all four of you are on the boat, then I have collected all I have, which is also everything I could have wanted."

That is how I found myself being smothered in the first

group hug I had ever received. Kisses pressed against my cheeks and shoulder, hands stroked my hair, and warm bodies pressed tight around me.

I had always tried to keep people at a distance, receiving as minimal an amount of physical contact as possible. Now I found myself dreaming of going to sleep and waking up surrounded by these men. I promised myself that I would find a way to make it happen.

Then, the delicious petting from my men reminded me of something I had forgotten.

"Storm! Are you okay?" I grabbed his face between my hands. He tried to pull away, but I used the tiny, microscopic cups on my palms to suction to his face. That made him freeze.

"Zosime, what have you done?" His voice was cautious, not angry, or fearful.

"I just wanted to see if you were okay, and you tried to pull away," I replied. "Now you can't get away from me until I am satisfied that you are okay."

I ignored the snickers of the other guys.

"We didn't finish bonding yesterday," I continued. "I thought I had to bite for my venom to work, but apparently the toxin can go through blood as well. You exhibited all the symptoms, as well as an added punch from ingesting my blood. How are you not sick? With the others, they seemed to get worse the longer we waited to—" I paused, suddenly shy and hating the feeling.

Fynn took pity on me. "We will need to conduct some

tests,"—his cheeks blazed red but he continued with a straight face—"but it does seem that once you inject the venom into us, your mates, we need to fully copulate for the symptoms to reverse. I'm not sure why that is, or what part of the process is working as an anti-venom. Is it the act itself? Maybe your venom is designed to ensure the species survival. Or maybe it is a chemical reaction you release that counteracts the venom? I'm still guessing here, but Storm most likely didn't continue to experience the effects of the venom because he also had your blood in his system. You aren't affected by your venom, so maybe the answer is in your blood. None of us have taken blood from you, so until we test some of these theories, we won't have more conclusive answers."

"Heck yeah!" Kye cried. "Sign me up for all these trials! I know it will be tough, but it is a sacrifice I am willing to make." Kye's twinkling eyes caught my gaze for a split second before Eason put him in a chokehold and dragged him from the room. Storm trailed after the scuffling pair, calling to me over his shoulder.

"Zosime, I haven't forgotten that you didn't claim me yet. When we are out to sea and away from this mess, you will be mine. Rest up, my love."

I shivered in delight.

Mine.

CHAPTER EIGHTEEN

ZOSIME

I sat alone in the room. Fynn had gone to make the arrangements as promised. I told him about my last kill, the man who had stabbed me, and how his victims had been buried and forgotten. Fynn passed the information on to Eason, assuring me it would be taken care of, and that a team would arrive to see that each girl was found. I would be able to leave the area knowing the girls would receive the dignified burials they deserved.

Kye had brought me a small box he called a television, claiming that it would help me to sound more natural when I spoke. I doubted he would be able to articulate naturally if he had to share his body.

I was still struggling to balance the different aspects of

my nature. The Siren was animalistic, enjoying our lethal talents, and pushing me to just take what I wanted. She saw little need in speaking unless it was to tempt someone. Less talking, more action.

The soldier in me also preferred to speak less, instead preferring to watch and listen. As a Promised, I had focused on my mission and little else mattered. When I spoke, it was concise and direct.

Just since meeting the men and hearing their thoughts, I was beginning to hear the flow in the language and sentences. That didn't mean it always came out of my mouth sounding the way I thought in my mind, but I would get the hang of it eventually. The words he called 'slang' made no sense at all to me. But Kye seemed to take pleasure in showing me his world, so I would try to have an open mind.

I had been alone in the room for several hours when I began to cough. My throat and mouth were dry, reminding me of the sensation of choking on dust during a dust storm. The water bottles Kye had pulled from the cold metal box lay empty around me. Maybe there were more, the alternative was drinking from the odd smelling tub. I shuddered.

I eased myself off the cot and onto the cold tile. Turning so that I faced away from the small box that held the water, I used my arms and fluke to push myself backwards toward my goal. Reaching it, I pulled open the door only to be disappointed when I couldn't find any more water bottles like Kye had given me.

All that remained in the box was ten tall, thin cans. I thought about the sweet soda I had enjoyed by the docks. The letters were not the same, but any drink had to be better than the water from rusty pipes, right?

It took several tries, but I finally managed to open the can. I sniffed it first, relieved when my nose didn't burn from the scent. In fact, this drink smelled amazing, like roasted fires and toasted cream. I started with a tiny sip, moaning as the cool sweet taste slid down my throat. This had to be sweet nectar from the Ancients! I finished the first in a few gulps, and quickly opened a second. I was draining the sixth can when the lock on the outside of the door jangled.

His thoughts began to batter the walls of my mind, forcing their way in. This was not Fynn. He was thinking about Fynn, but not in a pleasant way. Not sure what was going on and wanting a chance to assess the situation before this man spotted me, I looked around the room for a place to hide. The only place large enough to hide my tail was the wretched tub.

Grumbling under my breath, I scooted toward the tub and lifted myself up into the basin. I may be lean, but I had built muscle from fighting the ocean's currents every day. I arranged my fluke and contorted my upper body until I was confident he would not see me unless he walked over to stand by the tub.

The metal door opened slowly, and the man walked in. He shut the door softly behind him and next came the sound of a lock clicking into place. I didn't mind Fynn locking me inside four walls, but it was completely different knowing the man was locking Fynn out.

His thoughts continued to pour into my mind. I stiffened. He blamed my mate for his lack of success as a researcher. I stifled a snort. Well, duh. He was in here trying to steal research because he wasn't smart enough to do the work himself.

Duh? I didn't recall ever hearing the word. It must have sunk into my subconscious from the incessant chattering on the television.

I maintained my control as the man began to trash the room. Papers were ripped as he went through the files, clearly looking for something. I just couldn't figure out what. I nearly jumped out of my tail when the sound of things hitting walls and clattering to the floor echoed around me. This went on for nearly ten minutes, and then the room became still. Only the sound of his ragged breathing could be heard.

"You think you are *so* smart," he said to himself. "I know you are hiding something in here, otherwise you would have flown back to your mansion to do research. There is something in here that is valuable enough for you to padlock the door. Since I can't find it, I'll just wait for you to come back and tell me where it is."

This insane man was talking to himself. He wasn't touched by the Lure; he was just evil. Drawers were opened and slammed shut as he searched for something else.

"Ah yes. This will do. I'm sure Fynn will talk when I threaten to slice up his pretty boy face. Once he talks, I'll slice him up and toss him in the bay for the sharks."

The wall that had held back my emotions cracked under the intense pressure of my anger. It was like an aqueduct with a hole in it; I didn't have all my emotions at once, but they were coming back a lot faster than before. It was only a matter of time before they all rushed in with full force. But in that moment, the only emotion that I felt was searing rage.

It was decided. He must die.

Mentally, my Siren clapped in glee, while my warrior giggled behind her hands.

That was when I realized I had a far more serious problem than being locked in the room with an insane man holding a knife and planning a murder.

My body tingled, feeling like it was made of pure energy. Electricity sizzled through my body, and my mind felt like it could move at the speed of light. My heartbeat sped up and magik touched every cell. The humans had found a way to bottle magik from the Ancients.

This had to be what the man was looking for, an elixir that enhanced your body and made you more powerful. He couldn't be allowed to have it, a secret like this must be protected. It was time to do what I was trained to do.

I sat up, bracing my arms on the side of the tub, preparing to flip out of it.

The man spun around shouting, "Who's there?"

I answered in a shout of my own, "¡Hola! Soy Zosime."

Internally, I facepalmed myself while cursing Kye for the stupid television. Externally, I vibrated in excitement.

Confusion and fear crossed his face as he took me in. "What *are* you?" he gasped.

"That's right, you should fear me. I have drunk the nectar of the Ancients and its power courses through my veins." I propelled myself over the side of the tub and onto the floor.

"You have a tail?" His skin was turning a strange, mottled color.

"Oh." I looked at my tail and then back at him. "Yes, I am a commander of Atlantis and a Siren of the sea. Today you will take a one-way trip to Tartarus! Prepare yourself for death."

The speech was new. I tended to be more direct and to the point with my kills. Kye would be proud.

It was time to act. My vibrating body moved toward my prey, but not with the hypnotizing slither of a snake. Nor did it move with the sway of a giant cat stalking its prey. Instead, my body was so full of magik it bounced across the floor like a fat joyful seal.

For the love of the Ancients!

The man brandished the knife at me like he was trying to scare off a dog, not a terrifying creature of myth and legend who just told him she planned to kill him.

I bounced into his legs, knocking him to the ground. He grabbed for the knife as it skittered across the floor, but I knocked it across the floor with a flick of my fluke. It was harder to strangle a man on land, so eventually I bit into his neck and delivered my venom. He stopped struggling almost instantly, his body limp and eyes unseeing.

I didn't need to eat yet, but knowing we had a journey coming up, I decided it was best to drink what I could. I bit down again and sucked in a mouthful of blood. My stomach clenched and bile rose up my throat. I never enjoyed the taste of blood until I drank from my men, but I had also never had my stomach reject blood. It was necessary for my survival and blood was blood, right?

I drew in another mouthful, my eyes watering as I fought past my gag reflex and swallowed it. My breaths were coming in pants now, but I was determined to drink so I wouldn't be a burden to my mates.

My fangs were still deep in the man's neck, tears running down my face as I gagged down the blood, when I heard Fynn's voice.

"Zosi! What happened? Are you ok—" His voice trailed off. No doubt taking in the blood splattered across the floor, the ripped papers and destroyed items from the man scattered around us. His mouth opened and closed several times, but no words came out.

Retracting my fangs, I hurried to reassure him. "I can explain!"

I didn't get a chance to explain though, because the pressure of the call built inside me. The Lure was nearby, ebbing away at someone's soul.

An officer ran into the room, his gun drawn. But it wasn't pointed at me. He entered the room with it focused on Fynn.

Well, well. This was convenient. It wasn't often that the Lure came to me. And right now, the magik of the Ancients still ran through my veins.

He was about to sleep with the fishies.

CHAPTER NINETEEN

FYNN

I t would have helped if my new bride had come with an instruction manual. Maybe then I would have been more prepared for the scene I walked into upon my return. Something must have made her snap because the lab had nearly been destroyed. Shredded papers lay soaking up blood that was splattered across the floor.

Bloody drag marks smeared the floor, most of the drawers had been emptied of their contents and thrown around the room. The amount of rage it would take to do something like that was terrifying. Zosi sat on the floor; a man partially flopped over in her lap. A janitor's badge hung crooked from his blood-spattered shirt. His fingers were slightly curled, likely due to the paralytic effect of her venom.

She watched me through slitted eyes. Blood had splashed across her face and torso. Her chest was heaving as she breathed, and her body trembled.

Yanking her fangs out of his neck, she exclaimed, "I can explain!"

I couldn't think of a single thing to say. What was I supposed to do now? We had found a way to somewhat justify her other kills, but it appeared she had simply gone into a feeding frenzy with the janitor.

Running footsteps in the hallway had me turning to the door I had left open. An officer skidded into the room. How could I explain this away? They would take Zosime. What would it take for him to forget any of this ever happened?

It turned out I didn't need to worry about him talking.

Zosime's fluke hit the floor and she propelled herself into the officer's chest. He cried out and staggered back against the wall. The crack of a gunshot was followed by the crack of her fluke hitting skin. Their bodies dropped to the tile with a thud. My ears rang as I stumbled toward them. By the time I dropped to my knees next to them, the officer's eyes stared unseeing at the ceiling.

I pulled Zosime off the dead officer and into my lap. Cradling her against my chest, I breathed in her soft beach scent and tried to figure out what our next step was. I needed to think fast. The officer was going to be missed pretty fast.

"I couldn't let them kill you," she said, her words muffled in my shirt.

I stopped rocking her. I had assumed she had snapped and killed them because she couldn't help it.

"I know what you thought," she continued. "We have so much to learn about each other. It is natural that you would be suspicious of me."

She didn't sound hurt, but I was mad at myself. I had trusted her enough to bind myself to her, but not enough to hear her side of events before assuming things.

"The first man worked here as a janitor because he failed in his studies. He blamed you for his failures and he came to steal the research he thought you were working on now. When he could not find it, he found a knife to torture and kill you. I had stayed hidden until he got the knife. No one touches what is mine. Do not worry, he did not find the elixir. I would have stopped him if he got too close."

She had fought him to save me. He could have stabbed her. The thought of opening that door to find her dead knocked the wind out of me. I clutched her tighter, reassuring myself she was fine.

"Zosi, what do you mean by elixir?" I asked.

"I found it in the cold metal box," she replied, gesturing to the box in question. "Before he arrived, I drank several, and they enhanced my abilities and increased my energy. It is like the magik of the Ancients."

I glanced across the wrecked room to the refrigerator. Six cans of a coffee energy drinks lay scattered around it.

"That's not magic, it's coffee."

"There is a difference?"

She was adorable and I barely contained my laughter. "You are on a caffeine high, Zosi," I explained. "That's a lot of caffeine to drink at once, especially if your body isn't used to it. No wonder you thought they were magic."

We both jumped suddenly at the wail of police sirens. I looked around the room; there was no time to spare, we had to run.

I stood, holding her against me. Then I ran out into the hall and out the side door nearest the docks. The moment my feet hit the docks I started sprinting. If anyone spotted Zosime's mermaid tail, the hunt for her would be relentless. There was a small fishing boat at the end of the dock. I would find a way to pay the owner for it later, but right now it was our ticket out of here.

I jumped on board, settling her quickly. In less than a minute we were moving through the bay and out toward the open water. I felt for the phone Storm had given me, relieved that it was still in my pocket. Dialing his number, I listened to it ring. There was no answer. Cursing, I shoved it back in my pocket.

We traveled for almost two hours, never spotting a sign of anyone coming after us. My first clue that anything was amiss was the bullet embedding itself in the cushion of my chair. A second bullet hit the side of the vessel. I listened for their engines, but our boat's motor was too loud to hear anything over.

"Stay low!" I shouted. Zosi didn't respond. Panicking, I turned to see if she had been hurt, but the boat was empty. Should I stop, or keep going? I got my answer when she surged out of the water and grabbed the boat rail next to me.

"I was going to take out the shooters, but there are three boats," she explained. "These men look like experienced hunters. Their boats are dark, the lights are blacked out. They do not want anyone knowing they are out tonight. There is no way to outrun them in this boat, Fynn."

"We don't have a lot of options, Zosime!" I cried. All I could think about was what those men would do if they caught her. "Zo, you need to go," I insisted.

I clicked dial on the phone again. On the fourth ring Storm picked up. "Storm, listen!" I shouted. "Two guys tried to attack, and Zosime killed them. We made it out into the ocean, but there are too many and they are armed. I'm sending Zosime to hide—"

Another shot rang out. The new shooter must've believed we were far enough out for the sound to not matter. I dropped the phone and grabbed at my burning cheek.

Zosime caught the phone. "Storm, come to Key West. I love you all." She didn't wait for his response. Tossing the phone into the water, she lunged forward and wrapped her arms around my neck. She arched her body and flipped me out of the boat and into the sea.

I gasped in surprise as water rushed into my lungs. I

began to thrash, my need for air overwhelming all other thoughts. Above us, the dark of the night burst into blinding red and gold. I needed air or I was going to die. But if the men were up there, surfacing could mean my death as well.

"*Fynn, my love. Listen to my voice.*"

Her body moved against mine, her tail curling around my legs to calm my thrashing.

"*I need you to trust me.*"

"Whatever you want, princess."

Her lips pressed against mine. Thinking this was likely the last time, I kissed her with wild abandon, savoring every second. It took several seconds for my foggy brain to realize that I was tasting blood in my mouth.

"*Drink it, Fynn. Hurry.*" There was urgency in her voice. I obeyed without question.

My lungs burned, and stars sparkled against my closed eyelids. I was going to lose consciousness.

Then her lips disappeared. I barely registered the prick of her fangs in my throat. I relaxed, no longer fighting the inevitable.

"*I love you, princess.*"

"*Breathe, silly man.*"

She had lost it. I couldn't breathe underwater.

"*I said breathe. Obey me, stubborn human.*"

Her voice carried a power I hadn't heard from her before. I sucked in a shocked breath at her command... and the burning in my lungs eased. In disbelief I breathed again, pulling water deep into my lungs. With each breath, the burning in my chest eased and the fog in my brain cleared.

"I'm breathing. Underwater." I couldn't believe it.

"Yes."

"But how? Did you know you could do this?"

"I adapt with each challenge. When Atlantis fell, I was blessed or cursed, I still don't know which. I am meant to survive. Perhaps it is so I can fulfill my oath, or maybe it is simply to amuse the Ancients. You're my mate, and now your life is intertwined with mine. I knew I was going to lose you, and I wasn't willing to accept that."

"How long will this new ability last?"

"You will need to take my blood every few hours. When Storm exhibited the traits of my Siren after ingesting my blood and toxin, I began to wonder if he might have had borrowed other abilities from me. I had planned to test my theory when we were somewhere safe, and all together. I didn't want to say anything until I was positive. Tonight, I had no choice."

I wrapped my arms around her, holding her close.

"Now what?" I was out of my depth, literally.

"We wait for your ride." Zosi laughed a silky laugh and I started to worry.

CHAPTER TWENTY

ZOSIME

I smiled watching Fynn stroke the underside of Sheba's pectoral fin. It had been a relief when she had found us the night we had to run. There would have been no way I could have swum with Fynn for long distances each day. He wasn't a small guy. We couldn't risk going on land near the bay. It was best if we waited to until we could meet up with Eason, Storm and Kye. I had been relieved to find that my blood heated his body, keeping him comfortable during the days spent in the water. We still had to avoid the depths; those temperatures would be too much for him.

Fynn had enjoyed every minute of the journey, excitedly pointing to schools of fish or colorful displays of corals along the way. More than once he had awkwardly clung to rocks and kicked uselessly as he tried to explore crevices or hidden coves. When he strayed too far, Sheba would appear from nowhere and smack him with her tail. I laughed at the odd yet beautiful bond they had formed.

Fynn's love for the ocean shown in his eyes, and he was making the most of the chance to observe creatures in their habitat. Watching my mate explore the world that had become my home was a gift. I could spend time on land, but I wasn't truly comfortable there. When I was in the ocean, the water supported the weight of my tail and fluke, easing the strain on my body. I wondered if I would ever be able to call the land my home again.

Twice while we rested in kelp beds, smaller sharks had swum near us. Sheba didn't wait to see if they were friend or foe. Passing close enough to bump us, she made it clear she was the only one hunting in that area.

The one thing Fynn hadn't enjoyed was eating raw fish, but he had treated our ocean journey just as you would treat journey into the wilderness. You did what you must to survive. The past several days had drawn us closer. I hadn't thought I would ever have this type of bond with another human. In the peaceful world below the surface, we were able to speak and learn about each other, all without the world interrupting us.

Fynn had shared news about the recent ocean mining for the natural resource the humans called 'Orpati.' I had listened without commenting, but my brain was working overtime. Was the drilling what had woken me? I was also worried that what they were mining for, was pieces from the heart of Atlantis. I hated to think of what would happen if the world got ahold of the full heart, especially while the Lure was still claiming souls. I had to find Atlantis and secure our secrets. There was so much I needed to do, but I was growing weaker with each hour.

We had been traveling for nine days. I needed my bonded, all of them. The longer we were apart, the worse I felt. My body ached and my head pounded mercilessly. We had moved into warmer waters, but I remained cold. Feeding from Fynn helped, but that relief only lasted a few hours. I was struggling to hide how sick I had become, not wanting to alarm him while he was still relying on me.

With Sheba's aid, we had made good time. One more day until we arrived in Key West. I just had to hang in there. Sheba pressed her side against me, her massive pectoral fin sliding underneath my body, supporting my weight. I continued to pump my fluke and swim beside her. Her annoyance flashed in my mind. I was lagging and she could go faster if I accepted help.

With her massive body blocking Fynn's view of me, I allowed myself to be weak. I turned and flattened myself against her to create as little drag as possible. I used my palms to suction and secure myself.

"Take care of him."

I whispered my plea to her, not sure if she understood. Closing my eyes, I drifted to into the bliss of sleep.

CHAPTER TWENTY-ONE

LOKENE

I watched her sleep like a creepy stalker, but I didn't care. Thousands of years had gone by since I had last been able to sit next to her. The warm rays of the sun heated her skin, casting a golden glow and heating her feverish skin. She was a stubborn little thing. Until this moment I hadn't realized how sick she had grown. We had very little time to turn this around.

Reaching out a hand, I brushed the dark wet strands away from her beautiful face. Zosime had always been a stunning woman, although now her features had shifted slightly. She was inhumanely perfect, which wasn't a shock considering her lineage and the magik that had been used to save her.

If Atlantis hadn't been wiped from earth, I had no doubt she would have become the subject of paintings and sculptures. Her bravery as she fought battle after battle would have catapulted her into the human legends. Beauty, bravery, and brains. It was an alluring combination. Any man lucky enough to be loved by her, was given an incomparable gift. I had that once.

Water lapped at her skin, rocking her gently like a mother rocks her child. Zosime's scales glowed, the dim light flickering, one more sign of how ill she was. Her blue-green eyes locked on mine. The irises were pale and flat, the glow that should have been there was gone.

"Where are my mates? Are they safe?"

I heard her voice in my mind. Her heart was beating erratically as her panic began to rise.

"Fynn has gone to find the others, all are safe," I tried to soothe her, "It is okay, Soyale."

Tears pooled in her eyes at that last word.

Her tongue stuck to the roof of her dry mouth as she tried to speak. I conjured a bottle of water and held it to her cracked lips. Most trickled out the side of her mouth, but she managed to swallow some of it.

"I never thought I would hear my mother tongue spoken again."

My heart shattered at the sorrowful homesickness in her voice. She was longing for a time and place long gone. Hearing the language of the Ancients brought all those memories rushing back to her.

"Soyale." I wanted to say more, but the lump in my throat threatened to choke me.

She sucked in a sharp breath at that single word.

There was no direct translation for the word, the meaning too deep a concept to sum up in a single phrase. A love so deep it was limitless, the act of offering to trade their soul for just a day of your love, an oath of love and loyalty for eternity—it was all those things and so much more.

An ancient word that was never spoken unless the speaker was certain of their feelings. The word had been used with only a handful of couples for as long as the Ancients had existed. Ancients were immortal and could not break an oath, so the word was almost considered taboo. Eternity was a long time to keep a promise.

Her emotions and memories danced across her face like a movie. Emotions, pain, disbelief, joy, and confusion showed in her expressions. I knew the moment she recognized me. The mischievous young man that beautiful summer day in Atlantis. A day that was both forever ago, and yesterday to me. It was a day I would never forget. I had not been allowed to show myself to her again, and I knew she assumed I was killed in the final battle.

"How are you sitting beside me? Atlanteans were not fully human, but we were also not immortal. Even if you survived the fall of Atlantis, you would have died millennia ago."

"I am not Atlantean."

Her eyes narrowed and then widened as she figured it out.

"Soyale, I am an Ancient. I did not enjoy the games some of the Ancients played with the beings on earth, so I kept to myself. I heard rumors of the Lure and came to investigate. I had not been in Atlantis for centuries, but I needed to see for myself what was happening. The moment I saw you in Atlantis, I forgot my mission. We spent that one beautiful day together. In my immortal life I had never been that happy or had a day so perfect. I planned to promise myself to you for eternity the next day. Before I could tell you, my father summoned me.

"I was pulled from the earthly plane and into an emergency meeting of the remaining Ancients. These were the ones who had not let their own greed corrupt them. I was told the Lure had been released on earth, and we needed to keep an eye on the crown princess of Atlantis. She would wage war against the Lure, and one day she would prevail. She was going to save the world, and then she was going to change it."

She turned green around the gills as I spoke. Well, not around the gills, she didn't have those, but her skin definitely took on a green pallor. Her lips parted as her breath came faster.

"Ancients are limited on what we can interfere with, but we watched in awe as this princess rallied entire continents around her and struck fear in the hearts of those who opposed her. Her heart was pure, and she fought with everything in her."

Salty tears streamed from her eyes, slipping into the sea. I leaned forward and kissed them away.

"I am so proud of every battle you fought. The earth has never seen a warrior like you."

My tears mixed with hers. We cried for a lost city, for lost loved ones, and for lost time.

"I have waited all these centuries for you to awaken. Hoping and praying that the magik that was slammed into you those final moments wouldn't take away the woman I loved, or the princess the world needed. You awakened, and again you amazed me with your strength. You learned to adapt to your body, and the new instincts that tried to control you. I wanted to come to you then, but your emotions were still buried. I couldn't offer my love while yours was still buried."

"I never forgot you or the day we spent together." Her voice was weak and shook with the effort to speak.

"I have waited a long time for you to be mine. The council of Ancients opposed my intervention time and time again, but today things changed. The balanced shifted, the Lure is spreading. The Ancients are under attack from those who betrayed us. There is a war coming again, and you are needed. Claim your mates, raise your city from the depths of the sea, and declare your powers. You are the Royal Storm of Atlantis, and it is time this world is reminded of what a true queen looks like."

I had more to tell her, but she couldn't take it while she was this weak. Immortal Ancients had been slaughtered. It was an impossibility that had become possible. Bratty Ancients who didn't get their way had released the Lure as a tantrum. They believed they had control over it, and that by controlling humans they could make the rest of the Ancients miserable.

The Ancients enjoyed spending time on earth, working with the humans and teaching them. They weren't our pets; they were treated as younger siblings or children. Their joy in learning new things was exciting to us. Atlantis had been our gateway to the world, and the Atlanteans our ambassadors. We were able to give them knowledge to help all mankind. The rebel Ancients focused their efforts on destroying Atlantis, the jewel of earth, their obsession with being treated like gods turning their hearts to stone.

Today they had found a way to use the Lure to destroy more than just the earth. The Ancients' world was on fire. If we attacked the corrupted Ancients directly, we would break our oaths. A war had started, and if we didn't find the loopholes to allow us to fight it, it wouldn't just be Ancients that ceased to exist.

Humans were finding the Orpati, and that was stoking the fire of evil that was rippling around the world. The mining was wreaking havoc in the sea, even now tremors shook the earth. The ocean was agitated, and it was only a matter of time before it unleashed its rage on the earth. A perfect storm was brewing.

Gathering her in my arms, I blinked us out of existence. My skin prickled as we materialized on the earth plane again. I laid her gently on a bed stacked in silk cushions and hand stitched blankets. With a snap of my finger, four very confused men blinked into the room around us.

All five pairs of eyes slowly took in the room. Zosime's eyes glowed faintly with recognition. This was her palace bedroom. Piles of colorful cushions were spread around the room, and flickering candles cast a soft yellow light onto the smooth sculpted walls. Tapestries from dynasties long gone hung on the walls; memories of many incredible places she had traveled. A large wood shelf with intricate carvings stood in the corner; it was still full of hundreds of scrolls she had collected. Each scroll was filled with forgotten histories, hand painted maps, and stories of true heroes. I had watched her men since she had awakened. They were all intelligent men who loved to learn, those scrolls were going to blow their minds.

I had carefully constructed a bubble over this part of the palace and filled it with air for her men. The palace bedroom that had once looked out over soft green hills and sun-kissed gardens, now looked out over a dark expanse of the ocean. It was a surreal view, and I found I loved it. It reminded me of the contrasts of my Zosime. My Soyale.

I smiled as Sheba slid past the window. I had sent her to Zosime. My intention was to provide her some companionship by giving her a pet. What I hadn't counted on was the sassy and stubborn attitude the shark possessed. Controlling her had been impossible.

What I had given to the predator was an understanding of humans, and of Zosime's struggles. To my shock, Sheba had chosen to find Zosime and stay by her side, all of her own free will. Which was a relief since I had met very few creatures able to resist the will of an Ancient, and the female great white had made the list.

Kye, Eason, Fynn and Storm stared in bewilderment, not understanding what their eyes were seeing.

"Is this a 3D movie?" Kye stage whispered in Storm's direction.

"I assure you it is quite real." Everyone focused their attention on me. I couldn't deny I loved this surprise. The life of an Ancient was boring, I was ready for some fun! Joy stirred inside me, and I felt like I was that young man with the sparkling eyes and mischievous spirit Zosime had fallen in love with.

Their questions came in unison.

"Who are you?"

"Where are we?"

"My name would be challenging for humans to pronounce." Ancient names were made up of sounds that didn't even exist on the earth plane. "Just call me Lokene. And let me be the first to welcome you to Atlantis!" Bending I gave a flourishing bow. "Now, we really do need to discuss how the bond works, because you men are making a mess of it. Zosime cannot be away from her mates for more than a day or two. She will get sicker with each passing hour, and eventually her body will give out. Which is what would have happened exactly six hours, eight minutes, and twenty-three seconds from now, had intervention not taken place. Thankfully there is time to rectify the situation, so chop-chop."

My words were spoken lightly, and they probably assumed I was teasing them. But I knew more about bonding than anyone in the room, and the situation was dire. She was still hiding how close her body was to giving up. I wasn't about to let that happen, not when she had four bonded mates in the room to set things right.

They better hop up on that bed and show her some love or things were going to get real kinky. I had watched some crazy stuff from the Ancients' world. Humans were innovative, and ropes were considered fun now. That would make things much easier. I would happily string them up for her if needed. I wondered if she would like that. Maybe as a birthday present?

They continued to stare at me. Seriously, a naked woman lays on a bed and they want to look at me? Raising my eyebrows in warning, I made a shooing motion toward the bed.

Finally, they tore their eyes from me looked to where the love of my life lay curled in the middle of the massive bed. Reaching out, I felt for her emotions, needing to know she was okay with what was about to happen. She was overflowing with happiness and love. Her emotions fully returned, but her body grew sicker by the minute.

"Lokene, join us. It is time to finish what our hearts started so long ago. You are meant to be mine, and I am yours."

Her words floated into my mind. The world may be burning around us, but for this one night, my life was perfect. I was going to enjoy every second and do everything in my power to ensure everyone else did too.... And I had a lot of power. I smirked.

This was going to be too much fun.

"She has legs!" Kye cried.

I chuckled in amusement at the stunned faces around me. Zosime was sliding her hands along her legs as though this was the first time she had owned a pair.

"Indeed, she does."

AUTHOR'S NOTE

Yes, yes. I know you guys are probably ready to vote me off the island right now. Not that I could blame you—it was cruel stopping right before our fishy girl had her way with five very eager mates.... and this time with legs!

Hopefully you guys will find it in your heart to forgive me and read book two when it comes out. *Siren's Hunt* was important to set the scene for what's coming next and to establish the background for the characters and plot. *Siren's Throne* is going to be a wild ride, er, swim!

While this book is 100% fiction, our oceans and their inhabitants face real threats. There are many incredible programs out there working to replant corals, clean the ocean and beaches, protect wildlife, and so many more wonderful things! I encourage my readers to do some research and find a project they are interested in supporting. Remember, even if you can't financially help, sharing posts can still make a huge difference. If every person does just a little, imagine how big an impact we can have!

Anyway, if you are still reading (and haven't thrown your Kindle into the sea or set my book on fire), I want to thank you all for all the support you have given me! Your sweet reviews, encouraging comments, day-making private messages.... they all mean the absolute world to me! My readers are the best readers ever!

Hugs,

Sedona

xoxo

SIREN'S THRONE
ROYAL STORM OF ATLANTIS, BOOK 2

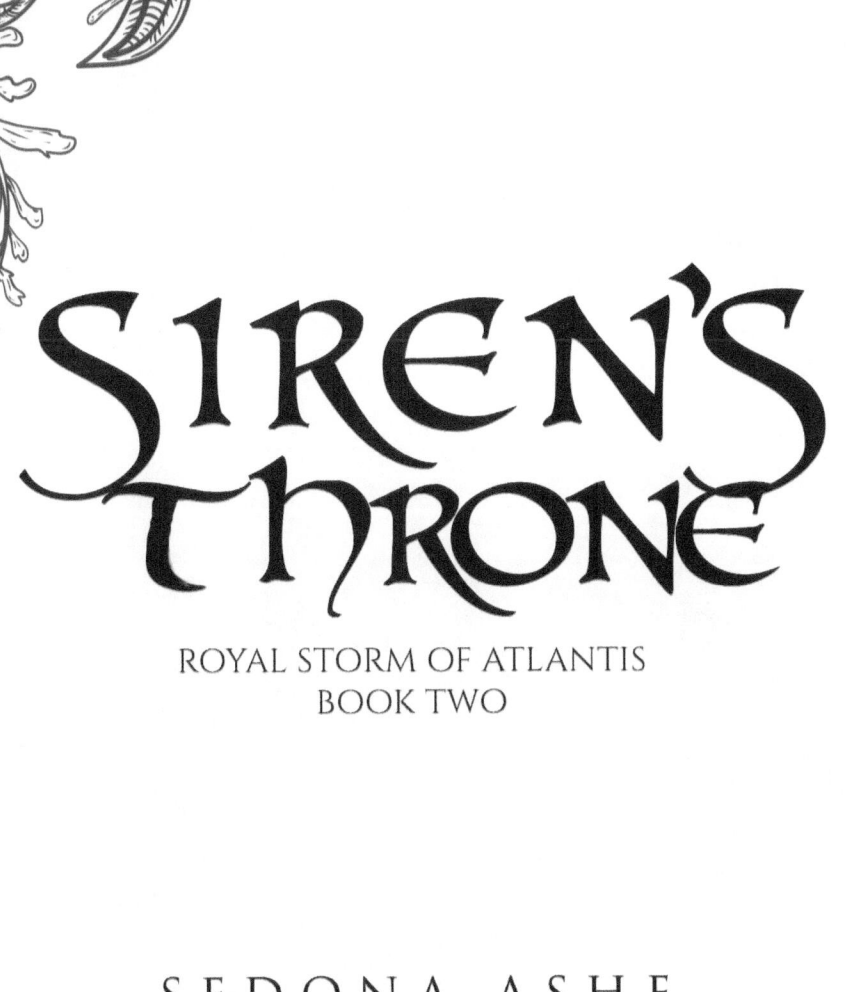

SIREN'S THRONE

ROYAL STORM OF ATLANTIS
BOOK TWO

SEDONA ASHE

I am dedicating Siren's Throne to my amazing readers!
I love y'all so freaking much!

"The more you embrace the weird crazy things about you, the
more you find your tribe."
~Jinkx Monsoon

CHAPTER ONE

ZOSIME

I wobbled my way down the tall, arching hallway, using the wall to steady myself. Deep male laughter came from the direction of the great dining hall. My legs threatened to give out beneath me. I sucked in a deep breath—and inhaled the aroma of food.

The loud rumbling growl from my stomach surprised me. I'd consumed a noteworthy amount of blood from all five of my mates last night and this morning, but perhaps a body with legs required more sustenance? Or maybe I had been far weaker than I had imagined.

Light radiated from the entryway as I neared it. Warmth washed the textured yellow walls in a golden glow. An unexpected pang of nostalgia sliced through me. I found myself equal parts annoyed and relieved at the return of my emotions. It had been a long time since I had walked on two legs, but it had been even longer since I had felt emotion.

Biting my bottom lip between my teeth, I thought about the work left to do. I needed to honor my vow to annihilate the Lure around the world, and now the realm of the Ancients needed me to help them stop the war that was destroying their divided world.

Would I be able to do what needed to be done, all while experiencing a full range of emotions?

Straightening my spine, I stepped around the corner and into the warm, inviting light. I took in the dining hall… or what used to be a dining hall. The long rectangular room that had once held a table nearly as long as the room itself was now full of shiny metal boxes and great slabs of stone.

"The metal boxes are appliances. The stone is granite, and the humans call it a countertop." Lokene winked from behind the steam emanating from the cup he held.

"What are 'appliances', and how did this stuff come to be here?" I asked as I walked toward the men seated around the long countertop in the middle of the room. My gait was slow, but to my relief, it was steady. These men were my mates, but I was a warrior and hated appearing weak.

Kye cleared his throat, opening his mouth to speak. I assumed he planned to explain things to me, but Lokene cut him off.

"I have opened my mind to you, Soyale. Take the information."

For a moment, I just stared at him, eyes wide and mouth hanging open like a whale collecting krill. Ancients did NOT open their minds, not to anyone. They were happy to read those around them, but they did not share their own thoughts. The information poured into my mind—stoves, cooking, refrigerators, cabinets, microwaves, and even a magikal thing called a dishwasher. What an era to be alive! People had been very busy in the last decades to have created such wonders.

Lokene spoke, his tone bored, "I blinked it here." He waved his hand carelessly. "You were planning to find Atlantis, so I assumed this would be our home base. It was several centuries outdated and in dire need of a facelift. I took it upon myself to get everything prepared before bringing you five here."

Unsure how to respond, I whispered softly, "Thank you." There was still so much for me to learn about this world, and it was difficult to not feel overwhelmed.

Strong arms wrapped around my waist, pulling me against a hard chest. Eason's scent, that of juniper and a warm sandy beach, swirled around me as he settled me into his lap. I breathed in the masculine scent and forced myself to relax against him. I needed to learn to control my body and mind because fighting against three sets of instincts and desires was exhausting. The Siren wanted to rip off his clothes and have her way with him. The girl in me, from so long ago, wanted to close her eyes and soak in every morsel of love and tenderness these men showed me. Meanwhile, the warrior wanted to scoff at his public display of affection.

"That's called a PDA. Humans enjoy shortening phrases into initials in this era," Lokene added helpfully. I narrowed my eyes in irritation at his invasion of my privacy.

Lokene's eyes sparkled, and he licked his lips. "I'd like to invade your priv—"

"Enough!" It came out as more of a squeak than the command I had intended. Where was the confident Siren voice when I needed her? No doubt she was snickering in the back of my mind.

Eason kissed my cheek, his rough, stubbled jaw brushing against my skin. "Good morning, soldier."

"Good morning, mate." My voice was all silk and smoke. Exasperated, I rolled my eyes. The Siren had sat up, deciding to participate. As I adjusted myself in Eason's lap, I realized she wasn't the only one to sit up and take notice.

"Be still, or we will head right back down that hallway to bed." His growl sent tingles of excitement racing through me. "Or maybe I will take you right here."

For the first time that morning, my warrior and my Siren were in complete agreement about what they wanted. Memories of his body moving against mine the night before, unhurried and oh-so-gentle, caressed my mind.

"How about we feed her first?" Storm set a plate of food on the counter in front of me before leaning down and pressing a soft kiss to my lips.

The moment he stepped away, I lunged for the food, far hungrier than I'd thought. I froze. Instead of fish, or something from the ocean, there were eggs and strange bread with a large hole in the middle. It was sweet that they prepared food for me, but it was clear bread-making wasn't a talent my mates possessed.

"Bagel," Lokene helpfully provided out loud and then followed up by mentally sending more information about the circular bread.

I eyed my plate doubtfully. They meant for the bagel to have this appearance? How odd. Tentatively, I took a bite, and my stomach rebelled. I gagged down two bites before Eason yanked away my plate.

"Stop! Don't eat it if you aren't enjoying it. Is it the taste?" Eason asked.

I had eaten far worse during my travels as a soldier, and I'd learned to be thankful for all food. There had been countless meals I had gagged down without complaint.

Fynn answered before I could, "Just because she has two legs now doesn't mean everything about her is fully human. It could be the taste, or maybe her body is rejecting something so different from her normal diet." He directed his words toward the others and then turned to look fully at Lokene. "Am I right? Is she human, or still a mermaid?"

"Siren," I corrected him automatically while picking at the edge of the bagel.

Lokene smirked at me. "No, she is not fully human. Zosi is not a fish either, although for now, her body is best suited for surf versus turf when it comes to her dining choices."

"So things from the sea and our blood?" Kye questioned, rubbing at his neck. A blush crept across his skin, and I smiled, knowing that he was thinking about my bite and the things my venom could do... The things it had done last night when I was between him and Storm. My skin flushed and heat spread through me.

One minute I was sitting in Eason's lap, and the next, my arms were around Lokene's neck and my legs wrapped around his waist. He had blinked me into his arms. Gasping, I lost my hold and would have fallen off his body had he not gripped my thighs and pulled me close.

"My naughty Soyale. Those types of thoughts will get you into trouble." His warm breath tickled my neck. My fangs ached with the need to sink them into the vein pulsing in his neck. I wanted to devour him—in more ways than one.

"It is natural to think about one's mates, and it's not my fault you refused to join in last night. I am sure I can ask Storm to satisfy my hunger." I purred the words, enjoying Storm's sharp intake of breath behind me and the way Lokene's eyes dilated. Was it anger or lust that had him tensing against me and his eyes narrowing on my face?

I smiled, the Siren cooperating fully, and teased my fangs with the tip of my tongue.

Lokene growled and captured my lips with his own. He kissed me with the hunger of a starving man. I returned his kiss, pouring my desire into it. His hand traveled up my back to twist into my already tangled hair. Need curled like a predator inside me. Lokene hadn't marked me, nor had I marked him. He had teased me into a blind lust several times the previous night, but each time he had stepped back and allowed one of my other mates to step in and satisfy my needs.

"We have to stop," Lokene whispered the words between kisses. "I want you more than I have wanted anything else in my very immortal life, but things will change once we mark each other, and I need time to prepare for that."

"We could make love without marking each other." Even as I made the suggestion, I knew it was an impossibility. It was taking every bit of control I had not to sink my aching fangs into his neck at that very moment. In the heat of the moment, there was no way I could stop the mate bond from happening.

"Soon. I have waited this long. A few more days won't kill me." His forehead rested against mine, our chests heaving while we caught our breaths.

Storm scooped me up into his arms and walked away from Lokene. The Ancient still hadn't caught his breath, and he leaned back against the stone counter. "That was hot as heck, but you need to eat. What is it going to be? Food, or my blood?"

The thought of blood made my mouth water. My stomach rumbled as if to ensure we all knew how neglected it was. Storm laughed and settled into a chair near the table.

"She needs both. Soyale, try this." A plate appeared in front of me, colorful bits of food decorating it. It smelled like the ocean, the earthy smell of seaweed, and the sharp scent of fish. I began cramming the small bite-sized pieces of food into my mouth, moaning at the explosion of flavors.

Kye gagged from his seat across from us. "You gave her sushi for breakfast?" He looked accusingly at Lokene.

"Since when did food become suitable only for certain times of the day? I will never understand humans." Lokene scoffed.

"You know so much about us, but we know very little about you. How about you enlighten us?" Eason's tone was casual, but his eyes watched Lokene the same way a falcon watches a mouse. "And while we're at it, why don't you explain what happened earlier. I'm guessing you are both telepathic?" The first part of his question had been directed at Lokene, but he directed the second part toward me.

Finishing my second plate, I took my time licking my fingers and then the plate. I used the delay to sift through his thoughts and decipher the meaning of the word.

"Yes. I am telepathic." Having answered Eason, I turned my attention to Lokene. "I have my own questions, but you already knew that."

Lokene nodded but remained silent.

I had so many things to ask him, but one question was more important than all the rest to me. "Can we raise

Atlantis?" My voice shook with emotion I shouldn't be feeling, and my eyes burned with tears that weren't supposed to be possible.

Lokene's heartbeat sped up, and worry flashed across his face. He covered it quickly with a broad smile, trying to hide something. "There would be a lot of red tape and politics with the Ancients, but the short answer is—yes. Atlantis could rejoin the modern world."

I sensed hesitation, Kye must have as well because he beat me to asking, "But?"

"I just don't know what they would think about having their homes and city ripped away from them."

My brow wrinkled in confusion, and my mind scrambled to make sense of what he had said. Lokene stepped to the far wall, the one that had once given a beautiful view of my childhood city. He pulled back the thick velvet drapes that covered the windows. The glass glinted in the light, distracting me for a moment before my eyes focused, and I stared out over the city.

My brain refused to believe what it was seeing. People. No, these were not people. I was looking at mermaids. I watched in stunned disbelief as their silhouettes darted between homes. Their powerful flukes undulated through the water in a movement no human could recreate.

Two thoughts slammed into me, stealing my breath and sending me to my knees:

I wasn't the only Siren on earth, and Atlantis wasn't dead.

CHAPTER TWO

STORM

She had been trying to hide how unsteady her legs were all morning, but now they gave out, and she didn't try to catch herself. I leaped forward and caught her right as her knees brushed the floor. I sank down and pulled her onto my lap, something I had longed to do all morning.

Shock rattled my mind when I caught the glimmer of tears sliding down her cheeks. Zosi didn't cry. She barely showed emotion at all. Until this moment, I hadn't been sure she had a full range of human emotions.

"Shhh... It will be okay." I swayed, gently rocking our bodies, my awkward attempt at comforting her. It must have worked because her sniffles stopped, and the large fat tears no longer fell onto my arm.

I took in more of the scene spread out in front of us. The guys had all moved closer to the large glass floor-to-ceiling windows to peer out into the dark lonely depths that surrounded us.

"This can't be real. I am standing in the Atlantean castle while watching mermaids and merdudes swimming around the bottom of the ocean." Kye's shocked voice broke the silence.

"Mermen," Fynn corrected him automatically.

That snapped Kye from his daze, and he snorted. "Yeah, because you know what they prefer to be called, right? How many merpeople had you met before our Zosi?"

"I don't know what they prefer, but I guarantee very few men on earth want to be called 'dude.'" Fynn pressed his hands against the thick glass panes, his breath causing fog to form on its surface. Doctor Fynn's curiosity must be through the roof.

"Where did they come from?" Zosime slid across the floor, making the movement appear smooth and graceful. She must not trust her legs to hold her up, but she was too stubborn to ask for help.

"Lokene, how did this happen?" Her voice broke, her sorrow tearing at my heart.

I looked toward the man, the 'Ancient'—whatever that meant—and watched his shoulders droop. His joking manner dropped, and he seemed to age several years in front of my eyes. Sitting down abruptly, he groaned when he hit the floor harder than expected.

"I'll try to explain things as best I can. It's a strange story, and to be completely honest, even the Ancients are unsure about the details." He took her slender, pale hand and held it between his own. "Soyale, you weren't ever fully human. Your mother was an Ancient."

Zosi recoiled like someone had slapped her. She tried to cover her cry with the back of her hand, and her skin paled to the point it rivaled the color of a ghost. "No! She was human."

I couldn't take seeing her pain anymore. "Enough. You've been giving us bits of information here and there. It almost feels like you are trickling it out for your own amusement. Give her the answers she deserves."

Lokene nodded. "Soyale, I'm telling the truth. You know an Ancient does not lie. Your mother was a pure Ancient who lived as a human."

"She was an Ancient..." Zosi whispered. I couldn't tell if it was a statement or a question.

"Yes." Lokene drew the word out, exasperated at having to repeat himself. Well, too bad for him.

"You couldn't tell? Does that mean not all Ancients are a pain-in-the-butt like the one we're stuck with?" Kye watched Lokene out of the corner of his eye. I couldn't blame him. The man hadn't hurt us, but he seemed to treat most things as though they were a game meant to entertain him.

"I noticed nothing unusual about how she behaved," Zosi sighed. "To me, she was my mother and the queen. I never knew her as an Ancient. She didn't display any other-worldly power or anything else of the kind." She gazed out the large windows. Her thoughts were on a time long ago and in a land that no longer existed.

A thought struck me with a jolt, shock rippling through me. "Wait. Do you mean queen? As in, the actual Queen of Atlantis?" Surely, she couldn't mean—

"Yes, the Queen of Atlantis. She was an incredible leader for our people." I didn't miss the wistful note in her voice.

"If your mom was the Queen of Atlantis, that would make you..." Fynn stammered, "the Princess of Atlantis."

"That's correct, although our girl never liked the title. She preferred to be known for her skills in battle."

Kye guffawed, his laughing echoing loudly and causing us all to jump. He grabbed his stomach with one hand and motioned at Eason with the other. "No wonder she looked like she wanted to kill you every time you called her princess."

Lokene snorted before succumbing to his own chuckles. "You are a brave man, my friend. I have seen her neuter a man for less."

Eason paled and slid a hand protectively over his family jewels.

Leaning toward Zosime, Lokene stage whispered, "They are finally catching on, although they are still missing the obvious. Where on earth did you find these men? Was this the best earth could offer?"

I would have been insulted if I hadn't caught the humorous glint in his eyes. Glancing around at the guys, their expressions were just as confused as mine was. We were way out of our depth with talk of Ancients, Immortals, and Atlanteans.

Lokene's eyes locked with mine over Zosi's head. "Ancients have been around for as long as anyone can remember. We are immortal. They based the mythology of the Grecian gods on the Ancients."

"Do you read our minds constantly?" I questioned, more curious than offended.

"Oh, Hades no! Having the thoughts of others constantly beating at your mind is annoying, not to mention most humans are mundane. I can turn off the ability when needed. However, right now, Zosime is still fragile from traveling so far and being separated from the lot of you. I want to know everything going through your minds."

Lip curling in disgust, his eyes landed on each of us. "One job. Keep her satisfied. Most human males would die for that type of opportunity, yet three of you go traveling the oceans and leave her behind. Idiots."

"We had no way of knowing that she needed us close by or that she needed physical contact to survive. That isn't a human thing. We can be away from our partners for long periods without dying for the separation," Eason spoke up, trying to explain our incompetence, but it still caused me to wince.

"Again, you show your ignorance. Sure, humans don't

physically die when separated by great distances, but their bond slowly withers away. Humans need closeness with their chosen partner as well. There is a magik in the mate bond, one that requires protection and nurturing. This is true of humans, immortals, Ancients, and Sirens. We all need love and to feel close to the one who holds our heart." Lokene absently stroked the back of Zosime's hand as he spoke.

"Lokene, even if you are correct about my mother, my father was human." Zosime's body trembled, and her eyes darted out to the ocean. There wasn't a doubt in my mind that if given the chance, she would have darted off into the safety of the depths of the sea.

"Your father wasn't fully human. This realm has its own energy, and the earth has her own magik. He carried a bit of that old magik in him." Lokene paused, taking a deep breath. "The old history says most Atlanteans had a bit of Ancient blood in them. Not much, but some. The same was true of earth magik. Over time, both bloodlines became diluted to the point that they were essentially non-existent. However, there were some who still carried a trace of that magik inside them. Your father carried more than anyone else on earth." Again, he paused before continuing.

"The story I've been told by Ancients who were hanging out on earth around the time is that your parents were dedicated leaders. Under their rule and guidance, the Atlantean people worked hard to take care of the earth and protect her people. The magik of this realm honored your parents. When you were born, the earth and the sea placed a blessing on you, their daughter. The Ancients, not to be outdone, also gave you their blessing. To our knowledge, there has never been a child blessed by the magik of two realms. You are unique, a love child of the universe."

The room remained quiet as his words sank in. None of us were sure what that meant for Zosi.

"So who gave her the fish-tail?" Kye broke the silence, going straight to the burning question on all our minds. How did she go from human to a mermaid?

"Zosime is Ancient, but also something other. She carries energy from the earth and the bloodline of those whom the humans consider gods. When Atlantis crashed into the sea, and the queen was being slaughtered by a soldier tainted by the Lure, she used the last of her power in a surge. She was trying to protect her daughter and the Heart of Atlantis."

Tears slid soundlessly down Zosi's face at her mother's last act of love. We all moved forward, kneeling around her, each of us trying to comfort her.

Part of me wanted to punch him to get him to shut up, but I knew he had answers that no one else did. This might be hard for my Zosi, but some small part of me knew that as difficult as this was to hear, she needed it to heal.

Lokene kissed her hand and then continued his story. "At the same time, I sent my magik toward the disappearing city. They did not permit me to intervene in the battle, and I nearly caused war among the Ancients by attempting to come to Atlantis' aid... to come to your aid." Lokene tenderly brushed her tangled hair away from her face with the back of his hand.

"It was a pivotal point in history, and while the Ancients enjoy meddling in less important things, they could not get involved in a battle such as that one. I tried, but the Ancients used their powers to overpower me.

"They kept me from preventing the city from sinking. In an act of rebellion and heartbreak, I tried to at least preserve the city beneath the waves. I wanted to keep its secrets and treasures hidden in honor of your memory. To my surprise, there must have been a loophole in the rules, and it worked." Lokene sat up, speaking intently.

"What I hadn't expected was your mother's burst of power or the surge of energy from the earth. A storm like none before, or since, bore down on the land and stirred the sea into a frenzy. Lightning streaked through the sky and water in a brilliant show. Screams filled the air as the world crackled with electricity and the lightning turned most of the enemy soldiers to ash.

"The combination of your mother's energy, the magik of the earth and sea, and my own power reacted in a way that still isn't fully understood. My thought was to preserve the city and keep it hidden. Your mother's power must have been focused on keeping you alive and protecting the heart."

Zosime interrupted him, "The last thing I remember

thinking was that I had failed my people. I wanted to live to protect them."

Lokene nodded. "I figured that was the case. When the magik-charged lightning hit the Heart of Atlantis, your body absorbed the energy it released. At that same moment, the power of two Ancients slammed into you. We all got what we asked for, just not how we had planned." A soft smile flitted across his face.

"You survived, your body going into a deep sleep, suspended in time, the Atlantean crystal forming a cocoon around you. The earth's blessing changed your body. It adapted to survive the environment it found itself in —water.

"The Ancients believe that the power of the Ancients slamming into you awoke your own latent abilities. Once that power awakened, it merged with your magik, and you changed the legs of your people to fins... Just like the sea had gifted you."

She looked down at her legs, brushing her fingers along the pale skin. "Will they be able to have legs again, too?"

"I don't know, Soyale. I wasn't even positive you could return to your human form. You are different, and your body adapts quickly, working to ensure your survival. The Atlanteans have a tail, but they don't have your bloodline, magik, or power. You are shifting and evolving at a rapid pace, and it is just one more thing we haven't seen before. The Ancients don't know what you are capable of, and it scares them."

"I have to talk to them, to apologize."

"Love, what happened before is in the past. A past that is so old it isn't even included in modern history books. We are myths and legends. You have no reason to apologize."

"Then I at least need to know if they are happy! I need to know if they want to return to the sun and the land." She was vehement in her response, fire sparking in her eyes. "These are my people. I could not help the time I was asleep, but I am back now."

I grinned, proud of my beautiful mate's determination. She held herself tall, royal, like a—

Lokene smiled, his lips twitching in amusement as he watched realization dawn across my face. I finally knew what he meant when he said we were still missing something.

My throat tightened, the shock causing all my muscles to tense.

"You are the Queen of Atlantis."

"But how am I going to talk to them? We can't open the doors; that would drown all of us." She waved a hand down her body. "I can't exactly go out there now that my tail is gone."

"You are thinking about what is impossible for

humans." Lokene tilted his head in our direction. "Okay, fine. If we opened the doors, they would die."

I narrowed my gaze at him in a warning.

You're not keen on sharing, are you? I thought, hoping he was reading my thoughts.

In response, he rolled his eyes. "Which we would, of course, never allow to happen. They will stay safe and dry inside the portion of the palace I have sealed with glass and made safe for humans. It's like a reverse fish tank!" He was far too pleased with himself. I, on the other hand, felt queasy, his words sending a wave of unease through me. I'd been in tight places before and had never been bothered, but I was feeling claustrophobic.

"I have an idea!" Before we could push for more information about his plan, he rubbed his hands together gleefully. With a sharp pop, the floor disappeared, and we fell through space. That's what it felt like, anyway.

We materialized, staggering to the walls for support or dropping to our knees. It was an efficient way to travel, but not pleasant. When the room stopped spinning, I took in my surroundings.

"This is the throne room of Atlantis!" Fynn shouted, staring at the massive, solid gold throne.

"What was your first clue, idiot?" Kye deadpanned, eyebrow raised.

He had a point; it was obvious exactly what this room was. We were in a hallway that ran alongside the main area of the throne room.

Lokene had separated us from the main area with a thick piece of his special glass so that we remained dry even while the great room in front of us was submerged.

It was like being at an aquarium and looking into one of the massive floor-to-ceiling tanks. If those tanks were around seven stories high, covered in sparkling jewels, and the pillars were gold-plated.

I would have expected time to have eroded and crumbled much of the beauty of the room and for the sea life to have claimed it and taken over. Instead, the room was immaculately clean.

Vibrant corals in artistic arrangements decorated the walls and vases, taking over the place with exotic flower bouquets. Rather than glossy palm leaves, giant sea fans waved in the gentle current. Gold covered nearly every surface, glinting in the soothing light that bathed the room.

I tried to find the source of the lights and wondered if it was another of Lokene's inventions. Before I could locate the source, Zosime's voice startled me from my dreamlike state.

"Why is there a man on the throne? My throne?" Her voice was low and vibrated with intensity.

My eyes snapped to what I had previously missed. Sitting on the towering gold throne was a merman. His long dark hair billowed around him, carried by the water. His eyes were blue and not a natural blue. Oh no. These were a hue I had seen before. They were the color of Orpati, a bright electric blue that was almost more shocking than the fact I was looking at a merman.

His tail was long, far longer than Zosi's had been. I would have guessed him to be around twelve feet long from the top of his head to the tapered tips of his massive fluke. His eyes locked on Zosime, widening for a moment before hardening. To my surprise, she bared her teeth and snarled.

"It's showtime!" Lokene shouted, sounding suspiciously delighted.

With a snap of his fingers, Zosime vanished. She reappeared a heartbeat later—on the opposite side of the glass.

"Zosime!" Everyone, except for the idiot that had likely just doomed her to a watery grave, screamed out her name. Rushing forward, we banged on the glass, knowing our efforts were futile but unable to stop ourselves.

Zosi clawed at her throat, her pale skin turning red. Had she been human, the pressure at this depth would have killed her instantly. She may be part Ancient and part earth magik, but she was struggling.

"Do something! Surely you aren't this crazy! You said she was your mate, too!" I lunged, preparing to throttle the insane man. Instead, I slammed against an invisible wall. I'd watched enough science fiction to recognize it as a force field. My fear stole all rational thought, and I slammed my body into the unseen barrier over and over.

Zosime had moved until she floated in front of Lokene on the opposite side of the glass. She was no longer ripping at her throat, and the panic had faded to resignation. Her lips moved, forming the word 'help.' It was her last plea.

Lokene smiled broadly, and, with a ridiculous flourish, he blew her a kiss.

I wanted to kill him. With a roar, I slammed against the shield, keeping him away from me. Logically, I knew he was an Ancient, and I didn't stand a chance, but I didn't care. Zosime was dying, and I would go out attempting to get justice for her. My brothers must have felt the same because they joined me, all of us rushing at the barrier.

"Oh! There we go! That's my girl!" Lokene puffed out his chest, proud as a peacock.

I turned to look.

"She's changing," Eason whispered in awe.

He was right. Blue energy spun around her body, shredding the robe she had worn this morning. The pale skin of her legs shifted into the charcoal color of her long, elegant tail. Webbing appeared between her fingers, and her ornate breastplate rippled across her chest.

I looked up into her face, taking in the way her hair danced playfully around the pale oval of her face. My breath stopped as I caught sight of her eyes. She had zeroed in on Lokene.

I laughed. "She's beyond livid." Bending, I clutched at my stomach as my anxiety turned to joy.

Lokene turned, an irritated look on his face.

I could barely get out the words. "You are so dead, Ancient."

CHAPTER THREE

ZOSIME

My mate just tried to kill me.

Not only that, the man had blown me a kiss. He was about to kiss something all right, but it wasn't what he was thinking.

I could feel my body caving under the pressure of the sea. My lungs burned with the need to draw in a breath, but I wasn't sure what would happen. How much of my body was still that of the Siren, and how much was human?

I got my answer moments later as rage boiled up from inside me. He dared to risk my life like this? To blow me a kiss like a cheeky idiot? How dare he look utterly lickable when he winked and flashed his dimples at me! I wanted to sink my fangs into him... To get rid of him or ride him was yet to be decided.

Ugh! Distracted by my warring lust and rage, the Siren took over my body. While my human body shifted easily into the familiar form I had grown used to, my mind flipped like a light switch. The control I clung to like a person drowning vanished in an instant.

The Siren had been created with earth and sea magik, while the power of the Ancients had surged through me. They had blended together to create the perfect storm: me.

It had also given me the ability to adapt and survive, and combined with my skills in battle, I was a predator the world had never seen. Yes, I had watched the Atlanteans swim outside the castle, and I had read their minds. They held the same spirit and heart as the human Atlanteans that I had loved and vowed to protect several lifetimes before. These people were not predators; they were gentle, preferring knowledge to killing.

My body was made to hunt.

That is why you are called a Siren, and they are called mermaids and mermen. You are a warrior, Lokene's voice flitted through my mind.

It didn't matter; they were my people, and I would protect them. I'd never wanted the role of queen, but I knew with certainty that fate had brought me home to care for my people.

Something moved in the water behind me, the faintest of ripples. Spinning around, I launched myself toward the blur as it moved in for the kill. Sinking my nails into the soft flesh of my attacker, I clung to him as he shot like an arrow toward the arched ceiling.

Twisting his body at the last second before impact, he intended to drag my body along the rough, textured ceiling. With a growl and a hard thrust of my own, I slid around his torso just as quickly, and the skin on his back scraped against the archway.

He snarled, snapping fangs at my face. Although strong, this man did not have the fangs of a predator. I did. Smiling viciously, I displayed my own fangs. I'd wanted to make it clear who the predator was, and the slight dilation of his pupils told me he was aware. This pleased the Siren in me.

He collected himself quickly. "You are an intruder to Atlantis. It is our law that all who find us must be put to death. There is too great a risk that you will speak of what you have found, and I will not risk the lives of my people. The men with you must die as well."

I couldn't fault his logic, but I questioned his sanity when he leaned forward and sniffed my neck. How long had the guys said these people had been down here? Maybe they were losing it?

I flashed my fangs again in warning. "No."

Seriously? I wanted to slap the Siren in my head. We could have explained things, but she was purposefully baiting him. I would have preferred to not play with my food...and boy, did dinner smell good!

"Who are you?" he growled. Or was that a moan?

"I am Zosime, Queen of Atlantis." While I had planned to sound haughty, as though the man pressing against me wasn't worth my time, the Siren had other plans.

Of course she did.

Each word that slid from my lips was pure silken seduction. The sound conjuring visions of long sweaty nights entangled in your lover's embrace.

This time, there was no confusion over whether he was moaning or growling. His long tail thrust hard, hurtling us through the water, the undulating movement grinding our pelvises against each other. Heat burned through me from my anger. It was anger that was causing me to feel so hot, wasn't it?

"I am the King of Atlantis. Zosime is a heroine of the Atlanteans, and someone that died during the last battle. Do not insult my intelligence by claiming to be her." The words themselves were cold, but his voice was a husky purr. Was he trying to seduce me like I seduced my victims? Could mermen even do that?

"I didn't die. In fact, I am very much alive." I leaned into the curve of his neck, sliding my fangs along the sensitive skin.

We crashed into one of the palace pillars, the force of our impact so strong that tiny bits of the ceiling drifted down around us.

"You speak lies. I am the ruler of the Atlanteans, and I will protect them from impostors." His hand closed around my throat, gentle enough that there would be no marks but firm enough to make his point.

I laughed, the sound melodic and meant to draw in my prey. His hand tightened, but his body quivered against mine.

"Submit, and you could be my queen," he spoke with a rough rumble that vibrated through me.

"Submit, and you could join my Kings," the Siren's voice purred right back at him.

WAIT. Hold on. He could join *my* men?

"I'll never submit, nor will I give up my throne." I admired the strength of his conviction. It was a shame the Siren would probably kill him for it.

What followed was a fight like none I had experienced before. I had fought men before, many times, and won. However, I'd never fought a merman, nor had I found myself in the strange position of fighting the urge to murder, or mate, my opponent. Usually, I was fairly clear regarding my intentions when going into a battle, and I knew the intended outcome. This time, I kept changing my mind.

The man fought well, a worthy adversary, and I had to be cautious about my technique so as not to hurt him permanently. He was growing tired and needed to submit before he injured himself.

I'd tried to read his mind, surprised that his thoughts hadn't simply poured out like nearly every other being on earth. It was intriguing to discover that I could only read his impressions and the random stray thoughts. I decided to try something and pressed my forehead against his.

His shock held him still briefly, and that was long enough for me to create a connection. Like the television Kye forced me to watch, my memories of that devastating day in Atlantean history played.

I closed my eyes, wishing it would keep me from reliving that day, but of course, it didn't. When I was sure he had seen all that he needed to see, I pulled away from him, panting hard.

"You are *the* Zosime." Wonder filled his voice.

"As I have stated." I lifted my chin.

"To think. My bonded is Zosime, Princess of Atlantis. We are the perfect couple to rule Atlantis. I have ruled for close to one hundred years but have yet to find my bonded or a woman worthy to rule at my side."

My heart jerked in my chest, and blood froze in my veins. Bonded. That explained my reactions to him and why he still lived. It would, however, be a cold day in Tartarus before I submitted to this arrogant man's bite. To make sure he was aware of that fact, I bared my teeth, displaying sharp fangs dripping with venom.

My family had ruled Atlantis since the beginning. It was our bloodline that had built the city and protected it for countless generations. The Ancients had blessed Atlantis with knowledge and gifts only for as long as my family remained in power and continued to use that knowledge for the good of the earth.

My heart wanted me to walk away and leave these people in peace. As long as he was a noble leader, he could continue to rule Atlantis. This man had ruled for nearly a century. Perhaps it was best for Atlantis to stay under his leadership?

The Siren and the warrior inside me joined as one. My scales glowed an eerie turquoise hue as their magik and power surged. They were not going to back down. There was a battle coming, and my people still needed me.

I eyed the merman. He was a capable leader, and I sensed no evil from him, just arrogance. He was a powerful ruler and worthy to rule... by my side.

"There is a war coming. A battle that will make all other wars throughout history pale in comparison. I am going to attempt to stop this war, but it may be too late. There is more than you know going on, but Atlantis needs me if it is going to survive. We can continue to fight, or you can step aside and allow me to fulfill the vow I gave to the Atlanteans and my family's vows to the Ancients." Still breathing hard from our fight, I shoved at his chest, trying to put some space between us.

"Mermen cannot submit so easily. I see the fire in your eyes and suspect that you would face the same challenge if asked to step down." A ghost of a smile lifted the corner of his mouth, exposing a fang. I'd split his lip during the fight, and it bled lightly, the blood drifting away in the current. Why was it so mesmerizing?

My brow wrinkled as I thought about his words. He

studied my face and then added, "I am a male; therefore I am a merman. Mermaids are female." His eyes slid along the length of my body appreciatively. Large hands moved to settle low on my waist, tightening and pulling our bodies tightly together.

"I am no mermaid; I am a Siren." I should have killed him for being so presumptuous, but I was too busy fighting to keep the Siren from sinking my fangs into his neck. My stomach growled. I was still hungry, and the pulsing vein in his neck was making my mouth water.

"Neither of us is going to step down. Let's get on with it." With a single hard thrust of his powerful fluke, we spun up toward the ceiling... again.

In response, I dug my nails into his skin and snapped my fangs in warning. I was hangry, and the sooner I finished this, the sooner I could eat.

CHAPTER FOUR

KYE

I was confused. Were they trying to murder each other or mate?

"Both."

My head snapped to Lokene, who stood grinning, his nose nearly pressed against the viewing glass.

"First, stop answering the questions I ask in my mind— those are private. Second, why are you so giddy?"

"Because everything is falling into place as it should."

It should have sounded ominous, but when he turned toward me, there was relief in his eyes, and he smiled softly. It wasn't a maniacal smile, as I would've expected from the strange man. No, it was a look of pure happiness. I rubbed at my temples, trying to fend off a migraine. This day continued to be ridiculously complicated, and I couldn't wait for it to be over.

"Look! See there?"

Every set of eyes in that hallway instantly snapped to Lokene. Had he just spoken in an Australian accent?

"Are you okay—" I began, only to be cut off by more of his special brand of crazy.

"Shh! It's the endangered Siren species. Would you look at her beauty? It is a rare treat to see a female in her natural habitat."

In unison, our mouths dropped open.

"Watch how the male is aggressively fanning his massive fluke! That is his way of impressing the female with his strength in the water. Now, watch as she shows him her fangs. This may look threatening, but it is actually a sign that she is interested," Lokene continued in his faux accent. Or maybe it was real? I didn't know where the Ancients lived.

"Please tell me he isn't narrating Zosime's bonding as if this were an animal documentary for television." Fynn's eyes nearly bugged out of his head.

That was exactly what he was doing.

"I think you missed the part where he said they were going to mate," Eason interjected, horrified, from beside me.

"It won't change anything for me. I love her." Storm's voice was thick with emotion.

"I feel the same." Eason then turned to Lokene, his

voice steely with anger. "This is too rough. I don't like it. You need to do something."

Lokene broke from his narrator's voice to reply, "You are judging what you see through human eyes. You forget, she isn't truly human. Have you ever watched lions mate? She is a predator, and it would be best that none of you forget that. Zosime doesn't need protection from physical dangers around her. She needs you guys to protect her heart because it is the only thing vulnerable about our mate. Should she lose control of her emotions, it won't be pretty."

He focused back on the scene playing out in front of us. "The merpeople have been separated from humanity for a long time. It did not affect them quite the same as Zosime, because of her proximity to the Heart of Atlantis stone when the city sank. Her bloodlines and latent magik also changed her in ways it did not change them. They are less powerful, less deadly versions of our Siren; therefore, they are mermaids and mermen. She is the only Siren.

"However, they are still more powerful than a human, and over the centuries, they have grown more vicious in order to survive against the predators and challenges of the sea. They have their own culture and their own rituals. Zosime has been safely asleep all this time, but the Siren in her is responding to the mating dance this male is performing."

The glass fogged as he leaned his forehead against it and breathed out a relieved sigh. "The future changes constantly, just like the tides of the ocean. I cannot see everything that is coming, but at this moment, things are how they need to be."

"You knew," I said it as a statement, not a question. "You knew she had a mate in Atlantis."

Lokene only tilted his head in acknowledgment.

A muffled crack and a man's groan startled me, causing me to jump. Still watching the strange Ancient from the corner of my eye, I took in the pair of mers currently fighting outside in the grand throne room. Zosi and the merman were thrashing and spinning.

She slammed his body into the glass wall. Hard. Keeping him pinned, she grinned evilly, showing him her fangs. I still thought Lokene was wrong about her being receptive to mating. She looked like she wanted to murder the merman.

Instead of doing the smart thing and swimming away fast, the man fanned out his flowing fin until it was nearly four feet wide, and his scales shimmered in the light. Muscles bulging, he positioned himself, still pressed against the glass, so she could see his peacock display.

I huffed. If Lokene was right, how were the rest of us supposed to compete with that?

"Oh, this is getting crazy! We may get to see the actual mating! Typically, male mers are very secretive and drag the female to a darkened cave to copulate repeatedly over the next few days. They have a real cave dweller style honeymoon!" Lokene looked way too excited at the thought of watching this aggressive merman mate our Siren.

"Whoa! Hold up! First, should we be watching? Second, he can't take her from us for days. You said she needs to stay near us, or she will get weak." There was panic in my voice.

I'd never seen her look as pale as she had looked last night when Lokene brought us to Atlantis. She had barely been able to lift her hands, and her entire body trembled for hours, even after drinking a significant amount of blood from each of us.

It had been a passion-filled evening, with lots of cuddling and gentle lovemaking as none of us wanted to weaken her more. Looking out at the merman, I wasn't sure he would treat her with that same level of care. His nails had left long scratch marks on her skin, and she had several bright red abrasions from being dragged along the walls and crashing into the tall golden columns.

I smirked when I caught sight of the man's injuries, though. Our Zosime gave more than she got. He sported a busted lip, deep marks from her nails, and several darkening patches of skin from her strategically placed punches. My heart swelled with pride.

The man's tail slid the length of Zosi's tail, and she shivered in response. The burning anger in her eyes flickered to something else. He repeated the motion several times before curling his tail around hers and pulling her close. They stayed pressed against the glass only a few feet from us, not seeming to care or even notice we were watching.

Her lips moved, but I couldn't make out what she was

saying. The glass rumbled as the merman responded. Fire sparked in Zosi's eyes, and she leaned in and caught his lips in a passionate kiss.

"Notice how the female has accepted the male's advances—"

Without thinking it through, I reached out and slapped the back of Lokene's head so fast, it shocked us both. He stared wide-eyed at me, rubbing at the back of his head.

"Guess you didn't see that tide change coming, huh?" I tried to sound confident, but the words came out with a slight stutter. He was an Ancient, and while I liked him, he could probably fry my butt with just a thought.

To my immense relief, he burst out laughing and threw an arm around my shoulder. I returned the brotherly side hug. I was growing fond of the little family Zosime had created.

CHAPTER FIVE

ZOSIME

We crashed into the glass, and I held him there, pinned like an insect. I had a sneaking suspicion he wasn't trying hard to get away, although if he had, it wouldn't have ended well for him.

There was no way I would allow him to see it, but I could tell my body was growing tired. I was still weak, and this mock battle was wearing me out more than I liked. It was time for both of us to make a decision.

His tail bumped against mine, and his eyes locked onto me. I remained still as his tail slid along the length of my own in an odd sort of caress. Biting the inside of my cheek, I held back my gasp at the incredible sensation. Each of his scales brushed my skin, a teasing touch that almost tickled but also had butterflies taking flight in my stomach.

Wrapping his tail around the base of my own, he drew me closer. There was no mistaking the fire in his eyes... He wanted me as much as I wanted him.

"If I kiss you, you will ingest my venom. I am unsure how it will affect you, as you are not human. In humans, it is a powerful aphrodisiac, and it is unlikely we will be able to prevent mating and bonding."

Two words were all he spoke, "Kiss me."

I pressed myself against him, and my lips found his. The kiss was raw, rough, and everything I wanted it to be. His tongue tangled with mine, still fighting for some form of dominance. I smiled against his lips at the continued stubbornness.

His tail rubbed against mine, a seductive suggestion that sent chills throughout my body. I was new to how mers bonded, but the Siren recognized the movements. He was coaxing me to let this thing between us happen, to give in and enjoy the moment.

I knew the instant my venom hit his system. His kiss became aggressive, and his tail locked around mine like a steel cable. I tried to wiggle free but froze when I felt the solid bulge rub against my scales. It turns out merman are not immune to the potent elixir. If anything, the man had a stronger reaction than my human mates.

Yay for me! I cheered internally.

My attempts to escape from his hold and put a little

space between us only served to excite him more. He ground his pelvis against mine. I groaned into his mouth, accidentally biting down on his lip and injecting him with far more venom than normal. Or maybe this was the normal amount for a bonding between Sirens and tritons?

Through the lust haze in my mind, I heard the thoughts of my mates. They were turned on, confused, and unsure.

Testing, testing. Is this thing on?

I paused mid-kiss at Kye's words. What on earth?

Zosi-girl? If you can hear me, can you give us a sign of what we should do? Like, do we go now and give you privacy with Fishboy? Or do we, um, stay? What am I thinking? I doubt she is listening to anything right now… Kye's thoughts trailed off.

It surprised me that he had tried to communicate with me, and I loved that he asked what I wanted. I pulled my upper body away from my mer mate and searched for Kye's face. I found him off to my right. When our eyes connected, he blushed.

Motioning for him to come toward me, I pressed my hand against the glass, spreading my fingers to reveal the webbing. Kye smiled, lining his hand up with mine on the opposite side of the glass.

I heard you. I mouthed the words.

Stay, or go? he mouthed back.

Stay. I waited to see his reaction. I had just gotten them back yesterday, after being separated, and didn't want them out of my sight. Not yet, anyway. While I didn't want them to leave, I needed them to stay because they desired it, not because I commanded it.

Kye's smile broadened, and he wiggled his eyebrows lasciviously. *Your wish is my command.* This time, he thought the words to me. Stepping back, he made a shooing motion with his hands, as if telling me to get on with it.

I blushed when I caught sight of the five sets of eyes watching me through the glass. It was then that I realized that the merman and I had put on quite the show. My face grew more heated. Maybe this wasn't such a good idea.

"Okay, I gave you time to reassure your worried mates. Now it is my turn to have your focus." His tail tightened around mine, holding me in place against him. His hands grabbed my waist and turned me so that my back pressed to his chest, and I faced away from him.

One thick muscular arm moved around my torso, sliding up until his hand could cradle my tender breast. His fingers stroked at the sensitive armored designs I guessed were magikal remnants of the Atlantean armor I wore the day of the great battle. I couldn't stop the moan that escaped.

"Yes, I want to hear you, Maridákia. I want you to scream and moan."

I stiffened, insulted that he had called me the Greek name for a small type of fish. I wasn't a fish, and I wasn't small.

"You are small to me. Now stop overthinking things."

His chest rumbled against my back as his lips nibbled my ear lobe.

I started to speak, but a gasp escaped as his fingers expertly slid along the outside edges of my most sensitive scales, the scales that hid my slick heat. His fingers teased and stroked, doing magikal things. This man knew the anatomy of a Siren. His finger found my slit, and with a hard thrust, he buried it deep inside me.

"Oh!" was the only word my addled brain managed.

His hips bucked, and his stiff erection suddenly pressed against my rounded butt. Where did it come from? I knew far less about our anatomy and planned to explore that train of thought... later. My body was too far gone to care at that point.

His finger explored, and then a second finger joined the first, stretching me as he buried his long fingers deep inside me. He began pumping his fingers in and out, setting a steady rhythm that slowly grew faster. His hips thrust in time with his fingers, his thick erection sliding along the curve of my butt.

Spinning me around in his arms, his lips captured mine again. I felt a pinprick of pain as his fang nicked my lip and a floral taste filled my mouth. His venom. Heat blossomed inside me, licking along every nerve ending from my head to the tip of my fins. It turns out I wasn't immune to his venom, not that I'd want to be with how the electric need was thrumming through me.

My gums ached with the need to taste his blood, and

other parts of my anatomy clenched with a need to feel him buried deep and move inside me. There was one thing holding me back—

"Bite me." His voice was hoarse with his own need and something much deeper that only he and I understood at that moment. He turned his head to the side, giving me full access to his neck.

Tears sprang to my eyes, and I blinked them back, refusing to allow myself the show of weakness. He was submitting to my claim and asking for me to mark him first. While his pride didn't allow him to say the actual words, his actions said them louder than any words. He was handing me the throne of Atlantis—he was giving me my home back and offering his heart.

Control? What control? I sank my fangs into his neck with the speed of a viper. He groaned, the sound of pleasure mixed with pain. Drawing in a delicious mouthful of his spicy warm blood, I moaned into his pale skin. It was so good. Each of my men tasted different, but this man tasted like the unpolluted sea, and it called to my heart.

I drank deeply, washing the blood around my mouth to savor every drop. His hands brushed along my skin and scales, exploring every inch of my body that he could reach with me latched onto his neck like a sexy suckerfish.

My hunger abated while other parts of my body begged for attention. His breath hitched, and the sound of his heart rate speeding up caught my attention. I pulled away to look up into his face and caught my breath. His pupils weren't just dilated; they were blown. Black, predatory eyes stared back at me.

"My turn." The two words were barely intelligible through the growl in his voice.

"Yes, please," I blurted out, then wanted to fin-slap myself. The seawater must finally be getting to me because this Siren was thirsty.

One large hand sank into my dark hair, yanking my head to the side. My skin flushed, heat burning my skin even at the frigid temperatures of the surrounding ocean. His fangs pierced my skin with no hesitation. I barely felt the bite. What I felt was the sting of his venom as it leaked into my bloodstream. Even with the water flowing around me, I felt myself becoming even more slick with my need.

"What's your name, merman?"

"Zeno." He pulled his fangs free and licked at the two puncture wounds in a swirling, slow motion.

"Zeno?" I murmured his name.

"Hmm?" He sucked and licked his way up my neck.

"If you don't stop, I am going to die before you have the chance to sheath yourself inside me," I moaned as he sucked my earlobe into his mouth.

"As you wish, My Queen." He was a man of his word. With a single smooth thrust, he buried himself to the hilt inside my channel. I cried out his name, clawing at his chest —whether to pull him closer or push him away, I wasn't sure.

The base of his tail, near his ankle, moved to circle my

ankle and pull me closer. His hands roamed my body, searching for those spots that were most sensitive. All the while, his lips sucked and teased my shoulder and neck before once again capturing my own lips in a long kiss.

I returned it with all the desire that was building in me and the fiery inferno that was being stirred up by his venom.

Moving away from the glass barrier, he let our bodies drift in the gentle ebb and flow of the surrounding sea. The current rocked our bodies, and Zeno timed his thrusts to the same rhythm. His strokes were slow and gentle at first but grew harder and faster within minutes.

The venom raced through our veins, and no matter how hard we fought to take our time, it was a losing battle. It was also the only battle I was fine with losing.

"Next time," he panted. "I promise our next time will be different."

"Now is not the time for speaking," I ground out through gritted teeth as our hips moved together.

Uncurling his tail from around mine, he gave a pump of his massive fluke and sent us crashing back into the glass. This time my back pressed against the chilled surface. His fangs pierced the tender flesh of my shoulder.

"Gentle, man! Don't break her!" I heard Kye's muffled voice through the glass.

I had forgotten they were all there, watching. This time, with Zeno's venom running through me, I didn't care. If I were to be honest, I'd admit that it made the fire in me burn hotter and my temperature rise. I wanted this.

Lokene's teasing voice filtered through the glass, "I just heard from my friend vacationing in Tartarus! He said it is freezing cold there today." He must have read my mind earlier when I had first met the merman and hadn't planned to let him mark me.

I'm going to murder you in your sleep tonight, I thought at him, not finding him nearly as amusing as he believed himself to be.

Who said anything about sleeping tonight? he responded with a wink before disappearing back into the shadows of the hallway.

With my body sandwiched between the barrier and Zeno's hard, muscled form, I could do little more than gasp when I felt his erection touch my slit and then push deep inside me. He wasn't overly thick, but he was longer than a human male. He moved faster, picking up speed with each hard thrust.

I could feel my belly grow heavy with need and my core growing tight as my pleasure drew nearer. I bit down on his chest, sinking my fangs in deep. The taste of his blood exploded in my mouth, and I nearly found my release on the spot.

In my excitement, I must have sent more venom through his system. I'd never injected this much into one of my bonded before. Was there a level that would prove toxic or fatal for my mates?

Zeno roared, yanking me against him and again wrapping his tail around me. I clung to him, my arms wrapping around him to keep the water from getting between our bodies, pulling me away from him.

He swam at the incredible speed of an ocean predator. I smiled in delight. My mate was strong. Each rhythmic undulation of his tail moved his erection inside me and rubbed me in all the right places. I didn't care where he was taking me. I just wanted to remain like this for the rest of my life.

He moved through the doors and out into the private courtyard of the palace. I glanced around, suddenly feeling shy at the thought that strangers might be around.

"No one comes inside the private courtyard. We are alone here. Besides, the Atlanteans are all out in a group to gather food. No one is here, except for your men and us," he answered my unspoken question, and I wondered if he had read my expression or if he could read minds as I could.

I nodded. There were so many questions I wanted to ask, but they would wait.

"Secure your tail around mine."

I stiffened at the command in his voice but forced myself to relax and obey. Curling my tail around his, I pulled our bodies close, enjoying the sensation of warm skin and scale touching nearly every inch of my body.

The moment he was sure we were together, he thrust upward. I tilted my head back to look above us. We were so far down that I could barely see any light coming from the surface of the water.

Around us, the ocean was a deep blue, and it extended almost as far as my eye could see in all directions. The only sign of which direction was up was the slightly lighter hue of the ocean, from navy blue to cerulean blue above our heads. There was no way we were going to be easily spotted by divers.

Zeno began a mating dance, spinning us around and moving from side to side as though listening to music that only he could hear. It was joyful, beautiful, and wild. Full of the playfulness of dolphins and the power of the orcas.

It called to my heart, asking me to bond myself with this man for the rest of my life. I knew it as surely as I knew my own name. It called to a primitive part of my being, one I had tried to keep boxed and hidden. One that was rattling its cage, eager to be free, just as my emotions were finding freedom.

From what I had gathered from the humans' minds, this would have been called a marriage proposal. Except this was so much more. It was a proposal and a marriage at the same time. If I accepted, we would be bonded for life. Our hearts and lives tied together for the rest of our time on this earth.

"Yes," I whispered the word but knew he heard me.

I sank my fangs into his neck, and he quickly reciprocated by burying his fangs in the tender flesh of my neck. His thrusting became frantic, his fluke beating the water, sending us higher while at the same time giving each thrust of his pelvis an added impact.

Scales brushed against me, sending chill bumps pebbling along my skin. The textures and sensations were overwhelming. I could feel the tightness in my core break free, and my release hit me in a wave. My body clamped down on his manhood, squeezing as I shook with pleasure, and my channel spasmed. He found his own release and shouted it to the depths of the sea.

When the aftershocks finally subsided, I rested my head against his chest. I had eaten well, but the bonding had still exhausted me. I smiled at how quickly life changed. An hour ago, I was considering killing this man, yet now I trusted him to hold me close and swim us to safety.

Life was strange, but I was beginning to like this new world.

CHAPTER SIX

ZOSIME

The call was back. I'd wondered if my returning emotions had dimmed the call, but that wasn't the case. The call was just as strong as it had been, perhaps even stronger.

After bonding with Zeno, we returned to the castle. He introduced himself to the other men through the glass. I had several alpha mates, and it was interesting to watch them adjust to each other's presence in my life.

While Zeno had left to speak with his advisers, Storm had insisted that we return to the bedroom, which I happily agreed to until they tucked me in and left the room... leaving me alone. The men claimed if they stayed, we wouldn't be sleeping, and I needed to rest. Spoilsports.

That was where I had been when the call came, sleeping like the dead in a bed covered with pillows and thick blankets. Still half asleep, I answered the call. It took some effort, but I finally found my way to the opposite side of the glass walls and out into the ocean. I suspected Lokene had something to do with that, but I hadn't caught sight of the confusing man since he'd left with my other mates.

Streaking through cool dark waters, I shivered, missing the warmth of my bed. However, my instincts refused to let me deny the call. As I drew nearer to the ocean's surface, men's voices tainted with the Lure filtered into my mind.

"How much do you reckon we drank?"

"Not enough to be seeing this, Todd."

"So you see it, too? The fish tail, I mean?"

"Yeah. I am guessing this is a mermaid, like from the television.

"Mermaids aren't real, idiot."

"Well, how do you explain that, then? She's got a woman's upper body and a tail instead of legs. She has to be a mermaid."

I stopped breathing. I was too deep for them to be talking about me. Surely I had misunderstood them, and they had not caught one of my people.

"How much do you think they will give us for her at the science center? I doubt they've ever seen anything like this before."

"I'm betting we are about to be paid enough to retire early."

Nearing the boat, I could hear their muffled shouts of victory and jubilation. My scales stiffened. They were celebrating the fact they were going to sell a life, all because they didn't see her as a life-form equal to themselves. Rage wrapped me in its warm embrace, and I no longer felt the icy bite of the sea. Good, it was one less thing to distract me from my mission.

Something slick and rough bumped against my tail, and I turned. My fangs descended, ready to fight my unseen attacker.

"Sheba." A brief flutter of joy ran through me at the sight of my friend. It relieved me to find she was safe, and she had sought me out like she might have missed me too. "Are you ready to eat?"

In response, she turned and circled the boat, her tail flicking in a gesture that reminded me of an angry cat. Oh yes. She was ready to return to work.

"Shark! Shark!" the man called Todd screamed in terror.

"Shut up and help me with the harpoon!" The second man shouted back.

My anger turned icy cold. They were holding one of my subjects captive, and now they planned to murder Sheba? Not going to happen.

I moved toward the back of the boat, where I knew a ladder would be. This boat was much longer than the smaller fishing vessels that had held most of my recent victims. There was a large crane and pulley system on one side of the boat to help lift nets filled to the brim with fish. Several guns and what the humans called a harpoon hung on the inside walls of the vessel. These were professional fishermen, which is no doubt the only reason they had managed to capture an Atlantean mermaid.

I bit my lip, worry clouding my mind. I wasn't yet sure how the Atlantean anatomy worked. How long could a Siren—or mermaid—be out of the water before her body deteriorated? I could spend a long time out of the water, but I wasn't the same as the Atlantean mers.

Was she injured? Had the nets hurt her during her capture? Had they hurt her afterward? Just the thought of her lying in pain and at their mercy made me sick. If I could get her into the water, I could get her back home. Maybe Sheba would even be in the mood to assist me, and we could get her back to the safety of Atlantis quickly. First, I had to do what the call had brought me here to do.

Hooking my arms over the bottom rung of the ladder, I hummed an old lullaby I remembered a nursemaid singing to me as a child. It was haunting, beautiful, and irresistible. Todd came to investigate, his face appearing and looking down at me.

"Hey, what are you doing down there, beautiful?"

Careful not to flash any fang, I gave him a small smile. "Enjoying a swim. Is there anything as amazing as a naked swim under a starry night sky?"

My voice had a husky edge, as though I'd spent the night screaming my lover's name until it was raw. If only my mates had let that be the case, then I wouldn't have to fake it. I could see by Todd's intake of breath and dilated pupils that the seductive tone had hit its mark. His body leaned toward mine, but not far enough for me to grab him. He just needed a little more motivation.

"You seem lonely. Care to join me?" I allowed a little purr to slip into my voice. If only I could release my venom like a perfume, then this whole luring-men-to-their-doom thing would be a lot easier.

The sensation I recognized as my magik moved through my body, a gentle brush along nerve endings. Just as quickly as it appeared, the feeling vanished. The man was saying something.

"I don't know about that. There is a shark in the water, and it's a big one. You'd best climb up here quickly."

I breathed out deeply in frustration and pinched the bridge of my nose. I just wanted to finish this and get home before my mates started freaking out. Knowing Kye and Fynn, one of them would peek in on me in the next hour, and I needed to be tucked in when they did.

I sucked in a breath, preparing to hum again, but gagged when I sucked in an obnoxiously sweet scent. What was that? It smelled like the water surrounding me had been turned into a perfume made from a field of flowers. A single drop would have been lovely, an ocean filled with the fragrance—not so much.

"Miss, hurry—" The man stopped mid-sentence, drawing in a tentative breath and then inhaling lungfuls of the sickening sweet aroma. "What is that delicious smell?"

His eyes turned a bloodshot red, and his breathing became ragged. I watched as his gaze landed on my face, and his face lit up. "It's you!" He sucked in another deep breath, licking his lips.

I shuddered. He was wrong. It couldn't be me. Could it? I discreetly sniffed under my arm and recoiled in horror.

It was me.

I smelled like a banquet hall overflowing with floral arrangements. This made no sense! Less than two minutes before, I had smelled of salty sea spray. What changed—

Todd jumped over the side of the boat, landing in the water beside me with a tremendous splash. A grown man had just willingly leaped into the pitch-black ocean with a strange woman and a monster-sized shark. Realization slammed into me with the force of an iron pan.

My magik had turned my venom into an airborne toxin. This was confirmed when the man surfaced, pupils blown, stripping off clothing, and reaching out for me. "You wanted me to join you. Come here, babe."

Ew and ew. Losing all my sexy Siren seductiveness, I doggy paddled backward in an awkward scramble to get away from Mr. Grabby Hands. If he touched me, I was going to ask Sheba to eat me.

He touched me. As his left hand brushed the edge of my breast, his right hand touched my waist, my instincts decided to kick back in. I threw my arms around his neck, twisting my body until I flipped over his shoulder. His neck gave an ominous crack, his body going slack. Sheba's blade sliced through the water between us, her rough skin bumping against my body. Todd's motionless body disappeared beneath the water. Good. I would just let her eat him instead of me.

"Todd? Who are you?" The second man's shout was far too loud for such a quiet night. He lifted a gun and aimed it at my head.

"Zosime. Todd is disposed." My emotions drained away, giving me the clear head I needed to complete this job. Todd had been tainted with the Lure, but that was nothing compared to the man in front of me. This man was a sadistic killer, and the Lure had completely eroded his soul.

"You mean indisposed," he corrected automatically while glancing around for his friend.

"No. I mean, I disposed of him." I heard the click of him cocking the gun, but it was too late. I'd already disappeared beneath the calm ocean surface.

I waited and watched from just below the surface. I couldn't risk him going back to where he was keeping the mer, but I needed him to leave the ladder area so that I could board the boat. It took ten minutes for him to lower his gun and give up his watch. He scratched his head, turned, and headed toward the bow of the boat.

This was my chance. Shooting through the water, I grabbed the bottom of the cool steel ladder. Resting my forehead against the bottom rung, I breathed in and out, focusing on what I needed from my body and magik.

Slowly, I climbed the rungs. For most people, this wouldn't be stressful, but stairs just weren't something I had been doing lately. I climbed carefully to my human feet, only wobbling for a moment. Once I was sure my legs were steady enough to walk, I moved cautiously toward the front of the boat.

Keeping an eye out for the man or the mermaid, I crept along the narrow walkway on the side of the boat. The sound of the man's angry voice startled me.

"Do you have friends out there? Answer me!"

I bit back a curse. He must be near the woman, which complicates things. I'd hoped I could flip her over the side of the boat. She would be safe while I dealt with the man and the boat, but that plan was off the table.

A loud crack broke the silence of the night. Bending my body, I leaned around the corner and took in the scene before me. The mermaid lay crying in a heap on the floor, her hand pressed to her crimson-colored cheek. Angry Man was pulling back the hand he had slapped her with while he leered in her tear-stained face.

I wanted her to rip into his throat and laugh in surprise when he realized he had underestimated our species. That wasn't going to happen. A quick glance was enough to tell me this beautiful mer wasn't a warrior. She was fine-boned and delicate. Her sagging posture and rapid terrified breathing told me she had already given up.

My emotions flared for a brief moment. I felt an overwhelming sadness at her distress and fear. Anger followed on the heels of my sorrow. It outraged me to see the cuts on her body, from a knife or a net, I couldn't say. As with Zeno, I couldn't read all her thoughts, only random phrases and words. I could also sense her feelings, and my anger boiled over at the heartbreak she was feeling at never seeing her family again.

The call pounded in my head, a steady drumbeat keeping rhythmic time to the mission. I breathed out quietly, letting go of the distracting emotions that were more a hindrance than a help.

Without a sound, I ran toward the back of the large man, pouncing on his back and intending to unbalance him so he would tumble over the side of the boat. The man must have had a very stable set of sea legs because he staggered a few steps before he quickly caught his balance.

"She-devil!" His screech threatened to burst my eardrums, and I fought the urge to cringe away from the loud noise.

"I'm back," I whispered in his ear. My arms slid around his neck.

He tried to gurgle a response, but my chokehold was too tight. Many people don't realize that choking someone until they pass out or die takes time. If you managed to cut off the blood supply just right, the process is faster, but that is a challenge. Especially when you weigh only a fourth of your opponent's weight and he is refusing to remain still.

He staggered and righted himself several times. All the while, I clung to his back like the proverbial monkey, only naked and dripping wet. I bit down on his neck, realizing too late that when I shifted to a human form, I must have willed away my fangs as well. With a growl, I tightened my arm until I feared it would break from the pressure.

"Just die already," I mumbled while mentally trying to call back my fangs.

Those three little words were a mistake. The man redoubled his efforts to survive. He slammed our bodies into the walls, the tiny cabin window, and even the pulley system.

It was when he rammed me into the rack that held the harpoons and guns that I felt the sharp bite of pain. The hooks that held the weapons stuck out from the walls, and the force of us crashing into the wall had embedded two of those hooks into my side and back. This time, there was no biting back my curse. I screamed but didn't loosen my grip.

Blood poured from my wounds in warm, slick trails, making it hard to keep my legs tight around his waist. I slipped, only a couple of inches, but it was enough. The man lurched to the side, turning at the same time. I crashed hard into the dark wood of the deck. My face and cheek bounced hard against the rough surface. That was going to leave a bruise and maybe a broken bone.

"You little witch!"

His angry shout was enough to rouse me from my stupor. Shoving myself up, I threw up my arms, preparing for his attack. A heavy boot collided with my forearm, and I nearly bit off my tongue to hide my cry of pain.

Click-click.

I wasn't an expert on this era's weapons, but I recognized that chilling sound. My arms would not shield me from what was coming.

Pop. Pop. Pop.

I might've had a chance for survival in my Siren form, the armored remnants providing at least some protection for the most important organs. This form was all pale, soft flesh.

I hated to die, but if I was going out, I would finish this mission at the same time. I threw up my hands, prepared to go down swinging.

CHAPTER SEVEN

ZOSIME

The first bullet tore through the skin of my bicep. His finger squeezed the trigger again. I threw up my arms, and a gust of air blasted from my hands. Not only did the wind stop the two bullets headed for me, but it flung them back at my attacker with a force strong enough to embed them into his chest.

Eyes wide in horror, he dropped the gun and clutched at his chest. The blood was bubbling from the wounds at a rate that guaranteed he would have died even if help had been only minutes away. Although once the call had drawn me to him, he was destined to die this evening, the only question had been how.

He staggered to the side, propping himself against the

wall for a moment before sliding down to the floor. A brilliant crimson stain smeared the wall, marking the path of
his falling body. Blood pooled around him as the life faded
from his eyes and his heartbeat slowed, giving one final
thud.

I tried to smile in satisfaction at yet one more completed
mission, but it came out more of a grimace. My own blood
was pooling around me at an alarming rate, leaving me with
a serious problem. Namely, how was I going to swim home
in shark-infested waters while clanging the shark version of
a dinner bell?

The second issue was the ship. It needed to sink. Preferably, further away from this cove. The last thing we needed
was divers exploring the area looking for bodies. I turned to
study the girl, who watched me with wariness in her eyes.
As long as she feared me, we would not be best friends like
the golden females on Kye's small television, but that was
fine with me. I just needed her to trust me enough so that I
could get her home safely.

"Wha-what's your name?" It surprised me she worked
up the courage to question me.

"Zosime." I paused. The manners of this time dictated I
asked her questions as well. I sighed. "What is your name?
Are you hurt?" The truth was, I didn't need her name or her
health status. When I tossed her into the water and told her
to swim for home, she needed to be prepared because she
had little choice in the matter.

"Kostantina." She hesitated, then added, "You can call me Kosta."

I tilted my head in acknowledgment before shifting my focus to cataloging the boat and the surrounding items. "Can you swim?"

"Yes, I think so. I injured my fluke when I got caught in their net. I can't believe I was so stupid. Fishermen never come out to this area. We've worked hard to create the myth of sea monsters in this area, and very few people venture here anymore. We stay out of sight while they visit unless they get too close to Atlantis. If they stumble on Atlantis, they disappear. It is almost like what happens in the Bermuda Triangle."

I did not know how the shape of a place called 'Bermuda' mattered, so I just nodded. She continued, "I was angry over a fight with my brother, and I wasn't paying attention. I got caught in the school of fish, and when I realized I was being scooped out of the sea, it was too late."

She ran her hand along her fluke, wincing slightly.

"Can you swim?" I had my doubts. Black dots had danced in my vision. It was time to finish the mission before I passed out.

"I don't know." Her face crumpled. "Thank you. I thought I was going to die, and then you showed up." Throwing her arms around my neck, she sobbed.

I stiffened. It had been an abnormally long time since I last comforted anyone, especially a sobbing woman. I murmured some soft noises of reassurance that sounded more like a pitiful whale calling while awkwardly patting her arm.

"There is an outcropping of rocks a few feet from the boat. If I help you into the water, can you wait there for me? I need to get rid of this." I waved a hand toward the man's body.

"Yes. I can do that!" Her tears dried, and a look washed over her face. It was one I knew all too well. She had a focus, a mission, and she felt useful. I didn't have time to reassure her that this one mistake was not her defining moment. It was only a blip in her life journey, and fate clearly smiled upon her.

"Okay. Give me a minute." I closed my eyes and breathed deeply, focusing on my throbbing wound sucking the life from me.

There was no guarantee this would work, but I was going to bleed out long before I got help if I didn't try something. I focused on what I wanted—my wounds to seal themselves shut.

To date, my body has continued to adapt to my needs as I grew into the power that Lokene told me I possessed. Hopefully, this time was no different. I needed the wounds to heal to continue on. Power rippled over my body, and my palms hit the planks. I opened my eyes.

Hades.

The good news was that my chest armor was back, and my bleeding had slowed. The bad news was that I had a tail again and was going to need to scoot around like a seal...

which would make everything that needed to be accomplished more challenging.

"Come on." I motioned for the girl to follow me. We slipped and scooted our way around the dead man and to the back of the vessel. "Slide into the water and move to the rocks as quickly as you can. I have a friend in the water, and I would like to introduce you to her with me in the water."

"Where's your—oooh!" She tried to speak, but it ended on a yelp as I shoved her through the ladder opening. She landed with a hard smack.

I waited to make sure she surfaced and started doggy paddling toward the rock formation that stuck up out of the water a few feet. With a sigh, I began the seal scoot back toward the bow again. It took almost ten minutes, but I managed to half roll, half squish the man down the narrow walkway until I could shove him off the boat as well. Sheba's dorsal fin broke the surface, and she jerked his body beneath the ocean.

Sighing, I leaned a shoulder against the side of the boat. "Come on, Zosime. You can do this." I was growing weaker, but my work wasn't finished.

I made my way to the boat's cabin. Once there, I found the controls. Boats were not something I was used to, but thankfully the vessel was still idling, and with some trial and error, I lifted the anchor and cranked up the speed.

As the ship raced along the dark ocean, I grabbed the lighter that had been left in the cabin. I had to gather everything flammable that I could find, and it took several tries, but at long last, I managed to start a fire in the cabin. Once started, it grew alarmingly fast.

I needed to get off. Like yesterday.

Making my way to the back of the boat took longer than I care to admit. I was no longer leaving a trail of wet, sticky blood everywhere I went, but my arms trembled, and my tail was a numb, useless stump from the massive blood loss —and possible internal damage. It wasn't looking too good for me unless I fed soon.

I made it to the back of the boat to the tiny ladder that was banging around in the sea spray and waves being created by the boat's dizzying speed. Glancing over my shoulder, I saw the fire fully engulfed the cabin, and the hungry flames were licking along the deck directly toward the gas. Even though that was my plan, knowing the boat was minutes away from a catastrophic explosion sent an icy chill down my spine. At least, I think that's what caused my skin to prickle from the cold.

Steeling myself for the impact, I threw myself off the back of the boat. The pain that shattered my body as I hit the churning surface of the water was far worse than I had imagined it would be, and I could hear my scream of pain over the roar of the boat's engine. My next scream was drowned out by the earth-shaking boom of the exploding vessel.

A pillar of fire and debris shot up into the sky, a beautiful display of destruction. It sickened me to think of the trash that was sinking to the ocean floor, but this was a necessary evil to protect my people. My one consolation was knowing the creatures of the sea would be pleased to have another broken ship to create their homes in.

I ducked below the water's surface and hid from the burning embers falling from the sky and crashing into the water around me. Several pieces of shrapnel from the boat slammed into me, but the damage I sustained was mild compared to my other injuries. Blood was oozing from where the bullet had sliced through my arm, the two ragged holes from the hooks that had partially reopened when I slammed into the sea, and from a large gash on my head from the ladder as I exited the doomed vessel.

With a flick of my long, tattered tail, I turned myself in the direction I needed to go. It had taken me longer than I thought to get off the boat, and I was many miles from the rock outcropping. That was good news for Atlantis, as any rescuers would not be searching the water closest to Atlantis. It was bad news for me since I was in no shape to swim a few feet, let alone many miles. But Kosta needed me, and I wouldn't let her down.

"Sheba?" I whispered into the midnight blue sea around me. "I need you."

Body trembling from exhaustion and fatigue, I began the swim toward my people and my home. There was no hiding my grin. Beat-up as I was, the night had been a success... And it had been entertaining.

Now it was time to face my mates.

CHAPTER EIGHT

STORM

An explosion rang in the distance. A plume of fire billowed up into the night sky. It would have been a stunning contrast of fiery oranges and midnight blue had I been able to admire it. Instead, my stomach turned itself inside out. Zosime was out there, and if I had learned anything about my girl, it was that she was definitely involved.

"Our troublemaking minx probably caused that." Fynn must have been thinking along the same lines as I had been.

"For us to see it at this distance, it has to be a large explosion. She did well."

There was no denying the pride in Eason's voice. He

adored our beautiful little soldier. I did too, but right now, I mostly wanted to find her so I could spank her... and not in the fun way.

Lokene had refused to come with us, his behavior continuing to confuse me. He had looked sick with worry but adamantly stated he couldn't come or he would risk changing events and bring down the wrath of the Ancients on us. He blinked us to the surface, sitting us inside a small boat, but stated even that was pushing the boundaries of what he was permitted to do.

Knowing that Zosime was likely near the explosion while we were so far away had anger burning through me. Couldn't he have blinked us closer to her? What purpose did any of our lives have if she died?

He claimed the Ancients needed her to save their sorry hides, yet he wasn't allowed to lift a finger to help us? I didn't understand their rules or their purpose, but I didn't care enough to find out... yet. I had one mission right now, and that was getting in this boat to find Zosime.

Thankfully, the boat had a motor. Unfortunately, it was a tiny motor, and we were miles from the explosion, which meant it would take time to make it to her side.

Zeno, our newest family member, claimed to have picked up on distressed emotions the moment we popped into existence. He ducked beneath the waves and left us behind without a backward glance. He had a lot to learn about how teams worked, but I would still be glad if he found her quickly, just so that one of us would be at her side quickly.

"Let's move out." I shook myself at the sound of Eason's voice. We were wasting time. Everyone pitched in to get the boat moving, excruciatingly slow but steady, across the glasslike surface of the water. The world was eerily silent except for the soft ripple of waves the moving boat created. What exactly had we missed?

"What's that over there?" Eason squinted at something ahead of us. He slowed the boat motor until we came to a stop. I stood, wobbling for a moment from the boat's rocking while trying to see what he was pointing at.

"Is that a shark fin, Fynn?" Kye asked. The fact he didn't so much as snicker told me how stressed he was feeling. Looking around at the tightly drawn faces around me, I knew we all felt the same.

"Yes. It's definitely a shark." Fynn scooted to the side of the boat closest to the shark that was heading toward us. Adjusting his glasses, he too squinted, trying to get a better look. "It's a great white shark fin."

"Sheba?" I knew my voice sounded pathetically hopeful. I didn't care.

"I have no way of knowing without seeing her full body. It is a very large shark, so I would say the odds are good." Fynn took off his glasses, wiping at the salt-covered glass anxiously.

"If Sheba is here, where is Zosime?" My hope was draining away quickly. I turned, taking in the flat, never-ending sea around me. How would we be able to find her? For all we knew, she was hurt and lying on the ocean floor.

The large shark fin disappeared. I held my breath, waiting to see what would happen next. Something bumped the bottom of our tiny boat, rocking it like crazy. The fin reappeared, slicing through the water as it circled us. The fin once more disappeared beneath the surface.

I yanked off my boots, tossing them to the side. Hauling my shirt over my head, I threw it to the side.

"What are you doing, Storm?" Kye asked. Suspicion sparked in his eyes as he tracked my movements as I finished undressing.

"I'm going in. This is Sheba; she wants something."

"You don't know that it is Sheba, and this shark could just be looking for an easy meal!" Fynn exclaimed.

"Oh well. It is a risk I am willing to take." Ignoring their protests, I dove into the sea.

I would love to say that I felt no fear, but that would be a bold lie. The instant my body hit the water, the large body of a shark slammed into me hard enough to knock the wind from my lungs.

Unable to see much in the dark water, I saw only the fuzzy shadow of the shark's body as she turned to head back toward me again. I put out my hands to fend off her attack, only to have soft hair run through my fingers.

Without thinking, I grabbed onto the shark as it moved by me. Making my way up her body, I found Zosi under one of the enormous great white's pectoral fins. Carefully clinging to Sheba's side, I curved my arm around Zosi's waist and pulled her free. The suctions on her hands came free, and I pulled her limp body against mine.

I kicked my feet, and we broke the surface.

"Are you okay?" I heard Fynn's voice first.

"Get out of the water, idiot!" Kye shouted in panic. He eyed Sheba as she circled the boat, his skin turning a sickly shade of green.

"Zosime!" Eason had spotted her first.

There was no way I could answer. I was too busy sucking in lungfuls of balmy night air. Clutching Zosi to my chest, I struggled to even my breathing and to slow my galloping heart.

Resting my fingers on her neck, I felt for a pulse. It was there, slow but steady. She must have either been knocked unconscious, or something had hurt her badly, for her to be unresponsive. What she needed was blood. If I fed her in the water and we spilled blood, we could attract sharks. Heck, for all I knew, Sheba would smell our blood and decide to have me as a midnight snack. As much as I wanted to feed her right that very instant, it was best we get back into the boat. Sheba could eat me for all I cared, but I didn't want to risk Zosi.

My brothers all rushed to the side of the boat and reached for our Siren. After much grunting and curses each time she was so much as jostled, Zosi finally rested on the floor of the boat. I sat beside her, her thin pale hand resting between my own. Her skin was nearly translucent, showing the purplish-blue lines of her veins. I hated seeing her like this.

"I'm going to feed her first," I stated in a no-nonsense tone. I lay down beside her, pulling her cool body against my chest. "Eason, your knife?" The man went nowhere without the tiny blade. His boots had a hidden pocket that made the knife nearly impossible to locate unless you knew what you were looking for.

Eason took out the blade and handed it to me. Without hesitation, I made a minor cut on the skin of my neck. I tenderly tucked Zosi's face against my neck, while in my mind, I begged her to drink me dry if she needed it.

Leaning down, Eason ran the back of his hand across her bruised cheekbone. "It looks like her cheekbone was broken, but she is already healing." His amber eyes darkened as anger flashed through them.

"We don't have a clue what she went through or how bad her injuries are. We can't do anything about that now. What we do know is that she needs to eat," I spoke with authority, trying to cover my gut-wrenching anxiety.

The boat rocked as Fynn kneeled down near Zosi's

head. With a tenderness born of love, he gently lined her mouth up with the pooling blood and pressed her lips against the open wound.

The look of love on his face was so raw that I almost felt like I should look away and give him privacy. We knew each other as men skilled in our respective fields, yet here we were, struggling with our most private emotions. Those were something that none of us easily shared, except when it concerned Zosi.

Zosi took a deep breath. I swallowed down the lump in my throat as she coughed, and her soft lips pressed to my neck in a weak kiss.

"Drink, Zosime. You need to feed." If she were stronger, she likely would have balked at the command, but she only stiffened slightly before I felt the slight suction as she began to feed. When her fangs pierced my neck, I felt only relief that she was eating. She was going to make it.

It didn't take long for the venom to have its effect on me. I'd hoped I would have longer before I needed to fight its effects, but so far, we had made zero progress on building up any type of resistance to her lust-inducing cocktail.

All the blood that wasn't flowing into Zosi's mouth rushed south. I ground my teeth together as my desire to be inside of her grew. My need for her was stronger than my need for a next breath. "Guys, I'm not sure she is ready for this, and I don't want to hurt her. Hold me down if you have to, but don't let me hurt her."

"She is tougher than you are giving her credit for,

Storm. Stop worrying, and just see how things go," Kye tried to reassure me.

As he finished speaking, Zosi's hand brushed up my chest. I grasped her hand in my much larger one, pleased to find she was no longer trembling.

I love you, beautiful. I spoke the words only in my mind, not sure if she could hear me.

"Mmm," she murmured against my aching neck.

I pulled her body tighter against mine, enjoying the contrast of her soft skin and textured scales against my skin.

The venom was boiling the blood in my veins. I fought the urge to move and give in to its demands for things I didn't feel she was ready for. She needed time to heal, time to recover from whatever this had been.

I understood about the Lure, and I understood her vows. Dang, we had been soldiers most of our lives, so we knew better than most what it was like to dedicate your life to a cause. Just because I understood didn't mean I had to like how she was required to put her life in danger every time she answered the call. I wanted to take the burden of the call as my own, so she didn't have to answer it.

My hand twitched where it rested against her hip. I wanted to stroke the soft skin, to slide it across the curve of her butt, but I knew if I did, I would lose control. Biting down on the inside of my cheek, I only barely resisted the urge. Sweat beaded on my brow, my body temperature was climbing steadily.

"Storm, I know you want to go easy on her, but you

can't resist the venom forever. You'll have to give in. Better to do it while you're still maintaining some semblance of control."

Fynn was right, and I knew it. He must have seen the indecision on my face because he added, "Her venom is part of her biology. You are going to have to accept the fact that our mate is different. You want to be a gallant hero for her, but in doing so, you are denying parts of her."

He paused, his expression softening as he looked at her. "She injects us with venom that sexually hypes us up. Her body, so far, has known exactly what it needed. She gave you the toxin, as long as she is a consenting partner, then give her what she wants."

He was right. Maybe I needed to let go of my human way of thinking from time to time. Still, I found my body unwilling to move.

"Stubborn man. Stop thinking." I jerked at the sound of Zosi's voice. She sounded husky, like she was thirsty.

"You're awake!" I exclaimed. Seeing her slight wince, I lowered my voice, "I was so scared for you."

She only raised an eyebrow at me.

I felt compelled to defend myself. "Yeah, yeah. I know you are this insanely talented warrior who could kick all our butts, but we are allowed to be worried about you. We love you."

An emotion I couldn't read skittered across her face, gone as quickly as it had come. Curiosity demanded I ask her about it, but as her fingers slid down my torso and brushed along my aching erection, I forgot everything other than having my way with her.

I groaned, and she growled... Or maybe it was she who groaned, and I was the one who growled. It didn't matter, because the next instant, we were all over each other like gravy on biscuits. Hands roamed, tongues explored, and my temperature continued to climb.

"You are too hot," she murmured against my mouth.

"Thank you," I managed between kisses.

She laughed, an alluring sound that caused my stomach to clench and my erection to jerk against her. "No, Storm. I mean, your skin is too hot. It is possible I gave you too much venom. We need to get you into the sea and cool you off."

This time, it was definitely me who groaned. A hot sizzle of pain ran along my spine, and I fought a wave of dizziness. I clenched my jaw and fought the urge to pass out.

"Um, guys? I think Zosi is right. We need to toss him overboard. Between the toxin and the blood loss, he is going to pass out if we don't do something." I must be hallucinating. Since when was Kye our voice of reason?

"Guys, I'm good." Instead of reassuring my brothers, the words came out slurred, and it caused even more panic.

Hands grabbed my arms and legs, lifting me and lowering me. The moment I touched the water, it steamed around me like I was hot lava. I clung to the side of the boat until Eason tossed me a small rectangular floating device to help me stay afloat. Seconds later, they lowered Zosime into the water beside me.

She slipped beneath the surface, and panic shot through me. They were letting her drown! My racing heart sped up even faster when I felt hands on my body. She surfaced in front of me. Her pale skin was marred with bruises and cuts, and there were dark circles beneath her eyes. She smiled at me, slipping her arms around my neck. I craved her touch more than a drowning man craved air.

I could barely speak as I croaked the words, "I need you, Zosime."

"You will never know how much I need you, my Storm."

At those words, spoken in her beautifully husky voice, the last of my control snapped like an overstretched rubber band. My hands grabbed her hips beneath the water, hauling her against me. Her scales pressed into my palms, and my thumbs immediately began rubbing the delicate patterns etched in them. She was a work of art, and she was mine.

I groaned as her lips trailed feather-light kisses across my chest. Without warning, her fangs sank into the skin just below my collarbone. I jerked in surprise, and my erection pulsed with the need to be buried inside her.

My fingers found the scales that hid her secret entrance. I slid one long finger inside her, enjoying the way she shivered and pressed tighter against me at my touch. Continuing my exploration, I found the pearls that provided her so much pleasure and stroked across them.

This time she growled into my neck, the vibrations going straight to my groin, nearly causing me to orgasm on the spot. I slipped another finger inside her, followed by a third, stretching her channel in preparation.

She pulled back. I glanced at her face and saw Zosi's soft features had hardened. "Storm. NOW." The snarling Siren didn't mince words.

In one swift movement, I sheathed myself inside her. Our bodies shuddered in unison at the incredible explosion of sensations. We remained motionless, allowing the ocean to rock us together while we caught our breath.

Zosime undulated her long, flowing tail to the rhythm of the sea. The rolling movement shifted me inside her, moving my erection, so it stroked the right places for both of us. She continued this steady undulation, her pace unhurried at first.

"Zosi, this feels incredible." My voice was low, needy, and roughening my vocal cords.

She must have recognized the sound of my desperate need, because water swirled around us as her tail moved faster. There was little I could do but grip her hips and hold on as she moved in a dance that was as seductive as it was mesmerizing. Each roll of her hips brought us both closer to our release.

We found our release together, our shots of pleasure filling the still night air. Zosime clung to me, panting hard. I kissed her forehead, murmuring sweet nothings into her salty, damp hair. She was the living embodiment of the sea, and I loved her even more for it.

CHAPTER NINE

ZOSIME

S torm held my trembling body to his chest. We were both panting hard from our exertion and blood loss. I was feeling less woozy, but I needed more blood. I turned my head from where it rested on Storm's chest and took in the three men that watched us with expressions of anxiety and raw lust.

I needed blood, but in my injured state, I had taken too much from Storm. These men needed a lot of rare steaks, and several days to rest and recover from nearly being drained dry less than forty-eight hours before.

I wasn't sure what I was going to do. What I had taken from Storm had stopped the bleeding, but the damage to my body was still very much there. Lokene had made it clear he didn't want to bond yet.

I thought about my merman. I wasn't sure he was going to be keen on sharing his blood when it meant he would be weak. I may be a Siren instead of a mermaid, but I recognized the same animalistic traits in them I saw in myself. The sea was wild and untamed, and that was the nature we carried inside ourselves. I looked across the smooth surface of the water. Where was my merman?

"Lokene wanted to come. He was frustrated and said he could not risk it since he would want to intervene. Zeno came with us, but he disappeared the moment we were on the surface," Eason spoke, having caught my swift glance around for my two missing mates.

Kye leaned over the edge of the boat nearest me. Reaching out, he brushed his knuckles across my bruised face, careful to not apply pressure or hurt me. "We thought he came to find you."

I shook my head. "No, I haven't seen him." Closing my eyes, I searched for the pull. If he was near enough, I should be able to locate him. I found him on the edge of my mental reach. Why would he not stay with my other mates? "He is out there. I feel him."

I pressed my head against Kye's warm hand, enjoying the skin-to-skin contact.

"Now that your bleeding has stopped, we need to get you somewhere safe. I don't like you out in the open like this." Eason, ever watchful, looked around us worriedly.

The problem was we didn't know where to go from here. I could swim to Atlantis, they could not. The men could go to shore and find a hotel, but dragging a beat-up mermaid with them was likely to raise some eyebrows.

"I say we head back to where Lokene teleported us and to where we last saw Zeno." I smiled, enjoying the sexy way Storm's chest rumbled against my cheek as he spoke.

We agreed, and Storm made his way back into the boat, turning to help me up. I shook my head. While I could be on land for periods of time, I just wasn't the most comfortable there. At least, not while I was in this form.

"I will stay beside the boat, but I prefer to make my way there myself." My hands slid beneath the surface of the water, reaching out for my calmly circling and ever-present friend.

"You're in no condition to swim—" Fynn started. He stopped when Sheba's dorsal fin breached the water's surface.

I watched as their eyes widened, and they held their breath. Fear. Or was that awe? Either would be a very human response, not only to the fact that she was a shark but also that her massive size made her a queen among sharks.

I laughed at their identical expressions of horror and awe... All except for Fynn. He looked jealous. I knew he had enjoyed his time traveling with Sheba and me.

"I'm not planning to swim back. My mother didn't raise an idiot." There is no way I would make it to shore, but as long as Sheba helped me, I would eventually get there. The best part was that I could stay in the water where I was more comfortable.

The men didn't argue, although their looks remained markedly uncomfortable. I couldn't tell if it was from Sheba's presence or being separated from me. They turned the boat in the direction of the rock outcropping, and with a sigh, I suctioned myself to Sheba, preparing for the long trip back.

THE SKY HAD TURNED A BEAUTIFUL PASTEL PINK FROM the rising sun when the vibrations from a boat engine in the distance caught my attention.

I let go of Sheba and surfaced near my mates' small boat. Grabbing the wooden side, I clung to it, partially lifting myself out of the water so I could speak with them.

"There's a boat coming. It's a decently large boat, if the vibrations are anything to go by," I started, getting straight to the point.

Eason looked at Storm. "What's the plan? If they saw the explosion and are looking for the cause, then we are going to need a reason to be out here."

The men spent the next several minutes creating a story in case the approaching boat was a patrol ship. Although, based on the information Lokene had given us regarding Atlantis, and its position on the seafloor beneath the waves, there shouldn't be any patrol ships in this area. While the men created a plan, I watched as a tiny speck appeared on the horizon, slowly growing nearer.

The boat was coming from the direction of the rock outcropping, although the rocks were still too far away to see with the naked eye. A thread of worry weaved its way through me. There had only been the one vessel in the cove when I began my hunt the night before. What was this ship doing in the area? Was Kosta okay? Had the unknown ship found her?

Letting go of the side of the small dinghy, I let my body sink below the surface of the water until only the top of my head and eyes remained visible. As the ship neared, I could see it was a luxury vessel, what the humans call a yacht. Why would anyone bring a yacht into an area where they believed there were sea monsters?

It relieved me that it was not a patrol vessel and that no one seemed to be searching for the two men I had executed just hours before.

My heart warmed as the bond glowed in my mind.

Interesting.

Zeno was getting closer. Was he following the yacht?

I moved behind the tiny boat, wanting to watch the approaching ship without being seen in the early morning light. My plan to stay hidden didn't last long when I saw who was standing on the deck, though.

Lokene was propped against the elegant railing, hands in his pocket, hair blowing in the salty breeze. He looked sexy as Hades. "I see you found our girl!" Lokene called out with a rumbling chuckle.

"We did, no thanks to you. It took us hours to get her, and she could've died before we found her!" Storm glowered.

My eyes rolled. Hard. I didn't need to be rescued. Sheba and I had been doing just fine. The words in my head sounded confident, but in reality, I didn't know if I would have made it if Sheba hadn't taken me to the men. I'd been in terrible shape.

"Hey!" Lokene's offended voice roused me from my thoughts. "Give me some credit! I did the best I could under the circumstances."

Kye snorted derisively. "Yeah, yeah. We know. Ancient rules all that." His voice dripped with sarcasm.

There was a part of me that was horrified by the blatant disrespect of the Ancients, but another part of me agreed... and secretly loved this bad boy side of Kye.

Lokene sighed. "You would think being an Ancient would earn a guy some respect around here."

Eason laughed. The sound was unexpected, and we all turned to look at him, wide-eyed. "Lokene, you are Zosi's mate, and that makes you one of us. You are my brother, which means you have our respect, but that does not mean you are safe from being messed with."

Lokene didn't respond, but as he turned away, moving

to lower the ladder at the back of the yacht, I caught the small smile that spread on his face. Joy bloomed in my chest. My mates, my new family, were getting along.

"Come on, then. Now that I missed all the fun, I can come to your rescue." Lokene's signature smirk was back in place, and his eyes sparkled as if from some inside joke.

We drifted to the back of the sleek yacht where, one by one, my mates stepped onto the light wooden deck to board. They playfully slapped Lokene on the back or jostled him with their shoulders as they climbed aboard. Then, just as they boarded, each one froze to take in the five layers of the eggshell-white yacht. Silver banisters decorated the edges and, while I couldn't see the vast array of fresh fruits aboard, their sweet aroma wafted to me, making me momentarily forget my thirst for blood.

Storm tied their pitifully small boat to the beautiful vessel. I wanted to laugh at the odd contrast between the woeful floating device my mates had arrived in and this monstrosity. He stood, taking in the polished wooden plank floors and shiny banisters.

Finally, his gaze landed on Lokene, and he raised a brow. "You can manage all this, but you couldn't be bothered to give us a decent motor?" His face was stony, except for the small twitch I saw at the corner of his mouth. Storm wasn't angry anymore; he was just messing with Lokene.

Lokene shrugged. "It's the rules, man. I can't interfere in most of the fun stuff. Not unless I want to risk setting off a butterfly effect that could send the world into chaos... Or at least, that is the belief of the Ancients."

"Fun isn't the word I would use. You couldn't even sit in the boat with us as we spent hours trying to get to her?"

"Oh! I totally could have come with you, as long as I changed nothing."

Storm's confused expression mirrored my own. "Excuse me? Come again? You could have come with us? Then why didn't you?" Storm's aggravation came through loud and clear.

"Because it sounded positively boring and utterly dull. Plus, I had a ship to build." Lokene turned toward me and winked. "I really wish I could have been here to help you when you were having fun blowing things up. Once you were safely off the ship, Sheba was all the protection you needed until the rest of your mates arrived. I wasn't needed."

I wanted to tell him I always needed him, but my pride wouldn't let me. Emotionally, I needed him, and my body hummed with desire for him. However, physically, I was more than capable of fighting my own battles. Sure, I was a little worse for wear, but I had survived to fight another day. That was a win in my book.

"Soyale," Lokene broke into my musings.

Raising my gaze, I met his eyes. "Yes?"

"I've missed you, beautiful! Now, come on." He blew me a kiss and then turned and waved the rest of my mates to follow him into the boat's interior. "Come on, the food is getting cold. She needs to greet the fish-boy."

The men hesitated, but when Sheba's fin sliced through the water near me, some of the tension left their bodies. They might not want to be in the water with her, but they trusted her to have my back.

"Wait!" I exclaimed, panic setting in. "I have to get back to the rocks. I left someone there."

Eason's eyes narrowed in suspicion. "What do you mean, you 'left' someone there? Is this person a threat to you? I thought you completed your mission and took care of the Lure?"

I narrowed my eyes at him. "I did, but they had a mermaid on their ship. I hadn't expected that, but I couldn't leave her at their mercy. There was no way I could have allowed her to be killed, so I had to help her off the ship."

Kye beamed at me. "That's my girl! Kicking butts and saving lives!"

"Was she injured? Do you think she needed a doctor?" Fynn asked.

A wave of jealousy shot through me, far worse than the pain of being shot, at just the thought of his hands on the beautiful mermaid.

"No. I mean, yes." My words came tumbling out, a jumbled mess, just like my thoughts. "She was injured and having difficulty swimming, which is why I left her on the rocks. She is waiting for me to return. Her injuries were not life-threatening as far as I could tell." I still hated the thought of him touching another mer, so I added, "I'm sure they have a mer doctor in Atlantis. I just need to get her there."

Zeno's head broke the surface of the water in front of me, a broad grin on his face. I had felt him drawing near, so I didn't so much as blink at his sudden appearance.

"Do not worry, Maridákia. I have taken care of the mermaid. She is safe in Atlantis."

The growing jealousy that had been simmering under the surface since I had thought of Fynn examining Kosta had finally reached its boiling point.

CHAPTER TEN

ZOSIME

*Z*eno had been with her. Alone. I snarled at Zeno, completely incapable of finding the words to express these unfamiliar emotions that threatened to undo me.

Zeno grinned, flashing his own fangs at me. "I find your jealousy amusing. Are you upset because I handled part of your mission? Or are you angry because I touched another woman?"

He touched her. He touched her, and he was telling me about it. The man must have a death wish. Why else would he be goading me like this? The Siren wanted to have another go at our dominance dance, and remind him she wasn't to be toyed with.

"You. Are. Mine." I ground my teeth together as I spoke.

My exhausted body longed to lunge for him, but I was still too weak.

"Calm down, Siren. The girl you saved is my sister. We had quarreled over an idiotic merman who she is determined to marry. She stormed off in a huff to sulk. Kosta knows better than to travel so far from Atlantis alone, but she was angry and had expected no one to be in this area. All vessels usually avoid it."

At the words 'my sister,' the rage that had been building inside me like hot lava in a volcano vanished just as quickly as it had come, leaving me more exhausted than before. "Your sister?"

"Yes, my sister. I have three sisters, and Kosta is the youngest. She is also the most headstrong and determined to gray my hair before it is time." He reached out for me, pulling me into his arms and tucking my head beneath his scruffy chin.

"See? I told you she would be fine. Now, come on. Time to eat." Lokene looked each of the men up and down. "You guys definitely need to eat something, especially if you're even thinking about giving Zosime more blood."

Fynn caught my eye and winked. "I definitely plan on giving blood. Do you have any rare meat, or do you plan on feeding me these grapes while I work on my tan?" There was a laugh in his voice, and he turned to push past Lokene on his way to search for food.

Each of my men blew me a kiss before following

Lokene and Fynn into the dark interior of the boat. They left me alone with Zeno.

I stiffened, not quite ready to be touched so soon after believing he had touched another woman. Sister or not, this jealousy thing had no bounds.

"Stop being so stubborn. You know we are bonded. There will never be another for me."

I forced my body to relax against him, relishing the pleasure of feeling his arms around me as it chased away the last of my jealousy. "Why didn't you come with the men? You could've reached me much faster than that pitiful excuse for a boat." I nodded toward the dinghy.

"Because we weren't even sure where you were. I knew the men could protect you if you could not protect yourself. I was raised to put Atlantis before my own needs and desires. I vowed to protect her people above all else."

He nuzzled the top of my head before continuing, "I sensed my sister was near and found her easily. Knowing that Kosta was out in the open, where humans could potentially see her, was a risk I couldn't take. I was the only one who could return her safely to Atlantis."

In the human world, it was assumed our mate would put their partner first. Love demanded it, right? However, that was not always the best decision. I would give my life to protect Atlantis, just as I would give my life to protect humans on earth.

If I knew my men were able to protect themselves, I would not hesitate to help the weaker person in need first.

He was not picking her over me; rather, he was lessening my burden by safeguarding Atlantis and her people when I was otherwise indisposed. Not only that, but the way he held me against him using his body as a barricade showed me he knew how weak I'd become, and he wasn't willing to let anyone else see me like this. My heart swelled. He'd taken his sister to Atlantis so her people would not have seen me weak, the ultimate disgrace for an Atlantean Warrior.

"Have you fed?" His warm breath blew tendrils of hair against my ear, and I shivered.

"Yes. Storm fed me," I answered tiredly.

"Tell me the truth, Maridákia. Are you injured badly? Will you need to feed again?"

I didn't answer him at first, not wanting to admit verbally to my powerful merman how truly weakened I was. Although, I had a sneaking suspicion that he already knew how bad it was.

"Bad enough." I tried to dodge his question.

"How bad? How many times will you need to feed to recover?" He repeated his questions, not satisfied by my half answer.

"If I were not a Siren, the injuries I sustained would have been fatal."

His arms tightened around me.

I continued, knowing that he would not let this go, "I will probably need to feed two or three more times to heal fully."

"I had wanted to introduce you to Atlantis tomorrow, but I think it is best we wait until you're at full strength. Perhaps Lokene will allow us to spend time on the boat for the next few days. This will give you time to feed on each of us, as well as time for your mates to replenish themselves. We could all use the rest." His large hand brushed at the damp locks of hair covering my face.

I looked at the monstrosity that he had called a boat. "How is this going to work?" I motioned at his tail. "Can you shift forms between legs and a tail?"

"No." He drew out the word, his brow knit in confusion. "Are you telling me you can?"

"Yes, I can shift between forms, although I am far more comfortable with my tail than with my legs at this point." I blushed as I thought about how I wobbled like a newborn deer on my human legs.

Interest sparked in his eyes. "Now that is something I would like to see." The look he gave me was filled with lust. Leaning in, he gave me a lingering kiss on my lips, one that had the tips of my tail curling.

Finally pulling back, he ran a finger along my jawline. "Come, Lokene seems to have thought of everything."

Grabbing my hand and slipping an arm around my waist, he pulled me under the cool water. We swam beneath the vessel's hull. The water caressed my injured body, giving me a moment of relief from my pain.

I gave Zeno a puzzled look, turning my palm up in a

gesture meant to ask where we were going. He jerked his head toward the surface and began swimming upward.

We surfaced on the opposite side of the boat, and I looked over to ask him what was going on. Before I could ask anything, the whine of an engine caught my attention. Studying the boat, I saw a small door on the side, lifting like a hatch. It wasn't large enough for a boat to fit through, but it was definitely large enough for Zeno and me.

"Is that—" I began.

"Yes." Zeno snorted. "It seems your Ancient has thought of everything. After I returned from delivering my sister to Atlantis, Lokene found me and told me to enter through this door. It was smart to save energy, and I suspected he already knew where you were, so I took him up on the offer."

Zeno reached out for my hand, pulling me along with him as we entered the ship through the small doorway. The area opened into a beautiful room with a large saltwater pool.

It wasn't the size of the glimmering bathing pools of Atlantis that I remembered so well, but neither was it a tiny pool. There was just enough room for Zeno and me to splash around comfortably. I glanced beyond the pool into the open area beyond it, and my mouth fell open in awe.

"Well, it's about time you joined us. I thought Zeno had decided to have his wicked way with you," Lokene joked. He strode toward us, an elegant glass of bubbly liquid in either hand.

Handing them to us, he dropped a kiss on my forehead and stepped back expectantly. I took a sip, wrinkling my nose at the cold beverage burning my nose. Why would anyone drink this stuff?

"Welcome to our new home, Soyale!" Lokene spun in a slow circle, indicating the ship. I couldn't help but smile; his happiness was contagious. My eyes trailed around the room, briefly landing on the small dining area that held just enough seats for our family. There was a cute little stove and a—what was the word? Oh! Refrigerator.

The floors were a beautiful natural stone that reminded me of the smooth sandstone roads that ran throughout Atlantis. Lokene caught my eye and grinned boyishly. He had read my mind again, and he had chosen these floors, hoping to ease my homesick soul.

For the world, Atlantis, if it even existed, had been gone for many millennia, but for me, I had lost my homeland, my family, and my troops only a few weeks ago. Now, with my emotions returning, I missed my loved ones and my home.

Blinking back the tears that burned my eyes, I took in the rest of the room. I couldn't help the gasp that escaped me when I saw the bed. Could that enormous pile of pillows even be called a bed? It took up almost a third of the room.

"Oh! I see you found my masterpiece." Lokene rubbed his hands together in... anticipation, I think. "It is large enough that all seven of us can fit in it at the same time."

"Um. All of us?" Kye squeaked, looking around at the other guys, discomfort showing on his face.

Lokene raised an eyebrow and gave Kye a smirk. "Yes, it's big enough to hold us with no one being forced into cuddling anyone else. If we put Zosi in the middle, we can all sleep around her."

My hands slid around Zeno's waist. "Almost all of us."

Lokene lifted one shoulder carelessly. "I can give him legs temporarily if you want me to. Heck, you can give him legs! If you do it, we are less likely to get in trouble with the Ancients."

"I don't know how to do that! I just learned how to give myself legs!" I appreciated how much he believed in me, but in this case, he was overestimating my abilities. I wasn't a full-blooded Ancient.

"It does not matter," Zeno cut into the conversation. I've had a tail my entire life, and I am not keen on giving it up— at least not at this time." He turned toward me, giving me a soft kiss on the lips. "I will enjoy my time with you, here in the water."

"Suit yourself." Lokene didn't look like he cared one way or the other.

"Is this yours? The boat, I mean?" I questioned Lokene.

"No, it belongs to Zosi. Our family has members who live in the sea." He motioned toward Zeno. "And members who live on land." This time, he motioned toward the men who were eating at the table. "It only makes sense that, for the time being, we have a home that can accommodate both the land and the sea lovers," he finished. I couldn't fault his logic.

"Thank you." I hated how inadequate those two words sounded. I'd been worrying for hours over how I could be with all my mates, and yet Lokene had found a solution. I let out a sigh of relief.

As I breathed in, I caught the tantalizing scent of fish, bread, and spices. My stomach growled, and my mouth watered. I still needed blood, but I also wanted food.

Fynn and Kye grabbed their plates and an extra plate from the dining area and moved to sit on the cream-colored stones near the pool's edge. Fynn handed a plate to Zeno.

I thought Kye would hand me the extra plate he had brought from the table, but instead, he took a fork and fed me bites off his own plate.

He didn't intend for it to be seductive, but I found it one of the sexiest things on earth. This green-eyed, blonde-haired god was feeding me... while my other five mates watched. I blushed. It was tenderly intimate, and I loved him all the more for it.

The rest of my men gathered their plates piled high with food and moved to sit around the pool. I couldn't help my smile. We were having our first family dinner. Maybe Zeno was on to something; surely we could spare a few days to rest, heal, and recover.

Looking at the tired but sexy faces around me, I knew I was going to enjoy the next few days.

THE SOUND OF A PHONE RINGING AWAKENED US.

"Hello?" Storm's sexy morning voice sent desire vibrating through me.

I could only hear one side of the conversation, but from what I gathered as his thoughts filtered through my half-asleep mind, their boss was begging them to come back to the field. This was confirmed when Storm got off the phone, tossing it aside with an irritated scowl.

"I can't believe this. Our boss, Dan, claims his boss called him and our presence is being demanded. There is new information that was discovered that they feel we need to look at." The muscle in his jaw clenched. "We were supposed to be on leave. The only reason we were willing to leave you and Fynn was so we could tell them, in person, to lose our number for a while. Yet, here we are just days later, and they are demanding we return. Dan says that if we don't report voluntarily, he is afraid they will send a team to drag us in. If we quit now, I have no doubt that they will still send men to collect us and force us to complete the job for the government as our 'American duty.'" I pinched the bridge of my nose, trying to stave off a headache that was forming.

We had contracted with and worked for several military branches over the years. I would bet money that multiple agencies would track us down if news of our resignation, and subsequent free time, were to spread.

"That can't happen! They need to stay as far away from Zosime and Atlantis as possible." Kye looked distraught at the idea of putting her at risk.

Storm chewed his bottom lip, his expression grave. "There was also a serious breach last night. They found several of our guards dead. A criminal mining crew came in last night, armed and with heavy equipment."

Storm sat down heavily on the side of the bed. "There was a devastating amount of destruction to the underwater rock face, which is where the last large pocket of Orpati was found. Who knows how much they managed to steal? There have been several tremors this morning from the area. The thieves escaped before they could catch them, which is why they want our help. They need us to see if we can hunt down a trail. It might still be possible for the miners to be tracked down." Storm dropped his head into his hands.

"We know who is behind this," Kye cursed viciously, shocking me.

"Of course, we know who's behind this. Richard Jack, the self-proclaimed king of the modern world. The problem is, the man isn't an idiot. He's smart, and tracing this back to him is going to be nearly impossible," Eason added grimly.

. . .

"It will be difficult, but it isn't impossible. We can nail this guy. He thinks he's above the law and smarter than everyone else, but he is not smarter than us." I admired Kye's optimism.

I didn't know this man, Richard, but I had known many corrupt leaders throughout my life. They were incredibly difficult to take down.

"Yeah, we can take him down; we just have to go hunting." Eason looked over at me, a sick expression on his face. "To do that, though, we will have to leave Zosi."

"I could go." Even to my ear, the offer sounded hollow. Truthfully, I wasn't ready to face humanity. Nor was I prepared to interact with people of an era so different from mine. I needed more time to grow accustomed to the speech patterns and customs of this time.

"No!" my men shouted in perfect unison.

"As much as I would love to show you off to the entire world, it's best for now that you stay hidden. These are nasty people we are dealing with, and they wouldn't think twice about killing you, or worse, to use you if it helped them succeed in their goals." Storm moved to kneel in front of me, taking my hands in his own.

I knew Storm was right, but I didn't like how he seemed to doubt my ability to be a useful part of our team. I wasn't worried about being able to handle the bad guys... That was 'no sweat,' as Kye would say. The part that worried me was trying to fit in with modern-day humans. I wasn't sure I could do it, at least not yet.

Lokene laughed. "They don't doubt your abilities, little warrior. We are aware that you are the deadliest of us all. What they are doubting is their ability to stay focused on their mission with your cute butt right there beside them. The only things these men think about is expressing their love to you and making love to you. I would say they were a bunch of saps, but the truth is, I find I'm not so different from them."

My brows rose, nearly disappearing into my hairline. I looked around the room at my mates. "Is that true?"

Eason refused to make eye contact and rubbed at the back of his neck, embarrassed. Kye blushed, his suntanned cheeks turning a rosy red hue. Zeno huffed and sank below the water's surface.

Storm was the only one to look me in the eye, his expression filled with such love that my stomach clenched, and my eyes burned with unshed tears. "Yes, it is absolutely true. After my dad died, these men were the only family I had. I love them, and I would give my life for theirs. I have dedicated my life to serving my country and protecting those around me. I love my work, but I have loved nothing in my life as much as I love you, Zosi."

Eason cleared his throat. "He's right, Soldier. I grew up with the family, if you want to call it that. I don't remember my Ma or Pa ever saying a kind word to me. What I do remember is how it felt to be beaten, how it felt to have their hands slap me for things I hadn't even done wrong. I joined the military the moment I turned seventeen, forging my paperwork to get in early just so I could escape from my home life. I didn't care if I lived or died. Storm found me and changed the world for me. He saved my life. Literally.

"The day Storm saved my life, I knew I would never walk away from our brotherhood." Eason's eyes swirled with dark emotion. "But I would, Zosime. Soldier, I'd walk away from everyone for you."

The tears that had burned in my eyes now spilled over, slipping down my cheeks and falling onto my lap.

Lokene leaned forward, kissing my tear-stained cheeks with a sweet gentleness. Pulling away, he smiled. "I've heard that mermaid tears are good luck." His voice dropped to a conspiratorial whisper. "There is even a rumor they can grant wishes."

I gave a watery laugh at his silliness. My emotions were a complete wreck. "It's too bad that I'm a Siren then, and not a mermaid," I choked out the words between sobs and hiccups.

"What if my wish was to spend the rest of my life with you? Would you grant that wish?" Lokene's playful demeanor turned somber. His eyes watched me intently, waiting for my answer.

Sliding my hand along his lightly stubbled jaw, I whispered, "Yes."

He pulled me into his arms, kissing me with an abandon that took my breath away.

CHAPTER ELEVEN

ZOSIME

One-minute Lokene was there, and the next minute he disappeared, leaving me kissing the cool air where he had just been.

"Lokene?" Confusion and panic seeped into me. Had he angered the Ancients? Had they taken him from me again?

His voice brushed against my mind, *I'm fine, and no, we're not in trouble. Right now, I'm not sure you could do any wrong in their eyes. They need you too much. I shouldn't have kissed you. It's not my turn—not yet. I just couldn't resist you, Soyale. I'll be back. I just need a chance to take a cold shower... Or maybe several of them.*

His voice disappeared from my mind, and for a

moment, I wanted to cry. When would it be our time? How many millennia did we have to wait?

Warm arms wrapped around me. "Shh, it's okay. It'll be okay. The idiot will get his head out of his butt at some point." Kye's voice held a teasing note. He playfully rocked my body from side to side, nuzzling my neck. "For now, though, I would be happy to take his time with you." I couldn't help but laugh and wiggle out of his arms as he began covering my face in wet kisses.

"Oh no, you're not getting away that easily!" Jumping up off the bed, he chased me, his arms outstretched.

Tripping and stumbling on my very human legs, I ran to the place where I felt the safest: The water. Still laughing, I dove into the pool, inhaling more than a little water before I thought to close my mouth.

Before I had even surfaced, powerful arms circled my waist, pulling me tight against a lean, muscled chest. Slick fins brushed lazily along my bare legs. My merman had come to my rescue.

Zeno brought us to the surface, where I coughed and laughed and then coughed some more. He kept my head above water, amusement twinkling in his eyes.

These last few days I'd spent with my mates, getting to know them and bonding with them, had been amazing. My emotions were continuing to grow stronger, and I'd smiled and laughed more than I remembered ever having done in this life or my past life.

I wrapped my legs around Zeno's waist and encircled

his neck with my arms. "My hero!" I grinned at the roll of his eyes and rewarded him with a quick peck on the lips.

"Mm. I think I like it when you have legs." Zeno's hand slid down my back, across my butt, and down my thighs. He nearly purred as he explored my naked body. It reminded me of Fynn's first examination of my Siren body. Heat flushed through me as I recalled how that had ended. Zeno's curious fingers were turning me on more than I cared to admit.

"Oh, do you now?" I raised an eyebrow, trying to ignore how breathy my voice had become.

"Yes." His lips captured mine in a kiss that sent my temperature climbing higher. "I've missed having you in the water with me," he whispered against my lips.

Several times, Lokene had offered to give Zeno legs so he could join us in the bed. Each time, Zeno politely declined. I could see the idea intrigued him. He just wasn't ready to accept, even temporarily. I think he enjoyed the connection between the ocean and her inhabitants.

Storm rose from the bed with a pained sigh. "I hate to do this, but I think it's best that we go check out what's going on, if for no other reason than to keep Dan's men from snooping around here."

Kye and Eason nodded their agreement, their shoulders drooping in disappointment at being pulled away from our little love nest.

Zeno grunted. "And I should probably return to Atlantis, at least temporarily. My advisers have been keeping everything running smoothly, but it is expected that I check in on everything myself. I also need to see my stubborn sister to make sure she is healing properly and not trying to take off with that mer-idiot she thinks she loves." He sighed. "Atlantis and I will forever be indebted to you for saving her."

The weight of his responsibility toward his sister showed in the tightness of his tone. I knew that weight. Blood family was sacred to Atlanteans. If harm ever fell on those who shared his blood, then his rule would come into question. Atlanteans believed that if you could not protect your family, then you could not protect Atlantis.

My hand rose, and fingers slid across the deep furrow of his brow. Just for a moment, our eyes locked, and his gaze flickered back and forth between my eyes, holding a hurricane of emotions. Tartarus! Had he been worried about me this whole time? That I might have been mad because of his choice to return his sister to Atlantis instead of staying with me when he was lessening my burden by doing so, securing our reign, and protecting his own blood?

"Oh, Zeno," was all I managed to choke out as both my palms pressed to his cheeks. Tenderly, I kissed my burdened mer-mate.

"You are a mate that most men can only dream of having as their own." Zeno brushed the wet hair from my face as he spoke.

"Hey! Don't be stealing our girl while we're gone!" Kye

growled. It might have been intimidating if his eyes hadn't sparkled with mischief.

Just great. It seems Lokene was rubbing off on him.

"If all goes well, we should be back in a day or two. Then we can return and make plans on how to confront Richard. With luck, we will hopefully gather enough evidence to arrest him this time." Storm dressed quickly and gathered his things from the small bedside table.

"Fynn, do you want to go with us? It might be wise for you to check in with your own company before they send out a search party for you." Eason, always thinking ahead, looked over at Fynn.

Fynn pushed himself off the bed with a groan. "I guess you're right. My team is used to me disappearing for long stretches of time, but the last thing I need is for them to start a search. They are good—too good—at their jobs. I'll have you guys drop me off somewhere with good internet access so I can chat with the heads of my company."

"How are you going to get there?" I asked the obvious question.

We were a long way from shore, and a yacht this size would definitely draw attention if we took it to a port. Lokene had finally admitted to creating this vessel out of thin air as a gift for me.

Anyone who was familiar with boat brands would quickly realize our boat was one-of-a-kind, and that would garner conversations and questions. Which was far more attention than we needed.

"Maybe Lokene will return and—"

The four human men vanished in the blink of an eye. My mouth dropped open as I stared at the empty places where they had just stood.

Lokene's voice whispered in my mind once again, *Don't fret. I just put them in a hotel a safe distance from us. They can call their boss and arrange transport. Return to Atlantis with Zeno, and I will meet you there shortly. Ta ta!*

I rolled my eyes but was thankful for his little update on the men.

"As much as I like this new body of yours, if we are returning to Atlantis, I think you might want to shift back into your tail." The way Zeno's hands were gripping my thighs, I wasn't convinced he really wanted me to shift back.

Pushing away from him, I sank beneath the salty water. Once I was fully submerged, I closed my eyes and thought about the magik that was hidden inside me, calling it forward. The water around me glowed a pale turquoise as the magik transformed my body.

When my tail replaced my legs, I opened my eyes to find Zeno's blue eyes gazing back at me. "Are you ready to meet the people of Atlantis, My Queen?"

Was I ready? What if they hated me? While being queen was not a role I had ever wanted, it was a position I had been born to feel. A pang of loss hit me as I thought of my parents. I wished they were here to guide me. I could only hope I was half the queen my mother was.

Taking a deep breath, I nodded. "As ready as I'll ever be. Let's go greet our people."

Pushing a button on the yacht wall, the small hatch lifted, giving us access to the ocean. The moment we were clear of the yacht, we began our descent into the navy-blue depths of the ocean.

A shadow fell over us, and I glanced up to find Sheba circling above my head.

"She's never far from your side, is she?" Zeno spoke, keeping a wary eye on Sheba.

I smiled as I watched Sheba move through the water, a magnificent predator. I nodded. "She appeared shortly after I awakened, and she has stayed near me since."

"Our people have a history with Great White sharks. I'm not sure they will feel comfortable having such a massive shark circling Atlantis." Zeno seemed hesitant to broach the subject with me.

I lifted my shoulder, indifferent. "They will grow accustomed to her presence. She does not attack without cause or reason."

"If you require a pet, there are many options that are less lethal and with far fewer teeth," he suggested hopefully.

I snorted. "Sheba is no one's pet. She's a queen in her own right. I have neither the time nor the energy to care for a pet."

Realizing that he would not win this argument, Zeno focused on getting to the city as quickly as possible.

Thank you for your help, my friend. I sent the thought

through the water, hoping that Sheba would somehow understand.

With a powerful thrust of my tail, I hurried after my merman. I was both looking forward to and nervous for what was to come.

CHAPTER TWELVE

ZENO

I flopped onto my bed, utterly exhausted. Had I ever been this tired before? I doubted it.

When Zosime and I had discussed introducing her as the Queen of Atlantis, I had assumed she would want to do a grand introduction in the throne room. I'd envisioned a royal ball with music and dancing, fanfare and fine dining, and attendees decked out in their finest.

Instead, my Siren mate had done the exact opposite. She asked to be taken door to door to meet each family individually. There were eighty mer families in Atlantis, and she had visited thirty-five families in two days. My fins ached just thinking about how many miles I had swum in forty-eight hours.

I'd let her drag me, the king, from one house to the next. Standing uncomfortably as Zosi played with children, cooed over pet eels, admired treasures, and shook hands with the heads of nearly half the mer families in Atlantis.

It was the most beautiful and demeaning thing I had ever witnessed. She cared deeply for these people—her people. From the expressions on our subject's faces, they had recognized her deep love for Atlantis' people as well. She was a queen from days long past, and we were lucky to have her with us.

Zosime snored softly from where she lay curled against my side. I watched her sleep, enjoying how soft and delicate she appeared while at rest. When she was awake, her face had a battle-hardened edge to it. Combined with her toned body and her quick wit, she was, without a doubt, the most dangerous predator in the sea. I was terrified of her, but I also loved her in a way I had believed impossible.

For the first time in my life, I had almost neglected my responsibilities to Atlantis. The pull to get to Zosime when I knew she was hurt and in trouble had far outweighed the pull I felt for my sister or my responsibilities to my people. It scared the crap out of me, knowing the power that my mate had over me.

The reality that I could have lost her felt like someone had ripped out my soul and allowed a hungry group of piranhas to feast on it. I'd never been so conflicted. I'd grown up being groomed for the throne, always knowing the exact thing to do in any situation. They'd taught me to never second guess my decisions, and until that moment, I had never doubted myself.

Logically, I knew I made the right choice to let Zosime's other mates care for her while I attended to my sister and, by extension, my people. Zosime had four mates and a fickle Ancient watching out for her. Zosi was, and always had been, a born and trained fighter. My mate could handle herself.

Unfortunately, Kosta lacked any survival skills. Atlanteans were no longer taught to fight as in the days of old, instead, they were taught to hide. If humans had discovered Kosta, who could not swim without help, our beloved Atlantis would have fallen. Treasure hunters would have descended on the city, and my people would have been hunted for both their knowledge and for sport. I would never have been able to forgive myself. Worse, I didn't think Zosime would have forgiven me for doubting her ability to survive and allowing her city to be put at risk.

Yet, even though logically I knew I made the decision that was required of me as a king... My emotions didn't agree. I still felt physically ill at the thought of how my mate must have felt betrayed by me.

I was such a coward that I couldn't even ask for her forgiveness, because every time I tried, the words got caught in my throat. Somehow, I believe she knew what I was asking, even without me speaking actual words. The kiss she gave me at the yacht was the most soul-cleansing experience of my life.

I watched her sleep, amazed at her trust in me. Wrapping my arm around her, I pulled her closer. She flopped her long tail over mine, wrapping our flukes together. I smiled, filled with contentment. Tucking her head beneath my chin, I closed my eyes and let the steady beat of her heart lull me to sleep.

I AWOKE TO THE SOUND OF GIGGLING. BLINKING THE sleep from my eyes, I studied the room. Zosi was still curled into my side, fast asleep; the events of the last several days had left her exhausted.

A shadow floated toward where we lay on the bed, and it took me just a moment longer to recognize my sister. "What are you—" I began, only to be cut off by a blur of movement.

One second my sister had been next to the bed peering down at us, and in the next, Kosta was pressed against the elegantly carved wall, with Zosime's nails at her throat. Frozen in shock, I could do nothing to stop the scene in front of me.

Zosime hissed, her long fangs glinting in the dim light of my room. She had gone from sweet angel to avenging reaper in the blink of an eye.

"What are you doing here?" Her voice deepened into the husky tone I associated with her Siren. Except instead of exuding sexiness, she was radiating pure power.

"I-I came to see my brother. Don't you remember me?" Kosta stammered.

Zosi's sharp gaze focused on the terrified mermaid. Not finding a weapon, she eased her hold, but only slightly.

"I know who you are, but that is irrelevant. Why are you here? You must have had a reason to enter the royal bedchamber." Zosime wasn't messing around, and it reminded me of our lovers' quarrel when we first met. Why was it turning me on so much?

Kosta turned her pleading gaze toward me, begging me to calm the angry Siren. I put my hands out in front of me in a defensive posture, signaling to her that I wanted to be left out of this.

"I have warned you about entering rooms without an invitation." Fine, yes. I was goading her. Kosta had always been the spoiled princess who did exactly as she pleased. Thankfully, she didn't have a mean bone in her body and had grown into a wonderful young woman, but she often acted before thinking. Like today.

"What if we had been having passionate sex? Is that an image you would have been able to purge from your mind?" Some of the tension had left Zosi's body, and I could've sworn I caught the spark of a twinkle in her eye.

She must've sensed that Kosta had meant no harm by

her careless action. Zosi's blunt question shocked Kosta, which was no doubt what she had intended.

"Sweet baby Hades!" Kosta cried in horror at Zosi's words. All the color drained from my sister's face. Apparently, that thought scared her more than the angry Siren who had very nearly killed her.

As Kosta gagged, Zosi stepped back and turned to rejoin me on the bed. With her back to Kosta, she caught my eye... and winked. This shocked me far more than her attempt to murder my sister. My jaw dropped.

Twisting and flipping elegantly in the water, Zosi settled against my side again. Reaching up a finger, she gently closed my mouth before stretching up to give me a quick peck on the lips.

Had she known it was my sister all along, and she was just messing with both of us? Or had my sister truly surprised her, and Zosi's instincts had kicked in?

Looking at the small smirk that played around Zosi's mouth. I had my suspicions, but I doubted I would ever get the truth from her.

With a long-suffering sigh, I spoke to the intruder—my sister. "Were you just coming to see me? Or did you have a purpose?"

"I was coming to invite you both to the dining hall. Breakfast is being served, and after the long day you had yesterday, I thought you might enjoy a large meal." Tilting her chin up, she sniffed as though she were the one who had been wronged.

This bit of information piqued my attention. We hadn't used the dining hall in at least a year. Was there a special occasion I forgot? I couldn't think of any other reason they would prepare a banquet in the dining hall, especially without informing me.

Kosta rolled her eyes. "You aren't normally this dense, brother." Using her hand, she motioned toward Zosi and then toward me. "Hello?! You, the most eligible bachelor of the century, took a mate and gave her the keys to your kingdom."

"I gave her the keys to the kingdom that belonged to her." My voice was firm. I wanted everyone to know the kingdom belonged to her by birthright.

"Semantics. Who gave who what is not really that big of a deal to me. What is a big deal is that my brother has a wife! A wife who single-handedly stole the heart of every Atlantean in the span of a day. Her fans couldn't wait to see her again, which is why there's an enormous feast in the dining hall prepared by the women of the city. Come or don't, it is your choice." Wiggling her fingers in goodbye to the both of us, Kosta sashayed her way from the room, fins streaming around her.

I thought that my heart would burst with pride. Food was a precious resource in Atlantis. We risked our lives to hunt for meat and to gather food from the wilds of the ocean. We had more gold, crystals, and precious stones than we would ever be able to use. Food was much harder to come by, and that made it our most valuable resource.

It was a rare occasion for an Atlantean to feed anyone outside of their immediate family. Royal balls were the only time there were large feasts, and those parties were few and far between.

The fact that our people wanted to share their food, to provide for their queen, was the ultimate honor. This was their way of showing their acceptance of her as their ruler, and I wasn't going to miss it for the world.

"When Kosta said all the Atlantean women had cooked for me, she didn't actually mean all, right?" Zosi's voice squeaked at the end.

Sitting up quickly, I stared at her as comprehension slowly dawned on me. She was afraid. I laughed. Not a little chuckle, but a full-blown belly roar. I laughed until my side ached and tears leaked from my eyes.

"Is my big, tough warrior scared of something?" I teased, using a voice reserved for cute pufferfish and small mer-babies.

Zosi narrowed her eyes at me, her mouth thinning into a narrow line.

"Oh! She is afraid! My beautiful bride is afraid of a party." There was no way I was going to let her live this down—not anytime in the foreseeable future.

Trying to look fierce, Zosime scowled but ended up laughing as well. She launched herself at me, and I caught her with ease. With a quick thrust of my tail, we surged off the bed and up toward the cathedral ceiling of the royal bedroom.

Holding her against me, I swirled and spun, dancing to the rhythm of the sea and savoring the feel of her body moving in tandem with mine. This was one of those memories that I would remember for the rest of my life; a perfect moment frozen in time.

"Are you ready for breakfast, Maridákia?" I placed kisses up her neck, wanting nothing more than to spend the day in bed exploring every inch of her body. Perhaps after breakfast, we could return to our bedroom and share a lazy day together.

I didn't mind sharing my mate with the other men, but I also wouldn't mind having a day with her, all to myself. The men were due to arrive back before evening, so if I hurried, I would have several more hours alone with Zosi.

"Do we have to go to breakfast?" my little temptress whispered, her hands trailing to places that were eager for attention.

I needed her to understand the full importance and symbolic meaning of this gesture from the people of Atlantis and how strong their desire to spend more time with her truly was.

Concentrating hard and ignoring my body's demands, I explained our customs to her. Once she grasped the situation, her chin lifted, and she pushed back her shoulders. One would think she was going to war instead of to a feast in her honor. Regardless, she was ready to face the room full of spectators.

Grabbing a comb from the nightstand, she quickly

brushed through her long dark hair, braiding it in a single thick plait that traveled the length of her back.

"Come, my love. If I must do this, then you must be at my side for support." Her voice was powerful, not a tremble or sign of nerves to be heard.

Linking her arm through mine, she lugged me down the corridor toward the great dining hall. The swim wasn't long, and soon, we were taking in the sight of the brightly-lit breakfast feast.

We entered the long dining hall. Bouquets of brilliantly colored corals and anemones decorated the table. They were living works of art. Shattered pieces of the Atlantean stone, what humans now called Orpati, sat in vases around the room, casting it in a beautiful blue light. Fish of all different hues darted around the room, keeping the mer-children busy as they chased the fish away from the food. Crimson and violet crabs dotted the golden columns, the small pests providing yet one more splash of vibrant color to the grand room. I tried to imagine the room before it sank to the bottom of the sea, but in my mind, nothing could have been as beautifully alive as the room spread out in front of me.

The moment we swam out of the shadows of the hallway, everyone in the room froze, their eyes locked on us. The sounds of clinking pottery, clattering silverware, and excited chatter ceased. It was so quiet I was pretty sure I heard the crab nearest me release a tiny fart. We had long given up trying to keep them out of the castle, and now we just looked at them as brightly colored and often amusing decor.

I cleared my throat, prepared to announce Her Majesty's arrival. Zosi's sweet, husky voice cut me off, "There is no need for long introductions. You know who I am, and I have met many of you. Yesterday, you invited me into your homes and allowed me to enjoy time with your families. Today, I'm happy to have you visit my home. I want to thank every one of you for the warmth you have shown me since my arrival in Atlantis. I hope I will be the type of queen my mother was, for that is the queen you all deserve."

A broad grin spread across her face. Clapping her hands, she shouted, "Now, let's eat this bountiful feast!"

There was enough food to feed the entire Ancient army of Atlantis. I ate until I felt sick, and I talked until my throat was sore. Out of the corner of my eye, I watched as my queen flitted from one guest to the other, gracefully moving up and down the long table that ran the length of the dining hall.

Zosime made sure that every guest knew we appreciated them and that she was happy to see them. It surprised me to find that she remembered every name and insignificant detail about each person's family.

If I had any doubts about her abilities or her place as Queen of Atlantis, watching her now would've squashed them all. Atlantis was beyond lucky to have Zosime returned to the city where she belonged.

I just needed to be patient. Right now, I had to share her with the people of Atlantis. However, if things went my way, I would have her to myself for at least a few brief hours. I smiled as I thought about everything I intended to do to her.

CHAPTER THIRTEEN

ZOSIME

S miling and waving goodbye, we finally made our escape. After swimming out of earshot and into the darkened hallways, I allowed my shoulders to relax. "That was the longest breakfast I have ever attended!" I was so full I wasn't sure I could swim.

"That was breakfast, brunch, and lunch," Zeno grumbled.

"Why are you so grouchy? I thought it went really well." I was confused. Everyone seemed to have a wonderful time, which is why they had stayed so long.

"That's the problem. It went too well. I wanted time with you before everyone else returned. This has really cut into my time." He was scowling in irritation.

"You're sulking!" I couldn't help but laugh. The man was being ridiculous.

"I am not." We were both quiet until he chuckled softly. "Fine, I am sulking. It seems you're bringing out emotions I didn't even know I possessed."

We made our way back to the bedroom, and I swam over to the large windows that looked out over the ocean floor. It was so desolate, reminding me of the way the Ancients had once described other planets. Rock formations created all strange shapes that dotted the sandy landscape and cast odd shadows on the sand.

Schools of fish swam by, twinkling in the dark sea like stars in the night sky. Occasionally, a gigantic shadow would fall across the watery tableau in front of me, and I would catch sight of a whale lumbering past.

As a child, I had looked through these windows at a scene so different from the one in front of me now. My dream since returning to Atlantis had been to figure out a way to bring Atlantis, and her people, back into the modern world.

I wasn't sure if that was what I wanted anymore. My soul was attached to the sea, and it was my home now. The ocean called to me, and I never wanted to be far from it.

Watching the mers as they tended to their homes and families, and as they laughed and ate this morning, I questioned whether trying to make them human again was truly what was best for them. They were happy, and for now, they were safe.

Zeno slipped his arms around my waist, pulling me back against his chest. "What are you thinking about, my beautiful mate?"

I hummed in contentment. "About how much I love our people and how much I love the sea." There was no way I could put into words everything that I was feeling, not when emotions still felt so foreign to me.

Spinning me in his arms, Zeno turned me to face him. "Do you know what I'm thinking about?" His lips brushed across my cheekbone.

The light touch sent a delicate shiver along my skin. Taking my time, I kissed my way along his chiseled jawline. He breathed out, the warm water a stark contrast to the cold water of these depths.

His hands slid up from my hips, across my waist, and up my ribcage. A fire burned everywhere his fingers touched. His fingers brushed along the edges of my soft armor, and need surged through me. How could something intended to protect me also be incredibly sensitive to the touch of my mate?

His long black hair floated in the current, a dark crown around his face. I sank my hands into the raven locks, running my nails along his scalp. This time, he was the one who shuddered.

"I want you, Zosime." His voice was all gravel and need.

"Then have me," I whispered against his lips.

I carefully pricked his lip with a single fang. I don't

think he even noticed. He was far too busy exploring every inch of my body with the eagerness of a horny teenager.

Zeno's breathing had already become ragged, but I still knew the instant my tiny dose of venom hit his bloodstream. He moaned, grabbing my butt and hauling me against him. Hard. I had wanted to tease him, but the feel of his hot bulge pressing against me sent liquid heat rushing to my core. If I wanted to play my little game, I needed to do it now, before we were both lost to the venom's lust-fueled haze.

With a single hard push, I freed myself from his hold. He stared at me blankly, confusion clouding his features.

"If you want me, you'll have to catch me." I blew him a kiss, performed an elegant flip, and darted through the doorway and out into the sea.

Even with my skills as a warrior, the merman quickly began to catch up. Trying to throw him off, I darted through rock formations and spun my way around the remains of two sunken ships. It slowed him down, but not nearly enough.

Thrusting my fluke hard, I veered skyward and swam as though a predator were on my tail—which was partially true. Glancing over my shoulder, I caught the glint of his glowing blue eyes and the flash of fangs. Gone was the tender lover, and in its place was a fierce hunter who was determined to capture his prey.

To say the Siren was thrilled would be the understatement of the century. She was almost salivating at the thrill of being chased by the sexy merman and purring at the thought of what he would do once he caught up.

The water lightened to a pale blue, and the sun's rays shimmered on the water's surface above me. Almost there. His fingers brushed the flowing tips of my fluke. I needed to be quicker than this if I was going to make it.

The hull of our yacht came into view. Reaching for the magik inside me, I used it to surge ahead. Rushing along the length of the boat, I made it to the secret hatch. Slamming my hand down on the button, I waited impatiently as the door rose, squeezing inside as soon as it had lifted enough to allow my body through.

I'd barely made it inside when I heard Zeno's body slam into the hull. He had to wait for the door to lift further before making his way inside. I was already speeding for the stairs. I called to my magik again, focusing on my human legs.

This time, the shift was faster. No sooner had my tail disappeared than I reached the steps and clambered my way up the slick stairs. I was giddy at the thought of leaving the water and being able to tease my merman from just out of his reach.

I laughed as I made it onto the stone floor. My laughter was short-lived as a large hand clamped around my ankle. I stumbled and caught myself. I was breathless, and my surprised squeal at being caught didn't help. Collapsing onto my back on the smooth floor, I went limp, my giggles turning to hiccups as the merman slowly pulled me back into the water. A thrill of excitement shot through me at the thought of what he might do.

Zeno pulled me back into the water, spinning around so that he sat on a step, with his hips and tail submerged. He adjusted me so that I straddled his lap, facing him. Blue eyes traveled my pale human body while his hands again explored my torso, only this time, I was naked, and no armor covered my flesh.

"I've never been with a human before." Zeno's voice was gruff and slightly distracted as he continued his perusal of my body.

"I should hope not." Jealousy flared briefly at the thought of another woman sharing intimacy with him, regardless of whether she had fins or legs.

Leaning forward, he kissed the tip of my nose, a playful gesture that I hadn't expected from him. "There is no one else on earth for me. You are my bonded, and there is no need for your jealousy."

"I didn't think you could read my thoughts?" I was momentarily distracted from my irritation.

"I cannot. Mermaids and merman are empaths. We feel emotions. Many times, we feel the emotions strongly enough to take a good guess at what the person is thinking. However, we do not hear actual words." He answered me while pulling one of my legs out of the water so he could examine it closer. "You wouldn't survive two days in the ocean with these skinny limbs."

"You aren't wrong. I much prefer my tail to the human

form. When I woke from my deep sleep, I was terrified of my own body, but with time I have grown to love it and appreciate the advantages it gives me." I squirmed as his fingers traced the edge of my foot. My human skin was much more ticklish than my Siren form.

Grabbing his shoulders, I tried to push myself away from his teasing hands. No such luck. One muscular arm wrapped around my waist like a steel band, holding me tight and preventing my escape.

I fought his hold, laughing as he tickled my foot again. As I wiggled, I bumped against his hard bulge, and I froze at the sensations that exploded inside me. I rocked forward slowly, and the feel of my most sensitive skin brushing against his scales nearly caused my eyes to roll back in my head.

"Oh!" The single word came out strangled. Zeno's eyes sharpened on my face, concern quickly changing to a smoldering heat as he realized the cause of my inability to breathe.

With a devilish smirk, his fingers dug into the soft skin of my hips. "I like how responsive this human body is." He rolled my hips against him, moving at the pace of a sea slug. I gasped. With an evil chuckle, he repeated the motion a second time and then a third.

Need built inside me, my core demanding release. I tried to rock my hips faster, but he held me firmly, maintaining control. I wanted to scream for him to move faster, but I couldn't catch my breath to speak.

Over and over, he rocked me against himself, allowing me to feel his own growing need. His pace remained steady, unhurried.

"I need more, Zeno," I growled.

"You are not in control, my beautiful little fish. I am." His lips traveled up my throat. I wanted him to move faster, to bury himself inside me, to bite me...

Bite. It was my turn to smirk. If he was going to play dirty, so could I.

Leaning forward, I sank my fangs deep into his neck. I didn't just give the merman a little venom—oh, no. I let the Siren give him as much as she wanted... which, in hindsight, probably wasn't the best idea since she had one thing on her mind and knew exactly how to get it.

Zeno groaned, rocking his hips up to grind against mine. The venom was working fast, but still, venom pumped through my fangs and into his veins. I finally took back control, afraid that she would give him a lethal dose. I still wasn't sure how much venom each of my men could handle.

"Oh, Zosime." The words were barely intelligible. "I-I can't control—"

One minute I was grinding against his bulge, and the next, I was impaled on his erection. Tartarus! Where had that come from? He was big, too big for me in this form.

Barely giving me time to adjust, he lifted me off his scorching hot rod and then slammed into me again. I cried out, from pain or pleasure, I couldn't say. My butt smacked the water, splashing water in an arc around us.

He continued his reckless pace, sliding himself free and then instantly burying himself inside me. Water soaked the stones around the pool, and the walls nearest us dripped water, but Zeno didn't care. He drove himself into me. I moaned, my release building to a wild crescendo as he rolled his hips, hitting my pleasure center perfectly.

I screamed his name, my body shuddering as wave after wave of intense pleasure flooded my system. The merman bucked his hips twice more and then roared his release. I clung to his shoulders, my body still trembling.

"I love you, my Siren."

"And I love you, forever and always," I whispered back.

CHAPTER FOURTEEN

ZOSIME

O ne minute we were alone, and the next, Lokene had teleported the rest of my mates into the room.

"Was one hour alone with our mate seriously too much to ask?"

All I could do was laugh at his frustration. The Siren was ready for round two, but his annoyance was providing an excellent distraction. Who knew that men were so whiny?

"Hey! Are you two going to say hi? Or just continue to ignore us?" Kye teased us.

"Oh, they will. Fish-boy is just pouting. It seems we interrupted them at an inopportune moment." Lokene's chuckles and Zeno's irritated growl added to my amusement.

I moved so that I sat on the stairs, the water coming up over my breasts to cover me. Muttering under his breath, Zeno kissed me and sank to the bottom of the pool.

To my surprise, Fynn kicked off his shoes and came down the stairs to sit beside me. He pulled me onto his lap. "Well, hello there, pretty lady. Do you come here often?" He wiggled his eyebrows suggestively.

Ignoring his silliness, I asked him the questions that had been burning in my mind. "How did your trip go? Is everything in your company okay? Do we need to worry about someone being sent to find you?"

Fynn gave me a little squeeze, holding me tight against his chest, not caring that his pants and shirt were now soaked. He just seemed happy to have physical contact with me. I couldn't help but smile that even as a human, he recognized the pull of the bond. Being away from each other simply wasn't comfortable, no matter if you were mer, Siren, or human.

Or Ancient, Lokene's voice floated through my mind.

"Yes, everything is fine. I don't know whether to be depressed or relieved over the fact that my company doesn't really think they need me for it to continue to run smoothly." Fynn sucked his bottom lip into his mouth, deep in thought.

"That is a testament to your skills as a leader and as a businessman. There are way too many companies that crumble the moment the founder steps away." There was a note of admiration in Storm's voice.

I knew my men held Fynn in high regard, but I loved that Storm was trying to reassure him.

"Yes, I guess you're right." Fynn buried his face in my hair, laughing as the wet strands stuck to his 5 o'clock shadow. "I want my companies to continue to do good in the world and make progress for marine conservation. However, the most important thing in the world to me is sitting on my lap, and I'm right where I want to be."

"Ugh. I think I might be sick." Lokene made fake dry heaving noises.

Fynn laughed over Lokene's antics. "Keep it up, Ancient. I can't wait to see how lovey-dovey you get after she gives you her love bite."

Lokene scoffed. "I've already kissed her, and her toxin had no effect on me. Ancients are not susceptible to human illnesses, nor do they have to worry about bites from venomous animals on this planet."

Fynn raised a single brow. "You don't know what her venom will do if injected directly into your bloodstream. According to you, she carries earth magik you don't possess. You've also told us that her body adapts in order to ensure her survival. Which means you have zero idea what her bite will do to you."

"Whatever, human." With a dismissive wave of his hand, Lokene walked to the refrigerator, pulling out food and piling it high on the counter. Just seeing that pile of food made me feel ill.

"I'm still too full to eat," I told them about the feast that was held in my honor and the amazing mers I had met while they were gone. I tried to play down my parts of the story, but Zeno cut in and added the parts I had left out.

"I'm so proud of you." Fynn squeezed me against his chest in a massive bear hug.

"I would've loved to have been there!" Kye was enthusiastic, and my heart melted at the interest he was taking in my world.

Turning to Storm and Eason, I asked about what had been laying heavy on my heart. "What did you find? Were there any other attacks while you were gone?"

"No. Thankfully, there have been no other attacks. Seeing the amount of damage they caused was devastating. Giant rock-face walls were blown up using small electric charges. This kept anyone on the surface from figuring out what was going on beneath the surface. Then, without the perimeter being checked by the security team, there was no one to stop them. They worked nearly all night without interruption."

Eason dropped his head into his hands. "They were good men and didn't deserve to be murdered. All because of one man's greed."

"I spoke with the families, letting them ask questions, although most of them I couldn't answer. I was able to tell them about my memories of working with their loved ones and a few amusing anecdotes as well. They appreciated having someone to talk to about their loss." Kye's eyes were red. I suspected he had shed a tear or two over the loss of these men whom he respected.

While my Siren admired their strength and intellect, and my warrior heart loved their skills, I loved seeing glimpses of the vulnerable side of my mates.

I knew how difficult it was to hide your emotions while working. That was one of the reasons I had allowed the Ancients to seal mine away. Now that they were coming back, I was far more aware of the amount of strength it took to control your emotions while also staying focused on the task at hand.

"It looks like they took a significant amount of the Orpati. In the process of collecting it, they collapsed two caves and caused a huge crack in the largest formation." Eason stared out the large window at the endless sea.

"While we were on the offshore base, there were two slight tremors. They were insignificant according to the scientists there, but we were told that the scientists have concerns about the possibility of more seismic activity," Kye added.

Fynn's arms tightened around me. "Which means that depending on how much damage was caused, there is an increased risk of a significant earthquake." Fynn's muscles were taut. I didn't know as much about earthquakes, but from the thoughts running through their heads, I knew they could be deadly.

"If it's out to sea, it shouldn't take many lives, should it?" I was struggling to understand what was causing their faces to look so strained.

"What we're worried about is a tsunami, Zosi. An earthquake out at sea seems innocent enough. After all, there's not many humans at sea compared to the population on land. The issue is that there are times when an earthquake at sea will cause a tsunami, and when that reaches the shore, it causes massive devastation. Thousands of lives may be lost, as well as peoples' livelihoods, their homes, and sometimes even entire cities are destroyed." Storm was patient with his explanation.

"The sea is powerful and uncontrollable, which is why humans are both drawn to it and fear it," I mused softly.

"Unfortunately, we cannot see how much damage has been done since the rock formation where most of the mining took place partially collapsed after they blew parts of it up. Who knows how deep they drilled inside before that happened?" Storm's hand balled into a fist, and I could see a muscle in his jaw tick.

I looked around at my mates, all of whom had somber faces. I wanted to cheer them up but wasn't sure how to do it. The Siren had an idea, the same one she always had. When she wanted to be cheered up, she enjoyed sex and violence, neither of which seemed to be an appropriate option for my men at that moment.

Lokene snorted, and I shot him a look of annoyance. *Quit reading my thoughts.*

You know I can't help it, no more than you can help it. Besides, I find that as your emotions return, you are becoming increasingly entertaining. Also, I'm a fan of the Siren's way of cheering a person up. Lokene was trying to get a reaction from me, so I ignored him and focused on trying to come up with a way to please my guys.

An idea came to me. Unfortunately, I wouldn't be able to pull it off without Lokene's help. I narrowed my gaze on him, unsure if I want to ask for a favor.

You're my mate, that means it isn't a favor, he answered my unspoken question.

I'm not your mate yet, because you keep dragging your feet, I replied before thinking better of it.

I know I'm hot, but are you that impatient to get me in bed?

I rolled my eyes and turned to gaze out the window. The sun was setting, casting beautiful gold and pink hues across sky blue water.

Yes, Soyale. I will help you cook for your men. I've missed the food of Atlantis and would enjoy doing this with you. His voice was sincere this time, not a hint of a teasing tone.

I grinned like an idiot, pleased I was going to do something nice for my mates. I quickly flipped through memories of the dishes my mother used to cook. Once I had decided, I sent out a mental list of the ingredients that I needed.

I would make a dish called 'teganites.' They were like pancakes and were made with olive oil, honey, milk, and flour. They were delicious when topped with cheese or honey.

Mm. Now you've made me hungry. Lokene casually waved toward the cabinets and then winked at me. *It's all there. Your wish is my command, Soyale.*

I prepared to stand up but blushed. I knew my men had seen all there was to see of my naked body, but the idea of parading around cooking for them with no clothes on was embarrassing... Or at least it was to me. The Siren thought it was a terrific idea.

If I was going to cook the food of my previous life, why not wear one of my favorite garments?

Lokene? I asked hesitantly through the mind link.

It's already in the bathroom, waiting for you to change. He strode toward me, rubbing his hands together until a fluffy white towel appeared in his hands.

"Here we go!" This time when he smiled at me, the smile was tender. Sincerity shone in his eyes instead of his usual mischievous twinkle.

I returned his smile with one of my own, and, holding Fynn's hand for balance, I stood. Lokene wrapped the towel around me, and I was surprised to find that it was warm, as though it had been heated.

"Only the best for my queen!"

After wrapping me up tightly in the towel, Lokene pulled me into his arms for a quick embrace. He kissed my cheek and then stepped back. Slapping me on my butt, he added, "Hurry back, Zosi. I find I am suddenly starving!"

Once in the bathroom, I took a quick shower, rinsing the salty water from my hair and skin. Lokene had left me bottles of shampoo and conditioner. Squeezing far too much at my hand, I was surprised to find it smelled familiar.

Frankincense, cinnamon, myrrh, with other spices combined to create the unique scent of a perfume I had worn daily when not heading out to battle. My mother had created the spicy and sweet scent just for me, saying every princess should have a royal scent.

How had Lokene remembered such an insignificant detail? We had been together only once, yet the scent of the shampoo was nearly identical to the perfume my mother had crafted for me. I could feel tears burning at the back of my eyes, both from the sudden longing to see my mother once more and from the realization of how much that one day with me had affected Lokene.

I finished my shower quickly and dried. I looked deject-edly at my soaking wet hair, knowing it would be hours before it dried. I thought about the way my hair used to fall in satin waves when I unraveled my long braid.

I wondered if my magik could style hair. Closing my eyes, I reached for the magik inside me. I called for it, hoping it would understand what I was asking. I felt the warm prickle spread across my skin, up my neck, and to my scalp. As quickly as it had come, it vanished.

I stood for a moment, afraid to open my eyes for fear that instead of soft waves, I would look as though I'd been struck by lightning. Finally, I managed enough courage to crack open one eye, peering at myself in the small mirror. My ink-colored hair was completely dry and glossy. I hadn't seen it look this beautiful since I had awakened. Gentle waves started on the top of my head and fell nearly to my butt.

Opening both eyes, I studied my reflection before focusing on my clothing. My aquamarine pants were made of soft silk, puffy and trimmed with brightly colored gold and purple fabrics. There was a long slit that ran from my ankle to my hip on either side and when I moved, flashes of my pale legs could be seen.

The top was similar to what human women called a 'bra,' except mine had straps that were larger pieces of fabric that draped over my shoulders like small puffy sleeves. My top was made from the same aquamarine material and was trimmed in gold and purple to match the pants. Gold chains draped elegantly from the top, which stopped just above my belly button.

I gave a happy little wiggle, breathing in deeply when the lingering scent of the spicy shampoo tickled my nose.

I smelled like me.

I looked like me.

Hades, I was even wearing my favorite outfit.

As I stared in the mirror, the only difference I saw between the Zosime from before the fall of Atlantis and the Zosime from after the fall of Atlantis... was my eyes.

While they had always been a startling blue-green hue,

they had only glowed after I awakened. *Is that due to me being a Siren now?* I might never know.

I took one last look in the mirror and froze. There was one more difference between the old and new me...

I looked happy now.

CHAPTER FIFTEEN

KYE

The coast guards' boat speed across the choppy surface of the ocean. We were headed to the magnificent yacht owned by Richard. We had finally been given the go-ahead to arrest him. He had finally stepped far enough out of line that no one was willing to stick their neck out for him.

A shell casing had been found near one of the dead guards, and we had been able to trace that weapon back to one of Richard's employees. From there, we had pieced together a timeline of the man's movements over the past months and had tracked down surveillance footage of the man's activities as he traveled to and from work and while he was at work.

Once Richard's employee was arrested, he had quickly cracked during Eason's intense interview. The man had been worried he might get caught by the feds one day and had been storing up intel to swap for a plea deal and witness protection.

We'd got most of the footage through our contacts and by less than legal methods, but we had agreed that Richard was a sick man who needed to be taken down by whatever means necessary. Our records showed he wasn't just into selling inanimate things anymore. No, this man had stooped to selling human beings, promising them better lives and instead showing them the worst life had to offer.

I would have happily put a bullet in his head and was honestly hoping he would try to resist. I knew everyone saw me as the happy-go-lucky 'surfer' guy, but I had faced demons in my life, not literal ones, but close enough as far as I was concerned. It had been easy to watch the life drain from their cruel eyes, and I had smiled while I watched.

Later, I would show up at the crime scene with the team they had assigned me to. I never felt remorse for my actions. I'd only felt relief that one more twisted waste of oxygen no longer walked this earth.

After Storm had taken me under his wing, I no longer went out on my side missions. I trusted him to guide us the right way, and the man always seemed to get results. Usually, he would take us down the proper channels, but there had been times when we had colored outside the lines in order to get justice.

We had been after Richard longer than any other target we had set our sights on before. He had greased the right hands, and that had made it challenging to get access to the information we needed, but now we had enough. After we had Richard in custody, we had warrants for his vehicles, homes, boats, and businesses. There would be enough evidence to bury him for the rest of his disgusting life.

As we drew near to the mansion-sized yacht, I saw our commander, Dan's, boat had already made it. We had opted to come on our own boat from a location Lokene had teleported us to—which was in the opposite direction of Atlantis.

The captain of the patrol boat sidled up to Richard's vessel and cut his engine. Deafening quiet surrounded us.

"Something isn't right." Eason drew his weapon and crouched low as we moved onto the ship.

"Richard Jack. You are under arrest—" Storm shouted, preparing to go into the long spiel he had to give for everything to be legal. It felt like he was putting a target on our back by shouting out our current position.

"Yeah, yeah. That is what your commander has been trying to tell me. Save your breath; I'm not going anywhere with you," Richard's bored tone echoed down the corridor.

Eason motioned for us to head toward the bow of the canary-yellow yacht. I am not sure what I expected to see when we turned the corner and walked into the open dining and seating area, but never in a million years would I have guessed I would find our commander, bound, and with a gun pressed to his head. Scattered on the floor and across the beautiful pastel-colored furniture were the bodies of his team, agents I had worked with and admired.

"He's set this up to make it look like you guys went rogue and murdered these men and attacked Richard," Dan blurted out the info but was cut off when he was back-handed with the gun that had been pressed against his temple.

"Don't tell them everything! I've worked hard to lay a trail of evidence that will cast just enough doubt to get me off the hook. When you guys suddenly disappear, that will add another layer of mystery, and everyone will assume that you stole the Orpati, sold it to the highest bidder, and then retired to an island to live out your days under an assumed name."

"We are not going to disappear." Storm's voice was flat.

Richard laughed, and it was not a pleasant sound. "Boy, you don't have a choice. Haven't you realized I hold all the power here?" He twirled his hand, motioning to the man guarding Dan. The man nodded. Twisting quickly, he kicked Dan's legs out from beneath him and rammed his shoulder hard into Dan's chest. Off-balance, Dan tumbled over the side of the boat, and as he fell over the glass railing, the guard raised his gun and fired two headshots.

He didn't miss.

"No!" Storm shouted. He raised his own gun and prepared to shoot the guard. Storm hadn't seen the second guard come through the corridor on the opposite side of the bow. This guard had a semi-automatic rifle, and he aimed it at Storm's head, pulling the trigger.

I yelled a warning but knew it would be too late. Lunging toward the guard, I threw myself in the path of the bullets. My body jerked as the first two slammed into my torso.

"Kye!" Eason and Storm yelled my name in unison. My shoulder hit the wooden floor of the yacht with a sickening crack. Excruciating pain burned through my body like a wildfire.

"Try not to kill them! I want to get some information from them first!" Richard jumped from his seat and ran for cover inside the boat.

Eason fired several shots at Richard's retreating form. Storm leaned over my body, providing cover as he pulled me behind a large couch.

"I forgot how much getting shot hurts." I tried to make a joke, but it came out as a wheeze.

"Shut up, idiot. Why on earth did you jump in front of me?" Storm sounded angry.

"Dang. I didn't realize still being alive would make you so angry. This is the last time I save your life." The pain disappeared as a coldness crept through my body. I sighed in relief, but it turned to a cough. Something wet was on my lips.

Storm began cursing. I admired his creativity. I hadn't heard most of those words before. It was rare for our calm leader to curse at all. I opened my mouth to make a joke, but only a sucking sound came out. I knew I should be panicking. Instead, I felt relaxed. A nap sounded nice.

Eason groaned, and then the floor shook as something hit it—hard.

I wanted to ask if Eason was alive, but my muscles refused to obey me. My eyelids drooped.

"They hit him with a tranquilizer dart. There are too many of them, Kye. I can't get us out of this." Sadness dripped from each word. I wanted to tell him it was okay, and it wasn't his fault, but my body no longer obeyed my commands.

A slick, warm liquid was pooling under my motionless fingers. It didn't take a genius to understand I was bleeding out.

I was dying.

A dart whistled through the air, embedding itself in Storm's shoulder. It must have been a doozy of a tranq, because he collapsed on top of me almost instantly.

These men better hope Zosime never finds them. I was just upset I wouldn't get to see it.

CHAPTER SIXTEEN

ZOSIME

I tossed and turned on the yacht's giant bed. Fynn had asked Lokene to teleport him to his home office. He had several friends involved in earthquake research, and he wanted to ask them some questions regarding tsunami risks.

Eason, Kye, and Storm had left at dawn to assist in the arrest of Richard Jack. They weren't expected to be back until the following day. Zeno had returned to Atlantis to check on his sister and make sure she hadn't eloped with the young merman Zeno disliked.

Family drama was not something I was prepared to deal with, so I opted to remain on the yacht and wait. The problem with my plan? I wasn't a 'wait at home' type of woman. I was more of a 'lead the charge into battle' woman.

I was bored out of my mind and had been uneasy all morning. Were they all okay? They were too far away for me to sense them, and I was struggling to handle the separation from all my mates at once.

Lokene blinked into the room, flopping onto the bed beside me. Without missing a beat, he pulled me into his arms. His lips captured mine in a kiss that made me light-headed. I was wearing the same outfit as the night before, and I shivered as his fingers found the slit in my pants and brushed along my bare skin.

I was not about to miss this opportunity to do some heavy petting of my own. I found the hem of his T-shirt and pushed it up. My breath caught. I had grown up around Atlantean soldiers, all of whom were in perfect shape... But Lokene was perfection.

The man didn't have a six-pack. Oh, no. He had a twelve-pack. I traced my finger along the chiseled edges of his muscles. He was built like an ancient god, no pun intended.

Lokene snickered.

I scowled at him for reading my thoughts. "I know it has been a long time, and perhaps my memory is mistaken, but I do not remember you looking like this back then."

"I've had a lot of time on my hands while I waited for you to wake up, Sleeping Beauty." Lokene kissed the tip of my nose.

"Can't you just make abs appear?" I thought the Ancients' power was pretty much limitless.

He laughed. "Actually, we can't change our physical bodies. We can change the bodies of others to some extent, and we can change things around us, but we cannot change ourselves. Do you really think any of the Ancients would be fat and bald if they could change it with a simple thought?"

"How strange. Although, perhaps there is some beauty in the fact that even Ancients must learn to be content with themselves."

"Very true, Soyale." His hands moved down my back, pressing me against him.

"How am I able to shift between my human and Siren forms? If I am part Ancient, I shouldn't be able to do that." The more I learned about the Ancients, the more confusing their many rules and limitations seemed.

"Have you forgotten your heritage and gifts, my love? You have powers from the Ancient realm and magik from the earth. The Siren is now an equal part of what you are. You aren't changing into a form that doesn't belong to you; rather, you are shifting into a form that is just as much a part of you as the human form. No one knows exactly what abilities you may possess." As he spoke, his hands continued to caress my body.

My fangs ached with the desire to mark him. Tartarus! I scrambled backward, nearly falling off the bed.

He sat up quickly, confusion clouding his features. "What's wrong, Zosime?"

"I nearly lost control." I held my bottom lip between my teeth. The Siren was tired of waiting for this man. She wanted me to jump him and ride him like a surfer riding a wave.

This time, his shoulders slumped in dejection. "Don't you want me?"

"Are you serious? You can read my mind! You should know how much I want you and to be claimed by you."

He flushed. Lokene actually flushed. "I was distracted and wasn't listening."

That surprised a laugh from me. Mr. Nosey was so distracted by my body that he wasn't paying attention?

Lokene slipped off his shirt and pulled me into his lap.

I stiffened. "Lokene, are you sure? I don't think I'll be able to stop myself." If he continued to kiss me like that, I certainly wouldn't be able to resist marking him.

"Yes, Soyale. The time has come for the bond to be completed. I've waited endless millennia to be with you. It's my turn."

Stretching back out on the bed, he pulled me down on top of him. Hooking his thumbs in the band of my pants, I thought he was going to push them down, but they vanished. My top was gone too. I gasped, staring at him in shock.

"What? I made your clothes out of thin air, and I can make them disappear as well." His hands cupped my face. Leaning in, he added, "Keep that in mind, naughty Siren. I can make your clothing vanish. Any. Time. I. Want."

"You wouldn't dare!" I was horrified and excited by the thought.

"I guess we will see." Lokene's cat-that-caught-the-canary smile told me he would most certainly dare to take my clothes if it pleased him.

Two could play this game. Maybe. I concentrated on his pants, calling to my magik and hoping it could do what I wanted.

For a moment, nothing happened. Lokene lay smirking at me, likely knowing exactly what I was trying to do. Then I was suddenly staring hard at a very naked and very excited male body. I wanted to cheer, but my mouth went dry.

Lokene's jaw dropped open, his eyes widening in shock. "That shouldn't have happened. I made those pants. You shouldn't be able to undo something an Ancient created!"

I crossed my arms under my breasts and lifted my chin. "You shouldn't underestimate me. Ever." I hadn't actually believed I could do it, but there was no need to admit to that out loud.

The movement of my breasts caught his attention, distracting him from the fact he had no pants. Which was good for me since I had no idea where the pants had gone. Did they disintegrate? Or had my magik sent them some-where random?

Grabbing my waist, Lokene rolled me to my back, pressing my body into the mattress with his own. Using his forearms to hold himself up, he kept from squishing me. I wrapped my arms around his neck, and my legs around his waist. This was one of the rare occasions I found myself preferring my human legs to my Siren's tail.

He kissed my neck, slowly moving down my collarbone and then lower to my breast. He paused, his hot breath blowing across the hard peak of my nipple. I arched my back, trying to hurry him along. With a soft laugh, he obliged, sucking my nipple into his mouth and teasing it with his teeth.

Heat bloomed through my body. As he kissed first one breast and then the other, need fanned the flames of my desire into a raging inferno. I was going to burn alive. I needed more. Digging my nails into the mattress, I curled my fingers in the sheets.

The ache in my fangs had gone from dull ache to throbbing pain. As long as he didn't get too close to my teeth, we would be fine, and he could take his sweet time. He must not have been reading my thoughts, or he was trying to tempt me, because he shifted his body and nuzzled my neck. This put his shoulder mere inches from my fangs.

I can control this, I can control—

My fangs sank into his neck in one swift motion. The exotic taste of his blood exploded on my tongue. It was intoxicating.

His body jerked, and he moaned. "I can't believe you are in my arms."

"Mmpf," I agreed, my voice muffled against his skin. I

was relieved that my venom wasn't going to affect him because I could feel it pumping into his bloodstream.

I knew we had a slight problem when his breathing sped up and his heart raced. Forcing myself to release my hold on him, I pulled back and looked into his eyes. His pupils were so large that his irises were barely visible. The thin sliver of iris that I could see glowed. The unnatural light in his eye was a shocking reminder he wasn't human, regardless of how human he appeared.

His erection bumping against my flat stomach distracted me for a moment, turning me on more than I cared to admit.

"Soyale?" he panted out the endearment.

"Yes?" My own breathing was ragged.

"I was wrong. Your venom works on Ancients," he growled, grinding his hips against mine.

My brain tried to focus. This seemed like an important piece of information, something that could make a big difference. A difference in what, I couldn't remember. All I could think about was the feel of his hard erection sliding along my wet slit.

"Oh, Lokene. Please." Great. I couldn't even piece together a coherent sentence.

Lokene murmured something against my neck, but I couldn't make sense of the words. He lifted his body away from mine, and I felt cold at the sudden loss of his body's heat. "Soyale. When we bond, it will change things in our family."

My brain struggled to concentrate. "What do you mean? Why are you telling me this now?"

"Because it had to be now. You had to bond with your other mates first. I had to be last." His face showed signs of strain. He was fighting against my venom's demands. "I'm an Ancient. When we bond, my power is going to surge through the bond."

My heart lurched. "Will your power injure the guys?"

"No, it shouldn't." He sighed. "I don't think it will. We are in uncharted territory, Zosime. I don't know an Ancient who bonded with a human harem, and no Ancient has ever bonded with merpeople."

His glowing eyes met mine. "Nor has an Ancient bonded with a Siren."

"Then how do you know your power is going to surge through the bond?" I demanded, my voice rising.

"I don't know for sure. All I know for sure is that when two Ancients bond, they share power, and it binds them together. It is logical that anyone you have bonded with will also be part of our binding through you."

That seemed logical. "How do we know it won't hurt them?"

"It won't." He closed his eyes. When he opened them, there was desperation. Had my venom done that? "We are out of time, Soyale. We must claim each other now. Say yes. Tell me you want me, that I am yours forever."

"Yes. You belong to me, Ancient." My voice no longer

trembled. It came out as a husky purr meant to excite him more. It worked.

He lined himself up with my slick heat and slowly pushed himself inside me, feeling me until I gasped for breath. I clawed at his chest and arms, wanting more of the exquisite pain.

He thrust into me hard and fast, taking me and making sure I knew who was in control, and I let him believe that was true.

"I love you, Lokene." I clung to his sweat-soaked body. Once more, I sank my fangs into him. This time claiming him as mine.

"You are mine, Soyale. I knew it from the moment I laid eyes on you. I will never let you go again." He placed his right hand over my heart and growled, the sound vibrating through both our bodies. Bodies that were... glowing?

I glanced down the length of our bodies, wondering if I had accidentally shifted into my Siren form, but no, I still appeared human... Except for the glowing tattoos that swirled on my skin. They flickered with the same aquamarine light that I was used to seeing from my scales.

"Our power is responding to each other. The binding has begun." His hips moved faster, sending us flying toward our release.

The exchange of Ancient power called to my earth magik, and the turquoise energy washed over my body like water.

My body felt like it had been set on fire, inside and out.

I needed a release of energy and of desire. "Hurry," I whimpered against his neck.

He didn't reply, but he tilted his hips in such a way that his erection rubbed against me in all the right ways. I felt the release coming only seconds before we came together. I couldn't scream his name. I couldn't even breathe.

White-hot energy exploded in the room, blinding me momentarily, as the power that had been building up released. Relief and contentment wrapped around me like the world's softest blanket.

That one moment of perfection was shattered as I was sucked into a vision. Thousands of short clips played in front of me. The same event playing out a thousand different ways.

I saw miners destroy the world from their greed. Then the vision reset, and I saw weapons made from Orpati decimate earth. Again, the vision reset, and I saw all of humanity tainted by the Lure. Over and over, I watched humanity come to its end. There were thousands of ways the world might end, but I saw only one that might save humanity. Was this just a dream? Or was I being shown what I must do?

I tried to shake myself free of the nightmarish images and finally succeeded, only to be drawn into a vision of Kye where I looked through Kye's eyes.

Storm hadn't seen the second guard come through the corridor on the opposite side of the bow. This guard had a semi-automatic rifle, and he aimed it at Storm's head, pulling the trigger.

I yelled a warning but knew it would be too late. Lunging toward the guard, I threw myself in the path of the bullets. My body jerked as the first two slammed into my torso.

"Kye!" Eason and Storm yelled my name in unison. My shoulder hit the wooden floor of the yacht with a sickening crack. Excruciating pain burned through my body like a wildfire.

"Try not to kill them! I want to get some information from them first!" Richard jumped from his seat and ran for cover inside the boat.

A slick, warm liquid was pooling under my motionless fingers. It didn't take a genius to understand I was bleeding out.

I was dying.

A dart whistled through the air, embedding itself in Storm's shoulder. It must have been a doozy of a tranq, because he collapsed on top of me almost instantly.

These men better hope Zosime never finds them. I was just upset I wouldn't get to see it.

The sound of agonized screams yanked me from my own personal hell. I blinked rapidly and stared around in confusion. My throat burned as though I had swallowed acid. Who was screaming?

I knew who was screaming. It was me.

I'd just watched Kye get shot. They had taken Storm and Eason.

Rolling to the side of the bed, I vomited.

Tears of rage and loss blurred my vision. My mate had laid dying, and his last thought was of me. He'd found pleasure in the thought that I would avenge his death. He wanted vengeance.

Then he would have it in abundance. They would pay for what they had done.

CHAPTER SEVENTEEN

ZOSIME

I heard Lokene shouting my name, but I didn't stop. Running to the bow of the boat, I leaped into the water. The moment my body was swallowed by the sea, I called my magik and shifted effortlessly into my Siren form. I was ready to hunt.

In the past, when I hunted, my emotions had been sealed away. I could do my job without distraction. Now, emotions fought a war inside me. Grief, rage, agony, loss, anguish, and anger swirled within me like a hurricane.

I had believed that emotions hindered me from completing my missions, but I was learning that wasn't completely true. My emotions were a driving force that pushed me harder than I had ever been pushed before.

The binding had done something other than show me my worst nightmares come to life. It had also strengthened the link between my mates and myself. They were still too far away for me to sense them individually, but the bond was strong enough to pull me to them no matter where on earth they might have been.

I focused, trying desperately to teleport myself. Surely, as a half Ancient with some crazy earth magik, I should be able to pull this off. I didn't manage to blink myself to my mates, but I managed to blink myself a few feet.

Come on, Zosime. You are the Queen of Atlantis. You can do better than that.

Focusing hard, I tried to pull at the power that lurked beneath the magik. It didn't move, but the earth magik responded.

This time I had focused on the horizon in front of me, to the furthest point I could see. Again, I blinked myself, and this time I went to the spot I had focused on. I had traveled nearly three miles in the blink of an eye. Smiling grimly, I focused on the horizon, blinking myself another three miles. Over and over, I repeated the process, my rage fueling my magik.

Fynn needs to tell you something, Lokene's voice whispered through my mind.

I'm busy. I blinked again.

Zosi? Lokene is helping me to speak with you. There was an earthquake, just like we feared. It was 7.5 on the Richter scale. Fynn's panic was palpable.

I don't know what any of that means. Can't this wait? I am busy. I wasn't in the mood to talk about earthquakes. My whole world had been shaken, and my focus was on finding my mates.

Zosime, a tsunami has formed and is heading for land. I could hear the defeat in Fynn's voice.

What do you want me to do? I ground my teeth together. Fynn was upset, and I wanted to be there for him, but I needed to take care of things first. Clouds had gathered overhead, blocking out the sun. Lightning crackled over my head as large drops of rain pelted the sea.

I don't even know. I just thought maybe you could do something... Fynn's voice trailed off.

Where is this tsunami going to hit? And when? I blinked again.

It's going to hit the city where you are headed, and it will hit there in about ten minutes, was his soft reply.

How do you know where I am headed?

Because I know where Richard Jack' headquarters is located. Lokene told me what you saw, and I know you are going after him. Fynn was somber. *Zosi? Make him pay. Make them all pay.*

Thunder boomed overhead, and lightning crackled across the sky.

In the vision, Kye wanted me to act as an avenging angel and gain revenge for his death. Fynn wanted me to act as a guardian angel and save the lives of countless strangers. Could I be both? For my mates, I would try.

If I was going to do the impossible and stop a powerful force of nature, I was going to need to pick up the pace. Closing my eyes, I once again reached past the magik and called for the power that lay dormant.

Nothing happened.

I didn't have time for this. What was that phrase about grabbing bulls by the horns? Instead of asking nicely, this time, I mentally reached inside and grabbed the power. Agony surged through me. Light exploded around me for the second time that day. It lasted only ten seconds before the light faded and the pain ebbed away.

I smiled. The different parts of me had just snapped together like a puzzle. I had been powerful as a Siren, but now this Siren had the power of the Ancients surging through her veins. It was time to see what these new powers could do.

I focused on the energy that was coursing through me. It was wild and out of control, and I worried it would slip from my grasp. I wasn't sure what would happen if I lost control of it, but I wasn't eager to find out.

Show me the city. I need to see a mental picture. My power surged and crackled around me as I begged my abilities to once again adapt to a situation. I shouted the command directly into Fynn's mind, knowing that Lokene had already pushed boundaries by connecting our minds for the first time. He could not risk getting involved with my plan.

Relief swelled through me when I heard Fynn's voice, weak but clear through the mental link. *How do I show you?*

Find a picture of the city's shoreline. Create the picture in your mind. I need every tiny detail. Just like an artist with his masterpiece, I need you to speak to me without using words. You are conveying your thoughts with an image. I will see it, just as I can hear you. I hoped I was right.

I found an image online. I am building the image in my mind. You have to hurry, Zosi. I caught the rising note of panic in his voice. The same panic was clawing at my insides, but this was my only chance to beat the deadly wave to shore. This had to work.

I focused on the mental link, sending some of my antsy power through the bond. A blurry image wavered in my mind. I let a bit more power trickle into the mental link. The picture faded, and my heart sank. Then there was a snap, and I saw the image as clearly as if I were looking out at the scene myself.

It worked! You did it, Fynn!

It did? Are you sure? His words were hopeful.

Yes! I have to go so I can focus. I started to cut the connection and then paused. *Fynn? My love for you runs deeper than the ocean. Never forget that.*

Zosi! What aren't you telling me? Fynn's voice had grown hoarse with emotion.

The mental link snapped like a rubber band. I had less than five minutes if I wanted to beat the wave to shore. I brought the image to mind, concentrating hard on the tiny details. If this went wrong, I could end up sitting in the same spot, or for all I knew, I could end up blinking into another realm.

Keeping my eyes closed, I pulled at my magik and power. I spoke about what I intended to do and prayed my chaotic abilities wouldn't fail me.

I blinked.

My body slammed into submerged rocks. I opened my eyes and saw to my relief that I was on the beach. The buildings and businesses from Fynn's image were exactly where they should be, even down to the placement of light poles and trash cans.

Water pulled at my body, dragging me across bits of sharp rocks and jagged shells. I had intended to teleport myself to the shallows and then shift before walking onto the beach. I must have miscalculated because I was lying on my stomach in water too shallow to cover myself. I glanced over my shoulder and instantly realized why.

The water was rushing out to sea, leaving the shoreline littered with shells and debris. Children squealed in delight and ran to collect treasures to put in their tiny rainbow-colored buckets. Adults lifted their cellphones, recording the strange scene in front of them.

"RUN!" I screamed until my throat ached. When several of the cellphones swung my way, I knew I had made a mistake. I should have shifted before drawing attention to myself.

"What is that thing?" a man's voice shouted.

"Is that what is causing the water to disappear?" a woman asked.

"I'm calling the police! Don't let it get away!" another male commanded.

Since awakening, I had thought often of introducing myself to humans. I'd played out one scenario after another. Every single one had ended badly, and now I was living one of my worst nightmares. I was an 'it,' a 'thing' to treat with disgust. My heart hurt from shame and anger.

"Stop! Jill! Come back!" a mother screeched in horror. Her daughter ran toward me, throwing her arms around my neck.

"Mermaid!" The tiny human clung to my neck, giggling happily. Tilting her head so she could look into my face, she placed her small hand on my cheek. "Pretty."

I awkwardly patted her back. It would take time to grow comfortable being touched by anyone other than my mates.

A roar in the distance brought my focus back to the dire situation we were facing. I looked out over the sea, my stomach dropping to the tip of my tail when I saw the wave rising from the sea.

"κοριτσάκι," I hesitated. She wasn't likely to understand Greek. I tried again. "Little girl, you need to go to your mother. The beach isn't safe. I need you to run."

"Help! She's got my daughter!" The mother was terrified.

"Go!" I ordered the tiny human.

She cried, but obeyed me and ran to her mother.

I called my magik and shifted into my human form. This time, as I shifted, I thought about clothing. If Lokene could make clothes appear, surely I could. Right?

I wanted my Atlantean armor but feared I wouldn't be able to create so many tiny details for my first-time creating garments. The outfit Lokene had made for me was still fresh in my memory. It was definitely not intended to wear into battle, but it was better than going to battle nude.

The change was seamless. When I stood, my body was covered in shimmering turquoise pants and a top.

I hurried toward the churning sea. The tsunami was bearing down on the shore. The wave had grown to a height of nearly a hundred feet. Its shadow fell on the sandy beach, the sheer size of it blocking out the sun.

People screamed, sirens blared, and the ocean roared in rage. Humans had caused this with their greed. The ocean didn't pick this fight, but it planned to finish it. These people were small-minded, but they were not directly responsible for the actions that set off this chain of events.

My heart cried in sadness for the pain of the earth and sea, but at the same time, I felt my heart break at the thought of the innocents, like the sweet child, who would be lost if the monstrous wave impacted the city.

With a battle cry of my own, I braced my feet in the sand and threw up my hands in preparation for the fight of my life. Magik rippled across my skin, flickering in an aquamarine glow. Strength poured into me, and I ground my teeth together as my body adjusted to the shift in my abilities.

I looked at the wave as it reached its tipping point and began crashing toward earth. I needed more. I screamed and did the only thing I could.

I released my hold on the Ancient power that was battering my insides in a bid for freedom, and I prayed it was willing to help.

CHAPTER EIGHTEEN

ZOSIME

P ower and magik swirled and danced inside me, each
fighting for dominance. They finally blended to
create energy that surged through my body, waiting to be
called.

The last of the wall that had sealed away my emotions
shattered into a thousand pieces. A torrent of intense
emotion was released and created more chaos inside me, the
devastation over the loss of my family. Agonizing sorrow
from the memories of Atlantis, the homeland I have given
my all for. Debilitating sorrow when I recalled the vision of
Kye getting shot and his blood pooling around him. Shame
for not being there for him when he needed me most. Rage
against the men who had kidnapped my mates.

The beach was cast into shadow as the tsunami hit land and began to collapse. My limbs shook from the strain. This was all too much. I was only one person, one woman. How could I take on a force of nature that demanded justice?

The humans were right in their disgust. I was an unnatural thing. I shouldn't even exist. Maybe I truly was a monster that lurked in the depths, dooming men to watery graves with nothing more than a look and a single word.

Tiny arms wrapping around my leg dragged me from my thoughts. My heart stuttered in shock. I hadn't heard the child approach.

My throat closed in fear and horror for this little innocent who was soon to pay for the mistakes of the generations before her. What had the mother called her? "Jill? Why are you here? You need to run! Please!" I tried gently to shove her away, but that only caused her to hold on tighter.

"I'm scared!" she wailed. "Mommy fell and hit her head. She's not moving." Watery brown eyes looked up at me, pleading for my help.

Water poured down as the wave arched over our heads.

The magik swirled in my chest, beating against the confines of my physical body, begging to be released. I breathed in and squared my shoulders. This is what I had vowed to do when I was little more than a teenager. Protect. It didn't matter if they were born in Atlantis, because I wasn't just a daughter of Atlantis. I was a daughter of the Ancients. I had been born on earth and changed by the sea. I was exactly what the world needed right now.

Tattoos glowed on my skin, the same ones that had appeared when Lokene and I bonded. Power exploded out of me, and the wave stopped.

It didn't collapse on our heads, nor did it recede. The great arching wall of water was suspended as though time had paused.

With the whimpering child still clinging to my leg, I braced myself and called to the sea. "I know you are in pain. You are taken for granted and abused. Thieves steal your resources, never considering the cost to all life on earth should the oceans be destroyed. They tossed trash and waste into your waters without a second thought for the creatures who live in the seas. Hurricanes, floods, and tsunamis are your way of drawing attention to these issues, but we need to find another way. This will only end with more lives lost and more sadness."

I didn't care if the entire world thought I was crazy; I knew the earth and her waters were very much alive. I could feel the earth's magik within me, filled with pain, but also a flicker of hope.

I moved my hands steadily out toward the sea. My movements were confident, as though I controlled hundred-foot walls of water on a regular basis.

The water calmed, no longer a raging torrent. I pushed it back until it collapsed onto the sandy seabed with a crash. The impact sent a gust of wind across the land, flattening grass, blowing sand, and tossing people around like dolls... But at least they weren't dead. I considered that a win.

As the wall of water collapsed, it displaced water and sent another wave surging onto the beach. This wave was much smaller, but it still stood nearly twelve feet tall. I scooped the girl up in my arms, throwing up my hand as the surge barreled toward us.

Water exploded around me as though the wave had hit a solid glass wall. We stayed dry as the power of the ocean slammed into my invisible shield. I watched as the sea washed away the debris and pushed vehicles around on the pavement.

There would be mild flooding in the areas closest to the shore, but it was nothing compared to the devastation the city would have faced had the great wall of water crashed into it.

I made my way through and found the sobbing mother frantically slogging her way through the water, looking for her daughter. When she caught sight of the little girl waving at her from my arms, relief and joy exploded across the desperate mother's face. She gently took Jill from my arms and cradled her against her chest.

"Thank you." The words were barely intelligible between her sobs, but I knew what she meant.

I made my way down the street, allowing the pull of the mate bond to guide me to my men.

I tried to reach out and create a mental link with Storm or Eason, like I had with Fynn, but I was met with silence. I hoped it was simply because Lokene had not helped us create a mental link yet, but I worried it was because someone injured them badly enough that they weren't even conscious.

The mate bond pulled me one street over. It drew me to one of the largest buildings in the area. The name 'Jackon Enterprises' was emblazoned on a gold plaque on the outside wall.

I'd found him. It didn't matter if he was on land or at sea. I was a hunter, and I always found my prey.

Reaching up, I grabbed the giant glass doors and pulled hard on the handles. They didn't budge, so I tried again. It was no use; they were locked. Peering through the glass, I watched as a man in uniform walked toward me. He stopped in front of me on the opposite side of the glass.

"We are closed, ma'am. Please call during business hours to make an appointment."

I scoffed. He wanted me to make an appointment? The Lure had contaminated this man's soul. It was black and eroded. The call beat like a drum in my mind, telling me what I must do.

There wasn't a doubt in my mind. My mates were in this building. A building that oozed the disgusting inky taint of the Lure. I wasn't leaving here without them, and I was tired of attempting to use human manners.

The water was up over my feet in this area of the city. This time, when I threw my hands up, I didn't have to tell my magik what I wanted. It knew intuitively what I desired.

The force of the water crashing into the imposing glass

doors caused them to blow off their hinges and be tossed inside the building as though they weighed nothing. One door crashed into the guard, knocking him so hard that he collapsed onto the ground, his head connecting with the marble tiles with a sickening crack. The doors slammed into the marble floor, shattering the glass and scattering it across the floor. Shrill alarms began to shriek throughout the building.

The pull of the mate bond stirred my rage. They had what was mine. Thunder rumbled, and the building trembled. Blinding lightning streaked across the sky. The lights in the building flickered. I stepped into the building like I owned it.

Seeing my grand entrance, a guard rushed out from behind the front desk, and four guards came down the corridor toward me. Water rushed into the lobby behind me. At the same instant, all five men drew their guns, leveling the sleek black weapons at my head.

"Stop right there! Take another step, and we will shoot!" The man's voice was cold as ice. The Lure's presence in this building was so thick, I could almost taste it.

I wasn't an idiot. The only reason they hadn't fired yet was so they could question me. There was no way they were going to let me walk out of this building alive. Funny, I felt the same about them.

I took another step, maintaining eye contact the entire time. They pulled the triggers, the sound of gunfire ricocheting off the walls. As the bullets neared me, I threw up my hand, and a wall of water intercepted the bullets, knocking them harmlessly to the floor.

I twisted my hand, using the water to sweep up the shards of broken glass. With a quick flick of my wrist, I sent the shards flying into the chest and necks of the guards who had fired at me. Their deaths were instant and far more merciful than they deserved.

The building had an open layout, and looking up, I could see each floor all the way up to the arched ceiling far above me. Each floor had solid glass, waist-high viewing walls, and brass banisters. This allowed guests to lean safely on the rails and look down into the lobby or call out to people on the other floors.

A large glittering chandelier hung from the golden ceiling. It dangled down three stories in an opulent show of wealth. A glass column rose on one side of the room, and a metal machine hummed inside it, moving from floor to floor.

Shouted commands came from the floors above me as guards poured out of the rooms. I looked up to find that on various floors, there were about twenty men leaning over the rails with their weapons trained on me.

I didn't have time for this; I wanted my mates, and I wanted to go home. I had stopped a tsunami; didn't I deserve a good meal and a fin rub?

The call drummed in my head. Its demanding command drilled into my skull, and I could feel a migraine coming on. There was just too much evil and so many Lure-tainted souls surrounding me.

This building needed to come down. It was a den of sadistic cruelty and obscene greed. I could swear the evil was a living, breathing entity that slid across my skin like a coating of slimy algae. It was suffocating me.

The machine in the glass column moved. From what I could see from where I stood, it was the only way up or down inside this building. Several armed guards rushed toward it. Heck no. I didn't need everyone moving around, and I sure didn't have time to stand here and wait for guard after guard to shoot at me.

Running toward the door of the glass column, I called the water and slammed it hard into the elevator. The elevator shook and groaned, but it was well constructed and did not give under the blast.

I spun around, gathering water around me like a minia-ture hurricane. This time when I sent the stream of water toward the glass box, the water drilled into the glass. The glass exploded, and tiny pieces rained down from three stories above. It would have been beautiful if I had been able to enjoy it... but I had found the man I was looking for.

Richard Jackon.

He leaned casually against the brass banister on the top floor. He was smirking down at me. "Those are some impressive skills you have. Too bad you don't have the brains to go along with them. I'm going to enjoy having my scientists take you apart and figure out how you've managed these impressive tricks."

I clenched my jaw. Even though he was eight stories above me, I could feel the palpable evil that rolled off him in waves. I'd never met someone with a soul as black as his. There was no light in this man. In all honesty, I didn't think he had a soul at all.

Sweat beaded my body as the call's steady drumbeat picked up speed.

Kill. Destroy.

My gums ached, and my mouth went dry. I needed to finish this.

Richard's laughter rang out, loud and nasty. "That elevator was the only way for you to reach this floor, and now it appears it will be out of order for a while."

I snorted. "I don't need your elevator."

My heart cried out to the sea, whose waters still flooded the streets around the building and the lobby. I called it to me. The saltwater rushed to obey me, wrapping itself around me like an eager puppy awaiting his master's command.

With a spin, I leaped into the air, the waters spinning beneath me, launching me toward the ceiling with effortless ease as it continued to surge up behind me.

Richard's eyes widened when he realized I was coming for him, and there was nothing he could do to stop me. The man didn't have a clue what I was capable of. Nor did he realize just how badly he had ticked me off.

"What are you all standing there for! Shoot her!" His voice held fear and panic, a beautiful sound that thrilled the hunter in me.

A flurry of automatic gunfire came from all around me.

I called to my magik, smiling as my body hummed with energy. He wanted to play?

Bring it.

CHAPTER NINETEEN

ZOSIME

I spun, the water dancing around me. For a moment, I felt as though I were back in the ocean, moving weightlessly through the waters as I flipped and dove.

The water that could be so gentle and playful morphed into something feral. It lashed out at everything around me, a hurricane seeking what it could destroy. The chandelier above my head swayed dangerously as though it were a giant pendulum.

The barrage of bullets hit the water churning around me, only to be batted away like pesky, buzzing insects. Many of the bullets fell harmlessly to the floor, which was now several floors below me. Other bullets ricocheted off the brass banisters and marble-covered walls, and ended up embedding themselves in the shooters. Not a single bullet managed to get past the water to me.

Even with many of their comrades bleeding out on the floors, the rest continued to fire round after round at me. It wasn't enough to defend myself; I needed to end this. Now.

Wind whipped around me, tugging violently at my clothing and tangling hair. A blinding bolt of lightning slammed into the ground just outside the building, shaking the earth with its power. All the lights in the building flickered, and then with a loud snap, the electricity went out. The massive storm that raged outside was blocking the sun, so when the power failed, it left us in semi-darkness.

Through the chaos, I saw Richard rush inside his office, slamming the glass doors behind him. I heard the click of locks as he tried to barricade himself inside the suite.

Yet the man called me stupid? What an idiot.

Those glass doors would not keep him safe, nor were they going to keep me out when I reached him.

An ominous groan came from above me, and I looked up sharply. The oversized chandelier swung wildly, the metal creaking as it bent this way and that. With a terrifying crack, the anchors holding it to the ceiling tore free, and the chandelier hurtled toward the earth, and I was in its path.

There was a moment where my heart stuttered in fear, and I believed the glass monstrosity hurtling toward me was going to impale and then crush me beneath it. The fear dissipated instantly when I remembered I was currently floating mid-air, on a pedestal made up of angry water.

Seawater that almost seemed to enjoy the chance to destroy everything within its reach. I didn't wake up this morning only to die by something as ugly as this chandelier.

Not today, Hades. Not today.

I concentrated on the magik and power that vibrated inside me, just waiting to be released. With a battle cry, I sent out a burst of energy. It exploded out of me, a wave that blew through the room. Nothing in its path remained untouched. The chandelier disintegrated as it fell in every direction, but not a piece touched me.

Spiderweb cracks appeared and spread through the floor-to-ceiling glass windows, and across the glass walls that surrounded each floor. There was a pause as everyone froze, mesmerized by the horrifying sight of the traveling lines that spelled trouble. No one dared to move or breathe.

Then, the glass exploded outward. Broken shards became weapons as they flew through the room, embedding into walls, furniture, and every guard in the room. The only sound in the large room was that of the falling glass as it rained down, a deadly sparkling shower, on the marble floors.

With no guards left to stop me, I let the water carry me to the top floor. I stepped from my watery pedestal, my chin lifted and body humming. I released my hold on the water, mentally thanking it for its help, and allowing it to return with a splash to the floor below.

I stared at the wall of glass. What was it with this man and glass? Richard stood on the other side, leaning back against a tall mahogany desk. His arms and legs were crossed casually, as though he didn't have a care in the world... as if I hadn't just destroyed his building and slaughtered his security team.

I looked closer at the glass that separated us. It was the only thing keeping me from finding my mates. Hairline fractures ran throughout the glass, and I smirked. This was going to be easy. Too easy.

Leaning forward, I opened my mouth and blew softly. There was no way he could have seen the energy I released at the same time. For a moment, nothing happened. Richard raised a mocking brow at me.

In slow motion, the glass shattered into millions of pieces, the tiny crystals exploding into the room. I flipped my long hair over my shoulder and walked in with the confidence of a visiting queen. Glass moved slowly, as though it was moving through honey all around me.

Richard's mouth dropped open, and he scrambled over his desk, seeking cover. There was no place for him to go to escape me. I took my time, allowing the glass to drop and skitter across the floor in all directions.

"Stop!" Richard held up a hand. He meant the gesture to be threatening, but it came across as desperate. "Don't come any closer!"

"Or what? There is nothing you can do to me. Your men are dead. No one is coming to save you. If they do, I'll kill them as well."

"There has to be something you want! Name your price!" He was openly begging now. Pathetic.

I tilted my head, studying this pitiful excuse for a human. "You already have something of mine. I am here to take them back."

"Yes! I'm sorry! Whatever it is, I'll give it back. I have money, I'll pay you back and include interest! Just don't kill me. I'm an important man; the world needs me."

I sneered at him. "You are not important. You have no value as a human, and when I kill you, the earth will rejoice. Even your death will not repay me for what you took from me."

"Wha-what did I take? I've never met you before!"

I stepped closer, leaning down until our faces nearly touched. "You ordered your men to kidnap my mates, and when they didn't come quietly, you ordered them to be shot."

Confusion clouded his expression. The man had killed so many that he struggled to guess which men I was talking about.

"Where are they? Storm and Eason. Tell me now, and your death will be quick. Delay, and I will make your death excruciatingly painful."

I stepped back, watching understanding dawning on him.

"Swear you won't kill me, and I will take you to them."

That might have worked if I hadn't been able to read

the man's thoughts. As soon as I said Storm's name, his thoughts went into overdrive.

I knew where my men were, which meant I no longer needed him.

"I gave you a choice, and you chose to delay. You will die painfully, and I will enjoy it. My shark will enjoy you."

"If you take one more step, I'll kill them!" he screamed, slapping a button on his desk and waving frantically to the wall furthest from us.

The white wall had no decor except a long smoke-colored mirror that ran the length of it. The tinted hue of the mirror shifted, and what I saw sent joy rushing through me, but it was followed quickly by white-hot fury. Never in my life had I experienced such strong emotions. I lost it.

Behind the mirror sat my mates. Pale skinned, with blood soaking their clothes. I turned to look at the man I hated more than I had hated anyone in my entire life. Hate wasn't even a strong enough word for how I felt about this man.

"I hope you like hot weather, because the only place left in this realm you can go to escape from me is Tartarus."

CHAPTER TWENTY

ZOSIME

I launched myself on his back. There was no need to waste time with this man or his pleas filled with lies. I willed my fangs to drop and prayed I wouldn't end up shifting fully into my Siren form. That would be awkward.

My fangs descended, and taking a quick peek at my body, I was relieved to see they were the only part of me that had shifted.

"You're a vampire? That's impossible." He grabbed for his neck, scrambling away from me. I wanted to laugh at his futile efforts.

The last thing I wanted was to sink my fangs into this man who was so contaminated by the Lure. I gagged a little at the thought. If I plugged my nose, could I avoid the rancid taste?

I stared down at him, biting my fingernail as I thought about the best way to kill him... slowly. Then I knew.

I let venom seep into my mouth, and then I slowly licked each nail, making sure to use just the right amount. Too much, and he would die far too quickly. Too little, and he could cause me more issues.

When finished, I sank my fingernails deep into the skin of his neck, not giving him time for a grandiose speech or to reach for a weapon. I was done playing games. It had been a freaking long day.

His body convulsed, and I smelled the acrid scent of urine as he lost control of his bodily functions. Leaning away from him, I looked down in disgust. He had already lost control of his muscles and was unable to speak. Silent, just like a good little victim.

I wanted him to know that he'd been beaten by a girl, and he hadn't even had time to lift a finger against me. I wanted him to see this sanctuary that he had built crumble before his eyes. Most of all, I wanted the last thing he saw to be Sheba's toothy grin.

A quick, merciful death would have been a kindness, and I wasn't feeling particularly kind. It had been a people-y kind of day, and I was beginning to think I wasn't a huge fan of people. I wanted to be where the people weren't... At least for a while.

His mouth may have been quiet, but his thoughts certainly weren't.

Who is she? If she worked for the government, I would have heard about her. Plus, they would've sent a team with her. Who sends out a single woman on a rescue mission? Is she even a woman? The stuff she did in the lobby isn't human...

I decided to answer him out loud. "I would've found you, eventually. I hunt for those who have corrupted souls like you. When you started paying your crew to destroy the seafloor in search of Orpati, you put yourself on my mates' radar. When you ordered my men shot and kidnapped, you put yourself on my radar. You didn't have hope of escaping me after that."

I walked toward the mirrored wall, talking over my shoulder. "I am the Queen of Atlantis, and these men belong to me."

I RAN MY HANDS ALONG THE GLASS OF THE TWO-WAY mirror, trying to determine how best to get them out of the tiny interrogation room. My hands shook, and tears burned my eyes. I needed to touch them, to feel their arms around me.

"Enough." I growled. Trying to find the hidden entrance to the room was taking too long. This time, I didn't even bother summoning my power before I rammed my shoulder into the wall. My power crackled around me, and the wall cracked, pieces of drywall falling like dust onto the plush carpeted floor.

I backed up and then ran full strength at the wall, throwing my hands up at the last minute to block the dust from my face. The wall turned to dust around me, and I launched myself straight into Kye's lap.

"I thought you were dead!" I sobbed against his neck. "I saw you die in my vision!"

"Yeah, I thought I was, too." Angling his head, he buried his face in my tangled hair.

"You were dead, Kye," Storm spoke up, his voice pained.

I smiled at Storm and Eason, blowing them a kiss before turning back to Kye. "How are you alive?"

He looked just as confused as me. "I can't explain it. I remember knowing I was dying, and then I woke up like I had just been asleep."

"He died. We were lying on the deck of Richard's yacht. There was something like a surge of power between us. It burned through the tranquilizers in our systems and healed our injuries." I had missed Storm's deep calm voice.

"And a lot of good that did us. Richard's guys beat the crap out of us once we got here, all for information about the Orpati, which we refused to give," Eason grumbled and then winked at me.

"Having our injuries be healed was incredible, but I got the biggest shock of my life when a very dead Kye suddenly gasped in air right next to me. No sooner had he started breathing, the idiot started laughing." Storm shook his head in bewilderment.

I had a sneaking suspicion that I knew exactly how Kye had managed to survive death. What I didn't know was why he would laugh. I looked back at Kye. "Why did you laugh?"

"Because my last thought had been how amazing it was going to be when you hunted Richard down. When I realized I wasn't dead, I knew I would get a front-row seat, and I couldn't wait!" He looked over my shoulder to where Richard was lying, wide-eyed and drooling, on the floor watching us. "Zosi girl, you were glorious!"

I smiled, placing a kiss on his cheek. "We aren't finished yet. Come. It's time to get out of here."

Placing my hands over the chains that bound their hands to the chairs, my power easily shattered the metal. They rubbed their hands and wrists, working on getting the blood flowing again. One by one, they took turns embracing me.

I wanted a lot more than a hug. I needed blood, a week spent snuggling in bed, and a long cry while Kye held me. My mind was refusing to believe he really stood there in front of me. Alive.

I led the way out of Richard's suite, dragging the man across the floor behind me as though he weighed nothing. My mates had offered to carry him for me, but he was my prey. It seemed I couldn't quite let go of the Siren's predatory mindset, whether I was in the sea or on land. This was just who I was. I felt myself smiling, and I was really okay with it.

Reaching the edge of the floor, I looked down at the shattered glass and realized we didn't have an easy way to get down. I slapped my forehead, annoyed at how dense I had been. I had the ability to teleport... An ability I had forgotten to use during this fight. Things might have been easier had I been using it.

Hoping that it would work, I closed my eyes and teleported the men, one at a time, to the lobby below. I then blinked Richard and me down as well. I walked out into the sunset; the storm had nearly cleared, and patches of blue sky could be seen.

As we walked away, I turned back toward the damaged building. Throwing my fist up, I brought it down hard. Richard's grand headquarters imploded, and fire flared from the rubble, quickly turning the ruins into an inferno. Richard's face reflected the orange and red flames, and I leaned down to whisper in his ear, "Get a good look at that fire, Richard. You will be seeing a lot of those in the underworld."

As we walked along the edge of the ocean, I reached out to Lokene. *Where are you, my love?*

On the beach, where you came ashore. Come to me, Soyale, he responded immediately.

I looked out to sea, longing to jump in, but knowing we needed to get to Lokene and return to the yacht, our home. A dorsal fin sliced through the water.

"Sheba!" I cried, thrilled to see she had come to check up on me. I wondered if the creature had learned to teleport herself or just always managed to be in the right place at the right time.

"I have someone I would like you to eat, I mean, meet."

Richard's thoughts screamed through my mind. Curses and pleas mixing into a jumbled mess. I tossed him in the water, knowing he wouldn't be able to swim or fight, not with my venom slowing shutting down his body.

There was a tremendous splash as Sheba turned and snatched him from the surface before disappearing into the depths. I brushed my hands together, sighing as the demands of the call faded away with Richard's death.

Without my needing to drag Richard's weight, we made quick time to the docks, where several people rushed at me. I covered my eyes as lights popped and a crowd pushed toward us.

"There she is! That's the woman!" a man shouted.

"She saved my daughter!" I recognized Jill's mother in the crowd.

"Who are you?" one man shouted.

I paused, glancing out over the sea to the faces of the mermaids and merman that bobbed out on the surface of the water.

They came to make sure their Queen was okay, Lokene whispered in my mind. There was pride in his voice.

With the grace of a Siren, I turned to face the flashing

lights, whirring camera gear, and faces filled with curiosity and a touch of fear.

I smiled, the Siren enjoying the attention. My voice dropped to the husky pitch that exuded allure and absolute confidence.

"I am Zosime, Queen of Atlantis."

"What are you?" A woman pushed from between the cowering men. I admired her bravery.

Thunder boomed over our heads, and in perfect unison, twin bolts of lightning hit the two large light poles behind me. The sound was deafening. Beautiful, fiery sparks showered down around us. The crowd stepped back in unison, giving me some much-needed space.

"I am the Royal Storm of Atlantis."

I turned to leave but stopped, looking over my shoulder at the woman who stood with her back straight as she watched me. Curiosity piqued, I asked her, "What is your name?"

"Erin." She straightened her jacket and put her shoulders back.

I could read her thoughts and knew she was terrified, but nothing in her posture or voice gave that away. I admired that. After all, fear was nothing to be ashamed of, and it often helped to keep us alive. It was when you let fear take over your life that it became a problem.

"Do you have a number where I can contact you?" Her eyes sparked with interest, and she eagerly fumbled to pull out a card and bring it to me. I looked down at the white slip of paper and the numbers printed there.

"Change is coming, and there is work to be done. I need a liaison between my kingdom and the governments of earth. You will be perfect for the job. I'll be in touch."

I strode toward the sea where my men waited, arms crossed on their chest like personal security guards.

I threw my arms around Lokene's neck, clinging to him and not caring who saw. "You knew. Didn't you?" Leaning back, I looked into his eyes, searching for answers, but knowing he wouldn't give me any.

"Knew what?" he asked, a twinkle in his eye.

"You knew Kye was going to get shot and that he would die." I ran my fingers along his stubbled jaw.

"I saw many timelines. I know you also had a vision after we claimed each other, so you know what it is like to see the past, the present, and the future now."

He was right. I did know. It was terrifying and overwhelming and not something I ever wanted to repeat.

"In how many of those timelines did Kye die?" My voice broke.

He closed his eyes, looking away from me. "All but one."

"You knew that when we claimed each other, and our powers bound us together, it would save his life. That's why you waited to bond with me, isn't it? You did it to save Kye."

Emotion crossed his face, but he quickly disguised it with a smirk. "I don't know what you're talking about. I just wanted to wait until we got some time alone so I could have you all to myself." He pulled me into his arms, holding me tight against him. "I want you to be happy, always."

That brought tears flooding into my eyes. "I can never thank you enough, Lokene."

"Putting up with me for the rest of your life will be thanks enough." His hand slid down my back and pinched my butt.

I laughed and shoved away from him. My heart was overflowing. My men were safe, all of them.

"Take me home." I paused at the word home. How odd. When I had awakened, I had felt homesick for the land. Now, I missed the comfort of being surrounded by the sea. A rogue wave broke on the shore, soaking us all in its salty spray. I eyed the ocean suspiciously. Was it messing with me?

My mates were dripping wet. Their now semi-transparent clothes clinging to bulging muscles. I licked my lips, unable to help myself. My voice was low and husky when I finally spoke. "Yes, let's get home. I'm starving."

SIREN'S TRIBUTE

ROYAL STORM OF ATLANTIS, BOOK 3

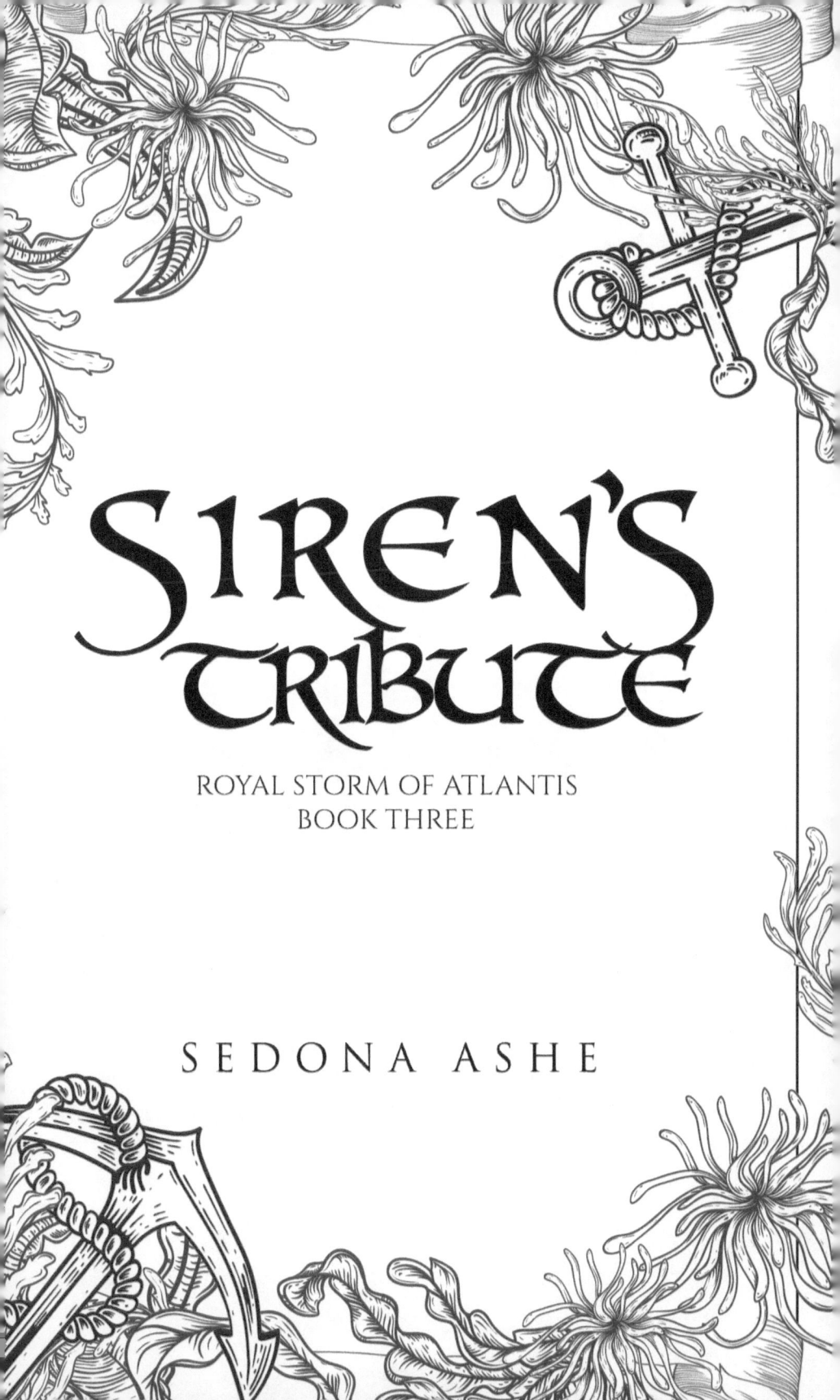

SIREN'S TRIBUTE

ROYAL STORM OF ATLANTIS
BOOK THREE

SEDONA ASHE

Warning:

This is a spicy read with detailed intimate scenes.
Check that your AC is turned on before you start reading. 😉

CHAPTER ONE

ZOSIME

I watched the guys flop around on the land like the fish out of water. Did I look that ridiculous when I was on land?

"You've made your point, Lokene!" Storm huffed.

"Yeah, dude. You could have at least done this when we were, I don't know, in the water?" Kye groaned into the dirt.

Eason lay flat on his back, silently staring up at the sky. He was probably plotting Lokene's demise.

"I was just trying to help. You have a siren mate who spends most of her time in the water. I thought it would help you understand her better if you experienced being half-fish as well." Lokene shrugged one elegant shoulder, a poop-eating grin spreading across his face.

"I might have believed you if you'd dropped us in the water where Zosime could spend the afternoon showing us her world. This—" Storm gave a hard thrust and twisted, trying to sit up. I bit my lip hard to keep from laughing when he too faced-planted in the dirt.

"You guys need to be prepared for the unexpected. Zosime is about to pick a fight with some very dangerous Ancients." The smile still played around Lokene's mouth, but his words held worry. He didn't like my plan, and it was straining our relationship. My body longed for him, but more than that, my heart needed the reassurance of our bond as I prepared for the biggest fight of my life.

Striding over to Storm, I helped him flip onto his back. He grunted his thanks, which I brushed away. There was no need to embarrass my mate any further. I trailed my fingertips down the length of his shimmery gray tail. It was the color of the swords of Atlantis, a brilliant flashing silver that would confuse predators and prey in the water.

"Your tail is as stunning as it is battle worthy." *Even if you wouldn't know how to use it,* I added silently. I hoped my words would soothe some of his humiliation over the situation Lokene had thrown them into.

Storm caught my hand and brought it to his lips. The heat of his mouth pressing against my palm caused my stomach to flip. With a laugh, I moved away from him before I could give in to the always-present need. It was a vicious cycle, and the need for their bodies and blood was a hard impulse to gain control over.

I moved to help Kye, only to find that he'd propped himself up on his elbow. With a clumsy flop of his fluke, he waggled his eyebrows, winking suggestively. "I bet you want a piece of this sexy tail."

Eason and Lokene snorted, bursting into laughter at a joke I didn't understand. Planting my hands on my hips, I tilted my head. "Why would I want part of your tail? I have my own tail, and mine is better suited to fighting than this showy tail with flowing fins that Lokene has given you."

Kye grabbed his chest over his heart and fell back into the dirt. "That hurts, Zosi. Way to kill my masculinity."

Rolling my eyes at Kye's dramatics, I walked silently to stand by Eason. Lokene had given him a tail similar to that of an orca rather than a fish. His lower body was covered in black and white skin, not scales. It was sleek, and his massive fluke would propel him quickly through the water. If Eason learned to use this tail, he would be a powerful fighter in the water. Unfortunately, on land, he was more vulnerable because trying to move the considerable weight of the fluke expended far too much energy.

"He's a beached whale. Get it?" Lokene started to snicker with the other men, but then he paused. His body grew stiff, and all playfulness drained from his face. When he spoke next, his words were clipped. "Enough, we need to go."

I tried to locate the source of his irritation, but there was no one but the four of us on this abandoned shoreline. I opened my mouth to ask what was going on but was cut off as the world tilted on its axis and inky blackness swallowed us.

CHAPTER TWO

ZOSIME

"Seriously, Lokene? You couldn't warn us?" Fynn groaned, pushing himself off the stone floor, where they had landed in a heap. Their tails had disappeared, and they were back in their fully human bodies.

Lokene had brought us to Atlantis instead of our boat. I turned to him, not missing the slight irritation that passed across his face before it disappeared, replaced by his ever-present smirk.

"Lokene, what's going on?" I strode to him, wrapping my arms around him and pressing my cheek against his shirt. He smelled of pure sexiness, and burning hot memories flashed through my mind.

"Nothing. I simply grew bored with the men's incessant

413

whining." His eyes didn't quite meet mine, and there was no hiding how tense he was beneath my fingers.

Lokene, you are hiding something from me, I whispered in his mind. *I want to know the truth.*

The truth? Lokene gave a harsh laugh. *The Ancients are a thorn in my side. Every day, they are becoming more demanding. At my last visit, they implied I was perhaps not a wise choice to send as an ambassador to you.*

Lokene wasn't one to show emotion, but I could almost feel the hurt bleeding from his tone.

I snorted. *That is absurd. Why would they think I'd care for the opinion of someone else over you?*

Lokene's arms tightened around my waist, drawing me tight against him. *The Ancients are scared, and they fight over everything. Half of the Elders felt that my sexual bond with you is causing the delay, and a woman should be sent. The other half of the Elders believe that perhaps if the sex was better, you would feel more inclined to assist and thus they want to send someone else.*

I wanted to laugh at how outrageously idiotic the Ancients were being, but I held back, not wanting to hurt Lokene. I'd once followed them without question. Now I saw that they weren't perfect, and right now, they were struggling with some of the same things humans did. Fear and the reality of death.

What was decided? I asked when Lokene remained silent, offering no further information.

I'm not sure. I stormed out of the meeting yesterday and

came straight here. Lokene twisted his face in disgust. *But there is something in the air today. I felt someone come through the barrier to Earth.*

I quirked an eyebrow at him. *That's why you brought us here beneath the sea? You know that will not stop an Ancient from finding us, right?*

Lokene's shoulders sagged. *I know, but I hoped to delay the inevitable.*

Fynn cleared his throat. "The whole telepathy thing you two have going on is fascinating, but we'd like to be in on the conversation as well."

"Yeah. Especially when it has Lokene, of all beings, looking distressed. That isn't a good sign for the rest of us," Kye added.

"The Ancients are questioning Lokene's abilities as an ambassador. They are trying to decide whether they should send a female to appeal to my mind, or a male to appeal to my desires. All this in hopes I will bend to their will faster," I stated bluntly.

My human mates stared at me, slack-jawed. Lokene groaned and pressed his forehead against the glass window that looked out onto the city of Atlantis.

"I don't understand. I have given my word that I would help them. Why do they doubt me?" I ground my teeth in frustration.

"Because they want you to act now. Things are growing worse," Lokene answered, voice tired. "There is reason to suspect that more Ancients have been infected with the

Lure, and things in our world continue to shift. I've tried to explain in the past that we don't see everything about the future, but rather we see multiple possible outcomes. Lately, those possible outcomes are becoming more devastating, and the chances of this ending well seem to become less likely."

"I needed a few days to recover with my mates and ensure things with Atlantis and the human governments were decided. Is that so much to ask? I'm not shirking my oath or my duty. I just need a chance to feed and rest." My frustration with the Ancients was growing by the hour. Lokene could be exasperating, but seeing my jokester of a mate constantly tired and anxious was alarming.

"Ignore the Ancients and take all the time you need, Soyale. You need to listen to your body." Lokene turned and pulled me into his embrace.

I tried to relax, but the tension continued building in my chest, unsettling me. Lokene was still hiding something, and I hated it.

"What aren't you telling me?" I murmured against Lokene's chest.

"Nothing that you need to worry about, Soyale." He buried his face in my hair. His hold on me tightened. The slight tremble in his arms dug up the unease I'd tried to bury.

"You're lying," Kye stated flatly. "I don't have your superpowers, but I know a lie when I hear one."

"Of course he is lying," a feminine voice purred.

Lokene stiffened, trying to pin me against him, but I scrambled free and spun around, blades in hand, ready to face the unknown intruder.

A woman sauntered from the shadows, hips swaying seductively. Her pale blonde hair fell to her waist, and her piercing eyes were so light blue they were nearly see-through. She focused on me before her gaze traveled the rest of the room. There was no question in my mind. The woman was an Ancient.

I tried to take a step toward her, hoping to position myself between her and my mates, but my body refused to obey my commands. Around the room, my mates stood frozen as well. Unable to move, I was forced to watch as she circled each of my mates in turn, her eyes traveling the full length of their bodies in a way that had fire burning in my veins.

The willowy blonde moved closer to Storm, her body just brushing against his. She stopped when their lips were inches apart. The siren in me thrashed against the invisible confines to get at this woman who dared to invade my castle and stand so close to my men. I struggled against the magik holding me in place.

"I wouldn't touch them, Lily." Lokene's voice was sharp as a knife blade.

"I can do as I please. None of you are able to stop me." She glanced at Lokene as she spoke, her bottom lip sticking out as she pouted. "Not even you, Lokene. You made the Ancients quite unhappy by departing from the meeting the way you did, and now they are working together to ensure you don't get in our way."

"Our?" Lokene growled.

She laughed, the sound a husky purr that could no doubt make people of any gender grow weak in the knees. It had the opposite effect on me. "Yeah, they plan to send Bion to seduce the siren into doing their will since you are unable to do the job." Her eyes dropped to Lokene's crotch, and she shook her head as though he'd disappointed her.

Lily's attention turned back to Storm, and her hand trailed up his chest. My teeth ground together, and my body twitched, magik forcing me back into place.

"Lily, stop. If you were sent to befriend Zosime, you are doing a really poor job of it. She is going to kill you, Ancient or not," Lokene warned, and I thought I detected wicked glee in his voice.

He wasn't wrong. I was going to kill her and not bat an eye while doing it if she didn't take her hands away from my mate. *MINE.*

"I was sent to convince her by whatever means necessary. Maybe if I take one of her mates as mine, she will be inclined to come to save him. I've heard she loves a good rescue." Lily's hand traveled up Storm's neck.

Storm's body stiffened at her touch, and anger overflowed his mind, pouring into mine. Lily may have thought herself a sexy seductress, capable of seducing any man she wished, but Storm was repulsed by her advances. Her abilities at seduction were nothing compared to the siren in me.

I struggled against the magik, ignoring the pain stabbing my body as I continued fighting its hold.

Leaning forward, Lily held her lips just centimeters from Storm's mouth. "And if she doesn't come to claim him, I'll be happy to keep him. He looks delicious."

She was going to kiss him. Another woman was about to taste the lips that belonged to me.

She was an idiot.

A very dead idiot.

I called my magik, both Ancient and Earth. Power surged through me and allowed me to slice through the silvery tendrils of her magik that held me still. I burst into action. With a twist of my wrist, I flung her against the wall. Keeping my hand out, I held her pinned there, just as helpless as I had been.

Turning to Storm, *my* Storm, I brushed the fingers of my free hand through his hair. *Mine.* I stood on my tip-toes and slammed my lips against his mouth, staking my claim and forcing the idiot female to watch.

I could feel Lily struggling, trying to free herself from my magik. I shoved her back, none too gently. She was a full Ancient, and I was not. There was no way I could hold her for more than a few more seconds, but I wanted her to spend those moments watching what she couldn't have.

The moment my lips touched his, Storm's body broke free from her magik as well, and his mouth moved hungrily against mine. His arms wrapped around me, traveling down my back to rest under the curve of my buttocks, hauling me against him.

"Mine," I murmured, his mouth devouring my favorite word.

"Yours," he groaned, nipping at my lip.

Knowing that I was barely keeping the siren under control, I reluctantly pulled away from the kiss before I jumped Storm in front of an audience. Facing Lily, I glowered and released my tenuous hold on her, and she crashed to the ground.

Lily rose to her feet with a sexy elegance that rivaled my siren. She gave me an appraising look and then clapped slowly.

"That was unexpected. Maybe you are strong enough to help against the Lure after all. It shouldn't be possible for a half-breed like you to break free of my hold."

"Stay away from what is mine, or you will need to fear me more than the Lure." I snarled.

Lily rolled her eyes. "You don't scare me. I could kill you before you had the chance to move."

I was raised to revere the Ancients, to bend to their wishes. If an Ancient wanted something that belonged to an Earth dweller, we would have freely given it.

But I would never give up my mates as long as I drew breath. If they were taken from me, I knew the siren would go on a rampage that would change the face of the earth, and I'd be unable to stop... not that I would want to. I'd already proven that when Richard took my mates and I'd thought Kye was dead.

"Lily!" Lokene snapped. "Stop!"

Lily ignored him and moved toward me, her steps slow and predatory.

My fangs descended, and I tasted venom in my mouth. Her confidence was amusing. She could probably kill me, but what she didn't realize was how quickly my body was adapting to every change, including the likes of her.

I wasn't sure if it was the strength of my mates or simply the effect of exercising my abilities so often as of late, but there was a chance my body would evolve fast enough to end her before she killed me. It was a chance the siren was more than willing to take.

"Your presence is required in the Iolatara, the realm of the Ancients," Lily said, voice commanding.

"I will come when I am prepared," I replied, the siren's voice a husky purr.

"Then I will take this man as a sign of your oath to come." Lily reached out to take Storm's arm. My eyes shot to her neck, prepared to rip it off her shoulders.

There was a flash, and another visitor materialized in the room. He was tall with brilliant red hair and a wry smile on his lips. His eyes met mine, and a delicious shiver traveled down my spine. He blinked a few times, like something about me had surprised him, before turning his attention away.

"Lily. The Elders wish to have a word." Blowing a kiss

at me, he rested a large fist on her shoulder, and they disappeared.

Lily's magik hold on the men vanished in the blink of an eye. We all stood there, gawking at the spot where Lily had stood.

"What was that?" Kye yelped.

"Who was that?" Storm asked, hauling my body against his.

"The female was Lily, and the man was Bion. They are both Ancients, and both of them are trouble." Lokene sagged into the chair nearest him.

Storm's body trembled against mine.

"Are you okay?" I whispered.

"I will be. Not being able to move or step away from her was an awful feeling. A lack of control is not something I am used to," he murmured, his lips pressed to my ear so that the others wouldn't hear.

"Will Lily be back?" Eason asked, his eyes continuously scanning the room as though waiting for her to pop out of hiding.

Lokene pinched the bridge of his nose. "I don't know, maybe? She was out of line. Had her tactic worked, the Ancients would have been pleased. But it didn't, and Bion is likely going to tell them just how badly it blew up in her face."

Personally, I'd prefer to never see her again in my life. If I did, I wasn't sure she would live to talk about it.

"And Bion? Will he return?" Fynn asked, cleaning his

glasses. It was an adorable habit he did when anxious.

Lokene sighed. "Without a doubt."

"He's the one sent to seduce Zosi?" Storm's chest vibrated as he spoke.

Lokene only nodded.

While he was pleasing to look at, one fact remained. "I do not want another mate." I was adamant on this point. Six men were more than even a sex-crazed siren needed.

Lokene laughed, a hint of a smile touching his lips. "That's because you don't know who he is. Do you know of the stories of cupid?"

The guys laughed, and I searched their minds for memories of this 'cupid.'

"He is not a tiny fat man," I stated the obvious. Bion was a tall dreamy crimson haired god—

"But if cupid existed, Bion would be the closest thing to the stories. There isn't a human on Earth who could resist his charm." Lokene dropped his head back and stared unseeing at the ceiling.

"Then it is a good thing I am a siren," I snapped back.

Lokene chuckled. "I believe that will only make resisting him harder."

I jutted out my chin and prepared to dig in my heels. Lokene was wrong. I could resist the mouth-watering man with ease. It would be a part of a cupcake.

You mean, it will be a 'piece of cake,' Lokene corrected, amusement back in his tone. *Avoiding your attraction to him will be interesting to watch.*

CHAPTER THREE

ZOSIME

I rubbed my temples, wishing I could disappear into the sea and avoid these boring meetings. Since I still wasn't comfortable inviting guests to Atlantis, there wasn't a chance I would allow anyone other than my mates onto our boat. Erin—the liaison I'd picked to help me communicate with the humans—invited me to her office to discuss proposals from several world leaders, an ocean research group, two movie studios, and a clothing brand.

I tried to look as though I were paying attention as she excitedly told me I was the best thing since sliced bread. What was sliced bread anyway? What made it so great?

"I have no interest in being on television." My voice was flat.

"But did you see how much they were offering you?" She spread several papers in front of me.

I pushed them away from me with a snort. "Money isn't important to me."

Erin sagged into the seat across from me. "If you are going to function on land, then money is important, Zosime."

I'd yet to trust her with all my secrets, so I'd not told her about the treasures of Atlantis. The last thing I wanted was treasure hunters descending on my city, which was the main reason I was in her office. I wanted to know my city and her citizens were safe.

Atlantis, and the water around the city, needed to be recognized as our own country with its own government. Now that the world knew of our existence, our boundaries needed to be respected. My people needed to be recognized and given equal rights as Earth dwellers, or we would end up as experiments or spectacles that people came to gawk at, which would lead to war. I shuddered at the thought.

"Where are the papers from the government leaders? Have they agreed to my terms?" I couldn't help but glance out the wall-length window over her shoulder. The aquamarine water sparkled, tempting me to forget politics and dive into the comfort of the sea.

Erin shuffled through her papers, pulling out several documents on creamy, expensive-looking paper. "Unfortunately, they aren't being cooperative. Several governments are trying to claim Atlantis as part of their country, and it is turning into a bit of a mess."

Irritation churned in my chest. How dare they claim what doesn't belong to them? "My men have told me that no country owns the ocean. Which means they can lay no claim to Atlantis."

"I know, and I agree with you. But they are trying to say that if you are to be allowed to claim Atlantis as its own city, with its own government, then you are trying to break international law. And if that law is to be amended, then they feel they have the right to claim the city and its citizens as its own."

"Atlantis was here long before any of the current world governments existed. If we are going to make ridiculous claims, then I am going to claim the land that used to surround my city." My irritation was quickly turning to anger.

"If you say things like that publicly, you could end up starting a worldwide war." Erin's voice had dropped to a soothing tone.

"I am already fighting a war, what is one more?" I snarled, my fangs lengthening as my fury surged. I was still struggling to come to terms with everything I had lost, and I would fight fang and fin for what and who I had left.

"Please, Zosime. Calm down." To her credit, Erin didn't flinch at my display. Even in my roiling anger, I felt the flicker of pride that I'd chosen well when I'd picked her from the crowd the night of the tsunami. "This is how politics work. Posturing and ceiling-high stacks of legal documents filled with weak arguments are part of it."

I forced myself to take a deep breath and release some of the tension in my body. I almost longed for the days when emotion wasn't something I had to deal with.

"Then what is the next step?" Relaxing back into my seat, I drummed my fingers on the table with another glance at the ocean beyond.

"I think we should schedule a meeting. This would allow them to make their points, and then you can state yours. If they can see how serious you are, I think they will back down. I have an attorney friend who is willing to help prepare everything for a meeting if you are open to it." Erin clicked the end of her pen repeatedly as she waited for my answer.

I had refused face-to-face meetings the last few days. My body had needed time to recover from fighting against an Ancient's magik, and I'd needed bonding time with my mates. I wasn't an idiot. There was a strong chance that when I traveled to Iolatara, I wouldn't be making a return journey, which is why I wanted to savor a few days with my mates. Clearly, that was too much to ask.

Still, I needed to know Atlantis would be safe, which was why this struggle of ownership needed to be taken care of immediately. I couldn't walk into the other world knowing that the city of my heart was unprotected. Zeno would care for our people if I didn't make it back, but I didn't want the mers to constantly be fighting off treasure hunters or dealing with tourists. How would my people survive if noisy humans scared off the large schools of fish?

"How soon can it be arranged?" I would do what had to be done, regardless of how much I despised it.

"Three days. We can have everything ready then." Erin's face lit up with excitement.

With a nod, I pushed to my feet.

Erin narrowed her eyes. "Zosime?"

"Yes?"

"You won't do anything crazy, right?" Her brow wrinkled, concern reflecting in her eyes.

"I have no plans to be 'crazy.'" Strolling to the door, I called over my shoulder, "But I will do whatever I must in order to win this quarrel."

Her groan echoed down the hall, and I smiled. We were going to become great friends... if I didn't die.

I stepped out of the towering office building and into the blinding sunshine. Breathing deep, I sucked in several lungfuls of salty air, clearing my lungs of the stale metallic-tasting air that filled the humans' air-conditioned buildings.

The pull was irresistible, and I took off at a run for the sea, knowing that Zeno waited below the surface for me.

We hadn't seen eye to eye on my upcoming trip, and Zeno had been avoiding me. I'd planned to hunt him down that evening if he didn't find me first.

With a happy yell, I darted down the wooden pier, racing to the end, and took a flying leap off. I dove into the sea without even the tiniest splash. The water closed over my head, folding me in its cool embrace.

Not bothering to shift forms, I allowed myself to sink, simply waiting.

A fin brushed against my leg, followed by a hand sliding up my thigh beneath my filmy skirt that flowed around me in the gentle current. Fighting the urge to shiver, I remained perfectly motionless.

Zeno's muscular body twisted around mine in a sensual dance. His hands gripped my waist, yanking me hard against his body. The joy that rushed through me at his touch was too much to resist, and I wrapped my legs around his waist and circled his neck with my arms. My lungs had begun to burn, but still, I didn't shift.

I was a warrior and enjoyed knowing my skill and strength, but there was something I loved about being in my weaker human form while pressed against Zeno's much larger body. For a brief moment, I could be protected instead of always being the protector.

Zeno's mouth pressed against mine, his tongue darting out to trace my bottom lip. *You need to shift, or we must surface.*

I deepened our kiss, opening my mouth to him so his

tongue could delve inside. Zeno's chest rumbled, and his fingers dug into the skin of my thighs as he ground the swell of his erection against me.

Shift. Now, he ordered.

I wanted to keep playing, enjoying the play of his merbody against my human flesh. The gentle scrape of scale against skin. But I was growing light-headed. I closed my eyes and allowed my body to transform.

The moment my body completed its transformation, the siren was pushing for control. Zeno and I had shared intimacy immediately after the fiasco on land with Richard, but then he had claimed to be busy and had avoided me. Sex with my other mates had been incredible, but I'd missed Zeno.

The siren wanted to seduce Zeno and remind him of what he'd been missing. I wanted to feel his love before I had to fight the hardest battle of my life.

Pulling my lips away from his, I slid down his body. I took my time kissing my way down his chest. My webbed fingers trailed down the scales on his hips and thighs, tracing along each scale's edge. Zeno's fluke twitched in an imitation of an irritated cat. Although his reaction was from being aroused rather than annoyed.

I wrapped my tail around his fluke, holding myself against him so the current couldn't pull us apart. Zeno's fingers threaded through my hair, eliciting a moan from me at his gentle touch.

Finally, I made my way down his body until I came to

his sizable bulge. He growled as I licked along the scales that covered his erection, and it didn't take long before the scales parted, and his erection sprang out, nearly slapping me in the face. I'd grown accustomed to dodging cranky eels and sneaky barracudas though, and managed to dodge the attack.

I licked the tip, staring up into his fathomless dark eyes. A muscle in his jaw ticked, and his fingers tightened in my hair, pulling it gently.

What are you doing to me? Zeno growled.

Reminding you that you are mine.

But this isn't how mating is done. Zeno tried to argue, but his words slurred slightly as my tongue traced the curves of his erection.

You haven't been tasted before? I questioned, thinking I'd misunderstood.

No. The word was a hoarse whisper in my mind, and his hand trembled. *It wouldn't make sense for producing offspring.*

True, but it is great at producing pleasure. Intense satisfaction filled me. I would be the first to give him this experience.

Not wanting to waste any more time, I took him deep in my mouth until I felt his tip touch the back of my throat. Relaxing my muscles, I swallowed him as far as I could before sliding him from my mouth. I repeated the move over and over, unhurried and savoring the taste of him and the ocean on my tongue.

Zeno changed from combatant alpha male to a blobfish, and I found myself needing to hold us together tighter so he didn't drift away. I sucked and swirled, watching him for every shudder and every minuscule reaction.

When his face tightened with a need that verged on being painful, I relented. I bobbed on his length, working my throat muscles to squeeze him with each swallow. Zeno's grip on my hair grew painfully tight, causing my eyes to water and my scalp to burn.

Just when I thought he was going to come undone, Zeno jerked himself free of my mouth.

Zeno? I questioned through the mental link.

He didn't bother to answer. Instead, his body and tail slid around me like a snake preparing to eat his meal. Zeno's mouth traveled down my neck, between my breasts, and moved slowly down my stomach.

When his mouth pressed to my hidden slit, my body trembled. The feel of his tongue tracing along the edge of the sensitive scales had me sinking my hands into his hair. He chuckled, sending vibrations through my core and causing me to grow wet in a way that had nothing to do with the ocean I was swimming in.

Zeno's tongue slid inside me, teasing me, and caused me to squirm desperately in an effort to get away from the intense sensations sizzling through me.

Please, Zeno. I need you. My voice shook with need. His tongue was doing amazing things, but I needed to feel him moving inside me. I craved that connection with my mate.

I didn't have to ask twice. Zeno lined himself up with my entrance and thrust inside with one hard push. I clung to him, my body trembling as he began to move. Burying my face in the curve of his neck, I closed my eyes and allowed myself to be swept up in the moment.

Zeno took his time, making love to me as though it were the first time and the last time. Unhurried and almost reverent, Zeno's hands trailed across my scales, and his mouth tasted my skin.

The heat inside me built slow and steady. It caused me to grow slick around his erection as the promise of release drew closer. The greedy part of me wanted to buck my hips and urge him to pick up the pace.

Another part of me wanted to savor this alone time with Zeno and allow myself to forget about all the worries weighing so heavily on me they threatened to sink me to the bottom of the ocean.

And so I lay still, resting against Zeno's chest and allowing him to take charge of this time together. The slow burn in my stomach turned to a raging wildfire, forcing me to fight against the desire to sink my fangs into Zeno's skin.

His breathing grew heavy as his hips moved faster, the water doing little to slow down his thrusts.

Bite me, Zeno commanded.

Trying to keep myself under control, I pressed my fangs against his neck until just the tips pierced his skin.

Harder, Zosime. His words were sharp—a demand.

With a growl, I released my hold on the siren and sank

my fangs deep into his throat. Greedily devouring the spurt of warm blood coating my mouth.

Zeno returned the favor, sinking his own fangs into my neck. I embraced the prick of pain, a moan escaping me as he began to suck in long erotic swallows. He was careful to not take too much from me, wanting to ensure I was never weak.

The siren was less careful, and I had to focus through the haze to avoid drinking him nearly dry. I managed to yank my fangs free as Zeno shifted his position and drove into me at a different angle. An angle that had my release exploding through me with the power of a missile.

Lights sparkled in my vision, and my body clamped down around his, determined to never let him go. As my muscles continued to constrict his thick erection, Zeno came. His shouts slammed into my mind, and his hips jerked repeatedly with his release.

We floated there for nearly half an hour, enjoying the peace of the ocean and the joy that comes from being in the arms of your mate.

All the while, I tried to keep at bay the thoughts of what was coming. This was going to be a week straight from Tartarus.

CHAPTER FOUR

ZOSIME

Two days later, I was sitting at a table in a large boardroom surrounded by the arguing leaders of every major government on Earth. All three parts of me were in complete agreement that we should kill them all to quiet the excessive noise.

If this was the way leaders of the modern world acted when discussing serious issues, then I would be doing the world a favor by silencing them all... permanently.

My head and heart ached. My head from the loud thoughts barraging me from every angle, and my heart from worry over Lokene. I hadn't heard from him since he'd been summoned without warning. The Ancients had never kept him in their world this long, and the fact they were willing to do so even while knowing the effect our separation would have on me showed they were growing desperate.

Which is why this meeting today had to go well. I was out of time and options. It was imperative that I had my assurances that Atlantis and her people were safe before I left. But at the rate we were going, it would be months or even years before a resolution was reached.

I glanced out the glass wall to where Fynn, Eason, Storm, and Kye sat watching the proceedings. Faint lines showed around their shadowed eyes and grimly set mouths. They hadn't been allowed in the room with me, and security had tried to usher them downstairs before the meeting started, but I'd refused to have them out of my sight.

This was their world, boardrooms full of politicians and arguing, and they were comfortable in it.

I was not.

Having their presence near me was the only thing anchoring me and keeping the noise in my mind to a somewhat bearable level. Kye was thinking encouraging thoughts to me nonstop, which was sweet but not exactly helpful.

This was why I never wanted to be the queen of Atlantis. My mother had been the one who'd been skilled at handling battles of negotiations over dinner with foreign dignitaries. I was the one skilled at winning battles with a sword.

The men and women at this table had never seen a war, and I doubted they possessed any skills with a sword. Just imagining them wielding a sword had me smirking.

I listened as one leader laid out his proposal for claiming Atlantis as a territory of his country. In his mind, since Atlantis had previously been attached to the country's coastline, it still belonged to them.

Another leader disagreed, claiming since Atlantis lay somewhere between their two countries, it should be shared. I'd refused to give away Atlantis' precise location, but when I'd laid out my proposal, I had marked the area of the sea I wished to claim. I hated even giving that much information, but it had been necessary.

A third leader slammed his fist against the table. "Atlantis lies at the bottom of the ocean. International law makes it clear that the ocean belongs to no one, therefore Atlantis and its resources should be shared, and access should be given equally to all countries."

A fat, balding man nodded his agreement. "Yes, although that begs the question about who is responsible for caring for the mers and where they would pay taxes."

One of the women lifted her nose in the air. "How are they supposed to pay taxes if their civilization is so back-ward that they don't even use money? Which country is going to take on the costs of educating them to prepare them for proper interactions with today's society? Not to mention the costs of their medical care."

A shifty-eyed man who'd been quiet up until that point spoke up. "We are happy to take on the costs of providing those things, and in exchange, we would be given sole rights to the resources they obtain from the ocean floor and all Orpati."

Utter pandemonium descended on the room.

I couldn't take it anymore. I'd tried to emulate my mother, but it hadn't worked. Now it was time to do things my way.

Standing, I raised my hand, calling the water from all the pitchers on the table to me. The water swirled around me, and slowly, the room quieted as they noticed the display of power.

"I believe there has been a misunderstanding." My voice carried across the room as though I were speaking to my troops, but there was a subtle husky note from the siren that had certainly not been present with my troops.

"Atlantis is not requesting reorganization as a country. We are demanding it. We do not need your charity, nor do we need your money. We provide our own health care and education. In fact, we might just tax you for learning from us. At minimum, my people expect to be treated with the same respect as every other citizen of the earth."

The bald man cut me off, "With all due respect, your people aren't fully human. Our scientists will still need to run tests to determine the cognitive abilities of the merpeople. After those reports are completed, we can discuss the rights they are entitled to. For all we know, they are like dolphins."

I was rendered speechless by the man's cold dismissal of my people. Several leaders nodded in agreement. Why was

I fighting so hard to save the human race from the Lure, when they were so full of their own self-importance?

It was time I reminded them who they were dealing with. Glancing around the room, I wasn't one hundred percent positive I could pull off what I wanted, though. If Lokene were here...

I didn't have a chance to finish the thought before the world pitched to the side and darkness enveloped us. Just as quickly, the world righted itself, and the meeting room's long table now sat in the middle of the oversized dining hall in my Atlantean castle. Stunned into silence, the world leaders looked around in disbelief before fixing their wide-eyed gazes on me.

Warm arms circled my waist, and I tried to ignore the lurch of my heart. I didn't need to look to know the owner of those arms wasn't one of my already claimed mates, and regardless of what my siren believed, I wasn't planning on accepting any more mates. Especially if they were forced on me by the Elder Ancients.

"Queen Zosime felt it was necessary to show you Atlantis." Bion's voice echoed through the hall, carrying with it a jovial confidence that had the men grinning amiably and the women swooning. This man could prob-ably get away with murder.

"Who would you like me to murder?" he purred against my ear. "For you, I'd gladly do it."

I ignored the way my warrior heart pounded a little harder and disentangled myself from his embrace as gracefully as I could, needing to put space between us. Bion chuckled, dropping his arms to his sides.

I turned to the humans. "Yes, I believe you have all misunderstood why I asked for this meeting. I was not asking permission for Atlantis to be viewed as her own city. I was informing the world that Atlantis exists, and if we are all to get along going forward, then the mers deserve the same rights as the other people of Earth."

I strolled toward the wall of clear windows that looked out over the city and pressed my hand against the glass. Within seconds Sheba appeared, her massive body blocking out what little light made its way down this deep onto the ocean floor.

I hid my grin at the startled gasps from behind me. Sheba opened her jaws wide, adding to my delight and further traumatizing my guests before slowly moving out of sight.

Zeno, bring the mers.

The mer people slowly appeared in front of the viewing window, eager to see their first humans. Mers with tails in every shade of blue moved into view of the large windows. Gorgeous women with long flowing hair billowing around them and mermen with bulging muscles pressed against the glass. Young mers peaked from behind their parents to smile and wave at the strangers.

I turned back toward the leaders, who remained frozen in their chairs.

"Incredible!" remarked an older gentleman who'd been

fairly quiet.

Several people murmured their agreement.

I dared hope for just a minute that they understood the basic human decency we were owed. And then my hopes were dashed to shreds like a ship tossed against a rocky shoreline during a storm as their thoughts filled my mind.

I need to get my scientists down here to study these creatures. There are millions to be made from researching them.

Is that real jewelry that they are wearing? It must be worth a fortune! If my country can get the rights to Atlantis, we can have them work for us to mine the seafloor.

Crowds would pay thousands to visit mermaids in aquariums, not to mention how much could be made by renting out the palace for celebrity events and overnight trips. This is a literal gold mine.

Instead of seeing us people, they were viewing us as creatures that could be put to work for their own greed. I was done.

"We don't need your permission to live or to thrive in the oceans. This meeting was nothing more than a courtesy to the humans on land." I worked hard to keep my words level and calm, a perfect imitation of my mother's voice.

Baldy laughed. "I think you are overestimating your power, young lady. We are doing you the favor by allowing you to bring your petition to us. We all took time out of our busy schedules to make this happen, so you would do well to remember that."

I bristled at the condescension in his tone, and I felt my

tattoos begin to glow.

"Who do you think you are to appear out of nowhere and start making demands?" a sour-faced woman in a stiff business suit asked, her lips curling into a cruel smile.

Apparently, the others at the table hadn't noticed my growing anger, because they joined in with their own chuckles and laughter.

Laughter which came to a screeching halt as the lights around the room began to flicker ominously. Even with my back turned to the glass wall, I knew Sheba had reappeared, her large form casting the room into shadow.

Light emanated from my tattoos, and my eyes glowed brighter. Righteous anger over their disrespect clogged my throat, and I struggled to swallow it so I could speak.

"What is *that?*" the woman exclaimed with her eyes on me.

A deep chuckle came from the corner of the room, and Bion stepped from the shadows.

"Who is she? She's the mother-fricking Queen of Atlantis." Bion sauntered toward the table, not caring in the least that every single person in the room was eyeing him with suspicion... especially me. Pressing his palms flat on the end of the table, he leaned forward as though letting them in on a secret.

"Do you remember all those amusing stories about Greek gods you learned as a kid?" One brow raised, Bion waited for an answer. It took a moment, but most of the table slowly nodded.

"She's the daughter of one of those gods. You think it is a cute trick she can shift from a siren to a human girl with two legs? If you only knew what else she could do, every single person at this table would be shaking in their shoes." Bion's eyes sparkled with delight, and I got the distinct impression he wished I would terrorize the people in the room just a bit.

Unfortunately for him, he was the most likely person to feel my wrath as soon as we were alone.

He glanced back at me and winked. "I look forward to it."

"I have no more time to waste, so here is my final offer," I said to the humans. "The area I outlined in the documents will be recognized as Atlantis. No drilling, mining, or treasure hunting will happen in that area. The area will be marked and will be off limits to leisure vessels unless they are experiencing an emergency and need assistance.

"Government ships will be allowed only if Atlantis has given approval. It is vital that the area around Atlantis remain calm to ensure the wildlife is undisturbed. I will not allow my people to starve simply because humans are too curious or selfish to leave the ocean above it alone." I paused, and when no one spoke, I continued.

"If a time comes that we are ready, Atlantis may host tourism and science expeditions to help spread awareness of how mers live and the importance of protecting the earth's oceans. But we will not be coerced into either before we are ready and feel safe. We will work with the governments of the world in any way we can, treating those on land with the same respect with which we wish to be treated.

"We will come to the aid of any distressed vessels or people stranded in the ocean that we come across. Atlantis will be an independent country, not belonging to any other country on Earth."

Baldy's face turned an alarming shade of red, and he exploded. "That is absolutely unacceptable. We"—he motioned at the faces around the table—"will decide what rights Atlantis will and will not be given, as well as the obligations that she will need to meet. You will not order us around or try to scare us with your pitiful parlor magic tricks."

The other leaders nodded their heads in agreement. The snobbish woman stuck her nose in the air, trying to look down at me.

"Yes, we will discuss this over the next several weeks. Once we've come to an agreement, you will be notified regarding our decision. Atlantis will be given ninety days to comply."

I listened for the call, hoping these people were tainted by the Lure. But no, they were just horrible all on their own. My heart sank at the realization that even if I wiped out the evil of the Lure, some of humanity would still suck.

What didn't sink was my rage over their cold, calculated dismissal of my proposal and the rights of my people. I saw red.

CHAPTER FIVE

BION

T hings were about to get really good. Sinking further into the shadows, I threw up a wall between the room and myself, shielding me from their view.

Leaning against the wall, I decided that Zosime's mates needed to see this too, and I popped them away from the office building that was currently undergoing some hardcore lockdown measures. Humans sure freaked out when their world leaders went on surprise playdates.

"What are we—" the shaggy blonde began.

"Who are you?" the giant brute—Eason, I think? —demanded.

"Shh! The show is about to start." I shushed them while

shoving bags of popcorn I'd pulled from thin air into the arms of the confused men.

"Too bad Lokene isn't here to see it," I snickered.

Whatever the men might have asked next was cut off as Zosime's voice carried through the expansive room.

"Is that your final decision?"

Chills raced down my spine at the reverberating echo of her siren's voice. It was magnificent... She was magnificent. Not that she was going to give me the chance to tell her that anytime soon.

The old guy with a mouth bigger than his brain stood, trying to use his height to intimidate Zosime. Big mistake.

Storm tried to storm through the glass, and I stuck out an arm to stop him from impacting against it.

"Sit down, man. I only brought you here to admire your mate. She doesn't need help out there," I grumbled.

"You don't tell us what to do," Fynn snapped.

"Right now, I do." Waving my hand, I forced them all to lean against the wall alongside me and closed their mouths.

Not for a second did my eyes leave the fearsome beauty facing off with the leaders of this world.

The man in front of Zosime refused to back down, even in the face of her flashing eyes and shimmering tattoos.

"Yes. That is our final decision." He spat out the words and some saliva in Zosime's face, but she didn't flinch. Her eyes shot to meet those of each person sitting at the table.

"And you are all in agreement?" Her voice was calm.

Too calm. They should have known better than to do what they did next.

One by one, each face at the table nodded their agreement. Alas, they were all idiots.

Zosime ground her teeth, frustration rolling off her in waves. Swallowing it back, she tilted her head in acknowledgment.

"Then I will give you a warning. From this moment forward, Atlantis does not view you as friends. We will protect our borders and our people. It would be best that you advise your people to stay out of the zone I outlined. Anyone inside our borders will be treated as a threat. While the Atlanteans will be more forgiving and less inclined to attack, the same cannot be said for our allies, the beasts of the ocean, who will help my people remain safe."

Taking a breath, Zosime continued, "I have been fair in requesting an area smaller than all other countries on Earth for my people. But if our borders are breached, or any effort is made to capture or exploit the citizens of my city, I will claim the entirety of the oceans of Earth as belonging to Atlantis. You will be given one month to remove your vessels from the sea and advise your people to stay out of the ocean. It will be a war."

Sorrow glinted in Zosime's eyes. "This was not the outcome I hoped for, but it seems I misjudged the people of Earth. Greed is more important than the betterment of all life on Earth."

"You can't do that!" several people spluttered in outrage. I snickered.

"I can and I will." Zosime's voice was resolute. Her eyes swiveled and locked with mine, which should have been impossible since we were hidden, but Lokene had been right about her having abilities that defied logic.

Send them back, Zosime thought to me.

You too? I asked.

No, only the leaders. My mates stay here with me.

So she could see not only me, but her mates behind my wall as well. The side of my lip twitched up. Interesting...

With little more than a thought, I sent the leaders back to the meeting room while at the same time dissolving the wall that separated Zosime from us.

"Zosi!" Kye ran forward like an eager golden retriever puppy, scooping her in his arms and twirling her around.

For a brief moment, Zosime relaxed in his arms. Until her eyes landed on me and her body stiffened. Confused, Kye set her down.

Stepping between the guys, Zosime made her way to stand in front of me. Crossing her arms under her breasts in a way that made them look even more tempting, she narrowed her eyes. I opened my mouth, fully planning to say something witty and sexy.

"Hi." I wanted to smack myself. What was I? Twelve and losing my mind over a pretty girl?

"Thank you for your assistance." Her words made my heart thud harder.

"You're welcome. Anytime you need to banish some-one, I'll be here." I hated how eager I sounded.

"Where's Lokene?" Zosime cut straight to the point.

"He was summoned to the Ancients' world. I'm supposed to bring you to him." I hated being the one to give her that little tidbit of news.

"You mean he is being held as a prisoner against his will, as a pawn to force me to do the will of the Ancients?"

She saw right through the tactics being used against her. I understood the panic the Ancients were dealing with over the Lure. Heck, I was terrified of it. But pinning the respon-sibility of solving all our problems on one distractingly beautiful woman, while treating her as less than an equal, was all kinds of wrong.

"Yes." I saw no point in denying it.

Something lit in the back of her eyes. Surprise?

"I have no intention of going back on my word. I will be going to your world as soon as I finish my work here. Kidnapping my mate, and robbing me of this time with him, was unnecessary." Zosime studied my reaction.

"Agreed." I narrowed the distance between us, unable to fight the urge to touch her.

Why was it happening like this? I was sent to seduce her, but instead of putting her under my spell, it was Zosime who'd worked her magik on me. I couldn't stand one more moment of not touching her. Catching her chin with my hand, I savored the soft brush of her skin against mine.

"When you are ready, I will be waiting. Take whatever time you need."

Not giving her the chance to rebuff my touch, I blinked myself out of the room. Zosime needed time with her mates, and I had some business to attend to while the Ancients were distracted. And I needed to get away before I lost all my dignity, as well as my ability to resist her.

CHAPTER SIX

ZOSIME

I n the blink of an eye, Bion was gone, leaving me with a lot of things I'd wanted to say. I was thankful for his help, but I was also irritated by it. If Lokene had been here, then Bion's assistance would have been unnecessary. But Lokene wasn't. And like it or not, Bion had my back when I needed help.

That didn't mean I would cave to the siren's desire to bite him, to claim him as hers. On second thought, I might bite him, but just not with the same intention as the siren. Bion was a complication I didn't need and definitely couldn't afford right now.

Tonight was my last night with my men, only they didn't know that. There was no way I could risk taking them into Iolatara. I could handle myself. Between my skills and my body's abilities, I had a shot at victory. My odds of winning would go down if my attention was divided between protecting my mates and completing my mission.

Only Zeno knew my plan, and while he despised it, he understood my reasoning. The only way I could walk into the world of the Ancients without distraction was with the knowledge that Zeno was protecting Atlantis. He'd been an amazing ruler before I knew the city still existed, and he would continue the city's proud legacy, with or without me.

Tonight, I wanted to forget I was a warrior and a queen. I wanted to forget the mission coming up. I just wanted to be a woman with her loving mates.

Looking at the anxious faces around me, I wished we were back on our boat so I could have all my mates with me in one room. Here in the castle, I had to pick between my mates with legs or my mate with a tail. I couldn't have both.

Yes, you can. Zeno's voice poured into my mind like molten chocolate. Decadent and rich and irresistible. He couldn't read my mind, but he must have felt my despair.

I spun in a slow circle, looking out into the endless blue sea for my merman. He swam into view, his dark hair drifting around him and his eyes glowing. Zeno flattened his palm against the glass, and I quickly pressed my hand against his on the opposite side of the thick window.

How is that supposed to work while you are out there

and we are in here? I purred to him, the siren eager to get started enjoying her mates.

Give me legs, was his quick response.

I stiffened, my mind struggling to comprehend his three simple words. He'd refused to give up his tail on every other occasion the topic had been brought up. Why was he suddenly changing his mind now?

Because tonight is about you and... He narrowed his eyes at the men pressing against my back, *our family. Tonight we should be together. However, I do not wish to walk around these men. I have no desire to hear their laughter at my childish attempts to walk on two legs.*

Of course, he wouldn't want to risk anyone laughing at him, even good-naturedly. The man was stubborn and proud. I nodded.

I can send you to my bed, and you can remain there until you are ready to return to the sea. At least I hoped I could send him there. My skills with blinking others were limited to a few feet of distance and only to a place I was looking at.

I trust you. Zeno sounded so confident in my abilities.

Closing my eyes, I pictured the massive bed in my palace bedchamber, and then pictured Zeno in it, dry and with two legs instead of a tail. My skin with the etched tattoos burned, but I ignored the discomfort and focused on my goal. When the burning stopped, I opened my eyes, my heart trembling with trepidation.

Zeno was gone.

"Where did he go?" Storm asked.

"Princess? Where did you put Zeno?" Eason asked.

"I bet I know!" Kye gathered me in his arms, laughing as I shrieked in shock. I could do little but cling to his neck as he sprinted out of the room and down the long hall... and straight toward my bedroom.

It was strange how Kye, the least serious out of my mates—well, besides Lokene—seemed to be the fastest to figure things out about me. He may not be the most physically intimidating of my men, but he had a quick mind and was sensitive to the slightest changes around him.

"I knew it!" Kye crowed as he rounded the corner and caught sight of Zeno propped up on the bed.

"You survived!" I blurted in relief.

"You questioned if I would?" Zeno asked, mock horror on his face.

I opened my mouth to lie, but the words got stuck. As a hot blush spread across my cheeks, Zeno chuckled.

"Do you have legs? Let me see, dude!" Kye tossed me on the bed, eagerly crawling up after me.

It was Zeno's turn to look uncomfortable, and he gripped the blanket a little tighter around his waist.

"Did it not work?" I sucked my bottom lip between my teeth and eyed the shape of his legs beneath the blanket.

"Yes, it worked fine. I am just unaccustomed to this form," Zeno growled, refusing to meet my eye.

"Don't tell me she gave you a tiny—" Kye choked on his laughter, and I elbowed him in the gut.

"Who has a tiny penis?" Storm asked as he came into view. Seeing us on the bed, he immediately began removing his shirt.

"Who said it was tiny? It is likely average. The average male penis is—" Fynn came into the room behind Storm, one hand pushing his glasses up his nose.

"It's not tiny!" Zeno shouted in exasperation, tossing the blanket to the side and giving us an unobstructed view of what had to be a record-setting erection for males with a human body.

Kye yelled, grabbing a pillow to shove over his face.

"What the—" Storm barked before looking to the ceiling as though praying for lightning to strike him down.

Eason only grunted and collapsed into a chair that faced away from Zeno.

Fynn stepped closer. "Fascinating. You were able to give him fully human anatomy, Zosi. Did you pick how large he was going to be, or was it a comparative swap based on the proportions of his merman phallus?"

"I was worried about performing the shift and the teleport incorrectly, so no, I did not spare time to think about how large I wanted his manhood to be," I retorted in irritation. "What do you think I am? A sex-crazed monster?"

"If the boot fits..." Kye mumbled into the pillow.

With a hiss, I flashed my fangs in Kye's direction.

"I heard that, Zosi. You are just proving my point." Kye's chuckles were muffled by the cushion.

Huffing, I turned back to Zeno. "If I did not mangle your body, why are you acting strange?"

Zeno shot Fynn a disgruntled look and yanked the blanket back over his waist. "As I said before, I am simply unfamiliar with this form. It looks like those pink worms that the fishermen use for bait—except giant."

Kye and Eason burst into loud guffaws, and Fynn tried desperately to keep a straight face.

"Well, while you get used to your legs, I want to admire Zosime's." Storm gave a playful growl and crawled up the bed, sliding up my skirt as he wedged his broad body between my legs.

Storm's large hand caught my calf, bringing it to his lips as he kissed his way up my leg and inner thigh. I groaned. Kye tossed the pillow on the floor, propping himself on his elbow so he could lean forward and catch my mouth in a searing kiss.

Careful not to bump into the still freaked-out Zeno, Fynn moved to my side so he was opposite Kye. My heart swelled with happiness as I was sandwiched between Kye and Fynn, with Storm moving ever higher between my legs.

Fynn made quick work of the buttons on my blouse, and with the speed of a magician, both it and my bra disappeared. His tongue teased my nipple for one breath-stealing second before he began to devour my breast.

My toes curled, and I tried to moan, but Kye swallowed the sound, refusing to let me pull away even to breathe.

When Storm's mouth pressed against my black thong, I nearly jerked off the bed. His warm breath seeped through the thin fabric that was the only barrier between him and my aching core.

Shoving my hand into Storm's hair, I pulled him closer, my legs wrapping around his broad back of their own accord.

"Please," I begged, gasping for air as Kye's mouth moved to lavish attention on my neck.

"Please, what?" Storm whispered while tracing his tongue along the line created by my thong pressing against my slit.

I knew exactly what I wanted from them that night, what memories I wanted to carry into battle with me.

"Show me how much you love me." The need was raw, and my voice cracked.

"Always." Storm's voice was rough, but his hands were gentle as he lifted my hips and slid off the tiny scrap of fabric humans considered attractive underwear. His mouth was pressing a soft kiss against my lady bits before the thong even hit the stone floor.

"Storm!" I groaned his name, collapsing back onto the pillows.

All three men moved in like sharks, ready to devour their meal.

Kye's hand gently kneaded my breast while his mouth sucked and kissed along my skin. Eason claimed my mouth, his velvet tongue sliding along mine. Storm was doing amazing things with his tongue as well... just much lower on my body.

I tried to wiggle on the bed as Storm's fingers parted my lower lips, allowing his tongue to slip inside me, but the men pinned me in place with growls of disapproval. Eason moved from my mouth to my neglected left breast, giving me a moment to suck in much-needed oxygen.

Blinking my heavy eyelids, I met Zeno's burning gaze. He'd always preferred our intimate times to be private, and I'd worried about how he would handle sharing long term. Seeing the undisguised lust in his gaze eased my worry.

If there was a problem, I would tell you. We are partners, my little fish. Seeing these men worship your body is torture of the best kind. I get to watch how you react to their touch, something I cannot do while I am mating with you. Stop worrying and let me enjoy this display. Zeno may have been chiding me, but his eyes sparkled. Was he teasing me?

As if to reassure me, Zeno pushed the blanket from his lap. He slid his hand down until he gripped the base of his erection and began to rub his hand up the hard length. I watched, transfixed, my mouth watering.

I might have given in to the need to explore his body if Storm hadn't finished lapping up the evidence of my need and shifted to his knees. My full attention was back on the man between my legs. Storm's pants were nowhere in sight, giving me an incredible view of his thick member standing at attention.

"Kye. Fynn," Storm barked.

Both men must have understood the unspoken command because they scooted slightly away from me, giving Storm room to move up my body until the full length of our bodies were pressed together.

Lining himself up with my entrance, Storm shifted forward, sinking inside me one slow inch at a time. The desire to claw at his back and push him deep inside me was overwhelming, but Storm was taking his time, and I forced myself to savor the moment.

Closing my eyes, I caught my breath as he moved in and out of me. Storm's rhythmic motion reminded me of the rocking of the sea, calling to the siren. I tasted my venom as it leaked into my mouth. I wanted to bite him, but I wondered if my mates resented the fact that we rarely had sex without them feeling the effects of my aphrodisiac.

"Bite me." Storm nibbled my earlobe.

Still, I hesitated.

"She's afraid," Zeno supplied.

My merman may have a big member, but he had a bigger mouth.

"Lokene and I have discussed this. Zosime fears that we may dislike that sex with her means we are injected with her venom." Zeno the Nosy revealed one of my darkest fears with an air of casualness that had me itching to spar with him so I could toss him around a bit.

There was a tense moment of silence, and then all four men burst out laughing. Storm collapsed on top of me, although he carefully kept the bulk of his weight from squashing me.

"Princess, sex with you is mind-blowing, and your venom is the cherry on top." Eason gave me a soft smile.

"Not to mention it is addictive," Kye added, his cheeks darkening.

That piqued my interest. "It's addictive? What do you mean?"

CHAPTER SEVEN

KYE

"Not to mention it is addictive." As soon as the words left my mouth, I wanted to slap my hand over it. Why would I tell her that?

Zosi's eyes sharpened with interest. "It's addictive? What do you mean?"

Eason and Storm groaned and shot me a look.

Refusing to look at Zosi, I tried to explain. "You're my mate, so I'm already addicted to your touch and to touching you. I can barely stand to be away from you."

Zosime twitched, and I glanced at her curiously. She wasn't the type to fidget. This time, she was the one who looked away. Weird.

Deciding to finish explaining, I continued, "Everything about being with you is incredible, and then you add your toxin into the mix. Zosi, it's better than that first sip of caffeine in the morning."

I laughed when Zosi's brow raised in skepticism. My little mermaid had grown obsessed with having the 'nectar of the gods' as soon as she woke up and then every chance she could throughout the day.

"It's true, Zosi. Your bite makes every sensation explosive; sounds are clearer, colors are brighter. Sex with that pumping in my blood is indescribable. I don't need it like a drug addict. But when we are intimate, it feels like it is just one more perfect thing you gift us. I want all of you. Everything you will give me. I'd want to feed you regardless of your toxin, but I'm definitely not complaining about how your toxin affects me."

A tiny frown crossed Zosime's face as she listened to my poor attempt at convincing her that her toxin was nothing to feel bad about. She looked at Fynn, Eason, Storm, and Zeno.

"And what about you guys? Do you resent my venom? Or do you view it the same as Kye?" Her voice was soft, and she almost seemed afraid of their answers.

I watched in amusement as both Eason and Storm shifted their gazes away from her.

We'd all had a nice long talk about this very topic and were in agreement over the fact that our little siren really knew how to make sex an out-of-this-world experience.

Fynn was the only one bold enough to speak up.

"Yes," he stammered. "Your venom is quite unique and definitely increases our enjoyment." Fynn's ears grew red.

Why was it that since meeting her, we did far kinkier crap than we'd ever have dreamed of doing, and we'd do it in front of each other... but admitting to Zosime that we loved the effects of her venom had us blushing like inexperienced teenagers?

Zeno was the only one who appeared completely unfazed by the topic of conversation, and when Zosi's eyes locked on him, he simply shrugged.

"I don't see what the problem is," Zeno admitted. "Yes, your venom is more powerful than the rest of the mers. However, I don't understand why you're viewing it as a negative thing instead of a gift for your mates and an effective weapon against your enemies." Zeno reached out a hand, running it through Zosime's dark tangle of hair.

"If I understand the modern world correctly, a woman is pleased if her mate's phallus is large. She would love him regardless of his size, but she is pleased if he has the added benefit of a larger size, correct?" Zeno spoke in a factual tone, as though he were talking about the weather.

Things were getting weirder by the minute. I was definitely regretting my sudden admission to Zosime that had sparked this increasingly awkward chat. When no one spoke up, Zeno continued.

"It is simple. You bring venom to the relationship. An aphrodisiac created to kill those you dislike and bring intense pleasure to those you love." Zeno shrugged as though it made perfect sense. "You take the blood of your mates and give them a gift at the same time. It is fair."

Part of me wanted to complain about Zeno's blunt and almost crude way of thinking, but apparently it made sense to Zosi, because her shoulders relaxed.

"It's a relief knowing you guys view it as a positive part of our relationship and bonding." She gave us each a soft smile that simultaneously melted my heart and hardened other parts of my anatomy.

It had the same effect on Storm.

"Bite me, beautiful," Storm growled against her throat where he was nipping and sucking. "Use me. Feed from me."

Personally, I'd like to think that I could have come up with a much sexier way of saying that, but Zosime didn't need it, nor did she need to be asked twice. Fangs flashing, she quickly sank them into his neck, eliciting a long moan from the both of them.

Watching Zosime cling to Storm's body as her throat worked to drink from him was something I'd never have thought would be a turn-on for me, but I found my hand drifting lower to grab the base of my aching erection.

Storm's whole body shuddered as her venom sped through his bloodstream, while at the same time, it was sending the tiniest wave of jealousy through me. I was fine with sharing, but waiting for my turn was a special kind of torture. One that I hated but would happily endure for my Zosi Girl.

Zosime's hand shot out, wrapping around my pumping hand. As the soft skin of her fingertips trailed up my length, my lungs seized, forgetting how to function. When she squeezed her hand around me, I blew out a curse.

Storm picked up his rhythm, burying himself inside her, while Zosime's hand moved at the same pace along my hardened length. Fynn groaned, and I glanced over to find she had a hand gripping him tightly, too.

"Zosi, you're going to have to stop. I can't take much more," Fynn croaked. "I want to feed you."

"There will be time. We have all night." Zosime's voice was pure sex, her siren in full control.

Chills ran down my spine, and I arched into her hand. My body knew how dangerous my mate was, and that tendril of fear made every second with her even more thrilling. I loved it, but not nearly as much as I loved her.

"Zosime." Storm gritted out her name through clenched teeth. Sweat dripped from his body and his eyes darkened with raw need. The venom was working through his system.

Hips thrusting, Storm pounded into Zosime like a jackhammer. She never lost her rhythm as she pumped Fynn and me in perfect sync, rushing us toward our release together.

My entire body stiffened, and my hoarse shout was echoed by Fynn and Storm as we came apart in unison.

Locking my eyes on Zosi's face, I watched as pleasure spilled across her features. She was beautiful. A real-life goddess in the flesh. How was she mine? I was the luckiest man alive.

CHAPTER EIGHT

ZOSIME

We all lay in a sweaty, sticky heap, basking in the glow of our multiple orgasms. I couldn't wait for the day when we could enjoy each other's bodies without the impending doom of the world hanging over our heads.

Storm rolled off me with a groan, and I stifled a laugh. His eyes were fluttering as he fought the aftereffects of my venom. It was no use, though; he was going to be asleep within minutes.

I gasped as arms wrapped around me, lifting me off the bed in one smooth move.

"Eason!" With a yelp, I clung to his shoulders for balance.

"Princess," was all Eason said in response as he strode into the bathroom.

Eason set me on the sink. I hissed when the cool stone pressed against my bare backside.

"Stop being a baby." Eason snorted, releasing his hold on me and moving to grab a soft rag from the shelf.

Curious, I watched as he wet the rag in the sink—another modern convenience Lokene had installed—and then, kneeling in front of me, Eason began to gently clean my skin.

"You don't have to—"

"I want to." Eason cut off my protest. "Let me take care of you."

I stopped trying to wiggle off the cold sink and lost myself in his warm amber eyes. Eason paused, releasing a deep sigh. My heart began to thud painfully at the sadness and fear etched on his face.

"You know," I whispered, my heart pounding.

"Yes," Eason confirmed.

"How?" I asked, wondering if Zeno had told him my plan.

"Because I'm a soldier too. It's what I would do to protect those I cared about." Eason's hand shook as he rinsed the rag, but he quickly steadied it.

"You aren't going to stop me?" I asked, confused.

"No." His voice was resolute. "That doesn't mean that I'm not also fighting the urge to tie you to the bed and never let you leave, though. But I understand your sense of duty and what you are fighting for. I wouldn't ever get in your way."

I'd thought I knew these men. Even though I'd tried to avoid reading their minds, I felt like I'd known how they'd react. But Eason had surprised me.

Eason finished and rinsed the rag out before turning to me. Standing, he stepped between my legs until our bodies touched, and his erection burned where it pressed against my skin.

"I don't just support the princess that you are. I support the siren and the soldier in you, too." As he spoke, Eason's lips brushed against my cheek, my jaw, and then my neck. "I love all of you, Zosime. Everything that you are and everything that you will ever choose to be."

My heart thudded painfully against my ribs, and salty tears blurred my vision. Once again, my unstable emotions were getting the best of me. Hearing him acknowledge the fractured parts of me, and not just accept them, but love them, was a gift I hadn't even known I'd so desperately wanted.

"Eason," I choked, wrapping my body around him like an octopus.

"Shh. Don't cry, princess." The mountain of a man rocked me in his arms, letting my tears wet his chest.

For several minutes, I relaxed in the safety of his arms, committing to memory everything about his embrace and the scent of his skin. It didn't take me long to notice how nice it was when his soothing rocking motion caused his ever-present erection to rub against me. Eason may have cleaned me up, but I was quickly growing slick with need...again.

Scooting forward, I wrapped my legs tighter around Eason's waist, drawing him to me. We both sighed at the deliciousness of his erection pressed hard against my velvet folds.

"I want you." I let my siren purr, my tongue darting out to taste his salty skin.

"That works out well, because I'm yours." His words were a whisper so soft only I could hear.

A siren could only take so much temptation.

I sank my fangs into him, enjoying his long exhalation that shifted from surprise at the suddenness of my 'attack,' to a burning need in a single breath.

I drew the warmth of his blood into my mouth, savoring the intoxicating taste that was better than all the fine wines of Atlantis. Which was saying a lot, since Atlantis was known for making wine better than the Ancients.

Eason's hands moved across my skin, and his touch stirred the fire of another hunger to burn hotter. His breath turned to harsh pants that blew across my skin.

Sliding my hand between our bodies, I wrapped my hand around his base, squeezing gently and delighting in the way his body shuddered at my touch.

I shifted my hips and lined Eason's erection up with my entrance. My brief pause was too much for Eason, who was already feeling the effects of the toxin quickly spreading through his body and ramping up both his need and desire. Without hesitation, he buried himself inside me with a single rough stroke.

Stars sparkled in my vision, and I nearly choked on his blood as I forgot how to breathe. Eason's hands slid under my butt, digging into the soft flesh of my thighs and lifting me off the stone sink. I wasn't sure where he planned to take me, but I was more than willing to follow him to the ends of the earth as long as his burning erection stayed sheathed inside me.

It turned out our journey was short. Eason turned and pressed my back against the smooth gold walls. With a feat of strength that had my muscles clenching around him in lust, he braced me there. This gave him a better position to thrust into me, and when he hit my hidden chain of pearls at the near-perfect position, I pulled my mouth from his neck to moan Eason's name.

Eason took my cry as encouragement and a sign he was doing things right. With a growl, he began to thrust in earnest, hard enough that my back slammed against the wall with each rough pump of his hips.

I clung to his shoulders, my nails digging tiny half-moons into his skin as Eason made love to me with raw, unbridled passion. My human mates tended to be gentler during bonding, and I secretly adored it when they let go of their inhibitions and embraced this side of themselves.

Need and hunger burned through me like an untamed wildfire. Unable to stop myself, I sank my fangs into his neck a second time, craving the taste of his sweet blood. I sucked deeply, drinking far more than I should have taken, but lacking the strength to fight my all-consuming hunger.

Eason's smooth rhythm stumbled a bit, and we lurched to the side as more of my venom leaked through his system. He quickly righted us, pinning me back against the wall again, although this time, more of his weight pressed into me as he worked to stay balanced.

We would have been more comfortable on the bed or even on the floor, but I was too far gone to suggest we move. Eason's biceps bulged and sweat dotted his brow as he slid in and out, faster and harder with each stroke, driving us both upward toward the heavens as we neared our release.

When my orgasm finally came, I pulled my fangs from his skin and hissed as a pleasure, so strong it nearly hurt, rocked my body. Eason roared his own release, and my siren purred in satisfaction at the knowledge he was going to have a sore throat the following day.

I thought he would set me down or move back to the bedroom with me, but Eason stood still, my body trapped between the wall and his thick frame.

"Come back to me, princess," Eason murmured in my ear.

I wanted to promise him I would, but I never lied. It was a promise I just couldn't make.

"It will take heaven and Hades to keep me from you, my love." It was the truth. I would fight to the death and beyond if it was necessary.

Eason moved away from the wall, pulling me with him. His arms tightened around my waist as he held me. The heat of his embrace warmed the ice that had formed in my veins at the thought of what the morrow would bring.

"Stop tensing up. Tonight is not for worrying," Eason scolded, voice rough with emotions he was working to hide.

"You are right, my love." Giving him a smile, I placed a gentle kiss on his lips.

Tonight I would enjoy my mates, even though my heart was aching painfully at the absence of my most troublesome mate.

CHAPTER NINE

ZOSIME

C losing my eyes, I blinked myself to the quiet cove above the castle. It was still dark out, the sun not yet awake.

Had I been human, I would have missed the man sitting on one of the rock formations a few feet away. But I wasn't human, and my vision was as good in the dark as it was in the bright light of day.

Last night, after everyone was asleep, Bion had stepped from the shadows to speak with me. I wondered how long he had been there, but I didn't ask. I'd asked him to meet me here this morning to take me to Iolatara, and to my surprise, he had agreed.

"Ready?" I asked, all business. Last night I could afford

to have emotions. Today I was going to war, and being soft wasn't something I could risk.

Bion shoved to his feet and moved to stand in front of me. Even in the dark, there was no hiding the swirling emotions behind his eyes.

"I don't want to take you," Bion bit out.

"You don't have a choice," I retorted. "Take me, or I will figure out how to take myself. With or without your assistance, I will be going to Iolatara today."

We stared at each other as the crickets chirped and the occasional fish splashed in the distance. Finally, Bion caved.

"Fine, I'll take you." He paused, rubbing the back of his neck. "There's something you need, Fishy Girl. Once we're in Iolatara, I'll be unable to blink or teleport us around the planet."

"What?" My mouth dropped open. "What do you mean? you won't be able to blink wherever you want?"

"I meant exactly what I said," Bion grumbled.

"But you blink all over the place here! Lokene is always teleporting around and scaring us."

"Yeah, but that is here on Earth, not Iolatara. On Earth, some of our magik works differently than it does in our realm. There are stones that are landing spots and they scattered around Iolatara. Those are the locations we blink to when we arrive from other worlds. We can also travel around Iolartara by blinking from one landing stone to another." Bion didn't look happy about the limitations of his magik.

"The good news is we can blink to another world from any location on Iolatara, not just the landing stones... which is good in case you cause trouble. But anytime we want to teleport back onto Iolatara, we can only arrive on one of the landing stones. So, once we blink onto my planet, be prepared to do a lot of walking." Bion gave me a wry smile.

That wasn't a problem. I could handle a walk.

"We will arrive a short distance away from where the Elders meet. Which is probably for the best anyway. If I blinked you directly into the Elders' meeting room, I think it would be a shock for not only the Elders, but also for you." Bion bit his lip in thought, and the simple action caused my body to clench in sudden desire.

I wanted to bite his lip. I wanted to taste his kiss.

Bion cleared his throat. "The landing stone is a safe distance from the city, and you aren't likely to be seen. That will give you a chance to get used to our world and how your body reacts to the environment, but it means we'll have to walk the rest of the way. Is that okay with you?"

Shaking my head to clear the lust, I spoke, my voice a little huskier than normal. "Yes. I'm in agreement with your plan. Enough wasting time. Let's go."

To my surprise, Bion bent down and caught my mouth in a hungry kiss. Unable to help myself, I curved my arms around his neck. The stars swirled around us as the earth I called home faded away.

Ready or not, here I come.

Bᴉᴏɴ ᴄᴀᴜɢʜᴛ ᴍʏ ᴀʀᴍ ᴀs I sᴛᴀɢɢᴇʀᴇᴅ, ᴛʀʏɪɴɢ ᴛᴏ catch my footing on the rocky ground. He steadied me, and I found myself thankful I'd had Bion to blink me into Iolatara. Without Lokene, I wasn't sure it would have been possible for me to have safely blinked myself to the Ancients' world.

It didn't change the fact that I wanted to be irritated at Bion, if for no other reason than because it wasn't supposed to be him at my side. But it was impossible to stay mad, especially when Bion was trying to be as unobtrusive as possible.

He was trying to give me my space. But he was also still trying to support me, and not just in my plans to help the Ancients. Bion had given his assistance, without my needing to ask, during the meeting with the human politicians as well. He'd helped me impress on their minds that they weren't dealing with another human. And now, he'd been the one to teleport me to Iolatara.

My cheeks warmed when I realized I'd been staring just a little too long at his chiseled, ridiculously handsome face. I yanked my gaze away, ignoring Bion's laugh.

Bending to catch my breath in the change of altitude, I took in my first view of Iolatara.

I am not sure what I expected, but this wasn't it.

It was incredible how many of Iolatara's features were the same as Earth. Things like the tall mountain peaks in the distance and the puffy clouds in the sky. But other things couldn't have been more different. Such as the deep purple tint of the grass and the two suns in the sky.

Bion followed my gaze and explained. "We have twin suns here. One rises in the south, and the other rises in the north. They pass by each other every day."

I nodded, too transfixed by the suns to answer. Instead of the warm golden glow our sun bathed the earth in, the twin suns radiated a soothing rose gold onto Iolatara.

Reaching down, I plucked some of the purple grass, running my hands along the thick blades. It was soft, like velvet.

"Smell it," Bion encouraged.

I narrowed my eyes. Was he trying to prank me?

Bion chuckled at my obvious distrust of him. "It isn't going to hurt you. Just take a sniff." His hand covered mine, and leaning over until our noses nearly touched, he brought the grass close enough for us both to take a sniff.

I moaned, and my stomach rumbled. It smelled like spicy cinnamon and warm sugar. Lifting my eyes from the grass, I asked. "How?"

"You have flowers that smell, and we have scented grass." Bion shrugged, his laughter fading as his eyes slid down my face. Our lips were nearly touching in this position, and the intimacy of the situation had me standing quickly and taking a few steps back. If I planned to resist him, I had to keep some space between us.

Looking down into the valley beneath us, I spotted the beautiful ivory buildings scattered at the base of the mountain.

At first glance, each building seemed to have a domed roof made from a rainbow, but taking a closer look, I could see it was some kind of iridescent material that shifted colors with every movement I made.

Another thing that appeared quite different was the water as it cascaded down the mountains on the opposite side of the valley in a breathtaking waterfall before crashing into a golden river at its base.

My eyes followed the path of the gold river as it curved through the city, weaving around some buildings while other buildings had been built over it.

In some places, the river was as narrow as a creek, but in other places, it was wide enough that swimming it would have been exhausting for a human. It was an incredible sight to behold.

"Is there actual gold in the water?" I squinted at the water, confused that it seemed to be transparent.

"No. Water usually reflects the color of the sky. In your world, the sky is blue, but on Iolatara our sky is a pale yellow, and it gives our water the appearance of molten gold." Bion paused. "Or like someone peed in it."

I choked on a laugh. "You're a strange man, Bion."

"That's not the first time I've been told that." Bion

averted his gaze, but not before I caught a hint of sadness. I filed that away, finding myself wanting to know what had caused his pain.

"See that building?" Bion moved to stand beside me. Our shoulders brushed, and I tried to ignore the alluring tingle spreading across my skin from the brief touch. My body recognized him as mine. If the siren were in control, she would have claimed him on the spot as she had done with Kye.

I couldn't take another mate. There was no more room in my bed, and I already struggled to ensure each of my mates had time alone with me. Taking another mate would mean Bion would get very little time with me, and that wasn't fair to him. Plus, if Lokene's comments were to be believed, Bion was a player, not the type of man to settle down.

The mates I chose had made huge commitments—to my other mates and to me. If I chose someone and they decided they didn't want this life... I truly didn't know what that would do to me.

Pushing back my shoulders, I took a step away from him. I had a mission, and I didn't need the distraction or the risk.

I followed the line of his arm to see which building he was pointing to. It was a large circular building in the middle of the city, one of the buildings that had been built over the river.

"That's the meeting house of the Elders." Bion looked

up at the sky. "The twin suns have not crossed each other yet, so the Elders will still be in session."

"Then it's best I hurry down and introduce myself. Let's go." Grabbing my pack and tossing it over my shoulders, I began the steep trek down the mountainside.

CHAPTER TEN

ZOSIME

" **A** re you sure you want to go inside?" Bion asked.

I didn't bother to respond. He could either read my mind to get my answer, or he could simply follow my actions, but now was not the time for words.

I flattened both palms on the double gold-plated doors. Releasing the hold I kept on my roiling anger, I blew the heavy doors off their golden hinges. The shriek of the metal and splintering wood as the doors crashed into the hand-painted tile floor was horrific.

The Elders scattered around the room covered their ears, and their faces twisted in surprised horror. Like a commander going in front of her troops, I made my way to the center of the room, shoulders back and chin lifted.

They wanted me here badly enough to make an attempt at forcing my compliance. Wish granted, μαλάκα.

Bion must have been listening to my thoughts because he snickered, although he quickly hid it behind a cough. *Did you seriously just call the Elders 'malaka?'*

He knew exactly what I had said, and I didn't bother wasting time acknowledging his question.

Every eye in the room was pinned on me, but rather than shrinking from the weight of their judgment, I stood taller. I was born ready to fight.

Not giving the Elders a chance to speak, I spoke first.

"I am Zosime, Queen of Atlantis. I pledged my life to fight the Lure and have honored my oath even into a world vastly different from the one in which I made that promise." Pausing, I waited to see if any of the Ancients would speak up, but they remained stone-faced and silent.

"You took Lokene from me when I needed him during the last battle at Atlantis, and now you have taken him from me again. He is not a pawn for you to use in order to control me." My voice echoed through the room as the siren and warrior blended together, compelling everyone to listen.

"If I didn't feel honor bound to fulfill my oath, I wouldn't be standing before you today. I worshipped the Ancients, but you have done much to destroy my respect." I was pleased there was not even a tremble in my voice.

I was only half Ancient, and I wondered if the Ancients would decide to silence me permanently for my open disrespect. No one moved, nor did lightning strike and turn me to ash.

Either I was too important to kill, or their oath prevented them from murdering even a half-blood, because I remained breathing.

An Ancient with a long white beard and pale gray hair that hung in a braid to his waist stood up slowly from his seat.

"Welcome to your mother's homeland, Zosime." A gentle smile split his face as he greeted me.

Was he serious right now? I was here for war, both against the Lure and the Ancients who'd dared to take my mate. This wasn't a social call. Despite my irritation, my mother's etiquette training pounded in my head, ordering me to show proper respect to the Ancients. It took everything I had to fight against those ingrained manners and remain silent.

A blonde-haired woman who appeared to be in her mid-thirties spoke next. "We understand your displeasure over the inconveniences you feel we've caused you, but I assure you, they were necessary. You were needed here immediately, and your delays were unacceptable."

"Then why not teleport me here? Why use my mate as bait to draw me here?" I snapped, not bothering to hide my anger.

The Ancients exchanged an odd look before coming to some type of agreement on what to tell me.

"Your Earth magik is an interference. We can claim you

as ours because of your mother's blood in your veins, but the earth has also laid claim to you. We tried to bring you here, but the earth blocked our attempts."

I kept my face expressionless but stored that information away for later. The Earth claimed me and had thwarted the Ancients' efforts to take me from her by force?

"We would never harm you or your mates. I hope you know that, Zosime," the female Ancient with the glowing sky-blue eyes added as though their intentions made taking hostages ethical.

I raised a brow.

"Zosime, stop acting like a child," the gray-haired man scolded me. "We are trying to be lenient with you, but you would do well to remember who you are standing in front of."

My anger had reached the point of no return, and while the warrior inside of me had long revered the Ancients, the siren definitely hadn't.

"And you would do well to remember that I'm not a human to be ordered about." My words were calm. The kind of dangerous calm that comes right before a storm.

Lifting my hands into the air, I fought the urge to grin maniacally as the water of Iolatara obeyed my command and exploded through the floor. The force of the water shattered the beautiful hand-painted tiles on the floor and sent shards of broken pottery raining down around me.

"Enough!" one of the Ancients shouted. His hands

began to move, and I braced for whatever magik he was about to throw my way.

Only it didn't come.

"No!" Bion cried, stepping in front of me, throwing up a wall to separate the Ancients from me. He groaned against the pulse of the other Ancient's magik and stumbled back. He cast a glance over his shoulder and my breath caught in my throat at the worry and tenderness he accidentally let slip through his carefree, flirtatious mask.

Lokene rushed in, stepping to Bion's side. It took less than two seconds for Lokene to take in the situation, and he threw his power into strengthening Bion's wavering barrier.

"Lokene!" His name was out of my mouth before I could stop myself. Having him near, where I could see that he was safe, was an immense relief, and some of the tension drained from my body.

You look beautiful, Soyale. Lokene shot me a wink over his shoulder and then gave Bion a begrudging look. *I'm fine, and it seems Bion has a knack for finding the weaknesses in the Ancients' magik to yank me from confinement. Once free, it was a bit of a jog, but it seems I got here just as things were getting interesting.*

I was growing suspicious that Bion enjoyed causing chaos and was an expert at creating the distractions that caused the weaknesses in the first place.

Bion grinned at me. *Nope. This was all you, doll. Your sudden appearance and the water show were just what I needed to free your lover boy.*

"Enough! Enough!" a deep voice boomed as a third Ancient stood. I eyed the man with dark, wavy hair as he motioned for both parties to calm down.

My war was with the Ancients responsible for the Lure, not these Ancients. Sure, I was less than pleased with them and wouldn't be doing them any favors in the foreseeable future, but I didn't truly want to fight them. I wanted them to stop toying with my mates and leave me in peace.

With that in mind, I lowered my arms, allowing the water to crash back through the holes in the floor to rejoin the shimmering pool beneath the floating marble building.

Reluctantly, the gray-haired Ancient lowered his hands to his sides again. With a fierce scowl on his face, he opened his mouth, but was cut off by the dark-haired man.

"So help me, if you are about to say she started it, I will beg the Lure to take you, Jacque." I got the impression from the raven-haired man that this was not the first time Jacque had tried his patience.

Jacque sat down with a huff, crossing his arms over his chest. Now who was behaving like a child?

That's your uncle. Lokene sounded positively delighted to drop that bit of news on me.

That cannot be the truth, I protested, searching the sulking Ancient's face as though I might recognize an uncle I'd never met.

Don't you see the family resemblance in the stubborn set of his jaw and the 'I-don't-give-a-crap attitude?' Lokene teased.

I glanced at Bion, hoping he would tell me Lokene was joking, but he gave a slight nod of his head.

Sorry, Zosi. He's definitely your uncle. Happy family reunion.

You know what is worse than not having a family? Having a family that doesn't care about you. The day Sheba learned to fly would be the day I would call this man my uncle and accept him as family. He could have stopped by to say hi anytime since I was awakened, but had chosen not to; instead, he'd been part of a plan to take my mate away from me. I wouldn't forgive that so easily.

Ancients can't interfere, Soyale. You needed time to figure out who you were and adjust to your new body and abilities. Lokene tried to ease my hurt, but I wasn't having it.

Ancients seem more than happy to involve themselves when it suits them and then claim the excuse of not interfering when a situation is messy and they want to avoid it, I snapped back.

They'd sure been happy to toss a war in my lap, take Lokene from me multiple times, and finally, they'd dumped Bion and psycho Lily on me.

Bion seemed to be working out for the best, but I doubted the Ancients had seen that one coming. I sure hadn't.

Bion quirked a brow. *Working out for the best?*

Don't read too much into that. I just don't feel like

killing you at this precise moment, which is more than I can say about Lily.

Dark-haired man turned to me, tilting his head in a polite bow. "Hello, Zosime. It is a great honor to meet you in person. I'm Anthony."

He paused, awaiting a response from me. I let things get to the edge of awkward before tilting my head in acknowledgment. Still, I refrained from speaking, preferring to let him explain things.

"First, I want to apologize for the manipulations which were used to bring you here. While I was not among those who agreed to use those tactics, I am nonetheless guilty for not making any effort to stop it." His eyes didn't flinch from my unwavering gaze, and a seed of respect began to grow inside me.

"What now?" I asked, voice flat. "Are the Ancients going to continue to interfere with my life? Or will I be allowed to do the job I dedicated my life to?"

"We are not your enemy. Please save our kind, your mother's kind." There was a raw note to his voice. "You've seen the effects of the Lure on humans and how quickly it can spread. Now that it has mutated and is tainting Ancients, there is even more at stake. Ancients who have given into the Lure have the ability to spread it to other worlds. There is more at stake than just our two worlds."

He was afraid, and I couldn't blame him.

Taking in each of the Ancients' somber faces, I realized they were all terrified. Unlike humans who lived with the knowledge that someday they would die, death had never been something for the Ancients to fear.

Now it was a very real possibility they would be wiped from existence, their memory nothing more than a handful of fanciful tales of fictional Greek gods.

Sucked to be them.

Lokene and Bion burst into laughter, earning them a quelling look from... everyone.

"Where do I find the Ancients who are tainted by the Lure?" I got straight to the point. We'd wasted enough precious time. Once I was near enough, the call would guide me to my prey, but I needed to be closer.

Anthony looked uncomfortable. "We have heard reports they are in the Caves of Zavionia. I would start looking there."

I would have preferred more specifics, but this would not be the first time I headed to war with little more than a vague idea of where the enemy lay. This was just another day in the building.

The office, Lokene corrected in my mind. *It is just another day in the office.*

I fail to see the difference. An office is a building, is it not? I narrowed my eyes at him.

Well, yes. But... Lokene trailed off when he realized I was correct.

You aren't correct. Lokene's words in my mind were little more than a mumble.

"You will leave my mates alone, yes? All of them?" I

addressed the Ancients but focused my attention on Jacque.

"Yes, you have our word that we will not use your mates to get your attention," Anthony spoke, and each Ancient around the room nodded their head in agreement. Several looked livid about it, but they gave a jerky nod of agreement anyway.

Satisfied, I turned on my heel and strode toward the door. "Good. Then I will take my leave. I have work to do."

I heard the rumblings of the Ancients behind me, but I ignored them. Excitement pumped through my veins.

It was time for war.

CHAPTER ELEVEN

ZOSIME

I t turns out the Caves of Zavionia made up an area of Iolatara the size of a large city. It had taken all day to make it to the mountain range that marked the beginning of the caves. We stood on top of a mountain precipice, looking out over slate-covered mountains as far as the eye could see.

"Can you sense other Ancients in the area?" I asked, carefully surveying the rocky valley below for any signs of life.

"I should be able to, but they've done something to confuse things. It is almost as though we're in a house of mirrors. I can feel the presence of Ancients nearby, but I can't pinpoint which direction." Lokene rubbed at his temples as though staving off a headache.

"How about you? Can you sense the Lure yet, doll?" Bion asked, standing behind me, close enough that the soft blue fabric of his shirt brushed my bare arm.

I'd been surprised Bion hadn't disappeared the moment we'd left the meeting with the Ancients. He'd delivered me to the Ancients, so his assignment from the Ancients was finished. When I'd asked where he was off to, Bion had made a joke about tagging along for a bit because he had nothing better to do. He'd not been able to meet my eye when he said it, and I wondered again what he was hiding. Pain? Loneliness? Maybe I'd find out on this journey. Secretly, I was glad I didn't have to say goodbye to Bion yet.

Belatedly remembering I hadn't answered his question, I sighed. "No, we aren't close enough yet."

"This would be easier if we could just pop from mountaintop to mountaintop like we could do if we were on Earth," Bion grumbled.

"No. I prefer doing this the old-fashioned way. I want to head into the valley and look for signs of life having been here. If we can find some well-traveled roads or paths, I will be able to track them. Lokene says they are near, but if they are confusing their location on purpose, this is our best chance." My bloodlust was eager to begin the hunt.

We spent the next several hours searching the valley for signs that the Ancients had been there recently. Toward the evening, when the light from the twin suns began to fade and their moon cast an odd purple light on the landscape, we decided to stop and make camp for the night.

Ignoring Lokene and Bion's complaints, I found an abandoned cave with enough room for a small fire. Lokene growled in frustration.

"I wish we could teleport back to the human world tonight, but the nearest travel stone to the caves is almost a half-day walk away. If we blink to Earth tonight, we'd be forced to spend hours hiking back to this same spot tomorrow. The caves seem to cause interference for those wanting to blink deeper into the cave systems. We've never found a place in this valley where it was safe to place a travel stone." Lokene looked around the dim cave and shivered. "There might be spiders in here."

"There are spiders on this world?" I asked, intrigued.

"Yes, butt-ugly spiders as big as the dogs in your world." Bion fake gagged.

"But you are the Ancients? Why can't you just make spiders cease to exist?" The more I learned of the Ancients, the less sense they made.

"We tried that, but it didn't work. So then we tried burning everything to the ground, but that didn't work either. All that did was force us to create a new planet to live on, and somehow, the spiders still found a way onto this planet, too." Lokene sat gingerly on a stone near the cave's entrance, not willing to rest his back on the cave walls.

I couldn't help my snicker. The big scary Ancients were scared of spiders?

"You won't be laughing when you see the size of these

things!" Bion warned. "And they infest like the roaches of your world."

"Oh no. I am shaking with fear." Rolling my eyes, I began pulling supplies from my pack. "I'm not leaving this world until I have tracked down the tainted Ancients and ended this. Plus, I doubt my other mates will be eager to see me after I snuck away from them during the night."

I grabbed my pack, unzipping it as I added, "This is not the first time I've been forced to camp while tracking an enemy."

Dried fruit, meats, and bottled water.

Bion gave a horrified shriek, and I jumped up, ready to defend him from a dog-sized spider.

Only there was no spider.

Instead, Bion's attention was focused on the rations I had laid out, as though they were pet food.

"Surely you don't intend to eat that stuff?" Bion asked, voice incredulous.

I stared at the food in consternation. "Of course I do. What's wrong with them?"

"Everything?" Bion responded, more a question than a statement.

"I brought enough for both you and Lokene." Unwrapping the food, I held out a piece of jerky out toward Bion. He shied away from it as though it were a venomous snake.

"No, thank you, but thank you for the offer?" Again, Bion sounded as though he were asking a question.

I turned to Lokene, preparing to offer him the meat.

Lokene shook his head and held up his hands. "Soyale, let me make dinner."

I watched as platters of perfectly cooked meat, bread, and vegetables appeared on the stone slab between us. When I had packed for this trip, I hadn't been sure how soon Lokene would be returned to me or how long Bion would stay at my side. I'd made sure I had the supplies I would need if I were on my own but seeing a beautiful filet of fish made me very thankful for my mate's abilities.

Bion whistled. "Now that is food!"

"It is all food. You are just spoiled," I shot back, but I quickly repacked the unappealing dried foods.

We spent the next two hours enjoying the impromptu feast Lokene had conjured and mentally going through the chaos of the day. Once we finished eating, both men complained loudly about being forced to sleep in a cave like animals.

"At least let me make it more comfortable in here. Lokene fed you, so I can bed you." Bion winked and then blushed as he realized what he'd said. "That's not what I meant."

My stomach did an odd flip at the thought of him bedding me, but I quickly buried it.

Soyale, is there something you want to tell me? Lokene purred in my mind.

Like what? I asked as innocently as possible.

Perhaps that you desire Bion as a mate? Lokene's arms wrapped around my waist, pulling me flush against his body. *Don't worry, I've blocked him from hearing our conversation.*

That isn't— I started. I couldn't finish my sentence though, not unless I wanted to lie to both Lokene and myself. *That isn't important right now.*

I tried to push away, to keep focused on my mission, but Lokene wasn't having it, and his arms tightened.

Bion is a good man. Obnoxious, but good. Lokene nuzzled my neck and my skin flushed.

Thankfully, Bion spoke, cutting into a mental conversation he was clueless about. "Yes, this should be more comfortable than sleeping on the cold stone floor."

Bion flopped down on a large mattress that was piled high with pillows. He patted the bed next to him. "Come on, you two! Give it a try."

I made my way over to the bed but hesitated to sit down. I was covered in filth from the day's adventures. Pausing for just a moment, I decided I couldn't bring myself to climb into a clean bed like this and began peeling off my clothing.

I'd thought Bion might look away, but his heated gaze left a burning trail as it traveled every inch of my skin that came into view. Ignoring him was the safest course of action, but certainly not the easiest.

Lokene stepped up behind me, his hands sliding across my flat stomach. My breath caught as he unbuttoned my jeans and then hooked his thumbs in the waistband. Tilting my head, I caught his expression as he stared at Bion.

"Isn't she gorgeous?" Lokene asked the other man while sliding my jeans down my hips with excruciating slowness.

"Yes." Bion's single word answer was hoarse.

Lokene wasn't finished. He pushed the jeans down further, catching the band of my panties and sliding them down together. I flushed hotter than the fires in Hades as Bion devoured me with his eyes. Lokene kneeled, kissing down my legs as he exposed more skin.

"Lokene, this is not the time," I choked out.

"I've missed you," he whispered between kisses.

"I missed you too." My legs trembled, but I braced myself and steeled my resolve. "But we should stay focused on the mission." *What are you doing, Lokene? I asked.*

"The morning is soon enough for that." Lokene gently lifted one of my feet and then the other, ridding me of my jeans.

Maybe sleeping in my clothes would've been a far safer idea.

Lokene, please. This is hard enough without you creating more temptation.

He sighed. *As you wish, Soyale.* Once he had me naked, Lokene scooped me into his arms and carried me to the bed, laying me gently between Bion and himself.

Bion reached out a hand, tracing my jawline with a featherlight touch that sent chills racing across my skin. "You are beautiful. The most beautiful woman in all the worlds and realms I have visited."

I swallowed past the lump in my throat. "Bion, I can't. There are too many—"

Bion's face grew wistful. "I know, doll babe. But if the day comes that you change your mind, I will be here."

The siren screamed in my mind, urging me to claim him as mine. He was willing, after all. But I had responsibilities to see to and mates to think of that I had to put before my lust.

"Thank you," I whispered, squeezing my eyes closed to keep back the tears.

Bion smiled and tucked the blankets up over my body. Lokene laid down behind me and pulled me against his warm embrace. To my relief, sleep came quickly.

IT WASN'T A SOUND THAT WOKE ME. IT WAS THE LACK of any sound. The crackling of the smoldering fire was still there, but the rest of the night's sounds had grown silent. With the firelight nearly gone, the cave had been plunged into darkness.

I was off the mattress and lunging forward with my arm around my assailant's neck in less time than it took to take a breath. A new sound drummed in my ears.

The call.

Except there wasn't just one person. There were two.

It was about freaking time! I needed to let off some steam after the chaos of the past few days.

Not wasting time, I sank my fangs into the neck of the attacker in my hold, quickly injecting my venom while simultaneously using my hold and training to snap their neck.

As an Ancient, she wouldn't die from a broken neck. But if I was correct, she would die from my venom. The issue was I wanted to keep that a secret until I had finished battling the Lure, and if the second attacker escaped, my secret would be known.

A hard kick to my mid-section sent me flying into the cave wall. No sooner had my body touched the stone than I used it to propel myself straight into my attacker's body. A resounding crack was followed by a wheeze, and I smirked, knowing at least one of the attacker's ribs had been broken.

I heard Lokene stir and had to admire that Ancients slept like dead people because Bion hadn't moved from his sleep position either.

As much as I might have enjoyed the chance to practice my hand-to-hand combat, I bit down on the attacker's bicep, sinking my fangs in deep enough to scrape bone and injecting enough venom to take down a small whale.

The hood fell back from their face. The woman cursed but didn't have time to retaliate before my venom spread through her body, permanently shutting down her nervous system.

It had taken only a few seconds to finish the fight. My

chest heaved from exertion, and I worked to steady my breathing.

Lokene chose that moment to jerk upright, eyes wide with panic. "Soyale!"

"What is going on?" Bion leaped to his feet, voice rising in pitch as he took in the tableau in front of him.

Shoving the dead woman off me, I rose to my feet with the elegance of a cat, thankful I was finally growing comfortable in my two-legged form. Walking over to the fire, I tossed on several pieces of wood, and then I used a stick to poke it back to life. That task finished, I reached for the first attacker. I ripped back the hood to find another woman. Her eyes were unfocused, and the life once held inside them was gone.

"Do you know her?" I grabbed the woman's braided hair, hauling her face up so the rekindled firelight would shine on it and give the men a good look.

"Yes, I do. She teaches the younger Ancients," Lokene answered, raking his hand through his hair as he struggled to understand what was going on.

Horror spread across Bion's face. "Did—did you kill her?"

Scoffing, I released my grip and let the woman drop to the ground. "Of course I did. She was tainted by the Lure."

"Are you sure?" Lokene's skin turned an odd shade of green.

"Because this is what I was tasked to do. Allow the call

to lead me to those tainted by the Lure," I responded, confused by his question.

"But as Ancients, we should have been able to sense the Lure!" Bion's voice held panic, but I couldn't understand why.

"Ancients don't always see the future or precisely how some things will happen. Perhaps this is one of those times?" Bending down, I picked up the second woman, angling her face toward the men. "How about this one?"

Bion collapsed backward on the mattress, biting his fist.

Lokene swallowed hard several times before answering. "Yes, I know her. She was in charge of the gardens and floral displays. Zosi, she was a really sweet lady."

"She may have been once, but now she is not." I wanted to be understanding of their shock, but I couldn't help feeling hurt by the way they doubted me. Did they really think I would kill two people for the fun of it?

"Of course we don't think that." Bion sat up, answering my unspoken question. "It's just that we've seen what the Lure does to those tainted by it. I saw these women only two days ago, and they were sweet as always."

Bion tried to find the right words to not upset me, but I didn't miss how his eyes cut to Lokene's. Nor did I miss the worried expressions they exchanged. They were talking about me. Purposefully leaving me out of the conversation.

"I just don't understand," Lokene mumbled. "Are you sure you couldn't be mistaken?"

"Everyone makes mistakes," Bion added. "If this was an accident, it's okay. We can help you."

These men might be Ancients, but they were also acting like idiots.

I wish I could say I did the rational thing. That I ignored my personal feelings and did my job like a good little soldier. But that would be a lie. My new and unstable-as-ever emotions got the best of me.

Stomping over to both women, I yanked open their jackets, revealing the weapons hidden beneath the fabric.

"I suppose the reason they were sneaking around the cave in the dark of night, with their identities hidden, was because they wanted to have a friendly chat with me and maybe show off their weapons?" There was no way to hide the derision in my trembling voice.

"Soyale, I wanted to believe your instincts are correct. But these women are Ancients. They were alive before life even existed on your Earth. It is hard to believe they have given into the Lure," Lokene tried to explain.

Bion hesitated, his eyes darting between me and the two dead Ancients. "Maybe they were coming to offer their assistance on our mission?" he suggested.

I held up my hand, cutting them off. I quickly laced up my boots and grabbed my backpack before turning back to the men.

"If you doubt my ability to recognize the Lure, or the call that leads me to it, then you need to question my judgment regarding every single person I killed to honor my oath to *your* people." Tears burned my eyes, but I refused to let even a single tear fall.

I was a warrior, not a tender-hearted princess, and I would not let these men see me cry. How could I trust them to have my back during a crucial moment in a battle if they would so easily doubt me?

Hoping that my body would continue to adapt to my needs, I did the two hardest things I'd ever done.

I raised my mental shields, blocking both men from reading my thoughts. Something that should be impossible for a half-blood like myself to do.

The moment the barrier sealed away my private thoughts, there was a prick of pain in my skull. Lokene must have felt it as well because he gasped and pressed his hand to his temple.

"What did you do, Zosime?" Bion's brow wrinkled in confusion, looking between Lokene and me. Pushing to his feet, he walked toward me like a human approaching an injured stray dog. "Why can't I hear you?"

Lokene's eyes widened as realization settled over him.

"Because I don't want you to," I whispered.

Before either man could respond, I did the impossible and teleported myself away into the dark of the night.

CHAPTER TWELVE

ZOSIME

T he only thought on my mind as I teleported away
from the men had been how much I needed the
comfort of being surrounded by water. So I shouldn't have
been too shocked when I found myself suddenly submerged
in it.

This wasn't like Earth's water, though. Oh no. If Earth's
saltwater helped a body float, Iolatara's water did the exact
opposite. It was like quicksand, quickly pulling me deeper.

There was one other terrifying issue with this water. It
was scorching hot, far hotter than any hot spring I had stumbled across during my time on Earth. My skin burned as
though I were floating in acid rather than water.

I thought about trying to blink myself out of the water,

but what if I sent myself into a volcano next? Or worse, what if I blinked back to the cave? I wasn't even sure if I could teleport again... especially since I wasn't supposed to be able to do it in the first place.

I kicked hard, fighting to reach the surface. It was no use. The weight of my backpack and boots weighed me down. I wasn't sure how deep the water was or what was on the bottom. Which meant if I kicked the boots off so I could shift into my siren body, there was a chance I wouldn't be able to find and retrieve them afterward.

Hades, I wasn't even sure I could adapt to such inhospitable water before it murdered me.

At this point, though, I had little choice. I may have phenomenal breath hold for a human body, but with the weight of the water pressing on my chest, I knew that my time in this form was extremely limited.

I let go of my pack, ignoring the flicker of anxiety it caused me to see it sink like a lead weight into the dark water beneath me. Working quickly, I undid the laces on my left boot.

Ignoring a wave of dizziness, I turned my attention to the right boot. It took more effort than I expected due to the lack of oxygen, causing my mind to grow foggy.

Eventually, I was able to loosen the laces enough to kick both boots off. They were already waterlogged and immediately sank toward the bottom.

I wanted to curse, but I couldn't afford to lose the last bit of oxygen in my lungs. I needed those boots if I planned to go back on land. Especially since I had just pulled a disappearing act on the two men who could make new clothes for me to appear from thin air.

Even though swimming with my tail was a definite advantage, my progress toward the surface was far slower than I would have liked. But at least I was moving, right?

Unable to help myself, I sucked in another desperate breath, my body screaming for oxygen. Once again, my lungs ached from the weight of the water.

There was oxygen in the water, but not as much as I was used to. A deep breath of Earth's water had about half the amount of oxygen as was in the air. This water was far less oxygenated, and I was being forced to work three times as hard to breathe, while only getting a fraction of the oxygen my body was used to.

Dizzy and lightheaded, I fought to stay conscious. My body reflexively sucked in one deep lung full of water after another while I choked and gagged.

The water above me grew lighter as I neared the surface. If I could just break the surface, I would be able to take in a deep breath. I was so close.

I was five meters from the surface when I slowed. Something had changed.

The darkness that had tinted the edges of my vision had cleared, and my lungs, although slightly sore, as though they'd just finished a workout, were moving the water more easily with each breath I took.

With wonder, I came to a stop, suspended in the water,

as I realized that my mind was clear again and wasn't in danger of passing out. My body's freaky blessing, or maybe curse, that forced me to survive, had once again come to my aid.

I suspected there were few fish or mammals on Earth able to survive, even temporarily, in this inhospitable water. Yet my body had evolved fast enough that while I wasn't completely comfortable, I was at least surviving in it.

Staying below the surface, I moved in one direction, knowing that at some point I would have to hit land since planets were round, right?

It took about ten minutes before I could make out a wall of dirt and stone in front of me. Digging my fingers into the dirt, I clung to the wall before slowly creeping up the side until my eyes were above the water's surface.

Changing directions, I swam away from the surface of the water, heading back the way I'd just come. I grew stronger with each passing minute in the water, but it still took several minutes to reach the bottom.

Thankfully, the floor of this body of water was only about three hundred feet down. The water at this depth was cold and murky, but I could navigate it easily in my siren's form.

It took some searching along the craggy bottom to find my backpack. My boots would have been a lot easier to locate if they'd sank to the same spot. I guess that would have been too easy. Instead, the pair had gone their separate ways, floating a small distance from each other.

Finally, gathering the last of my gear, I pushed off the bottom and began the challenging swim up toward the surface. While Iolatara's landscape was beautiful, the underwater world I was currently immersed in was less than enthralling. The water was murky and dark. I didn't mind dark water—Atlantis was surrounded by it—but there was something unwelcoming about these waters. I kept looking for signs of life like small fish or plants, but I could see nothing but dark slate stone slabs and sharp-edged rocks. It wasn't a vacation spot I would be eager to revisit.

When the water grew lighter, signifying I was nearing the surface, I slowed my pace.

While I wasn't currently hearing the call, I didn't want to risk surfacing in front of a predator. Who knew what types of predators could be lurking, of both the wild creature and Ancient variety?

I also wasn't too keen on talking with Lokene or Bion right then, and I wasn't sure how far I'd blinked from our tiny cave shelter. For all I knew, they were sitting on the bank waiting for me to surface. I wondered if they had a way of tracking me. They were Ancients, after all.

Then again, I'd blocked both of them from my mind, which shouldn't have been possible. Perhaps that would keep the Ancients from being able to track me as well. Exactly how 'all knowing' were the Ancients?

Without making a sound, my head broke the surface of the water just enough so that my eyes were above the water and I could take in my surroundings.

It was still dark out, but the sky on both sides of the horizon was growing lighter. It wouldn't be long before Iolatara's twin suns rose. Glancing around, I tried to figure out where I was and how far I'd teleported.

Even more importantly, how far was I from my prey?

It turned out I'd landed in their backyard. Well, I was in someone's backyard. I just needed to figure out who it belonged to.

I sensed no presences, and no unwelcome thoughts bombarded my mind. Yet looking around, I could see signs of life. Someone had been here recently.

Several small wooden buildings surrounded a large firepit, and a path had been trampled through the tall purple grass down to the shoreline. Upon closer inspection, I could see tiny wisps of smoke coming from the fire pit. They'd been here recently, and with any luck, they'd come back.

As much as it grated on my nerves, I needed to wait.

Who knew? Perhaps I'd get lucky, and they would come down to the water on their own.

With that thought in mind, I slid beneath the water and moved away from the trampled shoreline. I made my way over to an untouched patch of grass where I could stay well-hidden if someone came this way.

I could always sink below the surface for a quick escape, but unless they were flying overhead, I would be difficult to spot in my hiding place among the water and thick grass.

I just needed to be patient, like a lioness stalking her

prey on the plains of Africa and waiting for that perfect moment to strike.

IT WAS JUST PAST NOON WHEN THE SUNS HAD CROSSED paths that the sound of voices drifted through the clearing. My muscles were fatigued from remaining motionless for so long, but I dared not move now.

The call pounded in my skull before the new arrivals had even stepped into view. These people were tainted.

My heart raced. I'd found who I was looking for.

But were these the leaders or just more tainted Ancients? I didn't know, so fighting the urge to answer the call, I settled in to watch and listen. If I was lucky, these Ancients would spill some helpful information.

A tall blonde woman and two brown-haired men strode into view, laughing and talking. The woman's hands touched both men in a way that left little doubt that these men were her sexual partners or her mates.

I analyzed every interaction between the three Ancients, searching for signs of which of the three were in charge. They would all need to die, but if I wanted to defeat the Lure, I needed to go to the source.

The woman spoke first. "Nick, have you heard from the assassins?"

Nick, who was apparently the more muscular of the two men, answered. "No. I haven't heard from them. I can't even sense anything from them."

The woman fidgeted with the end of her long braid. "They should have returned by now."

Nick rubbed his chin. "I agree, Lexi."

The woman, Lexi, gave a strained laugh. "Well, they couldn't have been killed. There is no way the ever-pure Bion and Lokene would dare to take the life of another Ancient. They'd never risk becoming corrupted. The little half-blood wouldn't have the power necessary to kill an Ancient."

Both men chuckled.

The second man spoke up for the first time. "Although she has some impressive skills for a mutt. I heard about the damage she caused yesterday. It's going to cost a small fortune to fix the floor of the meeting building, since only the original Ancient artisans are allowed to work on it."

Nick shook his head. "They should just use their magik to repair it. Less time, less work, and less money. Although maybe there is something to be said about handcrafted work."

Lexi coughed, looking at the second man. "Raq, when will the others arrive?"

"We're still waiting on the two assassins, and then the last two are due to arrive within the next two hours."

Lexi smiled, squeezing his arm. "Wonderful! I'm sick of living in this hovel. Once everyone is back, we can take the final step. It's time we introduce both Ancients and humans to their new leadership."

Nick settled into one of the chairs in front of the fire pit. Closing his eyes, he seemed to be preparing for a nap. "I'm looking forward to that. It's been a long time coming."

"I know something else that would like to spend a long time coming." Lexi turned seductive eyes toward Raq. "We have time."

I tried not to gag.

With a laugh, Raq scooped her up in his arms, twirling her around. With a laugh, he jogged toward the largest of the buildings.

Lexi's face lost the menacing, hard edge as she smiled at him. She looked girlish and heartbreakingly beautiful. It was easy to forget that she was part of the madness threatening to rip apart both our worlds. A battle that had cost countless lives.

Watching them disappear inside, I was surprised to feel a tiny pang of pity for her.

Because only one of us would be alive to see the rising suns.

CHAPTER THIRTEEN

ZOSIME

The sounds coming from the cabin had me sinking below the water's surface to attempt to muffle the noises.

I appreciated the biological need for mating, but being forced to listen to the sounds emanating from the cabin caused bile to rise in my throat.

The man in the lawn chair gave an annoyed groan. Nick had been unable to nap due to the screaming banshee inside. With a long-suffering sigh, he pushed to his feet, stretching his muscles while looking at the cabin. Rather than heading inside to join the two Ancients doing the 'no pants dance' as Kye calls it, he turned and meandered toward the water.

Thank Atlantis! If I'd been forced to sit still another minute, I feared my muscles would have atrophied. My relief died a quick death.

Nick stopped, taking a seat on a large stone that sat midway between the wooden building and the water's edge. I couldn't wait any longer. It was time for action.

With slow, quiet movements, I slid my body out of the scorching water. The day was warm, but the difference in temperature caused steam to rise from my body and a shiver to rack through me.

Once I'd moved fully onto land, I shifted into my human form. I'd considered going for my gear, but doubted I could dress without drawing the man's attention. The best weapon in my arsenal was likely my naked body.

If Nick was dedicated to the woman inside, the shock of seeing me should still give me the precious seconds I needed to sink my fangs into him. But if they were friends with benefits, my siren should have no issues distracting him.

I crept through the tall grass, wanting to approach the man from one of the rock pathways rather than approaching from the path to the water. The last thing I wanted was for him to realize I was the siren his assassin friends had been sent to hunt down.

I staggered into Nick's line of vision, faking a wince when I purposely stumbled over several loose rocks. The man's eyes snapped in my direction, widening as he spotted me.

I pretended not to notice when his gaze trailed down my body. No happily claimed man would linger so long on another woman's nude body. My odds of success went up.

I tried to look helpless as I made my way toward him.

Nick shoved to his feet, quickly pasting a look of concern on his face, but it did nothing to hide the darkness in his eyes. Lust clouded his mind, which is why he didn't pause to think about the oddness of the situation.

The pounding of the call grew more demanding as I drew closer to him. This man needed to die.

"Hello, sweetheart. Are you okay?" Nick's voice was gentle, worried even.

"I need help." I slurred the words slightly, adding to the image of a lost and injured woman.

"Are you hurt?" he asked, his hands reaching out to grab my waist, presumably to steady me.

I wobbled. "Yes." I purred the word, allowing tears to fill my eyes.

"Where does it hurt?" he asked, his rough palms sliding across my skin, all under the guise of checking me for injuries. I clenched my teeth as his fingers brushed the underside of my breasts. He was taking every opportunity to touch me.

"My head hurts. Can you help me?" My voice was a needy whisper as my siren pushed forward, eager to play her part in this little charade.

It wasn't a lie. The call had grown so loud it was now a stabbing pain threatening to split my skull. The female

Ancient, Lexi, chose that moment to let loose with another ear-piercing-orgasm-announcing scream.

I jerked forward into Nick's chest as though frightened by the loud sound.

"Oh!" My cry was breathless as my fingers curled into my prey's shirt.

Nick released a low moan, his hands running down my butt and pulling me tighter against his body.

The bulge in his pants pressed hard against me, and I ground my teeth, disgusted at the feel of another man's touch on my body. I forced myself to relax against him, not wanting to give him a reason to be jarred from his little fantasy.

"Yes, let me help you." He spoke in a deep voice that he probably thought was sexy. He couldn't have been more wrong. It sounded like he was two hundred years old and dying from diseased lungs.

My mind wandered, thinking of Eason's rough, gravel-filled voice. It was just as erotic as his rough, calloused palms on my skin. I missed him so much it hurt like a physical punch to my gut. My resolve to finish this mission hardened. The sooner I finished, the sooner I could go home to my men.

My venom had worked on the two Ancient women in the cave, but this would be the first male Ancient I would be trying to execute with my special toxin. How much would it take? How fast would it work? I'd have preferred to sink my fangs into his flesh quickly and be done, but I couldn't risk that it would take longer, and he'd have time to call out for help.

Nick's hands continued to explore my body, and I forced myself to remain pliant and not recoil in disgust. I pressed my lips to the bare skin of his collarbone, letting my warm breath blow across his skin as I pretended to pant. Nick's thick fingers dug hard into my hips, yanking me hard against his crotch. Ancient or not, men could be predictable.

Almost there.

His eyes closed, and his breathing grew ragged. When he started dry humping against me, like a dog in heat, I made my move. Not wanting to bring him out of his fantasy, I carefully sank just the razor-sharp tips of my fangs into his skin.

Nick hissed. "I see you like it rough."

We'd barely made it to our knees when his movements jerked and then ceased. He opened his mouth to speak, but only a gurgled grunt came out.

"Finally! It took you long enough!" I grumbled.

Grabbing him under the arms, I dragged him toward the water's edge, ignoring the burning pain as my muscles strained to drag the dead weight of his body. His very dead weight.

I pushed the dead Ancient into the scorching water, allowing it to swallow his body. With no time to spare, I yanked several handfuls of the fragrant purple grass and rushed back to where his body had fallen. I moved swiftly, brushing the grass through the sand to hide the obvious drag marks his body had made.

They would look for him, but there was no need to leave an arrow pointing in my direction, either. Once finished, I discarded the grass out of sight. Without a splash, I leaped into the unwelcoming water while shifting seamlessly into my siren's body.

Moving through the water, I made my way back to the shoreline and resumed my original position.

It was time to plan the next part of my hunt. The prolonged pounding of the call in my mind was making it increasingly difficult to think. One thing was for sure, it would be almost impossible for me to take both the man and the woman at the same time since they were powerful Ancients.

I needed to watch and wait for an opportunity to separate them. Maybe I would get lucky, and one of them would come to the shoreline to look for their missing friend. If that happened, I could easily pull them in, and if I was fast enough to inject the venom, my prey wouldn't have a chance to teleport away.

As I swam to a dark corner, the heavy drumbeat of the call in my skull demanded I storm into the house and take out both tainted Ancients. If they were human, that would have been easy to accomplish. But they were Ancients, so I fought against the overwhelming urge to go after my prey that instant.

How long would it be before the other two Ancients

they mentioned arrived here? Looking at the sky overhead, I checked the position of the suns. Hopefully, I had enough time to dispatch the two Ancients in the cabin before the newcomers arrived.

How far was this place from the cave where I'd left the guys? Were they tracking me down? If Lokene and Bion popped up in the middle of this mess, would they try to stop me from completing my mission? Even if they were on my side, they couldn't kill another Ancient. The best they could do is keep them off me... maybe.

But after the fiasco in the cave, I feared the guys would rush into the middle of a fight, only to hesitate when they recognized an Ancient they respected. I prayed they waited just long enough for me to take care of what needed to be done here before they arrived.

The sounds of raw sex quieted, drawing my full attention back to the tiny wooden house. I sighed with relief. I'd been half afraid they would go for another round. My skin still crawled from the dead man's touch, and between that and the guttural sounds of sex, I was fighting the urge to vomit.

I wanted nothing more than to run into my mates' arms and rid myself of the memory of the tainted man's touch. I'd done my job successfully, just as I had countless times before. Killing was something I was used to. It was the emotions that were causing me issues now.

The sound of giggling grew louder as Lexi made her way outside, smiling over her shoulder at her lover. Both

Ancients radiated satisfaction. I studied the man; he didn't compare to any of my mates in the looks department, but apparently Lexi was pleased with him.

Lexi stumbled, coming to a stop when she spotted the empty chair. "Where did Nick go?" She looked around, confusion marring her beautiful face. "Nick!"

She continued to call out his name, but of course there was no reply. It's not like he could speak from the bottom of the lake.

"Where do you think he could have gone?" Lexi crossed and uncrossed her arms, eyes darting around in apprehension. "He's been frustrating lately. Maybe we should have included him."

"I'm sure he just needed to stretch his legs or wanted to check the perimeter. Stop worrying," Raq said.

He seemed far less concerned about Nick's safety, and I wondered if there was a rivalry between them. It was so different from my mates' comfortable camaraderie, and they would never experience this type of jealousy.

Hurrying off the porch, Lexi cupped her hands around her mouth, her echoing call bouncing off the surrounding stones. She stood on tiptoe, searching down the path, trying in vain to catch sight of him.

"Maybe he's down by the water?" Lexi suggested, her anxiety seeping through.

My heart skipped a beat. If they came together, I would have to choose which of them to attack. I could not take both at the same time.

I tried to mentally will them to search in different directions. To my delight, I did not have to make a choice between them.

Raq put his hand on her shoulder. "No, no. Go on in the house and get yourself something to eat. I'll go look for the idiot. I bet he wandered off and got lost." Grabbing Lexi's chin, he leaned forward and placed a lingering kiss on her swollen lips.

"Yes. Okay," she stammered breathlessly as he pulled away. "I'll do that."

Smiling, she made her way back into the house. The man watched her go, and once the door shut behind her, his shoulders squared. A scowl of irritation flickered across his face. He stalked toward the water and released a string of vicious curses.

Malice and evil rolled off him in waves to drift into the air.

How interesting. The call and my instincts had told me he was tainted and had given into the temptation of the Lure. But watching him playfully interact with Lexi, and being unable to read his thoughts, I'd thought perhaps he was newly infected. Now that he'd dropped his guard, I could see into his soul. I shivered.

Raq wasn't newly infected. The Lure had been festering inside him for a long time, and it had eaten away at all the good inside him. Ancients were just able to hide it better, far more effectively than a human. It made sense why the other Ancients couldn't sense anything at all from the tainted of their species.

"It's just like that idiot to wander off. The sooner he dies, the better it will be for all of us." Raq's scowl grew more vicious as he made his way down the sandy path to the water.

Yep. There definitely wasn't any love lost between these two. Deciding it was time to get into position, I slipped beneath the water. Swimming toward the trampled edge of the shoreline, I made sure to stay deep enough that I was out of sight to anyone looking down into the water.

The hard thuds of his heavy footsteps vibrated through the water, and moments later, his shadow cast across the water's surface. I longed to spring into action, but I forced myself to be patient. If I was lucky, he might squat down to inspect the water.

Using myself as bait, I floated up a couple of feet in the water. Not enough to where he could see me clearly, but just enough that he'd be able to make out the shape of something in the water.

The sound of the man carried through the water as he called for the missing Ancient while pacing the shoreline. I knew the instant he caught sight of me. The shadow stilled.

"Nick?" Raq's voice rose in uncertainty.

Slightly leaning over the water, his eyes narrowed as he tried to get a better look at what was just out of sight in the murky water.

With the call pounding inside me like a war drum, I gave a sharp thrust of my tail. I torpedoed myself out of the water, hooking my arms around his neck and simultaneously sinking my fangs deep into his throat. Clinging to him, I allowed my weight to yank him off balance and into the water with me.

I could feel the electrical buzz of Raq's magik as he tried to teleport away. But it was too late. My venom was already surging through his body, disrupting his magik.

His eyes widened, and a stream of bubbles exploded from his mouth. I wasn't sure which was causing him more pain—the scorching water he must feel on his skin or the fiery pain my venom was inflicting internally.

Wrapping my hand around his ankle, I pulled him deeper down into the water. Raq thrashed wildly for several heartbeats and then turned to weak spasms as his muscles stopped obeying his commands.

His heart slowed to an erratic flutter. When the life drained from his wide, horrified eyes, I released his body and watched as he sank into the nightmarishly dark waters.

Two down, one to go.

CHAPTER FOURTEEN

LOKENE

W e stared in shock at the empty spot where Zosime had stood moments before.

She'd left us.

And worse, she'd blocked me from her mind. That shouldn't be possible. So how had she been able to do it?

Closing my eyes, I focused all my energy on finding the shining beacon that drew me to her like a moth to a flame. There was nothing. My mind was dark.

"I can't feel the mate bond," I choked out, too devastated to worry about Bion witnessing my weakness.

Bion didn't say a word, but his hand gripped my shoulder in a silent show of support.

Bion and I had a strange history between us. Centuries

ago, we'd been best friends and so much alike that people joked we were twins. Somewhere along the line, our friendship had turned to rivalry. I couldn't even pinpoint when the competition between us started. Maybe he dated someone I liked? Or maybe I'd hurt one of his friends? A whisper here, a snarky comment there. We weren't bitter rivals, and we didn't hate each other, but he wouldn't have been the first person I'd have called if I needed help.

When the Elders had sent him to Earth, I hadn't been pleased. He was the last man on any world I would want around my mate.

What I hadn't expected was the way his guard had dropped around Zosime. Instead of being his obnoxious, arrogant self, he truly worried about what Zosime wanted and what she might need. He'd even shown a sensitivity for her emotions. It was incredible.

Bion liked women. No, that is an understatement. Bion *loved* women, and women adored Bion.

But never once in our long lifetime had I seen him show genuine affection for a woman, enough to defy our leaders to fight for. Something had changed in him, and I suspected it was the same thing that had changed in me when I met Zosi all those years ago.

When Bion had first blinked onto our boat, I'd been ready to do whatever it took to keep him away from my girl. But rather than doing the task he was sent to do, Bion had removed Lily, thus relieving Zosi's biggest stressor at that moment.

When the Elders had taken me and kept me locked in confinement with their magik, in order to use me as bait to draw Zosime into our world ahead of her schedule, Bion had been there for her. He'd even taken the time to visit me, giving me updates on how she was doing. It was unexpected, but I'd appreciated it more than I'd ever admit.

The Bion sitting beside me wasn't the same man I'd known for countless millennia. I found myself trusting him.

Closing my eyes, I tried in vain to find the mate beacon. I dropped my head into my hands. "It's not there. She's not there."

"What do you mean, you can't feel the bond?" Bion asked. "Did you bond correctly? A bond between Ancients gives them the ability to always know where their mate is. How could you have lost her?"

Okay, there was the Bion I remembered.

"I'm well aware of how bonding among Ancients works," I snapped. "But I'm telling you, I cannot feel her in the bond."

"What are we going to do, man?" The pitch of his voice rose an octave as the same panic that was flooding my chest was affecting him too. "How did this happen? It's supposed to be impossible! She shouldn't be able to teleport from place to place on Iolatara. No one can do that. She shouldn't be able to block us from her mind."

"And she shouldn't be able to mask the mate bond," I added. My mind was spinning, struggling to accept reality.

Bion stood and began hurriedly repacking our backpacks. I watched him, unable to pull myself from my heart-broken stupor.

"What are you doing?" I asked.

"Packing our crap so we can go after our girl." I raised a brow. *Our girl?* "She's a warrior and won't leave until her work on Iolatara is finished. If we find the tainted Ancients, we will find Zosime." Bion zipped the backpacks, tossing mine at me.

I struggled to think clearly through the fog in my mind. "What about these bodies?"

"Who cares?" Bion shrugged carelessly. "Lo, we made a serious mistake in doubting her. Clearly, the Ancients affected by the Lure had found a way to mask it from other Ancients. Why else would they be in here with weapons to kill us? That means Zosime is the only chance we have to cleanse Iolatara and Earth."

Bion was right. Zosime had known and had taken matters into her own hands. But instead of jumping up ready to protect her, we'd questioned her judgment and broke her trust. My stomach twisted. I pushed to my feet. "We need to go now."

Lifting my pack, I strode out into the cool night air with Bion hot on my heels. I would find my Soyale, and spend the rest of my life apologizing if necessary.

WE HIKED THROUGH THE MORNING WITHOUT stopping. All Ancients had the disadvantage of their powers being slightly limited since we were on Iolatara. For some reason when we'd established this planet as our home, we'd liked the idea of living a more normal life with dampened magik. But after trekking for hours on end, I was cursing my inability to blink wherever I pleased as I could on Earth. Sure, I could have created a vehicle out of midair, but the rough and ever-changing terrain would have made it impossible to use.

It was around noon when we came across a tiny smoldering campfire.

"This must have been where the two Ancients who attacked us in the cave camped last night." I kicked angrily at the ashes, needing to release some of the pain and fury that had built in my chest.

Bion nodded. "They weren't careful about covering their tracks. If we're lucky, we can follow their tracks back to the main camp... and hopefully, Zosime."

Without saying another word, we kept moving. The next hours were spent tracking. Several times we were forced to backtrack and try a different path because footprints had been disturbed or completely disappeared due to wading through a creek or walking across stretches of smooth stone. But thankfully, the trail was otherwise clean. They had truly expected to kill us all and leave no one left to follow their trail. A shiver traveled my spine. How could an Ancient break their oath and be willing to kill another?

It was around noon when we came to a steep outcropping of stones. Glancing below, I could see a small encampment. I couldn't spot Zosime, and the separation was bringing me to the brink of insanity, but I could sense the presence of other Ancients nearby, which meant Zosime was likely nearby... hunting her prey. This was it.

Motioning for Bion to stop, I signaled for him to stash his stuff in a hollowed-out trunk of a tree that sat behind some thick bushes. I didn't want us to be weighed down with my gear should I find an opportunity to assist Zosime.

Bion quietly stashed his gear alongside mine, and with careful steps, he settled behind another stone. His sharp eyes scanned the camp below.

Our attention was drawn to one of the chairs around the large fire pit. A man stood and stretched before wandering a distance from the wooden cabins. Sitting down on a massive stone, he stared at the water that lined the encampment on one side.

His body stiffened as something just out of my line of sight caught his interest. I didn't have to wait long to find out what it was.

Zosime limped into view, completely naked. On impulse, I tried to leap from my hiding spot, but Bion placed a firm hand on my arm, holding me in place.

"Let me go! She's injured!" I snarled, sorely tempted to rip his arm from his body.

Keeping his voice hushed, Bion tried to calm me. "No. I don't think she is. Wait a minute before you go rushing in like a useless knight in shining armor. If she isn't injured and you mess this up, she'll probably mess you up."

I yanked his arm from my grasp but forced myself to remain hidden.

Somewhat reassured that I wasn't about to do something we'd both regret, Bion also turned his attention back to Zosime.

I watched her move toward the man. Her beautiful nude body almost glowed. Now was definitely not the time, but I felt my pants grow uncomfortably tight from just the sight of my mate. I doubted I could ever see her without craving her.

The man walked toward Zosime. He said something, but I couldn't make out the words.

I saw my mate's mouth move in response. My muscles quivered when she stumbled.

The man's hands grabbed Zosime's waist, steadying her. The sight of his hands on her naked flesh had my body flushing in rage.

Zosime looked up at him, her lips moving. The man lowered his head slightly as he spoke again. I wanted to hear what they were saying.

The man's hands began to wander over her pale skin. When he teased the underside of her breasts in a way that only her mates should touch her, I began to shake.

Bion's hand shot out, clamping around my wrist. "Lokene. I've never wanted someone to die as badly as I want him to. You're bonded to her, so I can't imagine how those emotions are being amplified in you. But right now, we need to trust Zosi. Her hair is soaking wet. She was hiding in the water, and she could have stayed hidden there, but she chose to approach him. I'm telling you, she has a plan."

I hissed out a pained breath. "He's pretending to help her, but he's really just using it as an excuse to grope her."

"I know. And I'm pretty sure Zosi will make him pay for it," Bion said through gritted teeth. He was trying to calm himself as much as he was trying to calm me. "If she doesn't, I will. Oath or no oath."

The sound of a dying seal came from the tiny cabin, causing both Bion and I to jerk in shock.

"What kind of animal are they keeping in that building?" Bion whispered, trying to steady his breathing. "Are they sacrificing it for a ritual?"

"I don't know." Ancients didn't sacrifice living creatures, but maybe it was a Lure thing? I'd worry about that mystery later. Right now, my only concern was my mate.

Zosime gripped the man's shirt. His body shuddered, and his hands grabbed her butt. Even from this distance, I saw Zosi's jaw clench. She wasn't scared; she was irritated.

An anger like nothing I'd ever experienced before exploded inside me when the man's grip grew hard enough to leave bruises, and he started thrusting his hips against her like a mindless animal focused only on their release.

I saw the flash of her fangs before Zosi punctured his skin.

"That's right. Pump that maggot full of your venom," I murmured, wanting him to die an excruciating death for touching what was mine. With any luck, her venom would work on him like it did us, but instead of him turning into a raging pile of hormones, his length would explode. But one could only hope.

It took longer than I would have liked, but when the guy's body gave out and he collapsed in the sand, I finally managed to draw a deep breath. He'd gotten what he deserved. I only wished he'd suffered more.

Zosime stood over him, hands on her hips. I couldn't hear her words, but it was clear she was disgusted.

Wasting no time, she grabbed him under the arms, and, with effort, she managed to get him to the water's edge, where she tossed him in. My resourceful little mate used a clump of grass to sweep away all signs of her presence and the drag tracks left by the dead piece of pond scum.

Mission accomplished, Zosime stared at the cabin before disappearing into the safety of the water. Water that was anything but safe. Nothing survived in the death pools that dotted Iolatara's landscape. Being boiled alive would feel relaxing compared to being immersed in the pool's water. Much in the same way the venus fly trap plant on Earth caught and ate its prey, these pools swallowed and digested all who fell into their depths.

Yet, the siren was moving freely in and out of the water as though it were nothing more than a hot spring. Had she formed a symbiotic relationship with it? She was feeding it, and in exchange, it was providing her safety?

I wanted to rush to her side, but I could still feel the presence of other Ancients in the vicinity. And by the way Zosime had looked at the cabin, I had a pretty good idea of their current location. With a nod at Bion, we settled down to wait and watch.

CHAPTER FIFTEEN
BION

The door of the cabin swung open, and a couple stepped out. I couldn't quite make out their words, but I wouldn't have deserved the nickname cupid if I'd been unable to recognize the sexual satisfaction they were exuding. Which led me to a second realization.

"That wasn't a seal. It was sex," I whispered to Lokene.

Lokene raised a brow. "You have got to be joking."

"If a woman was riding me and released that sound during orgasm, I would blink up out of there so fast. But only if I didn't have a heart attack first," I responded.

"I don't think that Zosime is even capable of making that sound if she were to try." A ghost of a smile crossed Lokene's taut face.

The couple talked, and the woman called several times for the missing man. But instead of being genuinely concerned about the missing guy, both had agitation radiating from them. Lokene leaned forward, trying to get a better look at the Ancients. "They both seem really familiar, especially the woman. There's something about her..."

I hated to admit it, but Lokene was right. Even without seeing their faces, they were familiar. I growled softly for them to turn so I could see their faces fully. After several minutes, and without showing her face, the woman went back inside, leaving the man outside.

He stared at the cabin door before surveying the clearing and the surrounding area. No doubt he was looking for their dead companion, which meant we needed to be alert in case he moved this way.

And then it happened.

The man turned, giving us a glimpse of his full face. The air was knocked from my body as though someone had punched me in the gut.

"I can't believe it," Lokene hissed beside my ear. "I know him."

"Of course you know him. Everyone knows Raq," I whispered back.

"But him? I never would have thought he would give in to the Lure. He's supposed to be one of our ambassadors to other worlds! What if he is already trying to spread it there?" Lokene clenched his hands, knuckles growing white.

I couldn't blame him for feeling betrayed since I was feeling the same way. This man was one of the oldest among the Ancients. He was supposed to be a leader, guiding us on how to get through this crisis.

"It is a lot worse than we knew," I mumbled.

The news of Raq's involvement was going to shake the Ancient communities. He'd been one of the leaders who was most vocal about bringing Zosime here and about confining Lokene in his home here on Iolatara.

Lokene must have been thinking along the same lines. "He didn't want to bring Zosi here to save the Ancients. It was so they could more easily arrange her death."

Raq hadn't been at the meeting Zosi and I had crashed. No wonder he'd skipped attending the last few meetings. He didn't want to risk Zosime would sense he was tainted by the Lure, and he would be outed to the rest of the Ancients before he was ready.

A new thought sent an arctic chill coursing through my body. A thought that I doubted had occurred to Lokene yet.

If Raq was here, it was likely his latest partner was nearby, too. It didn't seem possible that she would be involved in this, but they'd become inseparable recently. And if I were right, we were so deep in crap we'd be lucky to ever see a blue sky above our heads again.

I opened my mouth, preparing to drop my bombshell realization on Lokene, but stopped when Raq strode down the grass-lined path toward the glistening water.

Toward Zosime.

He paused, calling out for his companion. Each step brought him nearer and nearer the water's edge and the waiting predator.

Fear tightened its claws around my heart. This wasn't just any Ancient. He was one of the most experienced with magik, and Zosime didn't have a clue about the power of the man she was about to attack.

I could tell the moment something caught Raq's interest because he stopped, leaning his body out over the water to get a closer look.

Just like a jumpscare in a movie, I knew what was coming, and yet I still jumped in shock.

Zosime's body torpedoed out of the water, her arms locking around the man's neck and yanking him into the water with a force that wasn't dissimilar to a shark leaping from the water to snatch its prey. I was once again reminded that her siren was a predator; wild, untamed, and heart-breakingly beautiful.

Zosime had proven time and time again to be one of the fiercest warriors born on Earth throughout all time. I'd never want to be on Zosime's list of prey. I might be an Ancient, but without my abilities, I seriously doubted I could protect myself from her.

I'd already lost my heart to her. And now I might have lost my chance to love her.

"Do you think she'll forgive us?" I asked.

Lokene leaned against the stone, eyes glued to the water's surface, which was smooth as glass. "We can hope.

The one thing we have going for us is our immortality. If we win this war against the Lure, we'll have a long time to convince her we're sorry."

FOR THE NEXT FIVE MINUTES, WE STARED AT THE water, watching for any sign that Zosime was alive. With each passing second, my anxiety was rising.

I tried to keep an eye on Lokene, not fully trusting that he wouldn't dart into the encampment. The levels of fear and anger seeping from him were so high I was almost surprised I couldn't see it wafting in the air.

"We could try to go around and behind the encampment and make our way to the water to see if we can locate her." Even I heard the doubt in my voice. I wasn't too keen to get near the murder water.

I glanced back at Lokene, and his heart was pounding hard enough that I could see it through his shirt. I understood the feeling, although Lokene would be experiencing it far worse since he and Zosi had completed their mating. I could only sit back and seethe with jealousy that she had claimed him and I was forced to watch from afar.

"If we head down there, it might alert them to our presence, which will just create more problems for Zosime. There is at least one more Ancient, the woman, but it's possible there are more. I don't want Zosi to get the wrong impression of our intentions. For now, we wait." Lokene's jaw was clamped tight enough to crack a tooth. "We need to trust Zosi knows what she's doing. She's already taken two of them out with terrifying ease."

It was easier said than done. The instinct to protect her was insanely strong and not something I was used to feeling. But if we messed this up for her, it might be the last straw in her ability to forgive us.

Watching the water's edge, we held our breath.

To our surprise, Zosime strode out from the rocky pathway behind the cabin. Her hair was pulled back in a tight bun, and she was clad in her clothes from yesterday. She made her way onto the porch, pressing her back along the wall and pausing beside the doorframe.

Zosime's hand shot out and gave three sharp knocks on the wood door.

I stopped breathing.

The woman pushed open the door and stepped out onto the porch.

Zosime sprung into action. Her leg moved faster than the speed of light, kicking the woman's legs out from underneath her. Zosi leaped onto the Ancient woman, following her down on the porch.

Wasting no time, Zosime sank her fangs into the woman's arm. The woman recovered quickly and slammed her head into Zosime's skull. Even from this distance, I winced at the audible crack.

Zosi toppled off the Ancient, her movements unsteady as she staggered to her feet. Had she been able to inject the Ancient with enough of her lethal venom?

"We need to do something!" I couldn't just sit here. I was an Ancient, but I'd never felt so useless in my life.

"Like what?" Lokene asked. "It's not like we can hold the Ancient down for Zosime. That would still count as assisting in the murder and would break our oath. We can't kill another Ancient." His words were filled with bitterness and pain.

I understood his feelings. We were trapped between breaking our oath, unheard of for an Ancient, or standing by and watching history unfold without interfering... which was the Ancient way. It was fine to play with mortals and their worlds, but never to help or assist in any way that might change history. We were a powerful and utterly useless species.

The woman scooted away from Zosime, pushing to her feet only to slide back down to the floor.

Maybe Zosi had injected her. Hope soared in my chest. This might be over!

While visions had never been my strongest ability, I never saw what happened next coming. It wasn't even one of the alternate futures.

Two new women ran around the front of the cabin and leaped onto the porch. The shorter red-haired woman wasted no time and launched herself at Zosime.

Lokene and I didn't speak as we hurtled to our feet. It

was three against one, and our girl needed help. We raced down the path, close enough to watch the horror play out in front of us, but too far to get there fast enough to intervene.

The second newcomer, a blonde-haired giant of a woman, slammed into Zosime with the force of a mountain lion, and they tumbled off the porch onto the soft sand. Kicks and punches were flying at an incredible speed. Zosi was an incredible fighter, but she had killed the others by catching them off guard; there wasn't a chance on Earth she could take on three skilled and prepared Ancients at once.

My thoughts trailed off as the red-haired woman ran down the porch steps and wrapped her arms around Zosi's neck in a chokehold. She tried pulling Zosime off her blonde friend, which was all the distraction Zosi needed.

Zosime's fangs sank deep into the red-haired Ancient's forearm. She ignored the woman's shrill scream of pain. Wasting no time, Zosime rolled, flipping her body until the red-haired woman lay still as death beneath her.

Seeing that her attacker wasn't a threat anymore, Zosi's sharp eyes cut back to where the blonde lay in the sand. The woman she hadn't bitten. But it was too late.

The moment that Zosime's attention had turned toward the red-haired Ancient, the blonde woman had jumped into action. Shoving to her feet, she bent and grabbed something from her boot.

Time slowed as I watched the woman thrust a knife into Zosime's stomach, quickly dragging it from belly button to rib and nearly gutting Zosime with that single move. Disbelieving horror numbed my body. This wasn't real. It couldn't be real.

Zosi never lost focus, not even when blood poured from her side in a crimson waterfall. It was a wound that no one but a full-blooded Ancient could survive. Zosime sprung forward, biting deep into the woman's thigh, all the while her hands frantically tried to hold the gaping wound in her skin closed.

The ticked-off siren must have pumped a heck of a lot of venom into that single bite because the woman crumpled to the ground, dead before her body touched the sand.

We were almost there.

Zosime staggered to her feet, not even glancing at the sand beneath her that had turned a brilliant crimson red. Her eyes were locked onto her final target: the woman on the porch.

A woman I recognized all too well.

Lokene lost his footing and fell to his knees. "Mom?"

The woman cast a quick glance in our direction and threw up her hand, sending a wave of magik crashing into us. I tried to stand, but her magik kept pushing us back. I'd heard Lexi had a gift with barriers, but I'd never tried to fight against one. I watched helplessly as Zosime took another step toward Lexi.

Lexi's voice carried across the clearing. "I have to say I'm impressed."

The Ancient's face split into a nasty smile. "I'm assuming you killed the two Ancients sent to murder you last night, and now you've taken out four more of the most powerful Ancients alive."

Zosime used the porch rail to pull herself up another step. Lokene and I fought against the magik, our need to get to Zosi pushing us forward little by little. We only had a few more meters to go, and I would be at her side.

"Sadly, it's not enough, little warrior," Lexi mocked. "You're dying, and I'm headed to the human world to finish what I started. Plus, I need to check in with Lily. I want to make sure that someone takes good care of your guys in your absence." Lexi blew a kiss to Lokene and disappeared.

Zosime lost her footing on the step that was slick with her blood, but quickly regained her balance.

I rushed forward, catching Zosime as she collapsed. I laid her gently on the ground, quickly making yards of gauze appear to press against the gaping wound. I wasn't a stellar healer, but I was desperate and willing to try anything.

Lokene pulled Zosi's head and shoulders onto his lap, stroking her hair and whispering things I couldn't hear to her.

Focusing on my magik, I tried to close the wound, but nothing happened. "Why won't this heal?" I roared with my pulse beating against my skull. She was losing too much blood, and her lips were turning a terrifying blue. Lokene and I took turns trying to heal it, but nothing happened.

"Check the knife!" Lokene snapped, his fear morphing to anger at our helplessness.

Using one hand to apply pressure to Zosime's wound, I grabbed the bloody blade from the sand. My blood chilled as a sweet scent—like the smell of Earth's honeysuckle—filled the air. With a curse, I flung the knife.

Lokene's questioning gaze met my tear-filled eyes. I didn't want to say the words aloud; somehow, doing it was going to make this more real.

"Nectar from the Caldera," I choked out, barely keeping myself from crumbling.

The Ancients had created the exquisitely beautiful Caldera plant. Unfortunately, the plant turned out to be deadly to all living creatures outside of this planet. For an Ancient, their pollen was as harmless as dust on a picture frame, but to a human, the Caldera's pollen was deadlier than anything on Earth. Thankfully, the plant and its toxic pollen couldn't survive off Iolatara, and no humans lived anywhere near the field of Caldera.

But Zosi was on our planet, and an Ancient had just stabbed her with a blade covered in lethal pollen.

I watched the snowy white gauze darken with her blood, and my throat burned with unshed tears. Zosime was the first person in my life I'd ever allowed myself to fall in love with, and I was going to be forced to watch her die.

CHAPTER SIXTEEN

ZOSIME

M y brain seemed to be filled with a thick fog. Unless a miracle happened, I was pretty sure I was about to die.

Anger burned through me like an out-of-control wildfire. I'd been so close to ending this. When my fangs had sunken into Lexi, scenes from the past had flashed in my mind. She was the creator of the Lure. The Elders believed the Lure had only recently started to taint the Ancients, but they were wrong.

Lexi had been infected with it since the moment she created it. The Lure thrived off her magik as an Ancient. She'd become the roots of the Lure as it spread between our two worlds, and when she died, so would the Lure.

If only the flash of the past hadn't stunned me, I would have pumped her full of venom, and this would have been over. Instead, she'd escaped to Earth. I groaned in frustration. I didn't have time to die!

What would my death do to my mates? The monster had said she was going to send Lily to check on my men. Furious at the thought, I tried to sit up.

Lokene gently pushed me back down, and I caught my breath at the raw fear shimmering in his eyes. "You need blood. Take it all. Please." My mate's voice broke, and he pressed his wrist into my mouth, but I hesitated.

What would happen to him if I injected him with venom and then I died? Would he die as well?

Lokene growled in frustration at my hesitation. This time, he pressed his skin hard enough against my fangs to slice open the skin of his wrist, and warm blood poured into my mouth.

I gagged when the thick liquid clogged my throat. Struggling to breathe and swallow took more concentration than my mind could handle. Especially when it felt like a rabid dog was ripping at my organs, and pain was overloading every nerve ending.

Lokene grabbed my neck with his free hand, holding just beneath my jaw. Tilting my chin back, he straightened my neck so his blood ran smoothly down to my stomach.

Dropping the barrier that had blocked them from my mind, I let Lokene and Bion back into my mind. I'd failed them all. I looked into his eyes, having much to say but knowing there wasn't enough time left to say it. Tears burned my eyes, trickling down my cheeks.

"Stop. Stop that right now." Lokene's voice shook. "You are not a failure. I've never seen anything like what I witnessed today. Soyale, you took down six Ancients as though they were nothing more than puny humans. No one has ever done that. If we'd just trusted you last night, we would have been here to—"

To do what? My words were a gentle caress in his mind. *You cannot raise a hand against your people. This is the way it had to be.*

"No, it doesn't have to be this way! Drink, Soyale! Drink every last drop if you need it," Lokene begged.

Already sweat dotted his brow, and his pupils were so wide his irises were barely visible. My venom was affecting him, and it terrified me more than my impending death.

"I don't care what happens to me," Lokene whispered, a single tear dripping down his cheek. "If you die, then I die with you."

The rush of his blood slowed, although thanks to my venom, his heart was pounding harder. I could not risk taking any more, even though I could still feel my blood leaking out of the open wound in my stomach.

Jerking my jaw from his grip, I clamped my mouth shut, refusing to allow him to give me more blood.

"Stop this and drink!" he cried, trying to open my mouth, but I refused.

Bion spoke up for the first time. "Lokene? Can we get

her to Earth? Maybe if she gets blood from the rest of her mates?"

"She wouldn't survive blinking between worlds," Lokene said in a choked whisper. "Please Soyale, take my blood. All of it." His eyes begged me to take more of his blood, but I would not allow him to die with me.

I love you, mate.

"Don't you dare, Zosime! You're a warrior, and this is just one more battle you have to fight!" Lokene yelled in desperation. "Don't you dare leave me!"

I wanted to fight, but I was so tired. My nerves had finally fried from the overload of pain, and now I felt warm nothingness. It was odd, but the sweet fragrant scent of honeysuckle tickled my nose. I'd always loved that scent.

"So that's it. You're tired, so you're giving up?" Bion's cold words shocked me.

If I could have chuckled, I would have. I was dying, and he was mad?

"Yeah. You bet I'm mad. I watched how you handled those arrogant jerks on Earth and here on Iolatara. Then I watched you systematically take down one Ancient after another, and not just any Ancients. Oh no, these were 'boss level' Ancients." Bion's face was turning red as he laid out his grievances.

It was a weird way to send someone into the afterlife, but Ancients had proven to be a strange species.

"Leave her alone! If the Ancients hadn't pulled her into this mess, she might have had a chance at a normal life,"

Lokene growled, and the muscles of his thighs flexed beneath my body. The warmth of his skin had me nodding away.

Tired. So very tired.

"Zosime wasn't born to be normal, and we both know it. She was a warrior among warriors. Atlantis' adored champion. She's done the impossible over and over. Yet now she is tired and, rather than fighting, she decides to give up." Bion's chest heaved with anger as he spoke, and it was a stark contrast to his eyes, which were filled with pain that I didn't understand. "Some warrior."

How dare he talk to me that way? I'd given my life, more than once, to serve Atlantis and the Ancients. But instead of sweet goodbyes, I had to listen to Bion ridicule me? If I could move without worrying that my insides would fall out, he'd be sorry.

"Lily was quite taken with your Storm," Bion added, and my scales flickered a pale turquoise as my temper flared.

My siren shoved forward in my mind, and taking advantage of my being too weak to control the siren's nature, she took full control. My form rippled, legs disappearing as my tail formed.

The rush of magik left me feeling woozy, but the siren wasn't anywhere close to being finished. If we were dying, she was going to go out with a bang.

I just didn't realize she planned to be so very literal about it.

Shifting forms caused the nerve endings in my body to flare to life again in a blaze of fiery, explosive pain. That agony, combined with the adrenaline from the fight and my anger at Bion's taunting comments was just too much. I screamed as excruciating pain flooded me.

I'd been getting better control of my emotions and learning how to blend in with modern humans, but that didn't change the fact that in my soul was the wildness of the earth, the raw power of violent storms, and the all-consuming hunger of the sea. There was no reigning in the feral monster inside me... the siren who was currently in control.

My pupils narrowed to thin slits, and I smirked at the apprehension flitting across Bion's features. He'd insulted the beauty, and now he'd deal with the beast.

Everything melted away except the heavy breathing of my prey. My fangs lengthened, and my gums ached with the overwhelming need to bury them in Bion's neck.

My tongue darted out, wetting my bottom lip in antici-pation. With a slap of my fluke, I launched myself at Bion. Only to feel Lokene's hands catch me around my waist and yank me hard down onto his lap, my back pressed against his chest. I fought to free myself.

"Calm down." Lokene's voice was a commanding purr in my ear.

I wanted to obey, but the raw hunger scorching my gut and the fact that Bion was still standing had the siren struggling against Lokene's hold. It took everything within me to not subdue Lokene and attack my prey.

Lokene's hand sank into my hair, his fingernails brushing against my scalp. With a sudden move, he yanked my head back hard, holding me in place while using my hair to maintain control of my writhing body.

To my shock, I felt myself growing slick with another type of hunger.

The siren hissed, snapping my fangs in his face. It was a promise of what was to come the moment he loosened his grip.

I should have felt embarrassed, but I didn't. Hunger and lust were the only two thoughts in my mind. The siren knew what she wanted, and she was just waiting for the moment she could take it.

"Stop fighting me, Soyale." Lokene's open mouth pressed against my throat, sucking, kissing, and fanning the wildfire inside me. Was the man crazy? I needed to be dunked in the icy waters of the Antarctic, not turned on even more.

"Zosime," Lokene moaned against my throat.

I squirmed, feeling his hard erection dig into my butt and smiling with satisfaction when my actions drew a groan from him. Using his grip on my hair, Lokene pulled my head to the side, giving himself better access to my mouth.

"Are you hungry?" Lokene asked, his mouth brushing across my lips and his tongue darting out to taste me.

"Answer me." His fingers tightened in my hair, pulling ever so slightly.

"Yes. I'm starving." My voice came out low and seductive, a full siren's call.

Lokene's chuckle was low and dark. His hips jerked hard against my backside. "Good, because I have a treat for you."

I wasn't sure what he meant until he tilted my head to look at Bion. In the lust of the moment, with Lokene's mouth and hands on me, I'd temporarily forgotten my need to attack Bion.

The tiny part of my brain still thinking rationally worried that I would be unable to resist the urge to take too much blood. I wasn't even sure if the siren planned to murder or mate him. Guess it was going to be a surprise for all of us.

Now, even through my feral haze, I recognized the raw need on Bion's face. He wanted me almost as much as I wanted him.

My heart stuttered in my chest. Even the siren paused.

I had a reason I wasn't supposed to bite him. Why, though? My mind spun, trying to regain some of the human emotions that would help me make rational decisions. But that part of my brain seemed to be off limits with the siren in control. I couldn't think of a single reason I shouldn't claim the smart-mouthed redhead in front of me.

Hungry. Eat. Make him pay. So wet.

Those thoughts pounded in my mind as loud as the call.

Lokene kissed his way down my neck, his hands sliding along my ribs to caress my aching breasts. "You want him, and you're hungry."

"Yes," I growled, trying to rock my hips against Lokene's lap. I desperately needed friction.

"Did you know Loverboy over there has been a mess since the first moment he saw you?"

This got the siren's attention. Locking eyes with Bion, I half expected him to deny it, but he didn't. Instead, his hand slid down to cup the large bulge in his pants. His breathing was ragged.

"You see? He hasn't ever had the chance to experience what it's like to mate with a siren—the sexiest woman on Earth," Lokene whispered, his warm breath tickling my overly sensitive skin. "And I think that's a shame. After all, it's only fair for Cupid to get a taste of his own medicine. Don't you think so?"

My stomach fluttered, and I pressed my hand against it and then froze. Looking down, I was stunned to see the jagged knife wound had sealed itself shut. I was weak, but I wasn't going to die. Had Bion baited me into shifting on purpose?

The siren forced the change back to my human body, leaving me naked and on display. Bion devoured me with his eyes while the siren preened. If I'd thought she would give back control, I was wrong.

Lokene pulled just a tad more on my hair, growling low

in my ear. "I know the siren is in control. So tell him, siren. Tell him what you want."

Even through the heavy fog of need, my siren hesitated, wondering what game Lokene was playing. Was he hoping that by stirring me into a feeding frenzy, I would accidentally or not-so-accidentally attack Bion during mating? It was a dangerous game, and I wasn't even sure if the siren had enough self-control to keep from harming Bion. Surely, Lokene wasn't that sadistic. I narrowed my eyes at my mate. Or was he?

CHAPTER SEVENTEEN

ZOSIME

Lokene's fingers slid lower, the callused tips of his fingers sliding across my overly sensitive skin. With a snarl, I renewed my struggle to free myself from his hold. The siren was loving that Lokene was in control and showing his strength while simultaneously hating him for it.

When Lokene's hand brushed along the inside of my thigh, I quivered, and my breath caught on a choked cry. My cry turned to a growl when his fingers stopped just shy of my aching core. Anger and lust blended together. This man was standing in the way of what I wanted.

The instant he let me go, I was going to kill him. I'd make wild, passionate love to him first, but then he would die.

"Tell him. Now," Lokene ordered a second time.

I hissed, struggling in his hold, my eyes pricking with tears from the burn in my scalp. While I was fighting to free myself, my traitorous body sent a wave of heat rushing between my legs at my mate's command.

Snapping my fangs in Lokene's face one more time, I locked onto Bion's face.

"I want you." I didn't clarify if I wanted to eat him or claim him, because honestly, the siren hadn't made up her mind.

Lokene had stirred the siren into a frenzy I'd never felt before. It was terrifying and exhilarating. The problem was, he thought he was in control, but the siren was biding her time. She was playing his game out of intrigue, but only until she'd had enough. What he believed was rational conversation was just the siren adapting to the situation to get what she wanted.

I'd wanted all my men, and I had taken them. Simple as that. But I'd been holding back my siren nature since I'd awakened, fearing what I didn't fully understand. With the siren's nature in control, all the pent-up lust I'd held back was released, and it was causing all kinds of internal chaos. How could sexual need be so powerful that it physically hurt? It felt as though I'd held my breath too long, and my lungs would explode without air.

Bion's chest heaved, and he took a step toward me. His eyes followed Lokene's hands as they roamed my body.

Yes. Come closer. The siren purred encouragement but kept the words to herself.

"That was decent. But you can do better, can't you, little mermaid?" Lokene cooed, nipping at my earlobe.

I wanted to snarl at my infuriating mate, and the siren half considered eating him instead, but I couldn't take my starving gaze from Bion. I was transfixed by the way he was staring at me with raw desire, but not like the other men with the Lure had looked at me. Bion stared at me as though I was the most beautiful woman he'd ever seen instead of a feral cosmic joke that had every intention of attacking him when turned loose.

The siren answered, putting the full force of the siren's allure into each word. I hadn't even heard my full voice. "Bion, I want to feel your body move in mine. I want to sink my fangs into your neck and taste your blood. I want my venom to give you a taste of the same need that is running through me. I want to do what I've fantasized about doing since that day you appeared on my boat."

I'd always held back, never using the full power of the siren's allure, and now I understood why I'd held a secret fear of it. Even my body had responded to the pure sexuality weaved through every silken word. Bion had stopped breathing and stood frozen as though my words had tightened every muscle in his body or I'd turned him to stone.

"Soyale," Lokene growled, his hips thrusting against my butt, and his body seeking relief from the sudden release of the testosterone in his body that the siren's tone had caused.

"Are you happy?" The purr caused Lokene to rock against me again, and the siren laughed in delight. He was losing control, and she loved it.

"Yes." Lokene choked out the word. "That was quite the little show."

Not ready to concede defeat, Lokene rested his hand at the apex of my thighs. His finger teased along my slit, and I shivered in delight.

With agonizing slowness, he slipped one finger inside. "Oh, my. You're soaked, Soyale," Lokene whispered against my ear, his tongue tracing along the curved edge, driving my need higher.

I whimpered, my mind a blur of lust and building release.

"Bion. You wish it was your finger sliding in and out of her right now, don't you?" Lokene addressed Bion, but he was watching my face. Studying my reactions.

"Goddess, yes." Bion swallowed hard, his eyes glued to where Lokene's fingers disappeared between my thighs.

Lokene chuckled. It was a devilishly dark sound. He was playing with fire and enjoying every minute of it. "Part your legs."

Without embarrassment or shame, the siren did as he asked, keenly watching Bion's every movement. He was barely holding on.

"Further, Soyale," Lokene coaxed.

And again, my body obeyed him, spreading my legs to

give him better access to touch me. It also gave Bion a full view of my naked body and my most secretive areas.

I should have been embarrassed and angry at being put on display. Instead, I felt like I was experiencing something forbidden. A fine sheen of sweat covered my skin as a lust so powerful it shook my body rippled through me. Never had I experienced something this strong.

The flood of raw unsatisfied desire ripped through me, and the feral instinct to do whatever was needed to survive kicked in. Hard.

I knew I could have blinked away. Lokene would've been unable to hold me there. But my mind was too far gone to care about the consequences of what was about to happen. All I felt was raw need.

Lokene slipped his finger into my slick heat, smirking at the wet sound it made as his finger slid back out. Bion watched with undisguised jealousy as Lokene brought the finger to his mouth and licked it clean, groaning like it was the sweetest dessert he'd ever eaten.

It took every ounce of willpower in my body to keep my muscles tight and not turn into a limp jellyfish in Lokene's arms.

Focusing back on me, Lokene's grip on my hair pulled until my scalp burned. Not hard enough to truly be painful, just enough to add another overwhelming sensation to my body.

"Do you remember how I told you Ancients weren't

able to change much about their bodies?" Lokene sucked my bottom lip into his mouth.

This seemed like a weird time for a lesson about the Ancients, but I nodded as Lokene shifted to begin placing kisses down my spine.

"Well, Bion is one of the few exceptions." Lokene's hand cupped my breast, gently cradling it.

"Oh?" I moaned, thrusting my breasts out, begging for more attention.

"According to Iolatara gossip, Cupid over there can apparently do some delightfully wicked things with his magik and the 'arrow' between his legs."

I didn't even know what he could mean, but my body clenched automatically, and the siren made her move.

Gathering my strength, I blinked from Lokene's grasp, reappearing fast enough to hear his shocked curse. The siren wanted to gloat, but her entire attention was focused on her prey.

Launching myself at Bion. I waited for him to flinch, or maybe even to do the smart thing and run. But he didn't. Bion opened his arms, catching me against him. The force of my attack knocked him backward, and we crashed onto the ground. Bion kept his arms around my body, absorbing the impact of our fall.

We hadn't even stopped moving before I'd straddled him and embedded my fangs deep into his neck. Just like with Lokene, Bion's blood carried a heady power in it. All my mates tasted delicious, but Ancient blood packed a punch that only served to further incite the bloodlust in the starved siren.

"Holy Iolatara!" Bion groaned, and his arms tightened around me to keep me against him. He needn't have bothered. I had no intention of releasing him.

Pulling my fangs free for a split second, I sank them into his collarbone, loving the way my prey squirmed with the bite. He was delicious, and I licked at his blood like a kitten licking up warm milk.

I drank until my belly grew heavy, and power hummed in my veins, and still, Bion did nothing to stop me. Was the idiot man going to let me drain him?

If that's what you desire.

Bion's voice penetrated the fog in my mind for the briefest of seconds. Yes, I did want to keep feeding. I never wanted to stop. And then Bion's jean-clad hips rolled, creating a delicious friction against my bare core and reminding me of my other desire. Everything in the world melted away until only the two of us existed.

With a flick of my hand, his clothes were gone, and Bion lay nude beneath me. Releasing my fangs, I sat up, still straddling his waist, and admired the sleek muscles and statuesque beauty of the man.

Tightening my legs around his waist, I rocked against his pelvis, sighing in ecstasy as his erection rubbed against my most sensitive places. I was so worked up that just the tiniest bit of friction almost sent me into an instant orgasm.

While Bion's blood was giving me a rush that no

amount of caffeine could replicate, my venom was giving him a different type of rush. His fingers grabbed my hips, grinding me down on him. At the same time, he thrust his hips up against me.

Bion's erection wasn't even inside me yet, and already I was far too aroused and sensitive to his touch. I screamed as an unexpected orgasm ripped through me. My body trembled as the aftershocks of my release echoed through me. But Bion wasn't finished.

Gripping my hips, Bion hauled me up his chest until the velvet heat of his mouth was pressed to my slick entrance. This wasn't a gentle, exploratory kiss. No, Bion's tongue plunged inside me, hard and demanding. He devoured my cream with the same enthusiasm I'd taken his blood.

Bion's tongue quickly zeroed in on the tiny bundle of nerves, and his tongue began to do things that tongues shouldn't be able to do. His tongue vibrated like a human's cellphone, and my thighs clamped around his head as he forced a second orgasm from me.

The pleasure was too much, and I tried to push away from him, but Bion's hands locked onto me, and his incredibly skilled tongue continued to send wave after excruciating wave of pleasure crashing through me until I thought my orgasm would never end.

When I finally managed to drag in a lungful of air, I looked between my thighs at the man who seemed content to stay there and flashed my fangs at him in warning. I'd enjoyed what he'd done, but I was in control. He was the prey, and I was the predator. But when I studied Bion's eyes, I could see a hunger almost as powerful as mine, and I wondered who was hunting whom.

Bion flipped me onto my back, drawing a surprised gasp from my mouth. Before I could retaliate, Bion's mouth was kissing up my neck and jawline. I wrapped my arms around his neck, pulling him closer to me.

Angling my head to the side, I caught his bottom lip between my teeth. He tasted of exotic spices, and I slipped my tongue inside his mouth, wanting more. Bion groaned as our tongues danced.

My siren nature was growing impatient. I needed more of him. Foreplay was nice, but I wanted all of him.

Mine. The thought spurred me on.

With a burst of speed, I wrapped my body around Bion and flipped us back over so that he was on his back. He started to smirk at the dance we were doing, but his expression shifted as I impaled myself on his stiff erection in one smooth move.

I moaned, and Bion's fingers dug into my thighs. He was perfect. Not too long, not too short. Thick, but not too thick. It was like he'd been made to fit my body. Lifting myself off him, I quickly lowered myself back down on his hard length. My thighs trembled, and Bion hissed my name.

Rolling my hips, I moved on top of him. I closed my eyes and tried to savor the sensations of his body stroking inside me for the first time. If I decided to eat him, it might be the only time. My pace grew faster, and Bion gripped my thighs while rocking his hips, driving us both toward our release.

My climax exploded through me without warning. My vision darkened, and stars fell behind my eyes. When my muscles clamped around Bion's erection, he roared his own release, bucking his hips up into me with a bruising force that had stars sparkling in my vision all over again.

I looked toward Lokene, who'd shed his clothes and was slowly stroking his hard length.

My mouth watered at the sight, but the siren wasn't quite finished with Bion. However, with my body as wobbly as a sea cucumber, I couldn't do much. I tumbled off Bion and collapsed in the sand.

"That's it?" Bion panted. "I half expected you to kill me."

He was goading me, and the siren, still unstable, rose to the challenge instantly.

"Oh? You're a male. I assumed you needed a break to recover," I taunted him. Each word was a seductive purr. I rolled to my hands and knees, preparing to attack.

Bion raised a brow, and Lokene's sharp bark of laughter confused me. I shot a look at Bion's member, and my mouth dropped open. He was rock hard. How had he recovered so fast?

Maybe there was something to his reputation...

Bion grabbed me, flipping me around so that I faced away from him on my hands and knees. I spun around, lunging for his throat. He'd excited my hunger, and it was back in full force.

With a snarl, his arms wrapped around me, spinning me around so that my back pressed to his chest. I hissed, clawing at the arms pinning me against him, but Bion only chuckled at my efforts. That was when I realized how much my siren liked him. I could have easily killed him and escaped, but I let him hold me down.

We were both on our knees, and I could feel Bion's erection bumping at my slick entrance. Bion turned us so that we faced Lokene, giving him a good view of our showdown.

Lokene's hand squeezed his hard length, and his breathing was ragged.

I gasped and squirmed against Bion's hold, but he didn't loosen his grip. With a single hard thrust, he buried himself inside me.

Keeping a strong arm around my waist, he moved his other arm up to my chin.

"Bite me. Take what you want," Bion growled against my ear.

Without hesitation, I sank my fangs into his forearm. We both sighed in unison.

Keeping his arms in place and my body pressed against his chest, Bion started pumping his hips. His erection slid free, only to plunge inside me with a hard thrust. Bion was rough, and it was exactly what I craved.

Lokene's eyes glazed over with lust as they roved over

my body. His hand slid along his hard erection, keeping pace with Bion's thrusts.

The siren delighted in having Lokene's full attention while, at the same time, she was taking blood from Bion at a rate that worried me. I finally gained enough control to pull my fangs free of his arm.

His hand moved to where our bodies joined, finding my clit and teasing it as his hips continued to thrust into me. I was not ready for his erection to start vibrating, and when it did, I came fast and hard. I screamed Bion's name. Clawing at the steel band of his arms, I tried to get away from the mind-melting intensity of the orgasm. Lokene shouted my name as he found his release, hips jerking until he collapsed back onto the sand.

Bion repositioned his hips and drilled into me at an angle that had a second orgasm threatening to rip me in two. I screamed, or maybe I sobbed as pleasure so powerful it was almost painful swept through me.

Bion stiffened, following me into bliss, and I could feel his release as he jerked inside me. I tried to pull away, but Bion pulled me into an embrace. Was the man insane? Who tries to cuddle the feral siren, who wanted them dead just a few minutes before?

To my utter surprise, the siren settled at his loving touch. I regained most of my humanity. We were quiet for several minutes as we caught our breath. Out of the corner of my eye, I caught sight of Lokene sitting and watching us with keen interest.

"You didn't claim me. Do you want me?" Bion whispered.

I tilted my head, and my breath hitched at the look of longing in Bion's eyes. He wanted to belong. *To me.* How could this incredible man, a living sex god, question if he was desirable?

Women want to sleep with Bion. He's a legend. If you can get him in your bed, it's something to brag about for the rest of your life, or so I'm told. Women view him as a sexual conquest and an experience, not someone to build a life with. He's been alone for a long time. Lust is something he's used to. Emotions like love? Bion longs for that.

I felt my heart break at Lokene's whisper in my mind.

Plus, remember the power surge you got when we mated? It is likely you will get the same when you bond with Bion since he is also an Ancient. It could be an advantage as you go back into battle, Lokene suggested.

"I didn't plan to take another mate." I chewed my lip. "It seems unfair to you, Bion. What if it means you won't get as much time with me? I keep hoping that one day I can stop fighting all the battles of the world and have more time for my mates. But it seems unfair to consider taking a mate now when I know we may not get a ton of time together—at least not for a while."

"I would give up everything for even just an hour of being your mate. If being claimed by you means I only get to see you on my birthday, so be it! I want to belong. I like your mates. Well, maybe not him," Bion joked, jerking his head toward Lokene. "But the rest of the guys seem decent."

Lokene snorted.

Guilt still ate at my insides, and I tried to get him to see reason. "We should wait. It's not right to claim you now when I know I'm likely to gain something from it. If we're going to become mates, I want to do it when you know there's no ulterior motive. I never want my mates to question why I claimed them."

Bion laughed. "Doll, if you think claiming me will help you in this battle, then I say let's go for it! We both want this. Why wait?"

I traced his face with my fingertips.

Mine.

Yes, he was. But I should wait.

Bion caught my face between his rough palms. "What part of this are you not getting through your thick head? Claim me. Take me. Use me. Just please make me yours."

I was trying to take the high road and wait for the right time, but the stubborn man was making it impossible. Time was running out, and I needed to get back to Earth. But it would not do any good to rush there if I didn't have a plan and was too weak to take down Lexi. I wouldn't be able to catch her off guard again.

Pushing aside any lingering guilt, I stepped into Bion's arms.

I kissed along Bion's red-stubbled jawline.

I had never felt this incredible in my entire life, and I'd

never felt so blissfully complete. Once these wars were over, I wanted to disappear and just enjoy my life with my perfect mates. I knew that wasn't possible as long as I was the ruling queen of Atlantis, but it was nice to have dreams.

I kissed the skin over Bion's heart. Pressing my cheek against his chest, I listened to the steady beat. I wanted to etch this moment into my memory. The moment we became one.

Releasing my magik, I watched it dance along his skin. Turquoise magik etched a shimmering tattoo from the skin above his heart. A mark all my mates shared.

"Αν έρεε να ζήσω τη ζωή ου ξανά, θα σε έβρισκα νωρίτερα," I whispered.

"If I were to live my life again, I'd find you sooner, too," Bion repeated in English, whispering the words into my hair.

"I'm yours, Zosime, Queen of Atlantis. Please don't ever let me go." Bion's words were hoarse, and his arms tightened around me.

"I never let go of what is mine."

CHAPTER EIGHTEEN

ZOSIME

The blood of my two Ancient mates swirled in my veins. The power Bion had released when I claimed him as my mate was vibrating inside me. I'd never felt more alive.

It was time to go home.

It was time to remind Lexi exactly who the earth belonged to.

It was time to remind Lily who she was messing with.

They both had to die. But it didn't have to be a horrible death... unless they'd touched what was mine.

Lokene and Bion both wore equally goofy expressions as they basked in their orgasmic afterglow and the lingering effects of my venom. They'd fed me a significant amount of blood, and even though they were Ancients, it would take a while to recover from that. Unfortunately, I couldn't wait around for their bodies to recover fully. I had places to go and people to kill.

Grabbing their hands, I gave them both a squeeze.

"Let's go home."

Before they had a chance to protest, I blinked.

We materialized in my Atlantean castle beneath the sea. I hoped I'd find the rest of my mates waiting there.

Kye and Eason sat in the dining room chairs. Their mouths fell open at our sudden appearance.

"Zosi? Is it really you?" Eason asked, standing slowly.

"Yes, it's me!" I ran across the room and jumped into Eason's arms. "I've missed you!"

Kye hurried to my side, stealing me from Eason's embrace to twirl me in a tight hug. "You have no idea how much I missed you, beautiful!"

"I missed you too, Kye." My words were breathless as he set me back on my feet.

"You're okay? Is it all over with?" Kye asked, and the hope in his eyes had my happiness at being home melting away.

"No, it's not over. Almost, but not quite. There are two

loose ends I need to tie up." I looked around the room. "Where are Storm, Fynn, and Zeno?"

Eason answered. "Fynn got a call this morning about an emergency at his company that required his attention. Storm went with him just to make sure he didn't go alone."

"We stayed here, so you wouldn't come home to an empty castle," Kye added.

My heart tripped in my chest. That was too convenient. Fynn's company hadn't really needed him since he backed away from operations, but suddenly there is an emergency when I am gone for two days? I hoped my imagination was being overly dramatic, but the sick feeling in my stomach told me I wasn't wrong.

"And Zeno? Where's he at?" I strode to the windows that looked out over Atlantis. A very chaotic Atlantis. Mers swam this way and that while agitated sharks circled overhead. Ice trickled down my spine. Something was wrong.

"There's been some problems, soldier." Eason sagged into a soft armchair. "Humans are planning to take Atlantis by force. They've launched boats and submarines, and they're headed this way. Zeno and the other mers are busy preparing to defend the city."

Furious tears burned in my eyes. "If I'd been a better negotiator, this wouldn't have happened. Why couldn't I have been more like my mother?"

Eason's arms wrapped around me, and he nuzzled my hair. "You don't need to be more like your mother."

I hadn't realized I'd spoken out loud.

"From everything I've heard, your mother was an incredible queen, an incredible woman, and she made an even more incredible daughter. You are a one-of-a-kind work of art. There is no way your mother could have ruled in today's world. But you can, princess. You've been sculpted by powers that humans don't even realize exist."

I gave a harsh laugh. "Yeah. I'm a half-blood."

Eason turned me around in his arms, forcing me to meet his eyes. "There's nothing 'half' about you. You're an Ancient, a Greek god, with magik from the earth and unimaginable power."

"Yes. Eason's correct," Lokene added. "Soyale, you're not weaker because you're only half Ancient. You hold an old magik—a magik that is just as powerful as anything us Ancients possess. Your body has blended the two into something unfathomable." Lokene hesitated. "If I'm honest, it's slightly terrifying."

Lokene was right. My power was growing stronger with every passing minute.

My body hummed with energy, preparing for what was coming. There was just one more thing I needed to do before I hunted down the two Ancients.

"I have to go get something. I'll be back." I kissed Eason and then Lokene before stepping back and preparing to blink.

"What do you mean? Where are you going?" Kye asked, running a hand through his messy hair.

"I don't have time to explain, but I promise I'll explain

everything later. Please try to get Storm on the phone and let him know they may be in danger. As soon as I finish my errand, I will go get them."

"We could go get them." Lokene and Bion spoke in unison.

"No. I can't risk that she will get her hands on any more of my mates." A growl rumbled in my chest just at the thought.

"If we go together, it would be two against one. I think we can handle that," Bion protested.

"Fine. See if you can find them and make sure they are safe, but don't get anywhere near Lily or Lexi. You may not be willing to kill an Ancient, but they don't seem to have the same set of morals." My stomach twisted with anxiety.

"Okay," both men agreed with a nod of their heads and disappeared.

Kye and Eason had twin looks of concern.

"I love you two so much," I whispered. Not waiting for a reply, I blinked away.

THIS TIME, WHEN I TELEPORTED MYSELF BENEATH A body of water, I did it on purpose and shifted forms at the same time. It was a relief to take a deep breath and start swimming when I materialized, rather than having to waste time and energy struggling in my human body.

I knew my guys would be livid if they knew how much energy I was expending, but it couldn't be helped. Lokene probably already knew what I was doing. That man was a walking mystery.

It was such a relief to be back in the salty seawater. This was my home, and I'd missed it terribly while on Iolatara. Especially when swimming in the scorching death pool.

I swam quickly through the twisted metal and debris left behind after Richard's mining disaster and the explosions he'd arranged. It was eerie, and I picked up my speed, not wanting to stay in the area any longer than needed.

Storm had told me this was where the bulk of the Orpati had been found.

My mates had explained how even small pieces were able to power large buildings and entire city blocks. I'd seen its many uses in the sunken city of Atlantis as well, but I was looking for a far bigger piece of Orpati.

Weaving between the huge chunks of stone, I located the large passage which had been created by the underwater miners. The entrance had collapsed, but I found a gap just big enough to wiggle through.

I made my way down the dark underwater tunnel, my anxiety rising as all around me rocks shifted and fell. I'd been ready to turn around when I felt the welcoming hum in the water.

It called to me, pulsing like a heartbeat through the

murky water. My heart synchronized with the throbbing energy that had once been the heart of Atlantis. Lokene had been right. My body had fused with the Orpati during the fall of Atlantis when both my mother's magik and Lokene's magik had blended and merged with the earth's magik.

It still held a significant amount of power. Not as much as before, but still unbelievably powerful... and I was betting I could use it.

Reaching the end of the cave, it narrowed before ending in a solid wall of stone. I cursed in frustration. Pressing my palms against the stone wall, I could feel the warmth radiating from the Orpati. It had to be on the other side of the wall. I just had to get to it.

I was going to need to blink, but it was scary to teleport with no idea of where I was going. Last time I'd done it, I landed myself in hot water. Literally.

Unfortunately, I didn't have time to come up with another solution. Who knew what Lexi and Lily were doing with my mates?

Closing my eyes, I imagined where I wanted to be... which was looking at the Orpati. The world swirled, disappearing and reappearing. Opening my eyes, my hands were pressed against the warm Orpati.

My mouth dropped open. It was huge. Far larger than I had expected. It was nowhere near the size it had been in Atlantis. The original undamaged Orpati had been the size of a large building that was several stories tall. This piece was small by comparison.

I swam around the glowing stone. It was six meters high and four meters wide. Maybe it would be large enough to help me. Swimming forward, I pressed my hands against the turquoise surface.

Pushing everything from my mind, I focused on what needed to be done. I began to pull the magik of the stone into me. Electricity crackled up my arms, and my palms burned. It was a slow process, but I was afraid if I hurried, my body would overload from the amount of energy flooding into it.

Little by little, the magik poured into me while the stone's brilliant glow paled. My tattoos glowed brighter with each passing second, and my skin burned as the magik licked across every inch of scale and skin.

When the last of the light drained from the Orpati, I slowly pulled my hands away. Powerful magik danced and twirled around me like a playful dolphin, eager to do my bidding.

Kneeling, I dug my fingers into the sand. I gave my magik a command, and it eagerly rushed to obey. I smiled as my magik quickly placed a barrier around Earth, blocking anyone from hopping between worlds. Lily and Lexi were trapped on Earth.

I dusted off my fingers. It was time to hunt.

If the world had been scared of me before, they were going to be positively terrified now.

CHAPTER NINETEEN

ZOSIME

My first order of business was to make sure my mates were safe. With my power crackling around me like a living creature, I didn't even need to close my eyes to feel for the mate bonds.

My magik locked onto my men, and their locations came into sharp focus. I knew exactly where they were. Not wasting any time, I blinked from the underwater cave. A heartbeat later, I appeared in a dimly lit room, fully clothed and completely dry. I was definitely getting the hang of this.

I took in the room with a single glance, and what I saw lit a fuse on my rage that burned so hot that the floor beneath my feet heated, and the acrid scent of scorched wood filled the room.

Fynn and Storm were tied to chairs. Fynn looked up at me, relief and shock in his eyes. Storm didn't look up and instead kept his gaze firmly on the dingy carpet. Using my magik, I scanned him for injuries, but there were none. What had Lily done to cause Storm to look away from me?

"I know you sent Lokene and Bion to look for me." Lily stood behind Storm, holding a knife to his neck and pressing deep enough that it pierced his skin. A thin trickle of blood trailed down Storm's throat and, for a moment, I stood transfixed as the siren tried to push forth and rip her throat out. Hasty and foolish choice. I tried to decide my next move.

"If you move, I will plunge this knife into his throat." Lily's unhinged grin left no doubt in my mind that she would do exactly what she said.

"Too bad you didn't know that I've learned to mask my presence. Your errand boys have been bouncing around the planet like idiots searching for me. It is a nifty trick when you need to spy on the Elders and pesky half-bloods." Lily spit in my direction, leaving no doubt which 'half-blood' she was talking about.

Lily sashayed in front of Storm, carefully keeping the knife pressed against his throat. In a single swift move, she straddled his lap and then leaned forward, preparing to lick at the trickle of blood trailing down Storm's throat.

Did she seriously think I would stand by while she took

what was mine? No one touched or tasted what I'd claimed as mine.

Energy pumped through my veins. My different magiks blended together into a single pulsing power that swelled in my chest. It was time.

Lily might be fast, but she wasn't as fast enough.

I blurred across the room. My hand was covering hers, and I was burying the knife into her throat before she'd even realized I'd moved. Grabbing her shoulder with one hand, I flipped her off my mate's lap before slinging her into a nearby wall as though she was a toy.

With nothing more than a thought, I blinked Lokene and Bion into the room. "Get them out of here!" I ordered the two confused Ancients.

I stalked toward Lily. The knife wound was slowly stitching itself back together. It wasn't a surprise. She was still going to die.

"Didn't I warn you about touching my mates?" My voice boomed.

Lily stood, brushing drywall from her clothing. "I'm an immortal Ancient. You're a half-blood. Do you seriously think I'm scared of you? What do you think you're going to do to me?" she mocked with a laugh.

"I'm so glad you asked." I blurred, magik crackling around me. Gathering the knife from the floor, I embedded it in her stomach faster than her eyes could track.

"If I wasn't so busy, we'd do this all day," I whispered in her ear. "But fortunately for you, I have more important things to do today than to play with you. What was your job again?" I tapped my chin, circling around her, a predator terrorizing its prey. "Oh, yes. You were supposed to deliver me to the Elders, right? How about we do that right now?"

Not giving her a chance to respond, I grabbed her arm and blinked us straight into the middle of a meeting being held by the Elders.

Shocked cries and shouts rang through the building.

"Lily? Zosime? What are you two doing here?" Anthony asked, his brow wrinkling in confusion. "What is going on?"

"I'm not allowing anyone to teleport to or from Earth until I finish with the Lure. It is temporary." I lifted a shoulder as though it was every day that Ancients were blocked from traveling to Earth.

"*You* aren't allowing it? By who's authority?" another Elder yelled in outrage.

"By my authority." The ground trembled as I spoke, sending fear flashing through the Elders' eyes. No one else dared to question me.

"I have something to say." I waited, but no one interrupted. "Next time you decide to send an ambassador to me, I highly suggest you make sure they're not tainted. I don't take kindly to having the Lure sent into the sanctity of my home, nor do I appreciate my mates being touched."

Murmurs rose from the Elders. "What are you talking about? We've known Lily for eons. There's no way she's been tainted."

"Don't deceive yourselves. The Lure has devoured her soul. Your ranks were infiltrated. The Lure adapted inside the Ancients to allow them to go undetected by other Ancients since Lexi created it."

Growing annoyed as the Ancients continued to argue with me and doubt my ability to recognize the Lure, I pressed my hand to Lily's back and sent a cocktail of blended magik pouring into her. The air around her shimmered and glowed. As the bright turquoise glow faded, the Lure was visible. The silence was deafening as the Elders watched the Lure continue to eat away at her soul like a living parasite. Moving my hand away, the magik faded, along with the view of the Lure.

The cries and shouts of the Elders as terror and distrust rocked through them were deafening. I waited for the chaos to die down before continuing.

"Don't worry. Lily and Lexi are all that's left of the tainted Ancients, and they won't be a problem soon." Stepping forward, I sank my fangs into Lily's shoulder, grinding deep into her bone.

I wanted to cause her as much pain as possible. Lily screamed, desperately trying to wiggle free of my grip, but it was no use.

"What are you doing? Someone stop her!" Utter pandemonium descended on everyone in the meeting hall.

Amused, I crossed my arms and waited, hoping someone would try to stop me. No one dared to touch me. Shame, a few of them looked like they wanted to die, and I was still holding a grudge against several of them. Maybe next time.

It didn't take long for the venom to work its way through Lily's body, and every eye in the room watched as she succumbed to my bite. Her body crashed to the floor. She was dead.

Several Elders rushed forward, checking for a pulse and trying to figure out what was going on and how an immortal had just died in front of their eyes.

"What did you do?" an angry gray-haired woman asked.

"I injected her with my venom. It turns out Ancients are susceptible to one venomous thing on Earth. Me. And you would all do well to remember that before you send another traitor into my home or kidnap one of my mates. Next time I will not be so forgiving."

Warning delivered, I blinked back to Earth.

CHAPTER TWENTY

ZOSIME

O nce back on Earth, I went straight to my mates. The men were scattered around our bedroom in the castle. Even Zeno sat with his back against the floor-to-ceiling windows, his gaze fixated out at the sea.

I breathed a sigh of relief at the knowledge they were all safe. It was exactly what I needed to see before I went after Lexi.

Storm sat on a large armchair, his gray eyes watching me with an unreadable expression. I blurred across the room, dropping to my knees between his legs so that we were at eye level with each other.

Storm reached out, brushing a strand of dark hair away

from my face, his knuckles brushing against my cheek. "I missed you, Zosime."

I leaned my face into his gentle caress. "And I missed you, my love."

When his hand finally dropped away, I spoke again. I hated to ask him, but I needed to know. "Did she do anything to you? Hurt you?"

I didn't need to clarify who I was talking about. Storm's eyes darkened, and I couldn't breathe. "No, she was still more interested in taunting you than doing anything to me. I'm just frustrated at being her pawn to get at you."

A dam broke, sending relief flooding through me. He was going to be okay. I'd made it in time. I crawled onto his lap, tears blurring my vision.

Storm's strong arms wrapped around me, pulling me close. It was always surprising how small I felt when being held by him. "Stop worrying, Zosi. We're all going to get through this. It will be over soon."

Storm was right.

"Yes, it will be over soon." Sooner than he thought.

Cuddled against Storm's chest, I studied each of my mates. "I've spent too many years of my life at war. I want a different life now. My life has been dedicated to serving the Ancients and Atlantis. I'll always protect my beloved city, but it is time I allowed myself to be a little selfish."

The solemn mood that had descended on the room was broken when Kye snickered.

Eason smacked the back of his head. "What is wrong with you?"

"Ow!" Kye grumbled, but his eyes sparkled with mischief when he answered. "Zosi's going to be little *shellfish.*"

Every single man in the room worked to keep their mouths from twitching at Kye's ridiculous humor, but when Bion burst into laughter, the battle was lost. Peals of hysterical laughter rang through the halls of the castle for the first time in many centuries. It was perfect.

"Oh yeah, now that you and Storm are back, you owe me twenty bucks." Eason nudged Fynn.

Shaking his head, Fynn pulled out his wallet and handed Eason a crisp twenty-dollar bill. "Here you go."

"What are they doing?" I asked Storm.

Storm rolled his eyes. "These immature idiots were betting on when you would claim Bion."

My cheeks burned. "You didn't think I would claim him?" I directed the question to Fynn.

"Oh, no. I knew you would claim him. I just thought it would be after you returned from Iolatara." Fynn spoke with such matter-of-fact confidence that I was stunned. "Eason was the only one who said you would claim him while you were there."

"Don't look so shocked, beautiful." Storm chuckled, kissing the top of my head. "We all knew. Your face when he showed up here the first time gave it away. You look at each of us the same way."

I snuck a peek at Bion, worried about how he would handle the teasing. His beaming smile as Kye and Eason exchanged fist bumps, welcoming him to the family, was answer enough.

My heart swelled with love for these men. There was only one thing still standing in the way of the life I wanted.

Lexi.

I pressed a soft kiss to Storm's throat, smiling when the knife wound glowed and healed without leaving a trace.

With the sound of my men's laughter echoing in my mind, I blinked away.

The siren wanted to hunt.

The warrior wanted to win.

I wanted coffee... and a vacation with my sexy mates.

And nothing was going to stop me from getting everything I wanted.

I STARED AT LEXI THROUGH THE THICK GLASS DOORS OF the opulent board room. What was it with modern humans and glass? Didn't they realize how fragile it was?

This entire floor was encased in glass, giving the occupants the illusion that they were floating in mid-air a hundred stories above the bustling seaside city below.

Lexi's shock at seeing me registered on her face, and I smiled as a new realization dawned on me.

She hadn't known I was coming. The Ancients in the encampment hadn't sensed my presence. Lokene and Bion hadn't known about my plans to visit the destroyed mining operation and absorb the energy from the Orpati. The Ancients had been shocked when I showed up in the middle of their meeting. And now, Lexi hadn't expected my arrival.

What a change. When Lokene had first come into my life, he'd usually known what was coming and had to stand by and let it happen rather than risk the wrath of the other Ancients by interfering with the outcome.

Things had changed. None of the Ancients knew what to expect from me or what my next move would be.

I'd adapted and evolved again. How could I thrive as a predator if my prey knew my next move and always knew my location? It was a threat to my survival, and my magik had changed the rules of the game yet again. Somehow, I was being hidden from the Ancients' all-knowing abilities, and it was giving me an incredible advantage.

I stepped forward, and the glass doors swung with nothing more than a thought from me. Lexi turned with a glare on her face. Around the table sat the head of every country in the world, and let's just say they weren't exactly thrilled to see me.

My vision shifted as my pupils thinned to catlike slits, and my stomach sank at the sight of the Lure spreading like spilled ink across the polished wood table. It seemed to be breathing as it reached out toward every person in the room, and I was horrified to see that it had already wrapped sticky tentacles around several of the leaders' hands. Could they not see it, or were they allowing it to happen?

"So this was your grand plan? Taint the world leaders so you could use them as your pawns?" I strategically chose not to act yet and took a seat at the far side of the table facing Lexi.

Lexi regained some of her composure and leaned back in the chair as though she'd already won. So imprudent. Putting her hands in the air, she laughed. "Guilty as charged. You caught me."

"To what end, Lexi? You're an Ancient—a god. You have the ability to go wherever you want. Why do you want Earth so badly?" I truly couldn't understand what she hoped to gain from alienating herself from the Ancients.

She laughed, the sound high-pitched and shrill. "What do I want from this? I'll tell you, brat."

Had she really just called me a brat?

"Among the Ancients, I was a shining star. I was the one who constantly created new things to delight the other Ancients. We were happy keeping to ourselves. And why shouldn't we have been? We were vastly superior to the pathetic life forms we'd found on other worlds." Lexi's nails clicked on the mahogany tabletop, and I bit back a smile.

For all her arrogance, she was agitated and venting. It was a terrible combination for her, but a definite advantage for me. I waited in silence for her to continue, knowing that my perceived lack of interest would add to her annoyance.

Curling her lip, Lexi continued. "Then your mother stumbled across this planet. The first planet we'd found that held a magik as powerful as ours while also being vastly different from our own. Even though the humans living on Earth at that time were unable to fully harness the strange magik, the Elders acted as though your mother had brought home their first grandchild.

"It was disgusting the way so many Ancients began to visit this world. Wasting their time trying to educate humans who could never comprehend half the things they were told." Lexi paused, taking a sip of wine to regain her composure.

"So, you were jealous?" I cut to the chase. Sure, I was curious about the past, but I wanted to go to bed early tonight. Besides, within the hour, the Lure would no longer exist. It would be relegated to the footnote in some dusty old book about ancient myths and legends.

She slammed her glass down on the table hard enough that wine sloshed over the edge.

Without thinking about it, I lifted my finger, suspending the wine mid-air before dropping every molecule back into the glass.

Several quiet gasps came from our human audience. It was the first sound they'd made since I'd walked into the room. They might not understand everything that was going on, but they at least had the intelligence to stay out of our fight.

Angry at the reactions my magik had garnered, Lexi threw the glass, where it shattered into thousands of sparkling shards as wine spread across the white marble floors like blood.

The alcohol loosened Lily's tongue. "I was not jealous, you stupid half-breed! I was disgusted that I was the only one of the few Ancients who realized how much time was being wasted on your mother's pets. She didn't deserve praise for her work in Atlantis. No more than a child deserves praise for building a crumbling castle in the sand."

Lexi's anger excited the Lure, and it was too late when I realized it had been inching closer to me this entire time. Hungrily, it threw itself at me.

CHAPTER TWENTY-ONE

LOKENE

Bion and I searched around the world, desperately trying to locate our mate. I'd seen the look on her face when she'd left. She was on the warpath. It was the same expression that had been on her face during the final battle of Atlantis.

Zosime planned to end this today. And I couldn't even see glimpses of the future to know if she had a chance to survive. I knew without a doubt if I'd seen any way that I could help to shift the outcome in her favor, I would do it regardless of our Ancient rules.

They'd bound me with their magik in that last battle, preventing me from going to her side. I'd been unable to help the love of my life.

I'd blamed the Ancients all these long centuries, but in Iolatara, I'd still stuck to my mindset as an Ancient. Refusing to cross the boundaries in order to aid my love. My Soyale.

If I lost her, what did anything else in this world matter?

Today I was going to fight by her side. If I could find her.

Blinking back into the castle, I cursed in twenty long-dead languages, frustrated at my inability to find my mate.

Bion blinked into the room several minutes later.

"Any luck?" I asked hopefully.

"No! Nothing!" Bion began to pace.

Kye snickered, and I shot him a dirty look.

"I was just thinking how much it must suck to feel powerless... like a human. You've fallen a long way from the arrogant, all-knowing jerk that we first met." Kye smirked, but quickly threw up his hands in mock surrender when I lunged for him.

"There she is!"

Fynn's victorious shout had everyone in the room rushing to crowd around his computer.

"I had to call in some favors, but my network of nerds helped to hack a few cities, and we found her." Fynn pushed back his chair, giving us a view of the large computer screen.

It showed a security feed of a board meeting. To a human viewing the tape, nothing would seem amiss. Oh, how wrong they would be. Nothing good could be happening in a room full of politicians, an unpredictable siren... and my mother.

"Address?" I barked, but then pulled the information from his mind before he'd spoken it out loud.

I appeared in the boardroom and was surprised when neither Lexi nor the humans reacted to my sudden appearance.

You're invisible. Don't make a sound, Zosime's voice warned in my mind.

How? It wasn't an ability I possessed or knew how to use.

It's an ability I possess, she answered, amusement dancing in her tone.

Ignoring me, Zosime's attention turned back to Lexi, and her amusement dropped away. "So, you were jealous?"

Lexi's rage was eating at her control. Her hand shook as she slammed her glass down with a sharp crack. A splash of wine leaped over the rim and then paused mid-air before returning to the glass.

I caught the slight movement of Zosime's finger and realized she'd controlled the wine, and it had obeyed her command.

Pandemonium erupted in the room. My ears rang with the sounds of shattering glass and my mother's screaming. But I wasn't focused on her. I was staring at Zosime with growing wonder and shock as I realized she was adapting faster than should be possible.

Something moved across the table in my peripheral vision. It was like seeing a ghost on a homemade film, and I questioned if I'd seen something at all... right up until it glinted again and crashed into Zosime's chest.

The instant the thing touched her skin, the air shimmered, and the thing's form came into clear focus.

The Lure.

It wasn't just a slow creeping infection anymore. Now, it was a disgusting living thing like a shadow from the pits of Hades looking to devour... and it was on Zosime.

My chest squeezed tight. Humans screamed, trying to push away from the desk as they saw the dark tentacles curling around their wrists.

I rushed forward, ignoring the slight chill I felt as I made my way to her side.

"Son?" my mother squawked, her voice shrill. Her fingers wrapped around my bicep, pulling me away from my mate.

I yanked my arm from her grasp. "Never call me that again, you monster!"

My ears popped as the pressure changed in the room. I glanced back at Zosime and watched as her tattoos glowed brighter. The lights flickered around us, bulbs exploding with the surge of electricity.

With an animalistic snarl, Zosime flung the thing onto the table, where it immediately spun around, rushing back across the surface toward her.

I lunged to grab my mate, but the woman I once called

mother threw a barrier up between us. "Let the Lure consume her, as it should." A cruel smile of victory curved her lips.

Zosime slapped the table, hissing in fury and releasing a pulse of energy rippling across the table into the Lure. The amount of energy in that single burst was more than most labs on Earth could have safely contained, and yet Zosime had used it as a precise weapon.

The blinding light temporarily stole everyone's vision, and I was thankful that, as an Ancient, mine returned supernaturally fast. The humans screamed in terror, but I ignored them for the moment. They would heal. Or, depending on how things went, they could still die.

As my vision returned, I could see a pile of ash where the Lure had been. It wasn't all the Lure that existed, just a piece. Even now, the inky tentacles still inched across the table, searching for souls to taint.

Zosime kept her palms pressed flat on the table. "I'm not scared of the monster you created."

Lexi's chest heaved as she stood. "You should be!"

Darkness enveloped the room, and thick smoke swirled around me, making it hard to keep my eyes on Zosime. I reached forward, determined to break the barrier Lexi had created between Zosime and myself, but it wasn't there.

Lexi appeared behind me, and when her voice spoke near my ear, my heart lurched. Something cold and slick crept down my neck, arms, and even my lungs grew heavy. The Lure.

Soyale—

I'd no more than thought her name before the entire roof lifted off the building in an eardrum-destroying symphony of groaning and screeching metal. With effort, I tilted my head to survey the damage, and my mouth went dry at the ominous clouds rotating over the building.

When the dark fog was sucked from the room, Zosime stood tall and proud.

And furious.

Her hair and clothes wafted around her as though she were floating beneath the water. Lightning crackled across the sky behind her, and her creamy skin turned a pale blue and pulsed with a power I'd never seen before. Where did it all come from?

It was like seeing one of Kye's favorite anime shows come to life. Zosime had powered up. But how? Zosime took in the tendrils of Lure that curled around my body, prodding for an opening. I could feel it slivering into my mind, attacking each and every thought I had, tainting it.

I shivered and collapsed to the ground.

"Let it in, my son," Lexi cooed. "Stop fighting it."

My hands yanked at my hair, and I gritted my teeth, trying to push it out. I couldn't let it inside of me, but it dug deeper, wrapping around old pains that I'd long moved past and pushing them to the surface. How easy it would be to give in.

A hiss like I'd never heard ripped from Soyale. Yes, Soyale. I needed to keep my thoughts on her. She flashed her fangs at my mother—both the top ones, and the brand new viciously sharp ones on the bottom. Had she gained those in the upgrade, too?

"How many times do I have to tell people to keep their hands off my mates?" Zosime's words were calm, but the rage in her eyes burned hotter than hellfire.

Mates. Yes, I was her mate. I belonged to her. Needed to focus on her. My Soyale. The Lure grew deeper, and I cried out as it pierced through my consciousness.

"I'm an Ancient, and he is my son. I will do as I please —" Lexi didn't even finish her words before she was ripped away from me and flung through one of the shattered windows.

I gasped in oxygen, clutching at my aching chest. It felt like I'd finally surfaced.

"No. You won't. This is my world, and I will decide what's best for it from now on," Zosime called out, presumably toward Lexi, but I didn't miss how her eyes bore into the human leaders still frozen in their seats and shaking with terror.

A shiver of unease licked down my spine. Zosime was more dangerous than anyone had even realized. With her ability to adapt and evolve, there was every possibility she could adapt to outwit any of the Ancients' god-like abilities.

Was there a limit to how far magik could alter her body? Because if not, the world of the Ancients might not be ready for what's coming if they ever cross her. And worse... what if she became tainted, and it was too late to stop her? For all we knew, it might already be too late.

If she'd merely been a mix of human and Ancient bloodlines, none of this would have been an issue. She would have carried only half our blood, which would've left her unable to use her powers. But a girl who carried both Ancient and Earth magik, and who had been blessed by both? That was another matter entirely.

Her body's will to survive had pulled her through impossible situations. She'd been tried by fire and had come out stronger every single time. The world had underestimated her and viewed her kindness as weakness.

I had a feeling she was about to set the record straight.

Or destroy the earth and all who lived on it.

Looking into her glowing eyes with their inhuman slits, I decided it really could go either way.

CHAPTER TWENTY-TWO

ZOSIME

"Soyale?" Lokene whispered.

I could read the fear in his eyes. He was afraid of me.

Not of you. I'm afraid for you. His deep voice tried to calm my mind.

I wasn't sure I believed him, but the sudden arrival of all my mates but Zeno distracted me.

"What are you doing here?" I growled. "You guys are supposed to be safe in Atlantis, not in the middle of the fight."

I pinned Bion with a look that said he would answer for this later, but he only shrugged.

The screech of chairs scraping against marble jerked my

attention from him. The leaders were trying to sneak their way to the door. Storm and Eason stepped in front of them, arms crossed over their chests.

Eason raised a brow in my direction. "Where do you want them, soldier?"

My heart began to race. Lexi wasn't dead, and I knew she would be back any moment. I wanted my men far, far away from here. Maybe I should have stashed them in Iolatara.

Soyale. You claimed powerful mates. You need to trust their skills. They are going to be miserable if you try to store them away in the castle forever. Let them do what they excel at doing.

Lokene was right. As much as it terrified me, this is what they were trained to do.

Lexi had killed the agents assigned to protect the politicians, and these humans needed to be protected and held here until I returned. I trusted my men to handle it.

"Keep them here. I want them to witness what is about to happen. Afterward, I wish to discuss an offer with them."

"We've already told you our conditions—" one of the presidents started to rant

I cut him off with a crackle of my power. "Things have changed, human. I will be back to discuss my list of demands once I finish with my previous engagement," I snarled.

"And by previous engagement, she means she'll be back

once she's stomped Lexi's butt into the ground." Kye cackled.

Bion gave a flick of his wrist and television screens seemed to be projected around the table. He gave me a wink. "I'll make sure they see all the good parts. Go get her, doll."

"Kye? Please find Erin for me." Kye immediately started punching numbers into his phone.

Fynn grabbed my hand. "Zeno is in the bay. He is waiting there as backup in case you need him."

I nodded my thanks. The pounding of the call in my head grew louder. Lexi was coming.

Lokene's eyes had lines of worry etched around them, and he couldn't quite hide his fear. *Come back to me, Soyale.*

I shared the same fear. If I lost control, could I come back? As Lexi appeared in front of me, I knew it was a risk I would have to take. Evil seeped from her, leaving an inky black pool that only I could see beneath her feet.

I didn't wait for her to attack.

Blurring across the room, I tackled her through the already shattered window. Tumbling toward the pavement, I tried to sink my fangs into her shoulder, but she'd prepared for my attack. A black tentacle snaked out, curling around my neck and holding me away from her.

I blinked, appearing just beneath her, and tried to bite her calf muscle. Again, the Lure slapped me away. With a growl of frustration, I blinked to the ground, waiting for her to appear beside me.

I wasn't worried she would try to escape because I'd seen the crazy in her eyes. She couldn't let me win. Beating me mattered more to her than her own safety or her getting away.

Sure enough, she materialized on top of a nearby car. Her chest heaved as she tried to catch her breath, but I didn't wait. I blurred toward her, but she blinked at the last second.

I licked the edge of my knives, soaking them with my venom. Our bodies met mid-air and slammed hard enough into the pavement to leave a two-meter-deep hole. Around us, the sky had darkened, turning day into night. Lightning cracked around us, sending sparks showering down on the streets.

At a speed faster than human or supernatural could track, I tried to stab my blades at her. But the Lure was quick to defend its mistress, deflecting my blows while also stabbing out at me with its pointed tendrils. I dodged the blows, but my blades were knocked from my hand. I rolled away and called a streak of lightning from the sky. At the last moment, Lexi disappeared.

Jumping to my feet, I moved to call my blades to me. But Lexi reappeared before I had the chance. She dropped a merman at her feet, while in her hand, she gripped the hair of a terrified mermaid. "If you so much as twitch, I will turn her to ash."

I froze. I knew both these mers, just as I knew all my people. They were a newly bonded couple who'd been excited to start a family. Both mers were so young, with so much life ahead of them.

"That's a good little half-breed," Lexi mocked. The dark evil of the Lure billowed around her like an imposing black gown. "Now, just so you know I'm serious..."

She glanced down at the angry merman, a vicious smile on her lips. And in the next instant, his body had turned to stone.

The mermaid let out an anguished wail that would haunt me for the rest of my life. Tears burned my eyes as I stared in disbelief at the statue. The merman's expression was one of proud defiance.

"Here's what's going to happen—"

I didn't let her finish the sentence.

The girl disappeared.

"Where did she go?" Lexi screeched.

I remained calm, not bothering to answer her. The girl was safely back in the ocean where she belonged, out of this demoness' clutches.

Lexi rushed at me, only to be crushed against the concrete as a wave from the ocean slammed into her. Instead of receding, the water curled around her, constricting her body as it lifted her to stand in front of me.

I blurred to her side, and there it was, the opening I was looking for. I sank my fangs into her arm. Her blood tasted of ash and rotten flesh, and I gagged as the taste of decay touched my tongue. Still, I refused to pull away.

The Lure's pointed tentacles stabbed at me, fighting me with the desperation of a wild animal. She was the original host, and it was her magik that provided magik for the Lure. With her death, the Lure would cease to exist. But that also meant this part of the Lure was stronger than all the others.

I refused to move even when I felt the first slicing pain in my stomach. Nor did I move when the second tentacle stabbed into my chest, slicing at the side of my heart. The third tentacle punctured my lung. Each time the Lure ripped through my body, it left a trail of its darkness behind to try to sear into my soul. With a hard slap, I was knocked to the ground.

I fell to my knees, and my grip on the saltwater released. Lexi fell to her knees beside me. Smoke rose from her skin as the Lure desperately tried to burn away my venom running through her veins.

My magik surged through my body, frantically working to slow my bleeding and stitch multiple organs back together. I knew I needed to get to her while she was weakened, but my power was too busy trying to repair lethal wounds.

Summoning my strength, I prepared to stop my healing process so I could use that energy to give Lexi the fatal blow. My heartbeat was slowing, and I knew that if I pulled the magik away from my wounds, I was going to die within minutes. But I also knew that I would take this evil out with me. It was a sacrifice I was willing to make.

I stopped in shock when Lokene appeared behind her. A streak of brilliant lightning reflected in the twin blades he held. My venom coated the blades. Without any hesitation, he slit Lexi's throat and embedded both blades into her flesh.

Lexi tried to speak, but only a strange gurgling sound came out as blood trickled from her mouth.

It was too much for even the Lure to repair, and her dead body tumbled to the cracked pavement.

"You might be willing to sacrifice yourself, but I will not allow it, Soyale. I don't care what law I must break or what the consequences are. I will never again stand by while you are under attack."

Tears burned my eyes. Lokene had just broken the Ancients' oath. He'd killed his mom, an Ancient, to save my life. But at what cost?

THE MOMENT LEXI DIED, SO DID THE LURE. WITHOUT its creator, it shriveled and turned to ash, ceasing to exist. The world was free. Those who'd only recently been tainted had a chance at survival. Those who'd been infected long enough to have the majority of their souls eaten away would have died along with Lexi.

The pounding in my head stopped, and for three blessed minutes, there was absolute silence in the world.

Lokene pressed his hands to my chest, pouring magik into my chest.

"You're interfering," I whispered.

He leaned over and brushed a kiss against my lips. "I think that is the least of my concerns at the moment."

I curled my fingers around his wrist. "I'm sorry about your mom."

"I'm not. She never wanted a child and left me in the care of other Ancients for most of my young life. I hadn't seen her in many years. Lexi only cared about Lexi."

As the last of my wounds stitched together, Lokene rocked back on his heels. "Ready to go home?"

I let him pull me to my feet. "Not yet." I tilted my head back to look up at the floor where the world leaders waited.

"Let's go then." Lokene's arms wrapped around me, and he blinked us away.

I hadn't even fully materialized before the shouting began. Each of the leaders seemed determined to talk over the others. Meanwhile, my mates watched with looks of misery.

"What is going on?" I demanded.

Seeing me standing in the room, alive, my men rushed to smother me in kisses and hugs. They took turns inspecting my healed wounds to reassure themselves I was truly okay.

Bion caught my chin and tilted my face up to his. "You did it, doll."

Not waiting for a response, he kissed me, long and deep. When he released me, I was panting and even more eager to finish this day so we could return home.

Then hurry up and take care of the humans so I can take care of you.

Straightening my shoulders, I marched over to the long table.

"Shut up!" I ordered.

The racket these people were making was far worse than the call had ever been. It seemed to have a similar effect on me, though... I wanted to murder some people to make it stop.

Erin rushed forward, hair askew, mascara smeared, and her face tight with worry. Leaning in close to me, she whispered, "I thought you said you weren't going to do anything crazy?"

"Brace yourself. It's about to get worse," I warned her.

"Listen closely. This is how things are going to be from now on."

The leaders opened their mouths to protest. At this rate, we would never get this finished. Flicking my wrist, I closed their mouths. I'd let them speak, but only after they'd listened.

"I've been fighting to protect Earth longer than any of

you have been alive. Today marks an end to an enemy that has terrorized humans for centuries. I've saved one of your cities from a tsunami that would have cost precious lives and countless millions of dollars.

"I've seen the damage your miners and overfishing have caused to the oceans. Humans do not understand how to care for the earth, and the earth will start fighting back if things do not change. The tsunami was a warning, and you were spared.

"From today forward, this is how things will be. I claim the seas as part of Atlantis. The water will be under my rule and my protection. You can continue to squabble among yourselves over the land, but you will not destroy the seas. The water is alive; it's the soul of the planet.

"If humans wish to drill or fish, they will need to seek permits. Erin will be in charge of bringing those requests to me. Just like every other country, there will be taxes and fees associated with these licenses, and the money will go into protecting the oceans and ensuring safety for the humans in the water."

I lifted my magik, and every single person in the room roared their indignation.

"You think you can get away with this?" my least favorite of the presidents asked. He punched something into his phone and turned a smug expression on me. "My ships are preparing to fire on Atlantis for this act of terrorism."

I snapped my fingers, and a projection showed his ships

as they sank beneath the waves. "First, your ships aren't near Atlantis. I'm not an idiot. It's amazing how real some illusions look. Second, the mers are saving your men from the water right now. We want peace and safety for both humans and mers."

"The oceans are huge! You can't seriously think you can control them all!" a woman called out.

I allowed the projections to shift from one scene to another. On beach after beach, vacations were fleeing the water as groups of sharks patrolled the shorelines. I smiled as I caught sight of Sheba's massive body in one of the projections, her size making the other sharks look like small fish. "The sharks are not going to attack, but they will keep the tourists out of the waters, and that will hurt the money you make from tourism."

Other scenes showed fisherman after fisherman with empty nets. "The fish have been scared away from these fishing vessels. We will continue to drive the fish away as long as you are trespassing.

"We will happily share the ocean with humans, but we will also protect it from them. I hope our people can work together on this." I prayed they would come to their senses and stop fighting me. This was the only way to stop the destruction happening and give me time to teach people how better to care for the seas.

"You are one city under the sea, and you think you have the power to order every political power on Earth to cave to your will?" The man laughed.

"I don't need more than one city, but if you feel it is necessary to prove our worth as a society, then perhaps I should take more land?" The ground rumbled, and the building shook as I spoke.

"Enough! Enough!" several of the terrified leaders shouted. "We agree. Have Erin, your liaison, send us the documents, and we will sign them."

One by one, they each agreed to the terms and rushed from the room, eager to get away from me. I couldn't blame them, although I knew in my heart it didn't have to be that way. It was their own greed that forced me to take such a firm stand.

I gave the stunned Erin a hug, promising to be in touch, and turned to my men.

"I'm exhausted. Let's go get Zeno and head home."

We all blinked to the shoreline where Zeno waited. I ran into his arms, enjoying the cold water splashing around us.

"You got justice for Atlantis today, my little fish. You've made our people proud." Zeno pressed his forehead against mine.

"Lokene."

I knew the voice instantly.

"Not today, Hades. Not today," I mumbled like a mantra.

"Lokene, you have broken your oath to not take the life of another Ancient. You must pay the price." Jaque's voice was solemn, but he didn't sound the least bit sad.

Lokene started to move toward the group of Elders on the shore, but Bion stepped in front of him. "I want to stand in for Lokene's punishment."

"Move, idiot. I am not ashamed of what I did, and I bear the consequences of my actions." Lokene shoved past Bion.

"Hold up," I snapped. "You had murderous Lure-tainted Ancients perfectly willing to kill anyone and everyone, but you didn't punish them. So why are you punishing Lokene?"

Jaque looked at me like I was stupid. "Because they are not here to stand trial. They're dead."

"Yeah! Thanks to Lokene and me! He should be honored, not punished." I wanted to throat punch this pompous jerk, and the siren was imagining our fangs sinking into him.

Anthony stepped forward. "We're sorry, Zosime. You have done both our worlds a great service and will be worshipped as a hero among our kind. But Lokene broke our most sacred rule. He must die as a reminder to others."

I wanted to snort. Great, I'm a hero, and as a reward for saving their entire world, they were going to take my mate from me... again. "No. He's not dying today."

The group of Elders stepped forward to place their hands on Lokene's shoulders.

"I said no!" I screamed, my bottled-up fury exploding out of me.

The Elders flew away from Lokene. They blinked to his

side and tried again, only to be blown on their butts again. I wanted to laugh, but I was too angry.

We faced off, and I waited for them to make the first move. My skin had shifted to a pale blue, and the water surrounding me glowed a beautiful turquoise. Magik hummed in the air, waiting to do my bidding.

The Elders studied the changes to my body and slowly stepped back, bowing their heads.

"We conceded. Lokene shall not face death for his actions. It is clear that taking a mate from you would not be wise for the stability of our worlds."

I was pretty sure he'd just insulted me, but they were going to let Lokene live, so I bit my tongue.

"He must still be punished." They looked at Lokene. "As of this moment, you are dead to the Ancients, and you are no longer welcome to travel to your home on Iolatara. You will be missed."

With a bow in my direction, the Elders disappeared.

I ran to Lokene, and he swept me up in his arms, twirling me around.

"I'm sorry you can't go home," I whispered.

Lokene's deep laughter had my toes curling. "Soyale, my home is here on Earth with you. I never wanted to return to Iolatara again. And now they can't yank me there whenever they want me to play messenger boy."

I looked at the faces of my mates, still unable to believe it was all truly over. We were alive, and it was time to start our lives together.

I couldn't help but glance back at the shore. There was something I wanted to try, but I didn't want anyone to watch in case I failed. "Bion, Lokene, please take everyone to the boat. I'll be there in a minute."

The men hesitated, but at my shooing, they teleported away, leaving me alone.

I blinked to shore and kneeled by the stone statue of the brave merman. It didn't seem right that I was going home to my mates, and he was not.

I pressed my hands to the merman's chest. The stone was cold beneath my palms, but it quickly heated and burned my skin as I pushed my magik into it. The statue remained unchanged, but I refused to give up.

Imagining my magik blending together, I blasted it into the stone. This would either work, or it would shatter the stone into a million pieces. I closed my eyes and turned my head away, not eager to be hit in the face by flying debris.

"Ouch! Queen Zosime? What are you doing?"

I screamed, falling backward at the sound of the male voice. My eyes shot open, and I saw a concerned merman watching me. He was okay. With a sob, I smothered the very confused mer in a hug.

After blinking him home, I thought about my beautiful boat home and the men who waited for me there. Heat warmed my belly, and for the first time, I felt truly happy. It was my turn to experience the joys of this incredible life.

INTERNATIONAL BESTSELLING AUTHOR

SEDONA ASHE

DINO MAGIC
BOOK ONE

DINOSAURS, DISASTERS
& Albert Einswine

I have huge man problems.

Literally, since one of my mates is a T-Rex.

Things are about to get interesting, because my day job
happens to be in a museum.

A museum full of dinosaur bones, if you know what I mean.

It turns out my bloodline is older than dirt, and an ancestral matchmaker decided to send me some gifts...aka, men. And not just any men, but dinosaur shifters from the past.

I've read enough paranormal romance to know all about fated mates, but I've never heard of fated dinosaur mates. These men are supposed to be my perfect match, here to help me learn about my magic. *Rawr*. Yes, they are as sexy as you are imagining.

My life had been a routine of working and spending time watching TV with my pet pig, Albert Einswine. Now I needed to learn to control the magic I never knew I had, learn more about my family line, and help these sexy dino shifters adjust to modern society.

All while hiding a T-Rex sized secret from the world.

To make matters worse, detectives are looking into the explosion I may or may not have caused when my blood mixed with some magic-infused ancient dust, which is a serious problem since the sexy green-eyed detective has my heart flip-flopping in my chest.

Dinosaurs & Disasters is a light-hearted romantic comedy with a whole lot of steam! This isn't a save-the-world type of story, but rather it focuses on Arizona's coming into her

hidden abilities and tracking down each of her fated mates.

*This is a paranormal series, not a serious true-to-science series. So, if you are hoping to learn about dinosaurs, this probably isn't the read for you.

I'm looking forward to getting to know y'all!

Please follow and join at the links below to share your opinions,
keep up with new book releases, giveaways, and for sneak peeks!
I cannot thank each of you enough for all the support and the wonderful reviews!
Thank you for helping to make this girl's dreams come true!

Facebook Page
Sedona Ashe Reader Group
TikTok
Instagram
Newsletter
www.sedonaashe.com

Sedona Ashe's Book Series

Dragon Goddess Series
Royal Storm of Atlantis
But Did You Die?
Three of Me

ABOUT SEDONA ASHE

Sedona Ashe doesn't reserve her sarcasm for her books; her poor husband can tell you that her wit, humor, and snarky attitude are just part of her daily life. While she loves writing paranormal shifter reverse harem novels, she's a sucker for true love, twisted situations, and wacky humor.

Sedona lives in a small town at the base of the Great Smoky Mountains in Tennessee. She and her husband share their home with their three children, adorable pup, five cats, two pet foxes, chickens, three crazy turkeys, two cows, and over a hundred reptiles.

When she isn't working, she enjoys getting away from the computer to hike, free dive, travel, study languages, and capture the essence of places and people in her photography. She has a crazy goal of writing one million words in a year and spending six months exploring Indonesia.

Hi beautiful readers!

If you are looking for something else to read while you wait for my next weird and kinda funny book to drop, please check out my other series!

<u>But Did You Die?</u>
<u>Dragon Goddess</u>
<u>Royal Storm of Atlantis</u>
<u>Three of Me</u>
<u>Dino Magic</u>

Or click <u>HERE</u> to see all my books!

www.ingramcontent.com/pod-product-compliance
Lightning Source LLC
Chambersburg PA
CBHW032251020726
47495CB00001B/51